0.4

"YOU'RE NOT TELLING ME THE TRUTH, JAKE...."

"You're not even admitting it to yourself. I've been putting you away from me, and now you come bursting back into my life. You can't play with me like that."

"I'm not playing with you, Alex. What do you think I am?"

"I don't know. A man who's been through a lot, a man who's afraid to take a chance."

"Come with me, Alex. Now. Forget all the rest." It was a groan, a kind of plea for help. He reached out and touched her fingers.

"I can't," she whispered, but her voice sounded weak, even to her own ears.

He broke the impasse finally. "Please, Alex. I need you."

He was reaching her heart, melting it until it was utterly his. Slowly she closed the distance between them.

Dear Reader:

We are very excited to announce a change to Harlequin Superromances effective with the February releases, title numbers 150–153. As you know, romance publishing is never static, but is always growing and innovative. After extensive market research, we have decided to slightly shorten the length of the four Superromances published each month, guaranteeing a faster-paced story.

You will still receive that "something extra" in plot and character development that has made these longer romance novels so popular. A strong well-written love story will remain at the heart of a Harlequin Superromance, but with the tighter format, drama will be heightened from start to finish.

Our authors are delighted with and challenged by this change, and they have been busy writing some wonderful new stories for you. Enjoy!

Laurie Bauman

Laurie Bauman,
Superromance Senior Editor

Lynn Erickson

THE FACES OF DAWN

Harlequin Books

TORONTO • NEW YORK • LONDON
AMSTERDAM • PARIS • SYDNEY • HAMBURG
STOCKHOLM • ATHENS • TOKYO • MILAN

All Hopi words have been spelled
according to a system worked out
by Mr. Charles Hughes of Columbia University.

Published March 1985

First printing January 1985

ISBN 0-373-70157-8

Reprinted with permission from *The Hollering Sun* by Nancy
Wood, copyright © 1972 Simon and Schuster, Simon and Schuster
Children's Book Division, New York.

Printed in Canada

The land was always our land
And the sun set upon it
The rain washed it
And the fire was kind in its fury.
It was so for all time.

. . . . . .

Sell the land, my brother?
You might as well sell
The sun, the moon, the stars.

From *The Hollering Sun*, by Nancy Wood

CHAPTER ONE

AT FIRST she saw the purplish dawn-darkness when shapes are just outlined: *qoyangnuptu*, the Hopi Indians called it. Alexandra Crawford lay still in her bed, watching the pale light crawl patiently up her bedroom wall, saying the name to herself. And then it was *sikangnuqa*, the yellow light that discloses man's breath—and then, presently, *tálawva*, the red sunrise glow in which man stands revealed in the fullness of his creation. She knew all the names, felt the subtle changes in light and gloried in them as her ancestors had. Then she offered up the daily prayer that Hopis had offered to their creator since the beginning of time.

As the first warming rays slid over her, touching her with golden fingers, she reached out symbolically, drawing the sunbeams to her, pressing them to her body, inhaling deeply and praying that she might be beautiful in body and heart. Then she felt the peace enter her, and she was clothed in good, protected from evil and strengthened to meet the day.

And then the phone rang.

The lovely peace fled quickly at the strident shriek. Alex almost laughed out loud. The present intrudes upon the past, she thought.

"Hello?"

"Did I get you up?" Janet Webster's voice was apologetic—carefree but apologetic.

"Course not. Why, it's late. It's at least seven!"

"Never mind. Are you coming out for our Sunday ride this afternoon?"

"Jan, listen, I've got a million things to do. I hate to get behind. . . ."

"Do them *this* morning. Come on, Alex, give in a little, *enjoy* yourself!"

"Janet...." Something inside urged her to go riding, to get away from duty, give in a little to pleasure. "Oh, all right. I'll be out."

"I *knew* it."

"See you, Jan," replied Alex dryly.

"Okay, okay. Later."

Alex lay back in her bed, ticking off chores in her mind. She'd do a couple of things this morning, then let the rest go till evening. After all, she worked hard all week. Wasn't she entitled to a little fun?

She puttered around the yard, watered the lawn, swept the porch and the front walk. Todd Lopez, a neighbor, walked his dog by and stopped to chat.

She was glad when it was time to put on her riding clothes—a red checked shirt, jeans and boots. She tied a silky blue scarf around her neck to complete the picture, pulled her heavy black hair back into a ponytail and put on her straw cowboy hat with the upturned brim.

She enjoyed the five-mile drive from the resort town of Sedona to her friend's ranch. The brilliant Arizona sun outlined everything with utter clarity: the red buttes, the eroded layers of sandstone, the dry, rugged hills surrounding the town. It was beautiful country—harsh, perhaps, but with its own kind of splendor.

Janet already had the horses saddled: Poncho, a gentle gelding for her, and Belle, a feisty little buckskin mare for Alex.

They had their usual token argument over where to go. "Bell Rock," suggested Janet. "The view's terrific."

"Too hot today. How about Wild Horse Mesa?"

"Too far."

They finally compromised on a shorter ride—across Highway 179 and up an oak-shaded canyon. That was Alex's idea.

"We haven't been up there in ages," she said. "I just feel like seeing it again."

She was to think later that everything that bright Sunday had conspired to bring her to a precise location. Then she even experienced a little the fatalism of the Indian, the feeling that she was being manipulated for some unfathomable reason. But those thoughts would only come much later.

It was a lovely ride.

Janet sighed, clucking to Poncho. "The scenery takes my breath away."

"It is beautiful," replied Alex. "I was raised here but I get so busy I forget sometimes."

"You mean when you're hidden away in your office in Flagstaff solving great crimes?" teased her friend.

Alex laughed, her face appearing young and carefree, her dark-blue eyes crinkling up with characteristic good humor. "Don't I wish! Mostly it's tedious. Paperwork. You know, my boss, Bill, doesn't think I'm ready to handle the whole shot."

"I *don't* know, thank goodness. I *wouldn't* want to be a deputy county attorney on top of everything else, Alex. I have enough to do with the ranch and the kids and a sheriff for a husband. I don't know how you could let yourself in for that kind of responsibility."

"Well, I went to school and passed the Arizona bar exam and here I am," Alex said playfully. "Simple!"

"Simple, my foot! You know darn well you're the first woman *ever* to be appointed to the county attorney's office. It's an honor! My Lord, it's a miracle!" Janet always spoke in italics, her honeybrown short curls bouncing with each emphasis, her huge brown eyes widening, narrowing, shining or filling with instant moisture. That was why, Alex Crawford often thought, she loved her friend so much: Janet Webster showed every emotion, every nuance, every reaction to the world with no poses, no affectation, absolutely no facade whatsoever.

How very different from her own more disciplined nature, Alex thought. But that was probably why they got along so well.

Opposites attract. And it was true of Janet and Alex. Not only were their natures entirely different but so was their appearance: Janet rode alongside Alex with her generous thighs bouncing, her short arms reaching across the horse's neck, her stirrups hiked up to the shortest notch. Cute. With a freckled face and turned-up nose, Janet had always been called cute. But Alex, with thick, raven-black hair blunt cut at the shoulder, high, almost too square cheekbones, and straight, fine nose, was a bird of a different feather. Her only really great facial assets were her striking, azure-blue eyes. Even her figure was entirely different from Janet's; Alex was long and lean of limb, almost boyish for her twenty-eight years, and had practically no chest whatsoever—at least when compared to Janet's abundant bosom.

Alex would never have been called cute. Her features, although individually attractive, did not add up to true beauty. She had an interesting face, striking perhaps, and one that would age gracefully. Janet always told her she should wear makeup more often and dress to show off her slim figure. But she was most comfortable in gingham shirts and faded jeans—sometimes a bright scarf tied at her throat. That was Alex. *Why try to be a knockout when you weren't? Just be yourself,* she often thought.

Alex mused idly as her dainty buckskin mare stepped between the mesquite, the creosote bushes and the various species of cacti. Perhaps it was the Hopi half of her that was more concerned with her inner life, the paths and patterns taken by her mind, the way she, as a human being, fit into the larger scheme of things. Her grandfather, her aged and very wise grandfather, would tell her as he had so many times, that she had a difficult road ahead of her.

"Chosóvi," he would say to her, and the soft sounds of the ancient Hopi language would caress her ears. Her Hopi name was Bluebird, and she adored it. "Chosóvi, my child. You have chosen the white man's path. It is an easier way in all external things, but inside themselves white men are not at peace with the world. They battle the land, they deface it, and it will always rebel and destroy them. We Hopi have learned how to live on the land. Our tracks mark it as lightly as the *tocha*, the hummingbird. We are the People of Peace. Our very name, Hopi, means peace, child.''

Peace. Alex steered Belle around a tall saguaro cactus. She was successful, she had friends, she was financially independent, in good health. What more could a person expect from life? She even had a steady man, a wonderful person who truly cared for her. And yet total peace, the kind her grandfather basked in, eluded her. Perhaps it always would. Her own mother, after all, full-blooded Hopi though she was, had never quite achieved it. Maybe peace was purchased at too dear a cost to the modern, ambitious person. And yet, what a marvelous goal to have in life, always dangling before one, always possible.

"Come on, admit it," Janet was saying. "You're proud as punch to have your position."

Alex smiled. "Okay, I admit it. To you and no one else. But I have a feeling being Judge Crawford's daughter helped."

"They'd never have given you the job unless *you* were capable of doing it," went on Janet doggedly.

"It's a challenge," conceded Alex. "One must rise to the challenge, you know," she finished dryly.

Janet glanced over at her. "Ambition's not so bad, Alex. I should know. I never had any except to raise a family, of course, and feed a husband with a bottomless pit." She sighed. "You know, even in high school, in our senior yearbook, I was named 'first to get married.' "

Alex laughed. "That's not so awful. I was 'most likely to succeed'! Ugh!"

"That's great, isn't it?"

"Are you kidding? All I ever dreamed of being was 'best looking.' "

"Really? I mean, *you* had one of those complexes?"

"You bet I did, Jan. It wasn't until I finished law school that I finally accepted myself just the way I was...am." Alex paused in the thought. "The only thing I'd like to change now is my nasty old habit of having to get too many things done immediately. It keeps me from getting in touch with myself."

"Overachievement."

"That's it. Good old dad's girl. Like father, like daughter." Alex frowned then shrugged.

It was then that Alex saw the owl. It flapped up from the twisted branch of a piñon and wheeled above them, its wings surprisingly large for its size.

"Look at that..." breathed Alex, her neck craned to follow its flight.

"An owl?" said Janet. "Aren't they night birds?"

"Yes," said Alex, a slight chill touching the back of her neck.

"Wonder why it's out now?"

Alex didn't respond—aloud. Still she could not help but think the answer: an owl, seen in daylight, was a lost soul, a ghost trying to return home. That is what her grandfather had told her; that is what the Hopi and Navajo believed.

A lost soul.

Janet pulled her horse up close to Belle's flank, took off her cowboy hat and wiped her forehead with a wrist. "Whew! It's warm."

"Gorgeous," murmured Alex, still held in the grip of her thoughts.

"Well, *you* don't burn like I do, you lucky thing. I spend a fortune every year just trying to cover up my blasted Anglo-Saxon-type skin. And you, you just turn golden tan! It's frustrating!"

"There are advantages," teased Alex, pulling down the brim of her Western hat, shading her blue eyes from the merciless Arizona sun.

"So how's Tom?" asked Janet casually a moment later.

"Tom's fine." Alex knew Janet was not terribly fond of Tom Farley, so she didn't elaborate.

"That's all?"

"Well, we're not getting married next week, if that's what you want to know, or next month."

"That's not what I wanted to know, Alex. What I meant was, how is your *relationship* with Tom Farley?"

"Well, you should ask, then."

"Lawyers!"

Alex laughed. "Tom and I get along wonderfully. He's polite, thoughtful, sweet, understanding. What more can I say?"

Janet pulled Poncho up, leaned forward on the saddle horn and stared thoughtfully at her friend. "You could *say*, for example, that you *loved* him, Alex."

Alex wheeled her horse away from her friend's suddenly penetrating brown eyes. "I do love him, of course I do." She kicked Belle into a smart trot. "Come on, I'll race you to the highway!"

"Last one there gets to unsaddle both horses!" yelled Janet.

They both bent low over the horses' necks, clapped their boots to the horses' sides and took off across the red-tinted rolling hills toward the Websters' ranch. Dodging clumps of sage and rabbit brush, throwing up puffs of red dust from their hoofs, the two horses raced across the startling landscape. The color that embraced them was mostly red; striated buttes and spires and ancient eroded peaks rose on every horizon, softened by the greens of the dry country growth of central Arizona: juniper and manzanita, sage, grama grass, mesquites, piñons and cacti. It was a strangely beautiful scene, hard cut and clear at the edges, diamond bright, lavishly colored.

Alex loved the feel of a good horse under her, the bunch and glide of powerful horse-muscle, the sensation of freedom, the smell of horseflesh and saddle leather and dust underfoot. She'd been practically raised on horses as a child. Strangely enough, it had been her Eastern father who had insisted on that. "You live in the West," he had always stated in his pedantic way, "and you follow their customs. The best of all possible worlds."

Janet had come to love horses later in life, when she married Randy, and was not quite the horsewoman Alex was. And so it was Alex who was ahead when the sudden flap of buzzards rising in front of Belle caused the little buckskin to slide to a stop on her haunches, then do a nervous dance, her ears perked forward, her red-rimmed nostrils flaring with fear.

Janet pulled up next to her. "What was it? You okay? My goodness, I would have gone right over her head!"

Alex was soothing Belle, stroking her wet shoulder with a calming hand. "I don't know. I mean, there were some buzzards, but I don't know exactly where they came from."

"Ugh, buzzards, I hate those hideous things!" Janet grimaced. "Do you think there's a dead animal or something over there? Should we look? Oh dear. Randy will be upset if one of the calves got out."

"We better look. It's awfully near the highway. Could just be a coyote hit by a car."

They steered the horses in the direction from which the buzzards had risen. Belle was still nervous, sidling and dancing, her shoulders dark with sweat. The sun touched Alex's back like a warm hand; the pungent smell of sage and crushed buffalo grass filled her nostrils as she walked her horse slowly, talking softly to the animal.

Then there was a rustle in the brush ahead. Belle snorted, then tried to back away. A lone, persistent buzzard flapped noisily up out of a stand of creosote bushes just ahead of them—and at the same time that Belle decided to spin away, Alex caught sight of an incongruous spot of bright red on the ground next to a large boulder.

"There's something over there on the ground," she called back to Janet, at the same time trying to calm Belle. Finally she got the mare quieted, dismounted and handed the reins to Janet. "I'll take a look."

She pushed through the dry, brittle branches of the shrub, feeling the twigs catch at her blue jeans like grasping fingers. Yes, there it was, a patch of red fabric. She took another step toward it, then stopped short.

She was to think later that at that point she already knew exactly what it was on the ground ahead of her, but that kind of surety only comes after the fact. She was suddenly, sharply aware of a sweetish, overpowering odor, the shape of the tattered red fabric and the coarse gray hair, a belt—a man's belt—faded blue jeans. . . .

"My Lord," she whispered to herself, rooted to the spot.

"What is it, Alex?" Janet was calling, a worried note to her voice, as if she, too, already knew.

Should she move nearer, make absolutely sure? She forced herself to step closer, her heart pounding, her stomach lurching.

It was. There was no mistake.

It was a man's body, face down.

She thought suddenly, foolishly: *maybe he's asleep.* But there was no mistaking the look of that body.

It was a dead man.

She was suddenly paralyzed, unable to take another step. She stood there for an interminable time, aware finally of the loud, gummy buzzing of a fly. Then Alex was stumbling back through the bushes to the horses, her normally peachy skin pale in the blazing Arizona sun.

"What is it?" cried Janet.

Alex, trying to calm herself, leaned against Poncho's warm shoulder. "It's a body," she managed finally, her voice breaking.

"A *what*?" Janet's eyes were huge and round.

"A man, a dead man." She gave a shudder, felt goose bumps rise on her neck and arms.

"Oh no. Oh my gosh." Janet stopped suddenly. "Is it—is it anyone—" She could not go on.

"No, at least I don't think so. It's...he's face-down," said Alex quickly.

"Should I look?" asked Janet.

"No," she answered firmly.

"We've got to call Randy," Janet breathed then.

"Is he at home?" asked Alex, taking up Belle's reins.

"I don't think so. He said he might go on into the office for a while this afternoon." Janet's eyes were dark pools in her face. "Sometimes, Alex, I really wonder why my dear husband wants to be a sheriff at all. He's got to come out here and—" she shuddered "—*look* at it."

"We'd better get on back to your place, Jan. It's the closest phone, isn't it?" Alex swung her leg expertly over the horse's back.

"It's only about a mile. The road is right there." Janet pointed at a speed-limit sign poking up about thirty yards away. "Oh, Alex, will we have to come back and show them where it is?"

Alex thought a moment, trying to collect herself. "I know what we'll do." She untied the bright-blue scarf from around her neck, cantered over to the road sign and tied the scarf to it. It flapped fitfully in the hot afternoon breeze.

"They can't miss that, can they?" she called to Janet. "Come on, we'd better let them know."

The two friends rode quickly across the highway—State Highway 179—and back to the Websters' small ranch. It was called Someday Ranch because, as Randy always said, laughing, "Someday we'll raise horses here, someday we'll build a new barn, someday the old irrigation pump will be replaced, someday...."

Janet swung down at the house and ran in to call the sheriff's office in Sedona. Alex led the two horses to the water trough and then began unsaddling them.

Janet came running out while she was brushing the sweat-caked dust off Belle's smooth sides.

"They're on their way," she half gasped, slowing up as she approached Alex. "Randy asked me who it was, can you imagine? Dumb question." Then, "Who *do* you think it was? Has anyone been missing recently?"

"Not that I know of." Alex shrugged. "Goodness, there are enough people around here that neither one of us knows."

"You didn't see its...his face?" ventured Janet, taking up a brush and beginning to clean Poncho.

"No, I wasn't close enough, and he was lying on his face. I could only see his back."

"Oh Lord, I *hope* it isn't anyone I know," said Janet, shivering.

"So do I," replied Alex thoughtfully. "I hope it's an utter stranger."

"Amen to that," said Janet fervently.

CHAPTER TWO

Jake Brannigan swore under his breath as he mopped the sweat from the back of his neck. Then he glanced over at his fourteen-year-old son who was sitting, or rather slumping, sullen faced, in the passenger seat of the old Pontiac.

"You want to turn back to Los Angeles, Bobby?" Jake snapped irritably in his low-pitched bass. "You think getting tossed into a juvenile detention center would be better than this?"

No reply. Bobby Brannigan merely shifted his lean frame a hair and folded his arms more tightly across his chest.

"No?" Jake pressed harder. "Then I guess we keep on driving. The only thing I ask is that you try to make the best of the situation." Jake would have said more, a lot more, except that ever since they'd left L.A. that morning and headed east into Arizona, he'd been harping on the same subject: the fact that if he hadn't decided to move away from the city, Bobby would more than likely have been tossed into jail before the summer was over. Jail, or worse.... That crowd his son had been hanging out with was the worst Jake had seen in a long time. Why just last month, in May, one of the little hoodlums had been caught robbing a liquor store—with a gun, no less. And Bobby? Bobby had been waiting outside in the car. It had taken all of Jake's influence in the police department to keep his son out of the courts.

He guessed he was like any parent whose son got into trouble: angry at the kid, angry at himself, guilty because it was his fault—or was it? Sad, confused. The whole gamut. He knew the divorce had left its mark on his son. Maybe not the divorce so much, but Linda's obvious neglect certainly had. Bobby professed to hate his mother, but Jake knew what kind of anguish lay behind those words.

Bobby was not a hard-core juvenile delinquent. He was a confused kid, left on his own too much. And then, too, Jake had difficulty being soft toward his son. He had a hard time communicating; he was more likely to yell at the boy than to sit down and have a heart-to-heart talk. It was almost impossible for Jake to say calmly, "I love you, Bobby. Tell me what's bothering you." It wasn't in him. He was the type that either kept silent or blustered and threatened out of anger and fear and pain. The kid needed someone to understand him, really talk to him. It was something Jake would work on—in Sedona, away from the city. He'd try his best.

He looked over at his handsome, fair-headed son momentarily, then back at the arrow-straight, sun-baked stretch of desert highway. Suddenly the needle position on the water temperature gauge caught his eye. "Hell!" he swore in a gravelly voice. "Car's overheating." He steered to the shoulder of Interstate 40, and rolled to a stop.

"Great," mumbled Bobby. "What're we gonna do now?"

The intense heat rising from the dark asphalt struck Jake's fair skin as he opened the car door. He tried to control his temper, to keep his voice calm. "We're going to open the hood of the car, Bobby, then sit here and wait until it cools down. Okay?"

"Here?" Bobby stepped out also, glancing in disgust at the huge, barren expanse of desert floor stretching away from them in all directions. "Here?" he reiterated. "A lizard couldn't make it in this place."

"Will you stow it?" growled Jake as he unlatched the hood. "Would you rather I keep on going and blow the engine?"

"Wouldn't be any loss," mumbled Bobby as he

scanned the faded chassis of the '66 Pontiac. Their heap
of possessions was tied on the roof and half falling out
of the trunk, which was so stuffed they'd had to latch it
with rope that morning. "Why'd you keep this old
wreck all these years anyway? Plenty of cops have the
latest model."

"I'm not 'plenty of cops.'" And on it went until the
water temperature cooled and they were able to limp
back onto the Arizona highway and head toward a service station forty miles ahead in Kingman.

They ate lunch at a truck stop while a mechanic
worked on the hole in the Pontiac's radiator. Bobby
barely spoke as he stuffed himself with two ham-
burgers, a large order of fries and a chocolate shake.
But Jake, who normally ate plenty to carry his six-foot-
one, hundred-and-ninety-five-pound frame, had lost
his appetite and merely toyed with a limp salad and
sipped on a tall iced tea. What he really would have
liked was a couple of beers over in that bar across the
way. But now that he didn't drink anymore. . . .

A lot of things had changed in his life these last
months. First he'd given up the booze. It had dragged
him down to a new low: blackouts, personality changes,
carelessness on the job. A familiar pattern in police
work. And then, five weeks ago, he'd turned forty-two.
Approaching middle age. Was there really such a thing
as male menopause? Lord, Jake hoped not. Then his retirement from the L.A. Police Department. It wasn't
full retirement but he and Bobby would manage. He'd
put in his twenty years, retired as a lieutenant in homicide. The pension he'd be getting now would almost
stretch as far as the salary he'd received, seeing how
most of it went to the mortgage on the house anyway.

The house—thank God—was finally rented. To a
nice young couple who'd just moved down from San
Francisco. The rent money would more than cover the
mortgage payments. That was good. And Jake's ex-
wife wouldn't see a cent of it, either. That had been the
deal when she'd walked out on him and Bobby seven

years before. She got nothing. It had cost Jake a half year's salary to beat her in court, but it had been well worth it. Besides, she had never given a damn about either of them. A hair appointment had been more important to her than taking Bobby to the dentist. And Bobby hadn't even gotten a card from her on his last birthday....

"So why Sedona?" Bobby was asking in between sips of his milk shake. "It'll be like living on the moon or something."

Jake shook his blond head. "It's a very civilized town, Bob. It's growing fast too. Lots of tourists, plenty of kids your age. And if I've got to find work, it should be easy."

"What you really mean," put in Bobby sharply, "is that your old pal lives there. What's his name?"

Jake's green eyes rested carefully on his son for a moment. "My 'pal's' name is Webster. Randy Webster. As you know perfectly well."

"He's sheriff. Right?"

"That's right."

"You guys are all alike...."

"That's enough." Jake leaned across the table slowly. "You're darned lucky we've got a place to go to and friends to meet us there. Sometimes I think I should have left you in L.A. to make your own way. If you'd rather be in jail...."

"Jail?" Bobby snapped. "Don't you think living in some dump named Sedona is about the same deal?"

Jake forced himself to calm down. They'd drive to Sedona. Check it out. Maybe stay there, maybe move on. They'd just have to see when they got there. But at least it could be a new start for his son. *Could be.* As for Jake, well, maybe it would be a new start for him too. A rare, clean life. But what was he going to do there? Bobby would be in school. How would Jake fill the hours now that he wasn't a cop? And he didn't even drink anymore....

Randy Webster had written in March that there was

an opening in the sheriff's department in Sedona. But did Jake really want that? He was used to the life of the big-city detective—a desk full of open files, rough city streets. Not a pretty life. But never dull.

The east-west interstate highway veered southwest following the Mogollon Rim of the great desert, a rim of giant, spectacular mesas twisted and carved by time, brutalized by ancient, fierce rivers and wind and drought to form the present-day, red-tinted mesa land. Millions drove the highway through the tortured land to wallow in its unique history. They pulled out their tour maps and exclaimed over the steep, perilous red canyons that, for countless centuries, had been home to ancient Indians, then to the Spanish conquistadores who had trudged recklessly up one canyon and down another in their futile quest for the fabled seven cities of Cibola. Then the Anglos arrived—mountain men, miners, sodbusters. The Anglos never left.

The Pontiac, as it climbed the south rim of one canyon, was running relatively well. Jake mopped his damp brow and mentally crossed his fingers. Soon the land would change subtly. The red, flat-topped plateaus and cactus-dotted expanses would give way to river land, green-spangled hillsides, jutting, horizontally striped red-and-ocher mountains, flat-topped still, but infinitely more hospitable than the land through which they were now passing. And then they'd see Sedona, at the mouth of a lush canyon. Jake had once driven through Sedona—years back—with Randy Webster when they'd just been discharged from the marines. Aeons ago. Before Jake's ill-fated marriage, before Bobby, before the out-of-control drinking.

"Is this joint we're going to in the desert?" Bobby asked, sighing. "If it is, I'm outta there. I mean it, Jake."

"Adults call me Jake. You call me dad...pop... father or *sir*, if it comes to that, Bobby, but not Jake." He drew a rolled-up white shirt cuff across his wet brow. "And to answer your question, no, it's not in the desert. You might just shock yourself and like it."

"Sure I will."

Even Jake did not really believe his own words. All he could do was pray.

Jacob Daniel—after his maternal grandfather—Brannigan was a ruggedly handsome man, a big man, a characteristic fair-headed mustached Irish cop. In his youth he'd been a great athlete—football, basketball, baseball. He'd been full of himself, bursting with pride and youthful energy, using his considerable strength and agility to its maximum.

But the years had squelched his exuberance: first, Vietnam, then the soul-deadening grind of police work and then the divorce. . . . Now, Jake knew, he was jaded, disillusioned, an athlete gone a bit seedy around the edges from lack of care and exercise.

Sure, he'd been a marine, like his father. And a cop—third generation. A real tough guy like all the Brannigan men. And a drinker, a beer-and-Irish-whiskey drinker. The Brannigan men had always done that well too. Now, after weeks of sobriety he realized the "macho" side of him had sometimes been brought to the fore by the booze. Well, that was one trait he'd never miss. Still, that surface machismo had helped keep him alive in the city "jungle." It was known on his beat that no one pushed Jake Brannigan around.

But now those days were over. The old ways wouldn't work for him anymore—especially in a decent, quiet community like Sedona.

Jake drove on, thinking about the implications of his new life. What was he really tackling? As the highway began to snake its way up the Verde River Valley toward Sedona, Jake finally forced the host of thoughts away from him. They were a little too unsettling.

"Let's stop," Bobby urged suddenly as they passed the sign Montezuma's Castle. "That's one of those old Indian houses. . . . ''

"A cliff dwelling, Bob. But we can't stop yet, we're almost there," said Jake, mildly surprised at Bobby's request. "But I promise we'll go to the site one day soon. It's only a few miles from Sedona anyway, okay?"

"Sure." He became sullen once again.

The valley seemed to narrow as they approached their destination. Jake tried to see through Bobby's eyes the clean, brilliantly blue mountain sky, the endless variety of green vegetation mingling liberally with myriad cacti, the grand red-hued mountains looming above the fertile river valley. It was breathtaking. Even Bobby must see the awesome beauty of it, be aware of the comparison to the smog-filled city.

"Cooled off some," Bobby finally commented grudgingly.

"A lot," put in Jake thankfully. "Must be about eighty here. It's sure a better climate than the city."

"Oh yeah, I'm betting everything's a lot better here than in L.A.," mocked Bobby.

Jake threw him a disgusted sidelong glance, then steered the car through the rolling terrain on the outskirts of Sedona. The town, on the banks of famed Oak Creek, drew thousands of visitors to the area every year. The Pontiac passed countless art galleries, Indian jewelry shops and fine-looking restaurants. Jake stopped to ask directions to the sheriff's department.

"It's a mile or so up the road," he told his son as he ground the car back into gear.

"You know what this place is?" Bobby slumped down into his seat.

"What is this place, smart guy?" Jake could hardly wait to hear.

"It's a big tourist trap. Artsy-craftsy. *Real* exciting, Jake...dad."

"At least it's clean....."

The sheriff's department sat on a sloping hill off the main road. It was in the basement of a one-story, clean-looking sandstone building on Forest Road.

Jake parked in a no-parking zone—old habits are hard to break for a cop—and stretched his long limbs by the side of the car.

"Won't you get a ticket?" commented Bobby dryly as he pointed to the No Parking sign.

Jake shrugged. Then, "You know, you're right. Why don't you hop in and back it over to that spot...?" But before Jake could finish, the distinct clatter of boots on concrete steps caught his attention, and then Randy Webster was rushing around the corner of the building.

When the sheriff saw his old friend, he stopped in his tracks. "Jake? That you?" he called.

"Yeah...what's the rush?" Jake walked over to pump his friend's hand warmly.

"We got a deceased John Doe lying on the highway southwest of town. Look," said Randy, "if you can stand getting back into a car, why don't you and Bob pile on into the Blazer with me and we'll talk on the way." Then the sheriff glanced toward Bobby. "If you think your boy ought to be along, that is."

Jake frowned, shrugging his large shoulders. "Bob's seen plenty already for his age."

"Okay then. Let's go."

The three of them piled into the sheriff's official four-wheel-drive vehicle and sped out of town, siren screaming, red and blue lights flashing in the late-afternoon sun. Jake sat back comfortably and familiarly in the passenger seat as he let the air conditioning cool his hot face. Once he turned in his seat to see Bobby thoroughly enjoying the wild ride through town. It never ceased to amaze Jake how much excitement was required to stir the interest of a teenager—these days, the kids had seen it all by the time they were fifteen. Things sure change....

"Never get away from it, do you?" called Randy over the siren's wail.

"What?" asked Jake.

"Police work."

Jake grinned to himself. "Guess not."

"Well, we'll see what's going on out there and then we'll get you settled over at my place for the night." He paused. "You know, it was Janet who called this in."

"Janet?"

"Yeah. She was out riding with her friend, Alex."

The Blazer took the curves easily, screeching to a halt finally about four miles from town, near a fifty-five-MPH speed sign that had a bright-blue scarf tied to it, a scrap of fabric that lifted faintly in the warm breeze. Jake guessed that Janet had tied it there to mark the spot. Cool-headed woman. But then, a policeman's wife had to be.

The three of them climbed down out of the Blazer and began walking west, toward the blinding sun, across the arid brush-dotted land.

And then they spotted it—the body—about thirty paces from the highway lying facedown next to a boulder.

"Maybe Bob here better not see this." Sheriff Randy Webster removed his official Stetson, wiping a muscular forearm across his damp brow.

"Look, Mister...I mean, sheriff," said Bobby quickly. "I'm no kid...."

Jake nodded and put a hand on Bobby's shoulder. "You're right there. You'll be a man soon. Guess it's time you saw the real world."

"And I thought this place would be dull."

Jake and Randy exchanged grim glances as they approached the body.

"Holy Moses," whispered Randy when he crouched over the inert figure, "guess it's been here a spell."

Jake, too, took a closer look. It was an old man, an Indian, lying facedown on the hard, sandy earth. There was brown, dried blood caked on the left side of the back of his neck...as if he'd fallen or...been struck.

Randy slowly, carefully, eased the body over onto its side. "Oh my God!" he exclaimed. "It's Joseph! Old Joseph Twelvetrees...."

"Who?" came Jake's rough voice.

"A real old time Navajo 'round these parts. Got some of his own land not too far from here. Good, fertile river land. It's a real rarity for an Indian."

"How's that?"

"Most of them stick to the reservations up north of here."

"Wow!" said Bobby abruptly, seemingly unshaken by the scene. "Look at those awesome marks on his neck...."

The body did have odd marks on its neck, as if an animal had clawed at it. What had caused death—the blow to the neck, an animal?

"Well, look," said Randy, "I'll head back to the Blazer, call in the coroner and an ambulance. It'll take a little while and I'm afraid we're stuck here. I want to get some pictures of this too."

Jake led Bobby away from the scene as soon as Randy went back to the car. "We don't want to disturb the area any more than we have to," he explained. Idly he walked the few yards to the road sign, thinking he would untie the blue scarf and give it to Randy to return to Janet. It had a silky, cool feel in his hand as he touched it.

"I know all that, dad," Bobby was saying. "I wasn't born yesterday, you know." Then, "You think it's murder, dad?"

Jake shook his blond head. The blue scarf gave off a faint perfume, a sweet, alluring aroma that filled his nostrils. Funny, he didn't remember Janet Webster using that kind of perfume. She was more the bouncy, talcum-powder type.

"Well, dad?" demanded Bobby.

Jake looked up quickly, stuffed the scarf into a pocket and frowned.

"Who knows? I just feel bad for the poor old man, lying out here alone like this."

"You do? I mean, I woulda thought you'd seen it all, dad. I mean...."

Jake smiled grimly. "I have. But it still stinks every time. Guess your old dad is just human after all."

CHAPTER THREE

WORD TRAVELS FAST in a small town; Sedona was no exception. It was shortly past six in the evening when Alex's phone rang, catching her as she was cutting vegetables at her sink.

"It's Janet," said the familiar voice over the line.

"Any word on that poor man?" She took her glasses off, setting them on the countertop.

"Yes," replied Janet in a concerned tone. "And I'm afraid it *was* someone you knew...."

"Oh Lord, who?" Alex's heart squeezed.

"It was Joseph Twelvetrees, Alex."

Shock held her silent for a moment. "Oh no," was all she could finally whisper.

"Randy called me just a few minutes ago, Alex, and I thought I'd better let you know immediately. I'm sorry." Janet added kindly, "I know you were fond of him."

"Yes." Alex wiped her hands on her apron, and felt tears pressing hotly behind her eyelids. "I went to high school up in Flagstaff with his oldest son, George. We saw one another from time to time, and I got to know his father quite well."

"Well, Randy is calling George right now. I understand that he lives permanently in Flagstaff now."

"Yes. He married several years ago. I think he has a child now. He's a good-hearted man."

"Did you know the rest of Joseph's children? He had several sons, Randy said."

"Three. But they're scattered all over the southwest now. One's in Phoenix and I think another is teaching somewhere in California. I'd have to ask George. I guess," breathed Alex, "that I'd better give him a call myself."

"Yes. Well, I'll hang up then. Look, Alex, I *am* sorry...."

"Thanks, Jan. I guess these things just happen. Joseph was quite old, you know...."

Slowly, Alex put the receiver back in its cradle. Then finally, she let the tears flow. That tough old man, she thought miserably, dying so alone like that, with no dignity at all.

It seemed hours before she rose, went back to the sink and put the chopped vegetables into a plastic bag to keep. Dinner was out of the question, feeling the way she did.

It took several long minutes, but finally she pulled herself together and let a kind of calm fill her. Death, as her grandfather would tell her—*had* told her many times—was as natural as birth or breathing or a golden leaf falling from a tree. All were inevitable. Simple laws of nature. It must have been the white man's side of her that had reacted with such shock to the news. The half of Alex that was Indian—at one with nature—took over, soothing her, surrounding her with an aura of peace.

Calmly she dialed George's number in Flagstaff. Of course Sheriff Webster had already informed him, but he thanked Alex for her concern.

"You were always very kind to my father," George told her. "That is why he loved you so. And, Alex, I insist that you attend the burial ceremony...."

"But George," Alex protested, "I'm not even a Navajo."

"I insist! My father would be angry if you did not attend. Please."

"Well...."

"I'll let you know when. You will honor the tribe." He paused, and then added, "And I also must congratulate you on your new position. Deputy county attorney. You must be very proud, Alex."

Alex felt herself blushing. "Thank you," she said softly. "I never thought you'd be congratulating me, George."

"Ah yes," he reflected, "you would not go out with me in our senior year at school because you said I was a chauvinist." Again, Alex colored hotly. "But the truth was," said George, "that I was merely jealous of your intelligence and tried to make myself a taller man by belittling you. It was not fair. And here, after all these years, you remained a friend to my father. I wish you could have been out walking with him those last moments before his spirit fled."

An image winged through her mind and a cold hand seemed to brush her flesh—the owl rising in front of their horses from the brush-spangled landscape. The owl that was a man's lost soul....

"Alex?" came George's voice.

"Yes, I'm here," she breathed.

"I said, I wish you could have been with him those last moments."

It was a very high compliment, given from one Indian to another. And in the true Indian spirit, Alex finally said, "Thank you. I, too, wish I could have seen his spirit fly." And yet, she wondered if she really had.

After her conversation with George Twelvetrees, Alex telephoned the sheriff's department and spoke with Randy for a moment. Strangely, he asked if she could stop by the office—not in the morning, but right then. Alex said that of course she would, immediately. What could Randy want of her, and on a Sunday evening?

She didn't dress up. But then, Alex rarely did. The truth was, when dealing professionally with men— which she did on a daily basis in her position—the less they thought of her as being a "woman," the better she liked it. Alex far preferred to hear the words, "Nice job, Miss Crawford," as opposed to, "My, you look nice." Unconsciously she played down the feminine side of her appearance. It certainly did make things simpler.

She arrived at the sheriff's department in the main business district of Sedona wearing blue jeans, a blue-and-white checked shirt and a pair of plain sandals that clicked on the tiled floor. Her ebony hair swung casually just below her shoulders; her reading glasses, as always, were shoved on top of her head, leaving several stray bangs touching her dark, curved brows. A little breathless after half running down the stairs leading to the sheriff's office in the basement, she took a moment to straighten her hair and tuck in her shirt. After all, she *was* a deputy county attorney. This just might be official.

Randy Webster saw her around the corner of the dispatcher's desk. "In here, Alex," he called from his office.

"I got here as fast as I could." Alex smiled tiredly, seating herself across from her friend's husband. "It's been quite a day, hasn't it?" The smile faded.

"Sure has." Randy leaned back in his swivel chair, folded his tanned arms across his barrel chest. "I'm sorry you and Jan had to go through all that today."

"So am I, Randy. Joseph was a very good friend."

"I remember, Alex." Then he drew stubby fingers through his dark, thinning hair. "Listen," he said slowly, "I wanted to talk to you for two reasons. First, I just wanted to say how sorry I am about all this."

Randy had called her in, on Sunday, to say he was sorry? She was beginning to think it must be official. And then she wondered: if she were a man, would Randy be walking on eggshells around her? If this was official, she certainly wished he'd come to the point.

Alex decided to press him, gently. "When will the coroner's report be in?"

"Tomorrow sometime. And that's the other thing, Alex. I kind of feel bad telling you this, but there were a couple of peculiarities surrounding Joseph's death."

"Peculiarities?" What was he trying to say?

"Well, you recall how his . . . body was positioned?" he asked carefully.

"He was facedown, Randy."

"That's right. And on the back of his neck there was a wound."

"I didn't see that."

"Yes, well, it looks as if he fell, or tripped. Maybe he had a heart attack, Alex, but somehow it appears as if he struck a rock."

"On the back of his head? But, he was facedown. . . ." How odd, Alex thought.

"Well, it looks like he fell somewhere else. Crawled to the spot where he died."

"Yes. I suppose. . . ."

"Or. . . he could have been struck."

Alex sat straight up in her chair, her heartbeat quickening. "Struck? But by whom? And why? Why would someone want to harm old Joseph?"

"Now that, Alex, I can't rightly say."

Then Alex sat back, expelling a long breath. "That's quite a hypothesis, Randy."

"There's something else." He paused, as if weighing his next words carefully. "There were some odd marks on his neck."

"Marks?"

"They looked, mind you I said *looked*, like an animal's claw marks. A large animal."

Alex sat silently for a long moment, thinking. But of course, she finally concluded, the marks were made by a predator. Joseph had been out there on the desert for some time. How dreadful! Perspiration began to damper the back of her neck.

"I think the answer to that is pretty obvious, Randy," she said quietly.

"No, I'm afraid it isn't, Alex." Finally, Randy rose from his chair, and came around his desk to sit on its corner, in front of Alex. "Of course, we don't have a medical examiner's report yet, but I'm sure he'll question the fact that if an animal got to. . . to the body, there would be teeth marks as well. Clawing the throat alone just isn't done by any animal I can think of."

"I see," she replied slowly. And then a strange feeling overwhelmed her, so strongly it became a physical reaction—it was as if a cold breeze had swept through the small office and suddenly she was chilled to the bone.

"Are you all right?" Randy was asking.

But Alex couldn't answer, not immediately. She was still too overcome by the sensations sweeping her, and her mind was working furiously. Claw marks. What was it about claw marks?

Finally, gradually, the chill that had seized her abated and she could hear Randy saying her name. "What?" she managed to whisper.

"Are you okay? You look as if you've seen a ghost, Alex."

Perhaps she had, Alex thought. Aloud she said, "I'm fine." She gave a short little laugh. "It was nothing. Really." Then she rose. "I guess all we can do is wait for the coroner's report tomorrow. I'm sure there's an answer, Randy."

"Of course there is." He walked her to the door. Suddenly he snapped his fingers, remembering something. "Say, Alex," he began, "that apartment of yours over your garage wouldn't be empty, would it?"

She had a moment's difficulty making sense of his question. "Why, in fact it is," she said halfheartedly. "The tenant moved out last month."

"You interested in renting it for a spell? Maybe a month or two?"

Alex smiled, shaking her head. "I don't think so. It really needs painting. And I promised mom that I'd have the couch redone. There're springs popping right up in it."

"Oh, my friend wouldn't give a hoot about that sort of stuff."

"Your friend?"

"Didn't Janet tell you? My old buddy from the marine corps, Jake Brannigan, got in town today with his son. He's a real good guy. Just retired from the Los

Angeles Police Department, and he's looking for a place to resettle. I'm trying hard to talk him into Sedona. Even got an opening here at the sheriff's department if I can talk him into it. He's a helluva good cop.''

"I see," said Alex. "And I really wish I could help but. . . ."

"Come on," urged Randy, "that painting can wait. And wouldn't your folks appreciate the rent money coming in on the place? I mean, if it's empty, it's just costing you. Come on, Alex. You know how hard it is to find an apartment here in the summer."

"Well. . . ."

"Come on. Look, you'll really like him. And he's been sort of down lately. There was a messy divorce. He could really use a break."

"If he's got problems, Randy. . . ."

"No. Nothing like that. It was just all those years on the streets. Homicide. Guess he's kind of burned out. That's why I talked him into coming here. Sedona's worlds away from the city life." Alex finally focused her attention and thought hard. The rental income would help her parents—their mortgage payments were pretty high down in Scottsdale. And the painting could wait. Besides, if it was to help Randy's friend. . . .

"Okay," she said, smiling. "You're pretty persuasive, Sheriff Webster."

Randy grinned, patted her on the back. "I'll send him around tomorrow."

ALEX'S TELEPHONE WAS RINGING as she unlocked her front door. She tossed her car keys onto the coffee table and rushed to pick up the phone.

"It's Tom," came the voice over the line. "I just heard. . . ."

"It was pretty terrible," replied Alex. "I've been sick about it ever since the body was identified. I'll really miss him."

"I know." Then he asked, "Would you like to have dinner? I'll take you to Rene's."

She frowned, running tanned fingers through her thick hair. "I don't think so, Tom. I'm really not hungry."

"I understand. Would you rather I got a bottle of wine and stopped by?"

"The company would be nice," said Alex, grateful.

She thought, as she waited for him, that she could really come to love Tom someday. In time. Perhaps they could marry, have children of their own. Although Tom was divorced, and already had two small children, Alex was convinced that he would like more. And he could afford them. His realty business in Sedona was successful, and Alex herself was now making a good salary. After she did a year's probation as deputy county attorney, she hoped they'd take her on permanently. She had, after all, been voted most likely to succeed in her high-school yearbook.

Tom arrived, wine bottle under arm, around eight, and Alex felt that familiar sensation of warmth the minute he smiled at her, took her in his arms and kissed her softly. She thought then that he was the most dependable man she knew. And he was her friend, too. As for their sexual relationship, that was fine, also. He never treated her like a sexual object. Tom actually liked her for her intellect.

"I'll get some glasses," he said, letting her go from his embrace, and Alex watched his tall, lean frame as he disappeared into her kitchen. *Yes,* she thought, *a man like Tom would never fail her, never try to interfere with her career.* She could easily let herself fall deeply for Tom. She just needed a little more time. . . .

CECILY WEBSTER took to Bobby Brannigan the moment she laid eyes on him. And it looked as if the attraction might be mutual. At least, that was what Jake had thus far witnessed.

And he was glad. Bobby could use all the friendship

he could get right now; changing one's whole life, one's whole environment was never easy, especially for a fourteen-year-old.

The evening was idyllic, cloudless; only a soft red hue illuminated the sky to the west across the desert expanse as Jake sat behind the Websters' comfortable house enjoying Randy's company.

"Desert's beautiful, isn't it?" mused Randy from his seat on a lounge chair.

Jake took a drink of his tonic and lime. "Sure is. I'd forgotten. You don't see many sunsets in the city."

"Wide open spaces. That's what we got here, Jake."

"You've made a good life."

"And you haven't? Come on, Jake, things will get better."

Jake glanced at Bobby, who was leaning against the corral gate, his head bent in conversation with Cecily. Things had to get better. . . .

"So what do you think of renting the Crawford place for a month or so?" Randy was asking.

"Sound's fine. But didn't you say Alex Crawford was a D.A. or something?"

"Deputy county attorney. We don't have district attorneys here. Just county."

"Well, yeah, but you know how attorneys and cops get along. They don't." Jake leaned back in his chair, putting his hands behind his blond head.

"It's different here. You'll get along with our friend Alex just fine."

"That the same Alex who was riding with Janet today?"

"Yeah."

"Want another beer?" called Janet from the kitchen window.

"Sure," replied Randy. "And bring our *sober* friend here a tonic." Then he asked, "Did you quit drinking to dump a few pounds, Jake?" He couldn't help glancing at Jake's slight middle-age spread.

"Damn it, Randy, give a guy a break. I'm forty-two. I wear the same size pants I did in the service."

"Sure, pal." Randy retreated quickly, muttering, "And my hair's just as thick as it was then, too."

"I quit drinking because I was turning into a falling-down drunk, Randy," he growled, adding bitterly, "A typical cop."

Randy was silent, obviously finding nothing to reply to his friend. The silence was filled with a slight tension for a time. Then Jake relented. "I guess I could stand to lose a couple of pounds," he admitted gruffly.

"Sure," said Randy. "If you'd do some weight lifting for a few weeks, you'd be as tough as in the old days. Remember?"

"God! How could I forget? A fight every Saturday night in some filthy bar in Saigon. Sure had fun . . ." he finished sarcastically.

"You know you liked it," disagreed Randy. "We sure could take them all on in those days, couldn't we?"

"We sure could," reflected Jake.

"You still get in one occasionally?"

"One what?"

"Barroom brawl. I know you, Jacob Brannigan."

Jake looked at his friend for a long moment. "I don't fight anyone," he said. "It's the new, sober me." Randy laughed, but Jake's lip just twitched a little, in a cynical parody of a smile.

"Here's your beer, honey," said Janet.

"Thanks."

"And your tonic." Janet leaned over and kissed Jake on the cheek. "Randy's missed you so. And so have I."

Jake turned his head a little, embarrassed. "It has been a while . . ." he replied half under his breath.

"You *are* staying," said Janet, pressing.

"We'll see." It was a low growl.

"Well—" she seated herself, adjusting her yellow-flower-patterned skirt "—you have to stay here. Who's going to listen to all of Randy's war stories? Not me!"

Randy grimaced. It was then that the Websters'

youngest, Brian, appeared at the back door of the house.

"Television blow up?" asked Randy of his ten-year-old.

"Nope." The boy walked over, hands stuffed in his pockets. "I was just gonna ask mom about the dead man. Mom, you promised after dinner you'd tell me."

Janet sighed. "All right. But it's not a very nice story."

"Ah, come on, mom. I'm not a baby." He sat on the lawn at her feet. Then Janet launched in from the beginning, and as she told the story, Jake found his thoughts drifting, back, back over the years to other times, other screaming sirens, other homicides.

His musings were neutral, just memories, neither threatening nor unpleasant, merely familiar. How many cases of death in his line of work had he been called on to attend? There were shootings at liquor stores, banks, seedy hotels. And sometimes there were children. Sad, confused, tortured parents took all their pent-up anger out on their offspring. *Those* deaths never failed to touch Jake deeply.

And then sometimes there was the sudden loss of friend. A fellow soldier in Nam. Too many of them. A comrade in the police department.

Janet's voice fell softly on his ear. He could see Brian's eyes wide in wonderment and fascination as the boy's mother spoke.

Yes, there were friends he'd lost over the long years. And yet, somehow, one in particular would always haunt him regularly.

Suzanne.

How could he ever forget the day he'd met her? Five years ago in the precinct captain's office....

The day had been steaming hot. Jake's light suit jacket had been glued to his back, the collar of his shirt irritating his neck in the heat, causing a pink rash to form on his skin. He'd been on edge all day—a typically hot day in the jungle of the city where nerves were raw and the rate of family arguments soared with the hot Santa Ana wind. So did homicides. He'd been on seven cases by three in the afternoon and was in no mood to be called into the captain's office. And there *she* sat, prim and puny and unattractively defensive. His new partner.

"A woman!" Jake had instantly hollered, his green eyes boring into her dark ones.

"That's right," the captain had said, quite unperturbed by the rude outbreak. "You'll be working with Miss Liebowitz while your partner is on special assignment."

"Like hell I will."

But in the end he had. And he'd been a real jerk to Suzanne from the moment they'd walked, together, out of the captain's tiny, cluttered office.

"I take it you aren't particularly fond of female cops," she'd said rather pertly.

Jake had growled. "I like them just fine. On the dispatcher's desk, as secretaries, maybe giving traffic tickets...."

"But not on homicide."

"My, aren't you the intuitive one." Then he'd looked her over, from head to toe, had shaken his head and disappeared into the safe haven of the men's room.

She was too skinny, only stopped talking to exchange feet in her mouth and wore horn-rimmed glasses. But she was the best detective Jake had ever worked with.

His partner's special assignment had lasted four months and at first, Jake had spent every waking minute of every day cursing his foul luck in having been saddled with a woman. But then Miss Liebowitz—Suzanne—had one day gotten the drop on a robber in a liquor store and saved not only Jake's skin but two hostages as well. He'd never seen a man—or woman—react as quickly and skillfully as did his partner that late night, and within minutes, she'd turned an impossible situation into victory. From that night on, Jake had looked at Suzanne through different eyes.

She'd begun to call him "Macho Man" or "MM" shortly thereafter, and he'd dubbed her WL—Women's Lib. And he'd even asked her out on a date once but she'd replied, "No way, Macho Man. I like 'em studious and small. Besides, you booze it too much and you're divorced."

So they'd become friends. The Mutt and Jeff of the homicide squad. And Jake had never once regretted their professional relationship.

"You asleep over there?" came Randy Webster's voice.

"Sort of," Jake replied in his characteristic, husky voice. "Just thinking...." And Janet's words once again filled the air.

Suzanne had died on a November 10 on a dark and lonely street.

It had been a routine call, which needed only a few minutes investigation that night, and then they'd headed back toward the precinct. It had been Suzanne's idea to stop the vagrant on the street and check him out.

"He looks out of place," she'd told Jake from her seat on the passenger side of their car. "Let's run his ID through the computer."

"He's just a wino." Jake had shrugged. "But if you want to roust him...."

Suzanne had only just stepped out of their car when the "wino" pulled his gun and shot her.

For months after that nothing mattered to Jake. He'd sunk into a deep depression and drank with reckless defiance until his fellow detectives poured him into his car and sent him home from the bar.

It hadn't been Suzanne's death. Not really. What had gotten to Jake was the simple fact that he'd never once told her that she was a good cop. He'd owed her an apology, and he'd been too gutless to issue it. She'd probably known how he felt about her, but still....

He *should* have told her.

Jake tipped his head back and gazed up at the brilliantly lit evening sky. Suddenly he felt restless and stood, stretching his long legs. He walked away from the family group toward the corral where his son stood talking to the cute little Webster girl.

He approached them, clearing his mind of the grim past. "And what do you do in the summer, Cecily?" he asked offhandedly, as he leaned elbows casually against the rail.

"Oh," she said, smiling prettily, "I ride a lot with my friends. And I'm on the swim team up in Flagstaff."

"You are?" chimed in Bobby.

"Yes. I've got all sorts of ribbons, too." Then she blushed, her small turned-up nose crinkling. "You wanna see them?"

"Sure," said Bobby, cow-eyed. "You know I was a diving champ myself," he boasted. "In L.A. I got lots of ribbons and three trophies."

"Come to practice with me on Monday and try out for the team," Cecily suggested brightly.

Bobby shrugged. "Maybe I will."

Jake smiled to himself as he watched the two head toward the house. How young they were. And really, so innocent. He hadn't seen Bobby so carefree and grinning in a long, long time. Jake guessed he should feel pretty darn glad they'd gotten out of the city.

To the east, stars made clear by the thin mountain began to shimmer softly in the darkening sky. Somewhere a frog croaked and a breeze hissed in the desert grasses. Jake leaned his broad back against the corral gate, glanced toward Randy and Janet, then toward the house where he could hear Cecily's tinkling laughter.

It was a warm feeling. A curious feeling. As if a long lost friend had suddenly appeared and he was at a loss for words. Still, he wasn't so out of touch that he couldn't recognize a good place when he saw it. And then he wondered cynically just how many married couples there were like the Websters. Wasn't a good family relationship a rarity these days?

The back door of the house swung open; Bobby and his new friend appeared.

"I'm going to show Bobby the pond!" called Cecily to her parents, and Jake's hooded eyes followed them until they disappeared down a bank.

They were pretty darn lucky, he thought, to have a whole lifetime stretching before them. At their tender age they had not yet suffered the pain of loving. They could not yet know how it could twist your gut and torture your brain until you thought you might go mad.

Silently Jake cursed his ex-wife, the lovely Linda, who had packed her bags and so easily walked out the front door. A week after the divorce had become final, Jake had heard that she'd gotten married in Las Vegas. He'd tied a good one on that night—gotten in a fight in a bar with a drunken cop from the Hollywood narcotics division. And for months afterward, he'd tried to stay drunk for as long as his stomach would allow.

Jake leaned over, picked up a small stone and idly pitched it into the desert night. Dear, sweet Linda. She might as well have cut his heart out—and Bobby's, too. But at least Bob would heal eventually, learn to love, to trust another human being.

Jake? He'd given up hope, seven years ago, of ever loving again. For a big, tough guy, he certainly was a coward. But for him, it was just fine that way. Put up the wall around him and make darn good and sure no one, *no one*, ever tore it down again.

Jake smiled that rare smile of his that almost seemed to melt whatever had frozen up inside of him, turned on his heel and strode back toward the peaceful family scene.

At least he had some friends....

CHAPTER FOUR

ALEX WAS STILL IN HER LONG BLUE ROBE and had just poured herself a cup of coffee on Monday morning when there was a knock at the front door. She left the cup on the counter and started across the living room. Now who on earth would be there so early? Perhaps something about poor old Joseph Twelvetrees?

The silhouette of a man showed through the leaded-glass pane of the front door. Randy? But no, this man was taller than Randy. Tom?

Inadvertently she pulled the robe together at the throat, and then opened the door several inches. A stranger stood there, the morning sun gilding his fair head from behind. He was tall, over six foot, had a not too neatly trimmed mustache and interesting lines in a rugged face. Broad shouldered and blond, he should have exuded a boisterous cheerfulness, she registered, and yet his eyes, deep set and shadowed, gave the impression of grimness while his mouth pulled down at the corners. His blond hair was fine and straight and a little too long; there was a thickening around his waist that did not seem to be in character with his bearing. One of the tails of his rumpled white shirt was almost hanging out and his khaki pants needed laundering.

All this Alex observed in an eye blink of time as the man stood, his hands thrust in his pockets, on her front porch. He stared at her, too; she was aware of his interested, yet distant gaze and felt suddenly, oddly, like blushing.

"May I help you?" she heard her own voice say, not quite sure from what deep well of habitual courtesy she'd dredged the words. She pulled the folds of her robe more tightly together.

"I'd like to see Mr. Crawford, please," the stranger said, and his voice was deep—weary and a little gravelly.

"Do you mean my father?" Alex asked. "He's retired to Scottsdale now. I can give you his number there."

"I mean Mr. Alex Crawford," the man said flatly.

It hit Alex suddenly exactly who this stranger was. She felt a small, instinctive smile curve the corner of her mouth; this was not the first person to make the same mistake.

She looked at him more boldly and saw that his eyes were green and that he had a longish jaw, a square-cut chin that was cleft with a vertical line. His skin was freshly shaven and there were a couple of nicks on one cheek.

"Come in, please," she finally said, opening the door, and wondering just how long she'd keep up the game. "You'll have to excuse my attire."

"No problem." He spoke curtly, then strode into the living room to look around quickly, automatically. Alex had the peculiar feeling that she could drill him a day later and he'd remember every detail of her house. A cop. He was a cop, after all. Yes, he had that look about him. From Alex's position behind him she tried to put a finger on her silent thoughts. What was it about this big rumpled man? Perhaps it was the way he moved, exuding an air of sheer physical competence, a controlled power behind the seemingly easy stance. She suspected that there were a few who had moved out of this one's way in his time!

He had turned toward her and she saw that he was scrutinizing her, hiding his impatience rather poorly now, waiting for the appearance of *Mr.* Crawford. She faced him in the middle of the room, and feeling his discomfort, relented.

"I'm Alex Crawford," she said finally. "Alexandra,

actually. And you must be Randy's friend, Mr. Brannigan." She held out her free hand. He stared at it for a split second, then shook it. His grasp was strong, his skin warm and dry, his fingers large-knuckled and long.

"Damn, of all the dumb. . ." he fumbled in the deep voice. "Randy never said. . . I mean. . . ."

Alex managed a smile. "I know. A deputy county attorney named Alex. Of course it's a man. Right? You're not the first, you know."

He shook his head ruefully, embarrassed. Then, abruptly he remembered, "You're Janet's friend, the one she was riding with yesterday. . . ."

Alex sobered. "Yes, I found the body. Poor old Joseph." She met his eyes. "I knew him, you know."

"That's tough." His low voice rumbled.

"Yes, he had a lot of friends in Sedona."

Silence hung between them for a moment, still and gravid. Alex had to pull herself from her thoughts as if from a pit. "But, Mr. Brannigan, you want to see the apartment, don't you?"

"Sure do. And call me Jake." A shadow of a smile pulled at his mouth, flitting uneasily across his face, as if he was long out of practice.

"Okay. . . Jake." She returned his impersonal smile, her blue eyes meeting his for an instant. "But give me a minute. I'll throw something on." As she hurried up the steps to change, she couldn't help but be acutely aware of this stranger's hooded eyes following her, and she was unaccountably thankful when she was behind the closed door of her bedroom.

She had a moment to think about him as she pulled on her clothes, and combed her straight dark hair back into a clip. He certainly wasn't her usual renter! He was an odd sort—the kind of a man who at first glance seemed to be a little too hard on the world, as if he *had* to be a tough guy. She was reminded of a character in a seedy detective novel—the good guy certainly, but one with more than his share of rough edges. And Randy *had* mentioned problems, a divorce. . . . What else, she wondered, lay hidden beneath the hard, unpolished surface?

Sitting on the edge of her bed as she put on her shoes, she envisioned him waiting below, imagined that he was the type to be pacing, impatient, ever moving. And there was that suppressed potential within the big frame for power and action and perhaps humor. Was he holding it all in carefully, afraid, perhaps, of letting all that emotion loose?

Curiosity snatched at her as did a sudden inexplicable female concern; the man looked like he needed some home-cooked meals, someone to iron his shirts, or at least send them to the laundry, someone to buy him new razor blades. He looked—she searched her mind for the word—neglected, as if no one, not even himself, *cared* about him.

She returned to the living room to find Jake Brannigan studying her collection of kachina dolls.

He turned, a little too quickly, sensing her presence. He moved well, fluidly, Alex once again reflected, like a big blond cat, quick on his feet for such a large man. "Just admiring your collection," he said. "Not that I know much about these things...."

"I'd be glad to show them to you some time. Some are very old."

Jake frowned. "And you leave them sitting out in the open like this."

Alex was momentarily taken aback. "You mean, someone might steal them?"

The frown remained fixed on his rugged face. He said nothing, but merely met her eyes as if to tell her the answer to her question was obvious.

Strangely, she felt the urge to explain. "There are very few robberies in Sedona, Mr.... Jake, that is."

He shrugged, his hands still in his khaki pants pockets. "Maybe it's none of my business, but I noticed your door wasn't even locked. It's an invitation to trouble."

Alex took a deep breath. "Well...yes, I suppose it

could be...." He was right, of course; still it really was none of his business. Her gaze fell away. "The apartment is just in back over the garage," she began anew. "It's a two bedroom, very small. I told Randy that it needed painting and the couch springs are, well, not so new anymore."

"I'm not fussy," said Jake flatly. "It's only my son and me. I don't know how long we're staying in Sedona anyway. It may only be a few weeks. I'm sort of...at loose ends, you might say."

"Well, let's go on out and take a look. I could let you have it for $150 month. I was going to raise the rent after it was painted and all but...." She shrugged her slim shoulders and led the way through the kitchen and out the back door. The garage was one of those old-fashioned ones, a carriage house, actually, that stood a hundred feet or so behind the house at the end of the driveway. Alex never used the garage anymore; years ago a carport had been added off the kitchen, and the garage was now full of dusty old odds and ends and pieces of broken furniture.

"Will $150 suit you?" Alex asked again. Didn't he care...?

"Sure. That's fine."

"Well," Alex said, smiling, "you better take a look first...."

They climbed the stairs at the side of the garage. Finally Jake stood behind her on the tiny landing. She had to reach up to the ledge over the door to find the key.

"I know," Alex said, "I shouldn't keep the key here...." Her fingers located it finally. But it wouldn't work easily in the lock. "Darn thing never turns," she complained, as intensely aware of his presence behind her as if he was actually touching her.

"Let me try." He took the key out of her hand, brushing her fingers with his in the process. A faint tingle ran up her arm from her hand. He had to squeeze past her on the landing to get at the door. It opened instantly with an obedient click.

"Thanks," she murmured, pushing open the door.

He gazed about superficially, but wasn't terribly interested in what it looked like, she could tell. He never even opened a cupboard or closet door; merely stuck his head into each of the two bedrooms and paced the length of the living room.

"It's fine. I'll take it," he said. "But I don't want to sign a lease or anything."

"Oh, that's okay. We're pretty casual here."

He pulled out a roll of bills and counted off two fifties, two twenties and a ten. "This is for a month then."

"Would you like a receipt?" she asked, surprised.

He looked at her closely, hesitated, then spoke. "Do I need one?"

"Well, no, I'm sure there wouldn't be any problem. . . ."

"Fine. I trust you."

"My, it's stuffy in here." Alex crossed to a window and pushed it open. "There's no air conditioning, but that big old sycamore shades the place, so it's not bad. At least, the last renters never complained. . . ." She found herself opening the cupboard doors about which he was so unconcerned, checking the refrigerator, turning it on, opening the oven door. "Everything works," she said, turning around to face him.

"I'm sure it does," he responded with faint sarcasm.

"Well, then. . . Jake. . . ."

"Don't let me take up any more of your time."

Alex glanced at her watch. "My, yes. I have to be getting to the office."

"We'll move in today, if you don't mind."

"The place is yours now. See you."

"Yes," Jake said. "We'll be around." And he turned away from her, disappearing into the bedroom as if, she thought, she was dismissed.

JAKE SAT ON THE OLD BROWN COUCH and looked around the small room.

Home sweet home.

It was comfortable, cheap, impermanent. Perfect. At least he wouldn't have to stay at Randy's indefinitely. It wasn't that Randy didn't want them; it was just that he detested depending on other people, feeling he *owed* them. He needed independence, especially now. He needed time. And peace.

Randy. Blast him. He *could* have mentioned Alex Crawford was female. Jake hated being caught like that in a stupid mistake.

But the girl had taken it well. Too bad he hadn't had the mental energy to joke with her about it. It seemed he had no sense of humor whatsoever lately. He used to be full of jokes and laughter and energy. All that was left of that now was a chafing restlessness, an inability to sit still.

His life sure had gone sour for a while there—the divorce, the drinking, Bob's problems in the last two years. And now Jake had a tremendous task before him; he had to somehow reshape that life, take it in his two hands and reform it, make something worthwhile out of the mess he'd gotten himself and Bobby into.

Bobby. He didn't blame the kid for being sullen and bitter. Fourteen was a hard year in anyone's life. A tough time. Puberty. He remembered his own teens—the pain and despair and dreams and hopes.

Sedona could be that new start. It seemed to be a nice place. Except, of course, for dead bodies by the side of the highway. But that, Randy had assured him, was most unusual.

He began to roam restlessly around the small apartment, looking out of windows. He put his hands in his pockets—an old habit—and felt the cool, silky fabric tangled up with his car keys and handkerchief.

It was Alex Crawford's scarf. Of course. The scent was hers; the blue matched her eyes. Beautiful, inquiring dark-blue eyes with thick, curving dark lashes. No mascara on those eyelashes. As a matter of fact, there was no rouge, powder, lipstick. No makeup. Not a bit. She had reappeared in a plain white blouse, and a pair of dark slacks. She'd dressed in a totally unremarkable manner as if to appear as inconspicuous as possible, as if to cover up her natural grace.

Why would a pleasant young woman like that want to hide her charms? Perhaps, he surmised, it was because she had to compete in a masculine world in her job. Maybe she didn't like the idea of using her femininity to advance her career. Or maybe she just couldn't come to terms with being a woman in what was still a man's world. He'd known policewomen like that.

A most unusual-looking woman. A good, honest face—not pretty exactly—and a certain intelligence there, a strength he hadn't quite put a finger on yet. But there was something vaguely foreign about her: the lustrous, black hair that was pulled back severely from straight bangs, the face too wide to be classic, the mouth full lipped but small. She seemed to be a combination of fragility and surprising strength.

Jake could only hope she'd be a good neighbor, which meant someone who'd leave them in peace. One thing he didn't need was a meddling female. Or *any* female for that matter. It was him and Bobby, alone against the world.

Jake paused at a window, scrubbing a hand through his hair. He'd drive back out to the ranch to get Bobby, and then they could begin moving all their junk in.

It was funny, but he almost put the key back over the doorframe as he left the apartment. Then he caught himself and shoved it in his pocket. Women. Some of them just never learned until it was too late. Of course, this wasn't L.A. or New York or Miami. But it never hurt to be cautious.

Then, as Jake slumped down into his Pontiac to turn the key, willing the old car into shuddering life, a strange notion occurred to him: this whole move to Sedona had gone awfully smoothly, *too* smoothly. Somehow he had the feeling that some trouble must be lurking on the horizon. But that, of course, must be his disillusionment speaking.

CHAPTER FIVE

ALEX WAS IN HER OFFICE in the county seat of Flagstaff when the call finally came late Monday afternoon.

"It's for you," said a fellow deputy attorney, handing her the phone.

Alex carefully marked a spot in the law book open before her, then pushed her reading glasses up on her head. It was Randy, down in Sedona, on the line.

"Glad I caught you in," he said. "Do you think you might head on down here and check out this coroner's report?"

"It's in?"

"Yes. And I'll tell you, the results sure don't help much."

"What are they?"

"Why don't you just come on back to Sedona, Alex? It's a bit complicated."

Curiosity ate away at Alex as she tapped on the county attorney's door.

"Bill," she began, "the report's come in on Joseph Twelvetrees. Sheriff Webster wants me to read it...."

Bill frowned. "I'd rather send Dave, but he's busy on that arson case. Darn. This is no case for you, Alex."

She knew what he meant: this was no case for a woman. She hated going through this every time she took on more than a traffic ticket. "The deceased was a friend of mine, Bill."

"That makes it worse. You're emotionally involved."

"I'd like to take this one," she said as evenly as possible. She would not beg. It was her job, for Pete's sake!

Bill pushed his horn-rimmed glasses back. "There

isn't even a case, Alex. There's no suspect, no clear motive. It was probably an accident.''

"It was no accident, Bill." She didn't know why she was so sure, but she was. Hopi sixth sense? Bill would hardly appreciate *that*.

He gave in—grudgingly, as usual. "Go on then, but I want a copy of that medical examiner's report."

"Yes, sir," she managed, then left his office, the familiar frustration making her face feel stiff and graceless.

Alex drove a small, front-wheel-drive red Saab. She needed a dependable vehicle, especially in the winter when Oak Creek Canyon, which led from the high elevation of Flagstaff down to Sedona, could become icy and treacherous during a storm. Generally however, it only snowed at the head of the valley, in Flagstaff. Sedona, far below, remained mild year round.

Still irritated, driving a little more aggressively than she normally did, Alex steered the Saab through the series of breathtaking switchbacks of the lush canyon, but was dismayed to run into heavy tourist traffic below. The drive, which should have taken a half hour, took nearly forty-five minutes. But without the tourists, she reminded herself, there would be no Sedona.

Randy was in his office, waiting. "Lot of traffic?" he asked, rising to greet her.

"The usual."

"Well, here it is. I'll leave you alone to read it. Then we better talk a spell."

"Okay." Already, before Randy had even left his office, Alex was putting on her glasses and burying her dark head in the three-page report. It was terribly disquieting reading through the lurid details of Joseph's autopsy, and she could not keep herself from envisioning the parts of the body described. Several times nausea swept her, but Alex managed to swallow and keep control.

It seemed that Joseph Twelvetrees—a full-blooded Navajo Indian—had been in good physical shape for his seventy years. Heart, respiratory system, muscle tone, organs all operating on a healthy level. So his heart certainly hadn't been the cause of a fall.

Alex read through the lengthy section about the head wound. When she was done, she reread the paragraphs more slowly, committing several phrases to memory. The wound to the head had been made by a rough object; the area of the abrasion was ten millimeters in diameter and the object was most definitely a rock, since debris—sandstone particles and red clay dust— was found surrounding the entrance to the wound, and particles of sandstone were also present in the blood samples taken from the base of the neck. There was also red river mud under the victim's fingernails.

"It must be noted," Alex read for the second time, "that this particular rock debris is found most often by the banks of a river or creek and not in the higher surrounding countryside." She read on. "Death occurred from complications resulting from the head wound. When examined by this coroner, the male body had been dead for approximately seventy-two hours."

And then Alex reread the section on the claw marks found on Joseph's throat and chest.

"It is the opinion of this examiner that the marks are authentic. They were made by the claws of a large wolf most definitely after death occurred. There are no teeth marks present nor is there any other torn flesh."

For long, silent moments Alex sat digesting the information, the report dangling from her fingers. And then, finally, it came to her—she'd been trying since the previous day, deep in the hidden recesses of her mind, to remember what it was about claw marks. . . .

Now she knew.

It was the ancient tales of the Navajo witch, a fearful wolf that does evil for its own sake—a demon.

The tug of the past pulled strongly at Alex. Her Indian blood pounded through her veins while tales of the witch's deeds came back to her. While before she'd always been able to reconcile the two disparate sides of her nature—Indian and white—now, as she sat rooted to her chair, her ancient Indian heritage would not release her.

"Some report," Randy Webster was saying. "You can see why I thought you'd want to read it right away."

"Yes," Alex breathed, "some report." Desperately, she tried to shake off the eerie feelings eating at her.

"And there's something else you ought to know, if you don't already. Fred Gaston stopped in here a few hours ago...."

"Fred Gaston?"

"Owns a gallery down in the Tlaquepaque area of town. Anyway, he has several Navajos working for him, and I guess they're talking up this strange theory. It's about a witch."

Alex felt the breath snatch in her throat. "The Navajo witch..." she whispered. Then she *wasn't* crazy.

"You know about it?"

Alex was about to tell him when suddenly Randy looked up from his desk toward the doorway over Alex's right shoulder.

"Come on in," Randy was saying. "Alex and I are going over this strange Twelvetrees business."

"I'm not interfering?" came a familiar, gravelly voice.

"No, no. In fact, I think we could use a little expert detective advice, Jake. Why don't you leaf through the coroner's report while Alex here tells me about the Navajo witch."

"The what?" asked Jake, sliding up a wooden chair. He nodded to her, growling briefly, "I didn't expect to find you here."

"Just doing my job," she stated, meeting his eyes levelly. Was he going to make some remark about women lawyers?

"Go on about the witch," said Randy.

Alex took a deep breath. How exactly to tell them without sounding like a complete idiot? She mustn't let her emotional involvement show—that was for certain. "The Navajo witch," she began in a professional tone, "is essentially an evil being. I've heard lots of stories about it."

"Then it's a man?" interrupted Jake, his green eyes fastened on her.

"It's. . .he's a witch. It would be incorrect to call him a man. But anyway," she said, pushing her glasses up on top of her head, "he does evil things. Like murder, you could say. It can turn into a wolf and always leaves claw marks on its victims."

"I see," stated Jake pensively.

Alex laughed lightly. "No, I seriously doubt that you do." Then she added, "I'm sorry. That came out all wrong. What I mean is, you'd have to be an Indian to give merit to the implications of the claw marks on Joseph."

Jake studied her impassively for a long minute. "Your Navajo witch, and correct me if I'm wrong, sounds a lot like a werewolf."

Alex thought. "A little, I suppose. Many cultures have tales of a man who turns into a wolf. The Navajo wolf is pretty much the same."

"Alex," said Randy, "you almost sound as if you believe in all this witch stuff."

Both men were studying her carefully; Alex felt their eyes resting uncomfortably on her, like small, rude feet treading on her flesh.

"Don't be silly, Randy." Her voice emerged light and tinkling. "You know me better than that."

It was finally Jake who broke the ensuing awkward silence. "Well," he began, tossing the report onto Randy's desk, "sounds more and more like Joseph Twelvetrees might have met with some foul play."

"How do you see it?" asked Randy, leaning back in his chair.

Alex turned in her seat, watching Jake intently as he spoke in that deep, rough voice of his. "I'd say he was struck on the head by someone, then taken up to the highway and left. The claw marks?" He looked at Alex. "They were left to point a finger at an Indian. Maybe an Indian did do it."

"You're saying he was murdered?" asked Randy cautiously.

"Appears that way to me."

"Couldn't he have stumbled down by the river," improvised Randy, "then collapsed later? Where we found him?"

"Could have. But why the claw marks?"

"Well...."

"They were left there as some sort of pointer or perhaps...a warning." Jake folded his arms across his wide chest.

"So you don't believe an animal got to him."

"No. Besides, why would a wolf...you *do* have them here...?"

"Yes..." Randy responded dubiously. "But very few."

"Why would a wolf claw him, then not make a meal out of it too?" Suddenly Jake caught himself and shifted his hooded gaze to Alex. "Sorry...I forgot you were his friend."

"That's all right," Alex managed, readjusting her glasses on top of her head with shaky fingers. "If there is a case to be made here, I'll have to consider all these things."

"I don't see where there are really any facts to base a case on, Alex," put in Randy. "We may have an open file...but a case?"

"Motive," said Jake. "Would anyone have a reason to harm him?" Again he looked directly at Alex, pinioning her.

"Everyone who knew Joseph liked him," she breathed. "I can't even begin to imagine...." Unless, she thought mutely, it really was the Navajo wolf....

"You know," Randy began, "something sticks in my mind here." He sat quietly for a moment. "I remember now. Joseph was in here, weeks ago, complaining to one of the deputies about some land speculator from the Phoenix area. Something about the guy bothering him about selling that tract of river land old Joseph owned.''

"A speculator?" repeated Jake, his brow knitted.

"Oh sure," replied Randy, "there're hundreds of them 'round these parts. All looking to make a fast buck. Anyone who owns any river land can expect a dozen or more of them to pound on their door every season.''

"That's right," agreed Alex readily. "Besides, murdering someone isn't going to get him to sell his land.''

"Maybe." Jake, putting his hands behind his head, rocked back on his chair. Alex couldn't help but notice the breadth of his chest, the muscled, all-male look of his lightly furred arms below his rolled-up white shirt sleeves. He really was a powerful-looking man. Strong. Interesting. She was suddenly acutely aware of his physical qualities. How bizarre, she thought as she forced her gaze away, that she would be aware of this big rumpled Irish cop, in that way!

And then, too, she was once again curious to know more about him. Why had he retired at such a young age? Why the disillusionment in those hooded, green eyes? And what sparked that note of toughness and cynicism in Jake Brannigan? He certainly was an enigma.

Alex let her thoughts drift. She could hear Randy and Jake tossing ideas back and forth, aspects of the Twelvetrees case. The same ground they had just gone over. Jake sure was still a nosy cop. She could envision him on the streets of L.A., chasing down hardened criminals, his gun flashing in a dark alley somewhere, risking his life—a life filled with danger, excitement, drama. What was he doing in Sedona anyway? And no wonder at all, she mused, that he was interested in this Twelvetrees business!

"That's right," replied Randy. "So it's hard to find a

motive there. All Joseph's boys are doing quite well, I understand. That right, Alex?"

"Ah . . . yes. They are all professional people." What had happened to her sedate, simple life? Ever since yesterday, on her ride with Jan, everything was topsy-turvy. First Joseph. Then opening her door that morning—a century ago—and finding Jake, who was somehow unlike anyone she'd ever met before, standing there like a bit of storm-tossed flotsom washed into her calm haven.

"I think, Alex," said Randy, "that you better tell your boss that we're going to leave the Twelvetrees file open. Do some checking around. There are too many unanswered questions here. Maybe we'll come up with some answers, maybe not. Tell Bill that I'll be in touch."

"All right," she agreed.

"Mind if I intrude?" came a voice.

Alex looked up to see Tom's tall, lean figure standing in the open door.

"I've been trying to track you down, hon," he smiled. "If I'm disturbing you, I'll wait outside."

"No, no," said Randy, rising, "we're all done here today. How're you doin', Tom?" Randy shook his hand.

"Quite well. Business is picking up. Summer season, you know."

"This is an old friend of mine," said Randy, leading Tom over to where Jake was still seated. "Jake Brannigan. We go all the way back to Nam together. Marines."

Jake finally rose, as if a touch bored, looked across into Tom's eyes and shook his hand. "Nice to meet you, Tom. Real estate, you say?"

Alex wondered how in heaven's name Jake had known that. Did that cop's eye of his place everyone so easily? And if so, what had he been thinking when she'd been sitting there, unabashedly studying him as if he were a lab specimen? The room seemed entirely too small for the four of them.

"Thought we might have dinner," Tom was saying, and Alex hadn't the least notion what she replied. All she knew was that she had an overpowering urge to get out of there, away from Jake and Randy and tales of Navajo wolves and open files on death.

It had been enough.

Outside, when the warm desert air fanned her once again, the effect was perversely like having a bucket of cold water thrown in her face.

"You look shaken, Alex," Tom remarked as he took her arm in his.

She smiled with no heart. "I am, a little."

After Alex had changed clothes, she and Tom dined at Rene's, the elegant French restaurant located in the Tlaquepaque Plaza. They'd had to wait nearly an hour to get a table; the summer tourist season had truly arrived. They had marked the time in the blue, Mexican tiled plaza, having a cocktail while they waited. Finally Alex had let the cooler, late-afternoon breeze renew her, had attempted to achieve that elusive calm, that tantalizing core of peace.

It was always difficult for either of them to relax. They both tended to pressure themselves. But when they were together, they tried to put aside the day's problems and attend only to each other. She liked feeling special in Tom's eyes. And she liked being seen with him—a pillar of the community, a fine, decent man, an attractive man with his well-fitting clothes, his neat, full head of sandy-brown hair, his genuine smile. Only occasionally did Alex find fault in him and then only due to someone else's thoughtlessness, the few times he'd been called away from her company by his office or a problem with his ex-wife or the children. But those things happen, Alex told herself, especially to a busy, productive man who already had a family.

She stood at her door, a little sleepy, replete from an excellent meal.

"I enjoyed tonight," said Tom, taking her hand.

"Want a nightcap?" she offered.

"Sure. Besides, it's early. My first appointment isn't until ten, anyway."

Alex brought them each a Grand Marnier. They decided to enjoy the drinks on the porch—it was a beautiful, cloudless evening and from Alex's porch, as from most Sedona homes, the red striated, flat-topped mountains seemed to loom over them, embracing the town in ageless beauty—a smooth blend of mountain and desert unique to Sedona.

Alex sat on the painted steps, letting the cool night breeze caress her, feeling the wind stir dark tendrils of hair against her neck. "Let's go somewhere this weekend, Tom. Just the two of us. Would you like to go backpacking?"

Tom was in a chair above her; she heard his sigh. "Gosh, Alex. I really wish I could. But Mavis has plans, and I promised to keep the kids for her."

"Oh," Alex said, fighting disappointment. "Well then, we'll go another time."

"That's right." He leaned over, and kissed the top of her head. "You're a good sport, hon."

Then silence fell comfortably between them and finally he was turning her toward him, his mouth descending over hers. Alex let the warm sensation of his kiss invade her, enjoying their nearness, their close, loving friendship. For a long time, Tom merely kissed her on the lips. Then he broke away, caressed her shoulder with his mouth and pulled her dark, heavy mass of hair aside to kiss the back of her neck.

"I'd like to take you upstairs," he whispered against her flesh. "I want to make love to you, Alex."

He always said the right thing; Tom always made her feel good. Whether he was holding a car door for her or asking her to bed, he had a distinct, proper way of doing it. It was as if he'd read the book on how to treat a woman, how to make her feel on equal footing with him.

"Oh, Tom," Alex breathed, feeling warmth toward him spread through her.

Alex heard a noise, a twig snapping followed by a

scuffling sound in her driveway. Later, she would be glad for the disturbance but at the time, she was merely irritated.

Tom's head came up. "What's that?" he half whispered.

Alex strained to see into the darkness. Walking up her drive, heading toward the garage, was a tall, lean shadow. "It must be Jake's son," she said softly, trying not to lose the intimate moment with Tom.

"Jake's son? Alex, I'm afraid I don't...."

"Oh my gosh! I forgot to tell you...I rented the apartment!"

"You did? But...oh, I see. To that guy I met today."

"Jake."

"Finnegan or something? But Alex, I thought you weren't going to rent it out."

Something in his voice, some hint of disturbance, surprised Alex. "Well, I just rented it. That's all."

"I didn't care too much for him," said Tom, rising and stuffing his hands in his trouser pockets, rattling his car keys.

Strangely, Alex's back stiffened and she, too, stood. "He's a perfectly decent person, Tom. I don't understand why you're acting like this."

"It's his type, Alex," he said sharply.

"And what *type* is that?"

"Oh, you know—Mr. Tough Guy. The old ex-marine routine. That went out in the sixties, for Pete's sake."

"It did?" replied Alex, taking the defensive. Tom was literally telling her that he didn't trust her judgment. "I found him quite likable, Tom."

Tom turned on his heel, glaring at her for an uncomfortable moment. "A man's man, is that it, Alex?"

There they were, standing on her porch, the best of friends—lovers, for goodness' sakes—having a silly, immature argument over a total stranger!

She told Tom as much, taking his hands in hers. Then

she smiled. "Why, I do believe this has been our first fight."

Finally Tom relented. "You're right. I apologize. I was a real idiot just now." He kissed her softly on the forehead. "Forgive me?" His voice, deep and melodic, was almost a plea.

"Of course."

Nevertheless, the spell had been broken. Tom left a few minutes later—alone—and Alex began to wonder if the whole thing hadn't been for the best. She had to work in the morning; the night was growing shorter. She snapped out the living-room lights, mounted the stairs and had her blouse half-undone by the time she entered her dark bedroom. Kicking off her sandals, she automatically went to her window to close the louvered shutters. Standing there, she couldn't help but notice the light shining from the apartment window. The drapes were moving in a silent breeze, the window was half open like hers to gather the evening coolness. And Jake Brannigan was sitting in the small living room, apparently reading. She could see only his profile, shadowy and rugged. Even at that distance, even in repose, there was a power and strength that filled him, that winked from his form like a kind of beacon.

Alex was not sure just how long she stood barefooted in the hushed darkness watching through the window, her blouse hanging from one hand. She didn't become aware of the fact that she was even doing it until he rose and walked out of the pool of light, disappearing from view altogether. Then slowly, she reached out in the cool night's breeze and pulled the shutters closed, fastening them carefully in place.

She wondered, as she drew a warm bath, if Jake Brannigan would stay in Sedona as Randy hoped he would.

But then, what did it really matter to her?

CHAPTER SIX

"DON'T FORGET THE PARTY this afternoon," Janet reminded just before she hung up. "I invited Jake and Bobby, of course. Say, how's it working out with them renting your place?"

"Fine," replied Alex. "I haven't seen a whole lot of them. Caught a glimpse of his son the other night. He's tall for his age, isn't he?"

"Yes, I think he's going to be big like Jake. I'll tell you, Cecily's mad over him. She's already called every one of her girlfriends and told them *all* about him. They're jealous as all get out."

Alex laughed. "Teenagers. Oh, I remember those days. And of course I'll be there this afternoon—with Tom."

"Make it as early as you can. We're having horseshoes, baseball, riding, all that sort of thing."

"Sounds like fun, Jan, but now, really, I've got to get back to work or I'll never get there. See you soon."

"Bye."

Compulsively she finished up a desk full of paperwork, reread the copy of the coroner's report on Joseph Twelvetrees once more, then packed it in for the day. It was Friday, after all.

On the drive back down to Sedona, she tried to rid her body of the week's tensions. Somehow Fridays were always satisfying, finishing up the work on her desk, tying up loose ends.

And this Friday had been singularly gratifying as she'd finally, after three court appearances, won the case for the "People versus Mr. Hodge Burson," a difficult one involving a wealthy drunk driver and his crafty lawyer. Thankfully the judge saw things the "peoples" way and gave the man six weekends in jail and a fifteen-hundred-dollar fine. Her boss, Bill, had grudgingly commented on it, making a congratulation sound like a criticism. "Your first case in court, Miss Crawford, and you won. Lucky."

"Thank you, sir," she'd said tightly.

He'd merely nodded his dismissal.

But she thought now as she steered the Saab through the difficult switchbacks of Oak Creek Canyon, that there was still one case—or semi-case—spreading large on her desk: Joseph Twelvetrees. She wondered if that file would ever be closed for good. It seemed she'd run into a dead end.

Once home, Alex just had time for a quick shower and was pulling on her riding boots when the phone rang. It was Tom.

"Listen, hon," he began, "I've got to work late. Can you meet me out at the Websters'?"

"Sure, Tom. But couldn't you put if off for once? You've been working yourself to death lately."

"Sorry, not this one, hon. I'll rush, really I will."

"Okay. See you soon then."

As Alex hung up, she reflected upon the fact that Tom had been doing this sort of thing more and more often lately. Oh, she was busy, too, and knew what the pressure could do to a person, but she tried with all her being to recognize it and keep her life in control. Poor Tom. Sometimes she wondered how he was going to make it through at all.

An idea occurred to her, although she hesitated mentally for a moment. She could ask Jake Brannigan for a ride out to the Websters' ranch and then she wouldn't have to drive herself home. But she had gotten the distinct feeling that the Brannigans—father and son—wanted to be left strictly alone.

But, really, just to ask for a ride. They couldn't object to that, could they?

She walked across the driveway, climbed the stairs

and rapped on the screen door. She could see into the living room; it was piled with boxes and suitcases still. The television was on—she could hear it. No one came to the door. She knocked again, calling out, "Hello? Anybody home?"

Finally Bobby Brannigan appeared at the door, a startling reminder of what Jake must have looked like in his youth.

"Yeah?"

"I'm Alex Crawford," she said, undaunted by Bobby's rudeness. "Is your dad around?"

"He's in the shower."

"Are you going to the Websters' party?" she asked.

"Yeah. I guess so. I'd rather stay here, but my old man insists. Sounds like a real bore. Horseshoes and baseball! Wow. What a lotta fun."

"I just wondered...."

"Somebody there, Bob?" came Jake's bass from inside. His wet head poked out from the hallway.

"I was just going to ask Bobby here if I could bum a ride out to the Websters' with you," called Alex.

The head withdrew quickly. "No problem," came Jake's muffled voice. "Have you met my son, Bobby?"

"Yes, I have," called Alex toward the direction of the hallway, but she held Bobby's gaze with her own. She felt a slight spurt of satisfaction when his stare fell first.

"Maybe you'd like to go for a ride this afternoon if horseshoes and baseball are not your thing," she offered sweetly, smiling.

"You mean on a *horse*?"

"Yes, a real live horse." She paused for effect. "You *do* ride, don't you?"

"Yeah, sure, I guess so. You only have to sit there, don't you?" the boy mumbled.

"Well, there's a little more to it than *that*, but never mind, that's a start, anyway." The calm courtesy in her voice never wavered. It was a little like being in court with a touchy judge.

She turned to leave. "See you in a bit, Bobby."

She was halfway across the driveway when Jake caught up with her.

"Hey, hold on a minute," he said. His hair was still wet, dripping onto the collar of his shirt—this time a pale-blue one, not yet tucked in and just as rumpled as the last. At least he hadn't appeared in a towel. "Look, I caught a little of your conversation with Bobby." His green eyes were narrowed against the sun. "I'm sorry. I apologize for him. He's a rude little snot sometimes. Too big to put over my knee, too small to knock down."

"Oh, there's no need to apologize. I know about teenagers." She turned to go but felt his hand on her arm, stopping her.

"Anyway," he said, "sorry for the kid." He made it sound like he was doing her a big favor apologizing for his son's behavior. Obviously he resented it; she was sorry now she'd ever had the idea of getting a ride with him.

And then there was his firm hand, still on her arm. She wondered if he was always so assertive or if it was just some reaction she provoked in him.

She thought to pull her arm away, but that would have been terribly conspicuous. And then he was drawing his hand back anyway.

"Please, don't worry about it," she said, trying not to show her agitation. How could a simple touch provoke such a turmoil in her?

"Okay. We'll be ready to go in a few minutes."

"Just honk and I'll be right out," she said shortly, turning away.

Once inside the relative dimness of her house, Alex had time to wonder at her ridiculous reaction to Jake Brannigan. He was attractive in a way, but he was not her type at all—too untidy, too overwhelmingly masculine, too rough around the edges for her. And he seemed to get her back up every time he opened his mouth. Well, at least Tom was meeting her at the party; she wouldn't have to put up with Jake for long.

Tom. She went into the bathroom, took out the rubber band that held her hair back and began to brush it out in long, thoughtful strokes. Then she rummaged around in the vanity drawer and found her long-unused mascara and some pale-blue eye shadow. She even put lipstick on, but then decided it was just too much and wiped it off roughly with a Kleenex.

She eyed herself in the mirror, seeing a stranger. Her eyes seemed larger, her high cheekbones even more pronounced; the width of her face was softened by the hair framing it, turning her into a mysterious, attractive woman instead of the everyday Alex—the lawyer and solid citizen. She felt a spurt of fear at the sight. Yet, perversely, she liked it, too.

Why was she doing this? The striking, inscrutable face stared back at her. Tom had always liked her just the way she was....

The party was in full swing by the time Jake pulled into the driveway off Highway 179 and passed under the sign that read Someday Ranch. There was an awful lot of beer floating around, a lot of laughter, the clink of horseshoes, the distinctive crack of a bat meeting a ball. Somewhere a stereo or tape deck spewed out country music. Most of the ladies were sitting under a big oak tree near the punch bowl.

"Alex," squealed Janet, running up to her, "at last! And Jake!" She kissed his cheek, unmindful of his impatience. Janet was like that—she noticed only what she wished to. "Randy's down at the horseshoe pit. Bobby, honey, the kids are over at the barn. There's a new foal down there. Come on, folks. What'll you have?"

"I'll help myself, Jan, thanks," said Alex, feeling the need to put distance between herself and Jake. Sitting beside him in the front seat of his car had been quite enough for a while.

"I know!" said Janet to Jake. "Tonic and lime. Right?"

Bobby hung back behind his father, sullen faced,

slouching. Alex felt pity for the poor kid, obviously uncomfortable, out of his element, a stranger.

There was a table of hors d'oeuvres set up—chips and dip, raw vegetables, crackers and cheese. Alex wandered around, nibbling, sipping on her glass of wine. She knew almost everyone there: the businessmen, doctors, restaurateurs, art-gallery owners, even a few artists themselves. The town's mayor was there, the entire sheriff's department except for a couple of poor souls on duty in town.

Jake headed toward the horseshoe game, Bobby in tow. Alex relaxed, spoke with the mayor's wife and some other women, caught up on the local gossip. Janet's parties were always casual and easygoing. Pleasant. Not elegant but a lot like Janet herself—fun and unassuming.

"Tom not here yet?" came Janet's voice from behind. "Oh well, he'll be along."

"Yes," Alex said, smiling, "shortly."

Then Janet stood close, her head bent toward Alex's. "You know what I like best about these parties?"

"What?"

"Looking at all the masculinity!" whispered Janet, giggling.

Alex laughed. Typical Janet. "I know," said Alex, "you're never too old to look."

Janet's eyes were on the horseshoe pit. "You know that Jake Brannigan looks even better than I remembered. Age hasn't hurt him at all." She turned to look at her friend meaningfully.

"Are you trying to suggest something, Jan?"

"And he lives right next door to you. Lucky girl," went on Janet, unperturbed.

"Janet, cut it out. He's not my type at all and besides, I'm spoken for and I'm quite happy."

"Of *course* you are!" Janet winked, drifting away with a little sway to her generous hips.

Alex finally saw Tom walking across the lawn toward her. Her heart jumped with welcome. Her man. She felt more secure all of a sudden, ready to enjoy herself without reservation.

"Hi, hon," said Tom, kissing her cheek. "I didn't see your car and thought you might have stood me up." He smiled tenderly at her, his smooth, clean-shaven face familiar and well-known.

"Oh, I got a ride with Jake," she explained. "So you could drive me home."

"You look absolutely beautiful today, Alex. Have you done something with your hair?" Good old Tom; he always noticed.

"Not really," she said, a little shy suddenly.

"Well, it suits you. Come on, I'll refill your wine. I'm dying for a drink myself."

Comfortably, Tom put his arm around her shoulders, and they walked toward the table that held the liquor and mixes.

"Tom Farley," she heard that familiar, slightly gravelly voice say, "isn't it?"

She was standing face to face with Jake as Tom's arm tightened imperceptibly around her shoulders.

"Yes. Mr. . . . Finnegan, did you say?"

"Brannigan. Jake Brannigan." They did not, Alex noticed, shake hands this time.

It was odd, Alex would remember later, but it seemed that every one of her senses was heightened, every nerve ending as sensitive as a tuning fork. She saw the shadowed cleft in Jake's chin, the whorls the whiskers made on his jaw, the way his green eyes seemed to narrow and recede behind a curtain of coolness, the way the cords in his strong neck stood out as he moved, the way his fine blond hair brushed the collar of his blue shirt.

And Tom. She turned her head ever so slightly and could see the flecks of gold in his brown eyes, the way every hair on his head lay in place perfectly, the exquisitely laundered and starched cowboy shirt, the well-cut Western-style suit, the glossy polished boots.

Inadvertently she leaned closer to Tom. She was making her statement: *This is my man, we belong together*. It felt good to do it—familiar, secure.

"Nice to see you again," Tom said, nodding as his arm steered her away toward a group of people that Tom knew.

She was relieved, surprised at the feeling, suddenly lighthearted. All at once she felt beautiful, desirable, a strange feeling for Alex, who recognized her plainness only too well and rarely let herself go beyond careful social talk in public. She laughed a lot, snuggling close to Tom. It occurred to her once that she was trying too hard but she didn't care.

"Are you having a good time?" whispered Janet in her ear.

"Oh yes, it's a great party, Jan!"

"Oh, good. Do you think it's time to start the barbecue, Alex?"

"Oh, not yet. It's way too early."

"Gosh," said Janet, "I've been a little worried about Jake. Being a stranger here and all . . . do you think he's having a good time?"

"Why, I haven't even seen him since you last pointed him out. I have no idea. But I'm sure he can take care of himself, Jan," she answered smugly.

"That's what I sometimes wonder about, Alex. The guy's been through a lot. . . ."

"Hey, Janet, don't worry. Introduce him to Polly Butler. I'll bet she's just his type."

"I don't think there's *anyone* his type anymore, that's the trouble." Janet's dark eyes glistened with concern.

"Oh, come on, he's a big boy."

"Sure, I guess so . . . oh, there's Randy. Hi, babe. You ready to start the barbecue?"

"Not yet, Jan. Actually, I was looking for Tom here. Mavis called. I told her you'd call her back."

"Thanks, Randy. Did she say what it was?"

"No, just to call. Go on up to the house. Use the phone in the kitchen."

"I'll just be a sec, hon," Tom said, turning to Alex. "It's probably just some little thing about the weekend."

Alex knew the minute she saw Tom coming back from the house. It was in the set of his head and shoulders.

"Alex, I'm sorry. . . ." he began, his brows drawn together.

"I know," she said with a sigh, "Mavis needs you."

"Jamie's sick, and she's got to take him to the doctor. It's just that it's Friday afternoon, and she's leaving for the weekend. I'll have to go stay with the oldest while she takes Jamie."

"Can't she get someone else? A neighbor, a teenager or someone? Tom, I really think. . . ."

"Alex, hon, I'm their father. She can't get anyone else. She tried. I'll just have to go."

I'll bet she tried real hard, thought Alex angrily, but she didn't say another word. It was not her place. She had to learn to accept the fact that Tom came to their relationship with baggage from the past.

"I'm sorry," Tom said once more, and he really *looked* sorry. Disappointed but resigned. "I was enjoying myself. Well, I'd better get going. I'll find Randy and Janet and thank them."

"Tom, I'm coming with you. You can drop me at home.

"I wouldn't think of it, Alex. You stay here and have a ball. The party's just starting."

"Tom, really, I'd rather go with you."

"Don't be silly, hon." He bent over and kissed her forehead. "Anyone can drop you off later."

"Tom. . . ." She reached for his hand, holding it like a drowning person would.

"I know, hon. It's a shame. But what can I do? Now you go on and have yourself a ball."

It was no use. She'd have to stay. It was either that or make a fuss that would be embarrassing to them both. Even as Tom turned and left her, she was not at all sure why she was so reluctant to stay at the party without him. It didn't make any sense at all

Perhaps she'd just ask around and see if anyone was driving back to town early. She could say she had work to do or she had a headache. No one would even notice. It was ridiculous the way she felt so conspicuous without Tom. She was sorry now she'd put on makeup and let her hair hang loose. People would think she was on the prowl or something; they were used to her more businesslike look, her ordinary, everyday appearance. She felt like a child in a Halloween costume at a grown-up's party.

She found Janet sprawled in a lawn chair, her cheeks flushed, her mouth open in laughter. Oh, to be so innocent and easy with oneself!

"Jan, is anyone leaving early? I thought I'd get a ride into town...."

"What's the matter, Alex?" Janet's brows drew together. "Something wrong?"

"Oh no. I'm just tired, that's all."

"Sit down then. For goodness' sakes!" Janet patted a tree stump next to the chair. "Come on. I saw Tom leave, by the way. Mavis again, I suppose. He should tell her to...."

"Janet, please."

"Oh, I know. Good old Tom to the rescue. I think he *likes* to do this to you. It proves your loyalty or something."

"Janet."

"Never mind me. But please don't go home. Hey, I just remembered. Bobby Brannigan was looking for you."

"What did he want? Last time I saw him he didn't appear to be the least bit interested in me. As a matter of fact, he was downright rude."

"Kids," sighed Janet. "Don't take it personally, Alex. It's only his way of showing he's cool."

"Oh, he's cool all right." Alex shrugged.

"There he is, Alex. Bobby, yoo hoo! Over here!" Janet yelled across the lawn.

Bobby sauntered over, hands in the pockets of his low-slung jeans. He certainly was *cool*.

"Are you having a good time, Bobby?" asked Janet.

"Oh, sure, Mrs. Webster." He turned to Alex, eyeing her carefully. "You still want to go riding?" he asked, his tone almost aggressive.

"Riding? Oh...." Alex remembered their conversation of that afternoon. She hadn't thought he'd really take her up on it.

"What a *great* idea!" exclaimed Janet. "Oh, yes, Alex, take him riding! Poncho will be perfect for him."

"Well, I don't know...."

"Oh, never mind, I didn't really want to anyway," grunted Bobby, turning away.

The poor kid. Here she was, rejecting him when he was a complete stranger here, without a friend in the world. And he seemed so sensitive. "Bobby, wait. I'd love to go riding." She stood, put a hand on his arm, and leaned close to his ear. "I've had enough of this social stuff anyway. Let's get away for a while, and by the time we get back dinner will be ready. What do you say?"

"Well, I guess so, if you really want to," he mumbled, allowing himself to be convinced.

"Have fun!" cried Janet gaily.

"You'd better tell your dad where you're going," said Alex. "He'll worry."

"Dad?" Bobby laughed. "He doesn't know where I am most of the time."

"Nevertheless, I'd feel better if you told him, Bobby."

"Okay, I think he's playing baseball. Can you believe it? Randy—Mr. Webster—talked him into it."

They came upon the baseball game just as Jake hit a double and slid into second. He got up, slapping the dust off his pants, grinning for once, while his team cheered. He had the moves all right, Alex noticed. An athlete. An *ex*-athlete, she corrected herself. But it was all still there, the fluid reactions, the power.

Jake walked over to them, his hair flopping loosely over one eyebrow, his cheeks flushed a little. "Hey, Bob," he said, "want to play for me?"

"Dad, I'm going riding with...ah...Miss Crawford here."

Jake looked at Alex intensely for a moment as if to question her motives, then nodded. "Great idea. Think you can stay on, Bob? I understand Alex here is quite a horsewoman."

"*Dad*, of course I can. I mean, we're not exactly running the Kentucky Derby, are we?"

"I'll watch him," put in Alex quickly. "The horse he'll ride is very gentle."

"Geez, you guys," said Bobby disgustedly. "Maybe you should come along, dad, and baby-sit. Or maybe you can't ride a horse."

"Bobby..." warned Jake.

"Come on, dad. I dare you."

"Maybe it's not such a good idea..." began Alex. "I mean...."

"Oh it's a great idea, Miss Crawford. Come on, dad."

"Well, Bobby, I don't know. Maybe the lady here doesn't want...."

"Oh, don't be silly," said Alex uncomfortably. She felt as if things were moving too fast for her, as if a current were carrying all of them to an unknown destination.

Jake was silent for a time, obviously weighing his choices.

"You're chicken, dad."

"Your father..." started Alex.

"Come on!" pressed Bobby.

"Oh, for Pete's sake, all right!" growled Jake, obviously exasperated.

Alex looked at Jake, big and blond and faintly angry, then at Bobby, smiling victoriously, a smaller version of his father.

Suddenly Alex wondered how this had all come

about and exactly why she was doing it. She felt a sinking sensation in the pit of her stomach. Then Bobby was saying, "Well, come on, let's go!" Jake shrugged, turning toward the barn, and Alex had absolutely no choice except to follow them.

CHAPTER SEVEN

JAKE COULD ONLY SEE HER NARROW BACK as she led them single file on horseback up behind the Websters' place and even then Bobby, riding between them, often hid her from view. He felt a little foolish and out of his element. Imagine, letting Bobby's childish taunts get to him like that! As if he were a teenager himself, having to show off in front of some high-school girl. He hadn't ridden in years and knew he'd be sore tomorrow, but the old habits came back quickly—the feel of the horse under him, the right tension in the reins that signaled intentions between horse and rider.

They seemed to be following a dirt road that they had encountered at the foot of Bell Rock, just beyond Someday Ranch.

"Where are we going?" he heard Bobby call to Alex.

She turned in the saddle, replying, "I'm not sure. It depends on how long you want to ride. We can turn around any time you want."

"I'm game," said Bobby proudly.

He was showing off, Jake knew. The kid had barely ever been on a horse before; he sagged like a flour sack, his toes hung down in the stirrups and he had a death grip on the big Western saddle horn.

Alex was still turned, one slim hand on the horse's glossy rump, one holding the reins expertly. Jake liked competence in a person. Alex Crawford was certainly competent—at a lot of things it seemed. "Then let's go on up to a favorite spot of mine. It'll take a while, though. It might even be getting dark when we get back."

"Whatever you say," said Bobby defiantly.

The dirt road climbed gradually, leading up a canyon that widened as they entered it. The late-afternoon sun gilded everything, turning red, striated rock so brilliant one had nearly to shade one's eyes. The sky, above the rough hills that rimmed the canyon, was deep blue at its zenith, paling to azure toward the horizon. Just the color of Alex Crawford's eyes, he couldn't help but think. Brush in shades of silvery gray green, olive and dark green studded the floor and walls of the canyon. The wash was cut into a crazy quilt of erosion by arroyos that emptied into it: this roughly sculpted disorder characterized the dry land. And yet it contained its own kind of spare beauty: it was not the overripe lushness of jungle or the neat, smooth fertility of farmland.

Small mammals scurried in the underbrush and once a family of quail erupted from under a clump of sagebrush, flapping away noisily. Magpies screeched at them, horned larks searched the ground for seeds, doves clucked gently in twisted trees.

Jake could hear Bobby asking questions; his voice was enthusiastic for once. It was a nice change from his usual "cool" boredom. Suddenly he turned around, excited. "Dad, we're going to a cliff dwelling!"

"It's just a small one," Alex called back over her shoulder. "Not exactly a national historical monument."

"Wow," said Bobby.

Jake urged his horse up beside Alex when the canyon widened out. "It's decent of you to do this for Bobby," he said, trying not to sound as if the words were forced; it really was good of her.

"Please, don't thank me. I wasn't so keen on staying and being social anyway. I love this place we're going to so it's really not any favor."

"Well, thanks anyway." Then, "Your ah... friend doesn't mind?"

She turned her head, her dark, glistening hair swinging at her shoulders beneath the western hat. "My friend?"

"Ah, Tom...." Now why had he gone and brought up that subject? Who cared what this Tom thought anyway?

"Oh no." She smiled. "He's not much for riding."

"Well, thanks anyway...."

She said nothing more, merely ducking her head a little shyly. A funny girl—too cool and in control one moment, vulnerable and young the next. And that boyfriend of hers, not much of a man by the looks of him, but then there was no accounting for taste. It's as if she deliberately chose a man who was no threat to her life in any way, one who would not touch her deeper emotions. Was she afraid of having her orderly life roiled up by a real man?

"We'll have to leave the horses here," she finally said, stopping. "It's a steep path to the top." She pointed up to the west wall of the canyon—a cliff, Jake would have said—and there, in a shadowed overhang was a jumble of pale cubes, as if a child had carelessly left his blocks in a pile there.

"How do we get to it?" asked Bobby, his head tilted up.

"There's a path."

If you could call it a path, thought Jake, as he struggled up the steep, rocky canyon wall. "This is for mountain goats!" he yelled once when they left him too far behind.

"Come on, dad!" Bobby shouted back.

He finally stepped out onto the ledge at the top of the path. "Whew! Didn't these people know about making steps?" He tried to laugh it off, pulling out a handkerchief and wiping his forehead.

"Here it is," said Alex, with careful diffidence. "It's not much. Mostly ruins now." She walked over to a crumbled adobe wall, stroking it as if it were fine mahogany. "I call it the House Made of Dawn. I'm sure it had a name—once—but nobody knows what it was so I named it from a line in a Navajo chant."

Jake stuffed his hands in his pockets and walked to

the edge of the ledge that held the pueblo; it was a long, straight drop to the valley floor. He heard a few dislodged pebbles roll over the cliff, tumbling and rattling all the way down. He stepped back; he never had particularly liked heights....

"It must be a thousand feet at least," Alex said beside him.

"I guess they liked it that way," said Jake. "For protection."

"I guess so," agreed Alex.

The ruined village seemed to have burst from the land. It was made of the red earth itself with spaces for doors and windows the color of the sky. And it was so old, existing long before the white man reached the Southwest, before the United States existed, before Columbus intruded upon the New World. As old as legend.

"Wow," called Bobby. "What kind of Indians lived here?"

"They were called the Anasazi," Alex replied. "The Ancient Ones. They lived here over eight hundred years ago."

"They built this eight hundred years ago?" asked Bobby in amazement.

"They were a very highly civilized race—the only Indians in the area north of Mexico who built actual, permanent towns."

"How'd you find this place?" asked Jake roughly.

"Oh, out riding when I was a kid. My grandfather told me about it. He says our ancestors lived here."

"Your ancestors?" asked Jake. "Wait a minute, I have a feeling I've missed out on something here."

She turned to him, faint surprise in her blue eyes. "Didn't you know?"

"Know what?"

"I'm half Hopi Indian. The Hopis are the descendants of the Anasazi."

"You mean, you're half Indian?" breathed Bobby.

"Bob..." warned Jake.

Alex smiled. "That's all right. I'm proud of it. He's allowed to be impressed." She walked along a half-fallen wall, touching it with sensitive fingers. "My mother is a full-blooded Hopi who chose to live in the white man's world. She was a lecturer at the University of Arizona. Anthropology. That's where my father met her." She went on, "My grandfather still lives on the reservation at New Oraibi. He's a wonderful old guy."

It explained a lot, Jake thought: that faintly mysterious look, the lustrous blue-black hair, the odd feeling that she did not quite fit into a neat category.

"This is the plaza where they held their dances. See?" She pointed at a crumbled pit in the hard-packed ground. "That was the kiva, the holy place where the secret ceremonies were held. And there is a storeroom." She stepped over a pile of adobe bricks. "I found a clay pot here once. Black and red. It was lovely. I gave it to my grandfather."

Jake found himself silently staring at her, not at the kiva, not at the ancient crumbling walls. He had the feeling that the girl—the woman—was as unusual, as mystical, as this ancient setting above the desert expanse.

She sure wasn't the run-of-the-mill type. Somehow he couldn't picture her dashing to the hairdresser's every week or having her nails done. Nor could he picture her with Tom Farley.

It had been a long time since he'd taken notice of a woman, other than admiring a pair of legs here and there, of course. And then he caught himself—brought his thoughts to a crashing halt. The last thing he needed in his life was to be looking at a woman. . . .

For a time they wandered silently, reverently among the ruins. The overhang was shadowed now in late afternoon, yet over the rim of the canyon the sky was still clear and dazzling blue. The sun-warmed blocks of adobe slowly cooled in the shade; a lizard scurried across the broken surface of what was once, eight centuries ago, a retaining wall.

"This is neat," said Bobby. "Did you ever find any bones of dead Indians here?"

Alex smiled indulgently, the color of her eyes precisely matching that of the southern sky. "No, they all just disappeared, all the Anasazi, hundreds of years ago. Very mysterious. There are theories to explain it. My mother firmly believes that a long drought caused them to move on and other anthropologists say warlike Indians, maybe the predecessors of the Navajo, chased them away." She brushed her bangs back absentmindedly beneath her hat. "Nobody knows really."

Jake did not feel the urge to say much. He watched his son and, in spite of himself, the woman. The boy was filled with the awe of his new experience. And the woman, too, had changed once again, chameleonlike. A kind of peace held her. An area around her was calm and untroubled, at one with her surroundings. If Jake closed his eyes, he could imagine this crumbled mansion of the past peopled by the Ancient Ones: men in their dance regalia, women grinding cornmeal, children running and playing on the warm stones, piñon smoke hanging over it all. And Alex would be there, too, belonging to the past he imagined. He felt a vague envy.

"Do you have an Indian name?" he asked, aware of the incongruity of his question the moment he said it. He registered her startled glance, wondering whether he had invaded her private dream.

"It's Chosóvi," she said quietly.

"What does it mean?" asked Bobby.

"Bluebird." Her glance fell away.

Slanted rays of sunlight still hit the top of the eroded bluffs above them, but it was tinged with red now.

"We'd better get going," Alex finally said. "It'll be late by the time we get back. Janet will think we've broken our necks somewhere out here." She gave a small laugh, reluctantly breaking the tie with the silent past.

"Can we come back?" asked Bobby. "I'd like to stay longer."

"Alex might have other things to do, Bob," said Jake.

"Of course we can, Bobby. Maybe you'd like to camp out over night here sometime."

"Wow! Would I ever! That would be really cool."

"Are you sure you wouldn't be scared?" Alex teased, leading the way off the narrow ledge to the path. "The Navajos are afraid of these dwellings. They say the magic of the Ancient Ones is older and stronger than Navajo magic and they won't go near these places."

"I'm not afraid!" said Bobby. "That's all superstition anyway."

"The Indians are a very superstitious people."

"Are you?" asked Bobby.

"No. Well, maybe a little," she confessed. "But not here. This feels like home to me."

The horses were dozing in the shade of a gnarled scrub oak tree. They mounted; Jake noticed a grimace as Bobby's rear hit the saddle. His own posterior was sore, too. Maybe he was getting too darned old for this nonsense. And yet Alex—Chosóvi, he remembered—sat as straight as ever, her body moving rhythmically with her horse, as if she could go on all day and into the night. He felt the contrast to his own weaknesses: his age, the lines of wear and worry that marked him, the extra flesh around his middle, the flabbiness of muscles that had once been taut. Was he supposed to accept all that with grace or fight against it with every ounce of energy he possessed? It was something he hadn't thought too much about—not for a while, anyway.

The ride back was quiet, punctuated only by Bobby's questions about the Indians and about when he could hike or ride back into the canyon to visit the House Made of Dawn again.

"I've got some books about the Anasazi at home, if you'd like to read them, Bobby. My mother left some of hers here. She has quite a collection, as you can imagine. The Anasazi were her special interest."

"Boy, I wish I knew about my ancestors like you

do," replied the boy. "Mine are dull, and they didn't even get here until—when, dad?"

"Around the 1900s."

"That's nothing compared to these Indians, dad," said Bobby with superiority.

Alex insisted on unsaddling the horses when they finally got back. It was dusk by then; a few stars punctured the velvety blue purple of the sky.

The babble of voices and laughter, the pungent smell of barbecued meat hung in the air.

"I'm starved!" Bobby was off like a shot. He stopped, turned and yelled back over his shoulder. "Thanks, Miss Crawford!"

"Alex!" she shouted back, laughing.

But he was gone.

"Here, I'll take them," said Jake, trying to help with the tack. "They're too heavy for you."

"Go on and eat," put in Alex. "Really, I know where everything goes."

"I'll be darned if I'll leave you here alone to do all this." He gestured at the saddles, the bridles, the sweat-soaked saddle blankets.

"You might think I'd never lifted a saddle before...."

And then he almost said something to the effect that putting up the heavy saddles and tack was darn well man's work but he caught himself. Alex Crawford would probably have been absolutely disgusted. Instead he lifted one of the saddles and easily hung it on its post.

Apparently, even that was too much.

"I said, I'll get these." Alex stood, hands on hips, her expression just hard enough to tell Jake to back off. Then she turned to resume her work in the barn. "Did you ever have to work with a woman for a partner?" she asked, straightening one set of reins.

Jake shrugged, leaning back against a stall, and crossed his arms. "I never did like working with a woman."

Alex shot him an amused glance. "I'll just bet you didn't."

He wondered if it would do any good to explain—to tell this defensive female that he couldn't help worrying himself sick when working with a woman, especially in homicide. But the moment passed. Let Alex think what she wanted. She'd obviously put him into a neat category: male chauvinist. But that was no business of his.

When she was done, she strode toward him, wiping the dust from her jeans. He could see the sweat dampening her hairline. He held his tongue.

"You know," said Alex, "you ride okay for a man." He'd have sworn he saw a spark lighting her eyes.

"Thanks."

"No. I mean it . . . that is, you ride well. Where'd you learn to handle horses?"

"There are, believe it or not, ranches in California. I worked at one the summer I was Bob's age."

"I see."

They walked together in the dark along the path toward the house. A cool breeze lifted dark strands of her hair, carrying the scent of it to Jake's nostrils—the same scent as her scarf. He thought to tell her he had her scarf, but that moment slipped away too.

"Oh there *you* are!" cried Janet as they walked into the circle of light in front of the ranch house. "You were gone *forever*! I almost began to worry, but then I saw Bobby. Did you have fun?"

"Not bad," said Jake.

"Very nice," put in Alex as her glance met Jake's for a moment.

"Cecily was *dying*!" whispered Janet in Jake's ear. "She would have gone along in a flash, but she was busy somewhere when you left. She's got a crush on Bobby."

Jake smiled crookedly, putting his arm around Janet's plump waist. "Aren't they a little young?"

"Girls are never *too* young, Jake," Janet said with a sigh.

Bobby was sitting at a picnic table in front of a plate piled high with barbecued ribs, corn and potato salad. Cecily Webster sat across from him, listening intently. Bobby waved a rib behind him, pointing in the direction of the House Made of Dawn. The kid was really impressed with the Indian lore, the old places and their secrets. Jake felt a momentary lapse in the worry that had grown in him like a malignant tumor. Maybe Bobby would turn out okay after all.

The party was still going strong. There were more than a few who had drunk their fair share and were laughing too loudly. Jake got himself a tonic and lime, and realized once again how distasteful it was to put up with drunks when you were sober. Once he too had been like that, and not so long ago, either. He sipped on his tonic and fought off the faint envy that he felt when he saw people drinking around him. Yet the envy was always mixed with a healthy shot of superiority. He was a better man for not drinking and that would just have to sustain him.

"How's it going?" Randy Webster appeared at his side, ubiquitous beer can in hand.

"Great, buddy."

"Have a good ride?"

"Passable."

"Nice girl, Alex Crawford," said Randy ingenuously.

"You didn't tell me she was half Indian . . . or for that matter, that Alex *is* a woman."

"You didn't ask, pal." Randy grinned.

"No, I guess I didn't." He paused. "She's been good to Bobby. I appreciate that."

"Like I said, nice girl."

"What's with her friend, Tom?"

Randy shrugged. "Janet can't stand him. Never could figure that out. He seems nice enough. His ex sure has him hog-tied, though. He and Alex, well, they've been seeing each other for a long time. Who knows?"

Jake was silent in the darkness against the old oak

tree, watching the party swirl around him. These were nice people, good, solid citizens. There wasn't any of the horror of the big city here, none of the hysteria or danger or ferocious excitement. It was a peaceful place; maybe he would stay, for the summer anyway.

He saw Alex Crawford across the lawn, sitting with Janet and another woman. As they laughed, the light from the house highlighted the curve of Alex's cheekbone and the line of the jaw where her heavy black hair hung down to intercept it in a graceful sweep.

There was a woman who was fascinating, yet who chose a dud for a partner, who kept an impeccable distance from anything significant or moving or profound in her emotional life. And he'd bet that went for her sexual life, too, not that he really cared.

Later he found himself sitting companionably with the men around a bonfire. The dry desert air was finally cool.

"What's going on with this Joseph Twelvetrees case, Randy?" asked a Sedona businessman. "It could be bad for business of it gets around."

"Could be good, too," replied another man. "This here talk of a Navajo witch; it'll bring in tourists like crazy."

"They're still talking witch, huh?" asked Randy, shaking his head.

"Well, couldn't it be some Indian grudge or feud? Maybe someone paid this witch to do it," said another man.

"Joseph Twelvetrees was a nice old guy, lived on his own land, off the reservation. Everybody liked him."

"Well, who knows? Are you going to pursue it, Randy?" put in the first man.

"Have to. It's my job."

"The funeral's Sunday. I read it in the paper. You goin', Randy?"

"No, the tribe doesn't invite many outsiders. The Navajos don't do much with dead bodies. They figure the spirit's gone and what's left is not worth much."

"Sensible," commented someone.

"Maybe," agreed Randy laconically.

The men fell silent for a time, tipping beer cans and looking into the fire.

Jake saw Alex rise, say something to Janet and begin to walk toward him across the lawn. She moved easily, with the grace of a person in fine condition, like a sleek thoroughbred.

"Look, I hate to bother you," she said, "but I wondered if you'd give me a ride home." She kept her voice low, as if reticent to ask. "I thought I'd get a ride with Tom, but...." Her voice faded.

"But your friend had to leave, right?" He caught himself—Alex's problems weren't his. "Sure, be glad to give you a lift. I've got to get Bob home soon anyway." Jake shrugged.

"I'd be grateful," she said softly.

"I'll go get Bobby. Then we'll be off."

"You're sure? I mean, if you want to stay...."

"If I wanted to stay, I'd tell you, okay?"

"Thanks."

They sat together on the front seat of the old Pontiac, but they were miles apart. Jake felt her distance like a tangible thing: surely she was thinking of her clean-cut boyfriend, was annoyed with him, missing him?

"Janet throws a nice party," he finally said, wanting to break through her impenetrable reserve.

"Yes, very nice."

Silence. The road unfolded in front of them as the headlights revealed it. A startled deer was suddenly illuminated at the roadside, leaping away into the blackness.

"Wow, dad, did you see that?" came Bobby's voice from the dim back seat.

"Sure did, Bob."

Only the swish of the tires, the tick and growl of the engine broke the silence. The lights began to get closer together, sentinels of civilization in an age-old land.

"I'd like to..." began Jake.

"Maybe you'd..." began Alex.

They both smiled a little.

"Go on," she said.

"Oh no, my mother always told me, ladies first."

"Well . . ." she hesitated. Then, "Oh, never mind."

"What were you going to say?"

"It's silly. And you probably wouldn't be interested in the least."

Now, Jake reflected, she was acting more like a human being. Then he gave her a sidelong glance and saw her eyes on him before she quickly looked away.

"Well," she said finally, "I was just going to ask if you'd like me to drive you out to the Hopi Reservation on Sunday. I have to go out there for Joseph's funeral. It's right on the way. Bobby, and you of course, could visit Old Oraibi."

"I don't really. . . ."

"Dad! Oh please. Could we? Come on, dad!"

"I do think Bobby would enjoy it," Alex put in hastily.

"It's not often that I get outvoted," grumbled Jake. "Sure, why not?"

"My grandfather can show you around. He loves to do it. He feels he's performing a necessary function— educating the ignorant white man."

Jake pulled up to the end of the driveway and turned the key off. "Here we are, folks," he said, opening his door.

"Thanks for the ride. I guess I should have driven myself. . . ."

"No reason," replied Jake curtly.

"Well, good night." She didn't wait for him to open her door.

"Good night."

He stood watching her dark form disappear into the shadows of the night.

"What'd she say her Indian name was?" asked Bobby.

"Chosóvi."

"That's kinda pretty."

"Not bad. . . ."

CHAPTER EIGHT

THE MORNING SUN glared fiercely off the back of the aluminum camper in front of Alex's Saab.

"Boy, that's bright," she said, shielding her eyes. "Would you rummage through my purse and find my sunglasses?"

"Campers ought to be outlawed on the highway," Jake grumbled.

Alex took the glasses from his hand. "They have just as much right to be here as we do," she commented matter-of-factly.

"Why don't you pass him?"

"Yeah, Alex," repeated Bobby from the back seat, "the guy's crawling!"

"He's doing fifty-five." *Men,* she thought, *put them behind a wheel and they're all at the Indy 500!*

"Pass him," growled Jake. "It's clear for ten miles up there, for Pete's sake."

"Who's driving? You or me?"

"I'll drive," chimed in Bobby. "Dad lets me sometimes."

"That's illegal," said Alex firmly. Finally she pulled around the camper. Once again they could see for miles ahead on the highway. "Are all you *boys* happy now?"

"Yeah." Bobby slumped down in his seat, closing his eyes.

It was silent in the car, save for the soft purr of the Saab's engine. It crossed Alex's mind that they could have been a family going on a weekend outing. Isn't that what families did? She was acutely aware of the way Jake sat beside her: one long, well-muscled leg crossed over the other knee, his powerful arms folded casually over his broad chest, the tanned crinkle lines around his often unreadable eyes.

His very silent presence was a little unnerving. She told herself, however, to concentrate on her driving, not Jake Brannigan. And too, he'd shown no interest in her other than as a mutual friend of the Websters. They were out for a drive, an interesting venture, she hoped, for both Bobby and Jake. It was nothing more than that.

They'd been on the road for an hour and a half and still the Navajo and Hopi reservations were a good hour away. North of Flagstaff, the highway ran along the top of a hundred-mile-long plateau, a seemingly endless expanse of high, rocky desert where the mountains to the east showed as mere cloud wisps on a distant horizon.

They passed a turnoff, finally, to the west. Grand Canyon—North Rim.

"Let's go!" cried Bobby, suddenly attentive.

"It's over a hundred miles up that road," explained Alex.

"Damn...." muttered Bobby.

"What?"

"I mean, darn, dad."

The highway, arrow straight, seemed to disappear at a pinpoint in the far distance. As they neared the western entrance to the reservation, they began to see tiny little huts on the side of the road, and homemade signs: Indian Jewelry, Navajo Rugs. The huts themselves looked as if a mild breeze might fan them away.

"Boy, are they poor!" commented Bobby.

"Bob!" said Jake, turning in his seat.

"It's all right," Alex said, laughing. "We Indians are used to it." She glanced at Bobby through the rearview mirror. "In fact, they are not at all poor. They just expect the tourists to think that and stop and buy something."

"Good gimmick," said Bobby. "Maybe I oughtta try it."

"The first light-eyed, blond-haired Indian." Alex smiled dubiously.

"You have blue eyes."

"From my father. He's as English as they come."

"Wasn't he a judge in Flagstaff?" asked Jake.

"Yes. And I know what you're thinking."

"You do?" Jake's eyes rested on her.

"You're thinking that's why I got my job."

"I wasn't thinking that at all," said Jake roughly. "I figure you got appointed because you're qualified."

Alex turned her head, glancing at Jake for a moment. Did he really think that? Or was he patronizing the little woman?

"I'm an overachiever, actually," she said evenly, keeping her eyes carefully on the road.

"I'm an underachiever," said Bobby proudly, leaning forward in his seat. "Really. I just goof off in school. I test real high, though."

"Do you want to go to college?" asked Alex.

"I dunno. College is for squares."

"Am I square?" Alex smiled.

"You? Naw. You're a real knockout."

"Come on, Bobby," grumbled Jake. "There *are* limits."

"I don't mind," Alex said quickly. "Women shouldn't mind compliments. Right, Bobby?"

"Yeah."

Twenty miles farther down the highway Bobby asked, "When are we gonna get there?"

"We've been on the Navajo reservation," replied Alex, "for the last fifty miles."

Bobby sat straight up. "You're joking!"

"The Navajo reservation runs a long way. It's larger than you can imagine, Bobby. And the Hopi Reservation is situated right in the middle of it."

"But, where is everyone? I mean...nothing could live out here! It's...it's all just desert! I don't even see a tree anywhere!"

"I think," said Alex patiently, "that my grand-father better educate you a little."

Finally Alex turned the Saab onto a small dirt road that wound across the valley floor before disappearing to the east of a tall, massive plateau. The going was slow, the road rough where it had been washed out many times by spring flash floods. They twisted their way through the desert, around masses of stunted juniper and across many arroyos—washes—that gnarled and scarred the arid land.

"The valley floor," explained Alex, "is virtually a wasteland. When we get higher, on the mesa, you'll see just how terribly eroded it really is." To the left of them, before they started to ascend the mesa, was a granite-capped plateau that resembled a stem with a tabletop balancing precariously on it.

"Now that's weird looking," said Bobby, pointing. "Looks like the top's gonna fall off."

"Someday," said Jake, "it will."

"In about a million years," put in Alex. "You see, the top is granite and the base sandstone; that's why the bottom eroded away."

"Boy, we should have brought our camera," said Bobby.

"It's just as well you didn't. The Hopi are very private. They don't like being photographed."

The road began to climb steeply, and Alex down-shifted. "Hold on. Gets real bumpy for a while."

"Want me to drive?" Jake asked.

Alex threw him an amused glance. "I've done it be-fore."

Jake shrugged.

They passed sheep and a few donkeys in the taller buffalo grass. Horses, rather weedy looking, grazed nearer the crest of the steep incline. And then, as they came to the top, the land opened up once again, affording a spectacular view of the valley floor and the distant, twisted mesas.

"We're on what's known as the Third Mesa of the

Hopi. It's our true, parental home. You might call it our promised land because we believe the creator gave it to our ancestors."

Shortly, they passed a cornfield, then several stands of peach trees.

"How can they grow fruit trees?" asked Bobby, staring out the window.

Alex smiled. "The land is bountiful here. We can grow a lot of things, and there are hundreds of kinds of game animals... but then, I suppose grandfather will tell you all about that."

"This place is kind of cool," said Bobby. "You can't see any of this from the highway."

"No, you can't," agreed Alex.

The village of New Oraibi, the center of Hopi civilization, lay sprawled before them. Essentially it was a collection of "new" type houses and pueblos, ceremonial plazas, a few melon patches, and corn and bean plots. Women sat in front of their houses quietly doing tasks: grinding the omnipresent corn into flour, shaping colorful bowls with capable hands, stringing bright beads, even making kachina dolls—fashioned after the spirits—for the children.

"My grandfather lives in a house near the central plaza," said Alex, pulling the car to the side of the road. "We'll have to walk from here. The road ends." Next to the Saab, several dusty pickup trucks were parked.

"Nice trucks," said Bobby. "Where do the Indians get the money?"

Alex was not put off by the question. It was fair enough. "Some of the men work down on the highway in Kayenta. It's what you'd call a tourist trap. Others are given the trucks by the federal government."

"Welfare?" Bobby asked.

"The Indians don't see it that way," she explained carefully. "You have to remember that this whole country was once theirs. It's been difficult since my people were placed on reservations. They always considered the land as a whole. Now it's no longer that way.''

"I guess it's a small price for the government to pay,'' reflected Jake.

"Very small,'' Alex said softly. "I'll introduce you to grandfather. You can call him Fred, if you like. Then I better head toward the Navajo village where George will be. I'll be gone for a few hours, I'm afraid, but if I don't go, George will be insulted. Besides,'' she teased, "I'll bet grandfather will entertain you pretty well.''

"What's his real name?'' asked Bobby as they stood in front of a pueblo.

"Fred Kwáhu. It means 'eagle.' ''

"Are there any customs Bob and I should know about?'' Jake folded his arms across his chest, his green eyes crinkled against the blazing June sun.

"Grandfather, I'm sure, will let you know. But it's all right as long as I brought you.''

He was elderly—a good guess would be near ninety—with a seamed face and a full head of yellow-white hair. He wore faded blue jeans, old climbing boots and a plaid shirt. Around his neck was a blue bandanna, and from his turquoise inlaid belt hung what Jake took to be a medicine pouch.

"I have been waiting to welcome Chosóvi's friends,'' he greeted from his place on a patterned rug. Jake realized that after introductions Alex had handily disappeared. So he and Bob were on their own....

"We are not old friends,'' explained Jake, "but my son and I greatly respect your granddaughter.'' He hoped that was the right thing to say.

"How'd you know we were coming?'' asked Bobby, seemingly at ease.

Fred Kwáhu kept a straight face. "An owl told me, Bobby.''

The boy shrugged, bemused, and then wandered around the central room of the pueblo. It was a simple room, only housing the bare essentials of life. Jake wondered if some of the Hopi had refrigeration or stoves and surmised that some must. Still, this old man had no such luxuries. Probably he did not want them.

"You are from a big city," said the old man.

"That's right. Los Angeles."

"I have been there. To Hollywood." That was all. No explanation. Apparently, none was necessary. To Bobby, he confided, "I could have been a movie star."

"You could have?"

"In Westerns. Forty years ago, my people were in a real movie. We met Alan Ladd in Sedona. Alex has seen the movie."

"You haven't?" asked Jake with a raised brow.

"I did not need to. I was there." Then Fred waved a leathery hand at Bobby. "Bring us some food." He indicated the heavy pot hanging over a fire pit. "You will need to nourish yourself before our walk."

Strangely, Bobby smiled at the old man and went straight to the task. Jake was amazed as his boy found three bowls and dished up what Fred called *nogkwivi*—a combination of mutton and hominy.

Jake prayed: let Bobby eat it without a complaint. To his further amazement, Bobby did just that!

"Where are we walking to?" asked Bobby between mouthfuls.

"To the center of my world. To Old Oraibi that was promised to us by the creator. No one lives there now."

"A ghost town! Wow!"

"I hope there are no ghosts, young man," said Fred levelly. "We will need powerful magic if there are."

Bobby was fascinated; his face lit up like a small child's at Christmas as they began their ascent to the oldest continually settled spot on the continent—Oraibi.

Stepping easily past clusters of mesquites and juniper, around stunted piñons, Fred and Bobby led the way. Fred, Jake decided, must be a mountain goat.

Jake himself was beginning to realize that he was pretty out of shape—he was huffing and puffing steadily, lagging some ten paces behind. Then, too, there was the lingering stiffness from his long horseback ride the day before.

At the crest of the rim they'd been following, the land once again opened up onto a wide plateau. At its center—just as Fred said—was old Oraibi, the very core, the umbilical cord of Hopi civilization. The old pueblo was now in ruins, but that was hardly a surprise as it had been inhabited since before 1100 A.D. until the early 1900s.

Now Fred stopped often. Jake was able to catch up, to listen to some of the things the old man was telling Bobby.

Fred knelt down once, took a handful of sand and gave it to Bobby. "What color do you see?" he asked patiently.

"Sand...well, it's brownish."

"There are maybe a hundred shades of brown," said Fred. "A Hopi reads these colors and knows if he can plant his corn there."

"In sand?"

"In the sand of our land. Yes."

They stood. Fred's yellow-white hair was swept back by a hot, dry desert breeze. His weathered brown skin glowed in the merciless sun. No perspiration showed anywhere on him, yet Jake's white shirt was drenched. Then Fred stretched out his left arm in a southwesterly direction. "That is blue. See the sky?" It was blue—cloudless, perfect azure blue. Like Alex's eyes, Jake thought inexplicably. Then Fred turned 180 degrees. "That is yellow."

"Wow," exclaimed Bobby. "It is!" Then he said, "So you have colors for direction. Neat!"

"The earth and the heavens are all colors. All different. That is one thing a Hopi must learn to survive."

"Can you hunt by colors?"

"Of course." Fred pointed due north. "There are the mountain lion and bear and badger." Then to the south. "And there are the wild pig and the parrot. To the east are the eagles."

"Wow!"

They entered the ancient village finally and Fred showed them the kiva pit—where the holiest of ceremonies were held—and the central plaza, the *kisonvi*, for dancing and sandstone painting and most Hopi social functions. They climbed over several fallen adobe walls, entering a few ancient chambers.

"Hopi," Fred told them, "means People of Peace. We are not fighters like the Navajo—the *Tasavuh*."

"The what?" asked Bobby.

"The head pounders. They came to this land from the north," Fred said distastefully, "and beat the heads of our people."

"Cool!" Then Bobby blushed a little. "May I ask you a personal question?"

Fred nodded, his deep-set brown eyes glowing amber in the sun.

"Did you. . . I mean, did you ever take a scalp?"

Fred looked at him intently. Jake cringed inwardly. "We are a nation of peace. My father may have taken a scalp or two. I think I buried them, though, back in the days before automobiles. I did not want the white soldier to avenge his brothers on my family."

Jake withheld the urge to laugh. Bobby, of course, let out a joyful "wow!"

They left Oraibi in the middle of the afternoon "when the yellow light turned to the color of the white man's gold." Fred showed Bobby how to tell the time by a long shadow that fell on the valley floor from the distant Second Mesa. Far to the east, a thunderhead moved over a clustered formation of ancient mesas. Wind, which Fred seemed to listen to carefully, stirred the sparse buffalo grass and nudged the twisted piñon branches.

"What a view!" said Bobby.

Fred smiled, his rheumy eyes resting on father and son. "It is our fourth world and *Masau* takes care of us."

Alex found her grandfather and his new friends where they sat on a red-clay slab overlooking the Third Mesa valley. "I knew you'd be here," she said simply, coming to sit by them. "Were they good students, grandfather?"

"Fair."

Alex smiled. "Did you like the tour, Bobby?"

"Fred says I can come and stay with him. I'm good medicine."

"Isn't it a lovely Fourth World?" She sat, her blue-jean-clad legs thrust out before her, long and lean, her head tipped back into the desert sun, the afternoon breeze catching at her raven-black hair.

"How did Joseph's funeral go?" asked Jake quietly.

"I don't like funerals," Alex replied uncomfortably.

"Nobody does."

The late, slanted shadows began to reach across the valley floor—it was time to go. Strangely, all were reluctant to leave this promised land of the Hopi, but civilization called.

It was Bobby who spoke aloud their thoughts. "I could stay forever."

"Come back, Bobby," said the old man. "I will call you Choviohoya."

"What's that?" His smooth-skinned face split into an eager grin.

"Deer. You will be Young Deer."

Jake and Bobby thanked Alex's grandfather, promising to return before harvest in the autumn. Jake, although he wasn't sure exactly why, had every intention of keeping his promise. Then Alex asked if they wouldn't mind walking on ahead.

"I'd like to have a few minutes with grandfather," she explained.

Jake nodded. "We'll wait by the car."

Alex walked Fred Kwáhu back to his pueblo and made sure that he was comfortable. "You were very kind to my friends." Her deep-blue eyes smiled at him lovingly. "And by the way, mom sends her love. She said to tell you that when it gets up to 120 in Scottsdale, she'll be here to visit."

"She'll come. Then she'll go back," he commented sadly.

Alex avoided his grief—it had always been there, since the day her mother had left the Third Mesa for college. She'd never really come back. So many never came back....

"You wish to speak of Joseph Twelvetrees...the Navajo."

"Yes," replied Alex, undaunted by her grandfather's uncanny knowledge.

"It was a wolf walker."

"A witch?"

"Yes."

"But why?"

"A Navajo witch does not need a reason. The moon was high that night. The witch had an urge to do his evil."

Suddenly Alex caught herself. What was she doing, sitting there, believing this insane tale of wolves and witches? Logic took over.

"I don't believe in the Indian ways," she said firmly, crossing her slim arms across her breasts.

"Yes you do."

"Think what you will, grandfather, but if you happen to hear any gossip about someone who might have wanted to harm Joseph, will you get in touch?"

"It was the witch."

Alex fell silent.

"You have a heavy heart, Chosóvi."

Finally she sighed. "I am troubled, grandfather."

"It is that man, your friend, Jake."

"No!" she said sharply. "It's not him. It's me... and Tom. He's so incredibly busy sometimes...."

"All white men are."

"Well, yes, but *he's* taken on so much. He's got his ex-wife and children, his real-estate firm, a hundred other obligations to the community."

"He does not know how to say no."

"I guess not. It's frustrating."

"He lacks a will of his own."

"Grandfather...."

The old man raised his weathered hands. "It is *your* conversation. I only speak from the heart. I do not know this white man, Tom. You have never brought him to see me."

"Well, I will someday." Then she thought silently, *But when? When will Tom have the time...?* "I guess," she said softly, "that my problem is very simple. I just don't really know where our relationship is heading. Sometimes I think I love him. Then...well, then I think we're just good friends." Alex ran a hand through her dark hair. "I just don't know what to do. He's one of the only men I know who treats me as an equal. You'd never believe how hard it is where I work. All men...." She shrugged. "My boss doesn't really trust me and one of the other deputy attorneys actually patted me on the bottom the other day when I was showing him my case file on a drunk driver!"

"You should have scalped him."

"Be serious, grandfather. I'm telling you how rare it is out there in that world to find a man who sees me as an intelligent person."

"But you are female."

"And *you* are old-fashioned! I'm asking for advice."

"I like this Jake man and his son. Both have strong wills."

Alex sighed. "Words of wisdom! Listen, he's too macho, you know, too...crude for me."

"Uncivilized."

"Sure."

"That is a good quality."

"Then it's no advice for me today." She rose, a little irritated. Sometimes her grandfather could be a tower of wisdom; at other times, a terrible old tease.

At the door to his pueblo, he said quietly, "Alex... Chosóvi...the Ancient Ones want you to go with your heart. Follow the shifting sands, my little bluebird. Do not be so afraid."

Slowly Alex turned back to face him. "Then you think my life is changing somehow. But I can't see it yet," she reflected quietly. "When will I know? How will I see it coming?"

"You already stand at the paths that fork. You just have not yet put your foot onto the path you will choose."

Alex's heartbeat quickened. "Will I choose the right path, grandfather?"

"For you, Chosóvi, it will be the only path...."

CHAPTER NINE

"I'M TOTALLY STARVED," complained Bobby. "When are we gonna eat?"

Alex glanced over at Jake, who was driving the Saab. "We could stop in Flagstaff...it's only about five miles."

"Or," put in Jake, "he could just fix himself a sandwich when we get home. What is it? About forty-five more minutes?"

"About. But it's late. Do you have anything at home? The stores are all closed...." She looked at her watch in the growing darkness. "Boy, we sure let the time get away." She turned toward Jake. "Sorry. I guess it's my fault."

"No apology necessary," he said gruffly.

Alex watched him out of the corner of her eye. He was a good, smooth driver and she'd been frankly glad when he'd once again offered to drive back at the turn-off to the paved highway. His eyes were on the road ahead; he switched on the headlights just then and she again found herself observing his powerful forearms, the crisp blond hairs, the capable muscles working beneath the tanned skin as he maneuvered the car through a series of curves in Flagstaff. She caught her furtive gaze rising, fastening on his profile, on the strength in his cleft jaw, the sensitive turned-down lips and the hooded eyes.

"I could cook dinner." The words came spilling out. Alex colored. What was getting into her? Was this another one of her attempts to prove she could do everything, take care of everybody, save the whole world? And what about Tom? It was one thing driving the Brannigans to the reservation. Cooking dinner for them was quite another matter.

"The kid could use a square meal," was Jake's succinct reply.

She'd asked for it, after all.

Dinner, due to the hour, was simple: leftover chicken, a tossed green salad, steamed broccoli. Alex hoped it was enough for two grown—or almost grown—men.

Jake sort of helped. "Where're the plates?"

Alex nodded toward a cupboard over the sink. "Up there." Then a twinkle lit her blue eyes. "Want an apron?" Now Tom, she knew, would say sure. . . .

"Are you kiddin'?" said that low, gravelly voice.

"You don't have to go into shock." She went back to slicing a tomato.

Jake grumbled something under his breath, placing the plates helter-skelter on the dining-room table. By the time he had the table set, it was all Alex could do to keep from commenting. She did, however, check herself and shifted the plates and silverware silently into a semblance of order.

"Didn't I do it right?" asked Jake, eyeing her from the living room, his shoulder leaning casually against the doorframe.

Alex looked up, catching his gaze. "I guess I'm fussy. Sorry. It's eccentric old age creeping up on me." She smiled, wondering what thoughts were running through his head. "Well, dinner's ready." She wiped her hands on her apron. "If you can drag Bobby away from the television."

Bobby literally gulped down his meal—there was a "great show" on TV, a Chuck Norris flick. Alex and Jake were left alone, eyeing each other occasionally, slowly eating their chicken.

Jake finally pushed his plate away, not quite finished.

"You weren't hungry?" observed Alex. Was it her cooking?

He put his hands behind his head, leaning back a little in the chair. "I've been trying to watch the weight."

He seemed a little defensive about it so Alex steered the conversation elsewhere. "I think grandfather really liked you. And especially Bobby."

"We liked him. What an interesting old character."

"That he surely is!" Alex poured herself another half glass of white wine. "You sure you don't want any?" She held the bottle in her hand.

"No...thanks, I don't drink...anymore, that is." Again, he seemed a touch ill at ease.

"Oh...sorry." Should she pry? Why not...? "Your health?"

"I was a pretty bad drunk," he said flatly. "It often goes with the territory."

"Police work?"

"That, and being a traditional Irish cop."

Alex smiled. "I'll bet your father was a cop, too."

"*And* my grandfather."

"Is your father alive? I mean...."

"No. He died from complications due to drinking."

"I'm sorry."

"So am I."

Alex studied him for a moment before her glance fell away. "What about Bobby?" Her voice was low. "He seems a nice boy." She smiled. "A little wise from time to time, but then, aren't all teenagers?"

"He's basically a good kid. At least," said Jake pensively, "he used to be." He leaned toward her. "Didn't Randy or Janet mention why we left L.A.?"

"Not really."

"Bobby had some problems. He'd been hanging out with some real thugs. And then my retirement came up...." Jake sat back, shrugging in his now-familiar manner.

"If this is none of my business," said Alex carefully, "I hope you'll tell me so. But what about his mother?" Perhaps she'd gone a little too far.

"I don't like to discuss his mother. Marriage was not one of my strong points."

"Maybe it wasn't all your fault."

His lips twitched, but the smile never quite reached his eyes. "Why don't we just blame it on the LAPD and leave it at that."

Alex still had no idea whether his ex-wife was dead or alive. And by the closed look on Jake's face, she guessed she'd never find out from him. Perhaps Janet knew.... Yet his omissions had spoken eloquently. She was beginning to understand what Randy had meant when he'd said Jake had problems.

A moment of silence between them stretched out awkwardly. Alex finally rose, glanced at him with constraint and began to clear the dishes.

"I guess I should help," said Jake, rising to hold the swinging kitchen door for her. She could have laughed at the lack of enthusiasm in his voice.

He ended up sitting at the small kitchen table having coffee while Alex put the dishes in the dishwasher. They could have been an ordinary couple, doing the usual after-dinner chores, save for the fact that there was a tremendous amount of tension in the room. Alex wished that she had never brought up the subject of his wife. How insensitive!

"Listen," he said at last, leaning against the counter, his green eyes fixed on her back, "I'm sorry if I was a little abrupt with you. I'm kind of . . . well, private, I guess you'd say."

Alex turned to face him. "You have a right to your privacy, Jake. Everyone does. I had no business asking." She half expected him to smile at her, or say, "that's all right," but he did neither. Instead, he simply sat there, solemnly watching her. His very existence in her home seemed to fill every inch of space.

She took her apron off, then put her hands on her hips. "Sure you got enough to eat?" Perhaps she should just talk about the weather.

"Plenty."

He seemed to have relaxed a little; at least he wasn't growling at her like a blond bear. But he certainly was a difficult dinner guest—a little short on the social graces.

Alex guessed she'd just have to count it as another challenge. She wondered again what on earth had possessed her to ask them for dinner in the first place.

"I hope you enjoy Sedona," she said, casting about desperately for a subject that was not sensitive. "It's a wonderful place to live."

"You ever live anywhere else?" His tone was belligerent, or was that merely the way he always sounded?

"I went to school at U.C.L.A."

"Good old L.A.," he said. "You like it there?"

She shrugged. "It was interesting. I made some good friends. I prefer Sedona, though."

"I'll bet." His voice rumbled in his chest. She wondered what would happen if he raised his voice.

He looked around her small, neat kitchen as if memorizing every detail. "You've got a pretty nice setup here." The words were wrung from him with difficulty.

"Thanks. It was my parents' house until they moved to Scottsdale. I guess it's really too big for me, but I like the old place. It just seems as if things are always needing fixing though."

"Yeah, I know...."

"You had a house, too?"

"Still do."

She wanted to ask if his wife—his ex-wife—still lived in it. Instead she asked, "Do you rent it out?"

"Yeah."

"So you might go back someday?"

"Maybe. Maybe not." Then his glance met hers. "You like your job?" My, he was absolutely garrulous!

"Oh yes. It's quite a challenge for me. They've never had a female in the county attorney's office before—except as a secretary." She snapped off the counter lights and sat down across from Jake with a cup of coffee. "It's very good for me."

"You find being a woman is a disadvantage in your job?" His green eyes met hers levelly. Did he really want to know or was he mocking her ambitions?

"Sometimes. Mostly when men insist on seeing my

gender instead of my capabilities.'' As soon as she'd said it, she felt his eyes on her, moving over every inch of her flesh. She felt herself go hot, then cold all over.

An uneasy silence fell between them; Alex felt terribly self-conscious, alone in her kitchen with this man who alternated between making her want to laugh and making her dreadfully uncomfortable.

Uneasily she sipped on her coffee, aware he was watching her closely, his big body deceptively relaxed. His mind, she suspected, was sharp, judging her every move and word, measuring her reactions as if to decide on her innocence or guilt. Jake Brannigan didn't miss much.

"You know, in Randy's office the other day,'' he rumbled, "I had the distinct feeling that you wanted to say more about that witch business.''

Alex shrugged her shoulders, feeling the tension pulse in the air. "Not really.''

"Then it's all just Indian lore. Right?''

"You know,'' she ventured, "I sort of feel like I'm sitting at an interrogation table, with bright lights shining in my eyes.''

Jake smiled, a slight uplifting of one corner of his mouth. "Am I being too pushy?''

"A little.''

"Once a cop. . . .'' He took a drink of his coffee. Then his eyes lifted to meet hers. "I still think that there's something you didn't tell Randy that day.''

"Why would I do that?'' Alex thought furiously: Had her reaction to the claw marks on Joseph been so noticeable that Jake thought she'd been hiding something? Apparently it had.

"You just seemed a little shaken when we were discussing the rumors about a Navajo witch. Look, you ever heard the expression, 'where there's smoke, there's fire'?''

"Of course.''

"Well, that's all I'm driving at. I've given those claw marks a lot of thought. Let's face it, they *do* exist. And

I'm sure not buying the Indian theory...but on the other hand...I can't believe a real wolf would have done it. Do you?''

She sighed, trying to summon up that inner core of calm. Why was she so edgy? "It's been on my mind, too," she breathed. "And I can't make any sense at all out of it. I wish it could have just been a simple accident.''

He nodded.

"Then poor old Joseph could have gone in peace to those great hunting grounds in the sky." Alex allowed a little smile.

Jake ignored her attempt at humor. "So what do you think is the explanation for the claw marks?''

Alex thought, avoiding his grave stare. "I tend to lean toward your theory. Either an animal, a wolf, if the coroner's report is correct, got to him, or someone—and Lord knows why—put those marks on him.''

"With authentic claws, don't forget. *And* after his death.''

Alex nodded silently, wondering if he ever missed a trick.

"And that's it?" His green, unfathomable gaze held her. "There's nothing else?''

"Why do you think there's something else?" She paused, shifting uncomfortably in her seat. "I'm not hiding anything, Jake Brannigan.''

"You're nervous." His tone was hard, relentless, the perfect cop.

Again Alex shifted. Should she tell him? He'd think her a complete, ignorant fool. But then, if she didn't tell him, he was still going to believe that she knew something more....

She cleared her throat, and searched his strong, unyielding face. "If I tell you," she began, "you have to promise it will never leave this room.''

He met her words with gravid silence.

"I mean it. Oh, you'll think I'm crazy." Agitated, she got up, stalking the length of the kitchen. "I can't imagine why I'm telling you this.''

He was quiet, his eyes moving over her for an agonizingly long moment. "Go on," Jake said finally, without inflection.

She could imagine him in a garishly lit interrogation room, calm, masterful. Her sympathies were all with the poor criminal, on the verge of an incriminating confession. Alex took a deep breath. "It *could* have been the witch. The Navajo wolf." She waited, the blood pounding like drumbeats in her ears.

Now the silence became unbearable. She never should have told him! And even to her own ears the explanation sounded completely insane.

When he spoke again his tone was so low she had to strain to hear. "Do you really believe that?"

Suddenly unaccountable moisture pressed behind her eyelids. She turned her head away. "I know it's crazy—in my logical mind I know it can't be true," she whispered, "but in my heart and in my guts, yes, I think there is truth in the old Indian beliefs. I don't know how to explain it to you. I don't even know how to explain it to myself." She laughed shakily. "Isn't it ridiculous?"

Then suddenly, just as she felt he was going to say something significant, the telephone rang shrilly.

Alex jumped. The phone rang again, insistently, and she was thankful for the intrusion. Her mind was still whirling as she picked up the receiver.

"It's Tom," came the familiar voice over the line. "I'd just dropped the kids off at Mavis's and was driving home. I saw your lights on. Everything all right?"

"Everything's fine," she said, quickly turning her back toward Jake. "I'm just up a little late."

"Where are you?"

"I'm in the kitchen, Tom," she said a little too sharply.

"You sound funny. You sure everything's okay?"

"Yes."

"I could come over . . . ."

"No! I mean, I'm just tired. I couldn't sleep." It struck Alex like a physical blow: she'd just lied to Tom, and with Jake sitting there listening, his green eyes boring a hole in her back. What was happening to her?

"Well, then, I'll say good-night, Alex." He added, "How about dinner tomorrow night?"

"Ah, well . . . sure. I'd like that. . . ."

"I'll pick you up at seven."

"That's fine."

"Tomorrow, then."

"Yes." She hung up, slowly. Tomorrow night she'd tell Tom the truth. She had nothing to hide from him. Jake Brannigan meant nothing whatsoever to her. Tom needed to know that.

"Your boyfriend?"

Alex turned. "Yes."

Jake put down his coffee cup. "I'll drag Bob away from the television, and let you get some sleep." He began to rise.

"Wait," Alex said, taking a deep breath as she ran her fingers through her dark hair. "I . . . well, you haven't told me yet what you think about the claw marks."

Jake's eyes never left hers. "I think your witch theory is a cop-out." He nodded toward the seat opposite his. "Sit down a sec." It was not a request.

A little rebelliously, she sat. "Well?"

"My grandfather believed in leprechauns until his dying day." Jake folded his arms.

"What?" asked Alex. What was he trying to say? Getting Jake to talk was like pulling teeth.

"I'm just telling you that there's nothing wrong with believing in Santa Claus. It doesn't make you crazy or anything. It also doesn't make the thing valid. Legally, anyway." He seemed embarrassed, caught off guard trying to be a "nice guy." Still, Alex didn't care. She'd gotten the message.

"Thanks," she said simply, almost embarrassed herself to see him shift uneasily in his chair.

The door to the kitchen swung open then, startling her. "I'm going back to the apartment," said Bobby nonchalantly. "Will you get me up early? Me and Cecily are going riding."

"Cecily and I," corrected Jake. "I'll get you up, and I'm right behind you. I'm sure Alex would like to get to bed."

Bobby smiled. "Oh yeah, thanks for everything today, Alex," he said dutifully.

Alex returned his smile. "My pleasure."

"See ya." Then he was gone.

Jake rose, putting his coffee cup in the sink as an afterthought. "Sorry if we kept you up. Thanks for dinner."

"My pleasure." She also stood, putting her hands on her hips, stretching her back a little. "I was glad to see Bobby enjoy himself today."

"Yeah. He sure got into the Indian lore."

"It's easy to do that." Alex glanced at Jake. "Well...." She pushed open the kitchen door, leading the way into the living room. Then she turned toward him. "You know Bobby's welcome to come over whenever he likes and use the video recorder. I could show him where I hide the key to the kitchen door."

"Don't spoil the kid."

Why did he always look on the negative side of things?

"It won't spoil him. I like Bobby." And she realized, surprisingly, she liked Jake too, in spite of his bearish growls.

Alex walked out onto the porch with him. "Beautiful night." She looked up, staring at the blanket of brilliant stars glowing in the inky-black mountain sky. Then she turned to face Jake. "Thank you for...for telling me about your grandfather. I would have liked him."

"He would have liked you."

She gave a little shiver hugging herself as the cool mountain air touched her bare arms.

"Cold?" His voice was suddenly softer; it could have come from a total stranger, a tall dark shadow in the night beside her.

"Not really." There was that sudden tension between them again, as if an electric current ran from one to the other. Jake was a strange man—a hard, rough man. He was a person impossible for her ever to feel close to, as foreign to her tastes and instincts as anyone could be. And yet . . . she detected a sensitivity to him that he tried to hide, and her powerful awareness of him as a man confused and unsettled Alex. It went deeper than like or dislike; it was above—or below—such prosaic emotions.

He did not leave, not yet. She felt his body lean toward her in the darkness as one feels a shadow on closed eyes. Her breath caught in her throat. She thought, in some distant corner of her mind, that he was going to kiss her.

His shadow came closer, covering her like the out-stretched wings of an eagle. She felt weak yet full of wonder. His face was very close now; his warm breath fanned tiny tendrils of her hair. She wanted to say yes to him, but her lips were held silent by age-old modesty.

His presence held her immobile; his powerful body was drawing her toward him. And she knew in that flash of time that she wanted him; somehow she desperately wanted this man, this stranger, to pull her into those strong arms.

But he didn't. Instead the moment passed explosively, and fled with the night breezes. Then he was gone, and she thought he'd said good-night, but she wasn't at all sure he'd said anything.

She stood, sagging almost helplessly against the porch railing, wondering just exactly why she'd wanted him so desperately in that passing moment. And wondering, too, just what would she have done if he had taken her in those uncompromising arms.

CHAPTER TEN

It was shortly after Janet and her daughter Cecily had picked up Bobby for the horseback ride that Jake received his first article of mail in Sedona. More than likely it was a check from his young renters—the Blacksmiths—in L.A.

He sat down on the sagging couch, tore open the letter and skimmed it, sipping his coffee.

"Dear Mr. Brannigan," it began, "we hate to get in touch like this, on our very first month in your place, but unfortunately the hot-water heater went out and we couldn't get a hold of you, so we had it replaced. The cost was $426.75."

Jake gnashed his teeth, putting his coffee mug down so hard on the tabletop that it sent droplets flying all over—even on the front of his yellow shirt, which happened to be the only clean one left! He let out a stream of oaths, thinking, no wonder men over forty suffer heart attacks!

He forced himself to read on.

"We weren't certain what to do. We waited until we got that postcard this morning from you and then wrote to you right away. We're really sorry for the trouble. We figured that because rent is $425 a month that we would just take the extra $1.75 off next month's rent. If this is not okay, please let us know."

Then, to put the icing on the cake, there was this little P.S. "The lawnmower won't seem to start so we thought we'd take it down to the Sears repair shop. Shouldn't cost very much."

Jake put his head in his hands, suddenly feeling like going out and getting a drink. And to top it all off, he'd been counting on that rent money to replace some parts in the Pontiac and now he'd have to scare up some used parts and put them in himself!

If there was one thing Jake hated to do, it was work on a car.

For several minutes he paced the floor, feeling suddenly caged in, restless. Retirement was just great!

If he wasn't going to take that drink, what then? There had been the police-department baseball team and in the autumn, football. And Jake had really let out his frustrations on the playing field. They all had.

Suddenly Jake knew exactly what he needed to do: go for a run. It wouldn't hurt any, either, to tighten up that gut of his. Jake remembered Randy's remarks of the other night.

His bedroom was still in disorder—of course he'd made Bobby put his stuff away the night they'd moved in—but Jake still hadn't unpacked his own things. He began tearing through his possessions, searching for a pair of running shorts, his shoes, socks, an old T-shirt. Finally he came up with a pair of brown nylon shorts and an old LAPD softball team shirt. They'd do fine.

It was about eleven by the time Jake hit the pavement. He figured on jogging till noon. The temperature must have been about eighty already, and he wished he'd remembered a bandanna for his brow.

He took off down Alex's road, down the long hill leading toward the floor of the valley—where the road crossed over Oak Creek—then up the other side toward a dirt road leading up toward Brin's Mesa.

Downhill had been easy. The winding, steep incline up Brin's did him in. Finally, detesting himself for quitting, he sat down on the edge of a boulder, the sweat dripping off his head and arms onto the red-clay road while he let a wave of nausea pass. Then he cursed himself, stood, and headed back. It had seemed simple, the run from Alex's downhill to the creek, but now his chest heaved with the effort and his long thigh muscles ached unmercifully. Still, he wasn't about to stop this time.

At last, almost dropping, he made it back into the driveway and sucked in gulp after gulp of air. Abruptly he straightened, suddenly aware of the possibility that someone might be watching. He thought, *It's the altitude.* But deep inside he knew the sad truth.

"I'll do better tomorrow," he grumbled to himself as he unlocked the apartment door and headed straight for the shower.

For long minutes, Jake let cold water run down his straight blond hair and onto the breadth of his shoulders and back. He could have stood like that forever.

But the phone rang. And rang again. Jake would have ignored it, but suppose it was Bobby?

Draping a towel around his hips, he caught it on the last ring.

"I was about to hang up," came Randy's voice. "Got a minute?"

"Yeah. I was just showering." From where he stood next to the old couch he was facing "the big house" and could see Alex's upstairs windows through his own. A soft breeze stirred his curtains and cooled his wet torso.

"I could take off an hour early tonight and swing by and get you for a little fishing up Oak Creek Canyon. You game?"

"Sure. Bobby won't be back for some time. Janet asked him to stay for dinner."

Randy laughed. "You mean Cecily talked her mother into having him!"

"No doubt."

"I'll swing by 'round four. That suit you?"

"That's fine." Jake hung the phone up, then went to the window, pushing the pane up higher to let in more air. Across the way, the curtains in the windows of the big house were also faintly stirring. He wondered if Alex was home but thought that most likely she wasn't—it was a weekday; she'd be in Flagstaff.

He dropped the towel onto the living-room chair, went to the bedroom and dressed—the usual: khaki pants, an old faded green sports shirt, sleeves rolled up to just below the elbow. Socks. Why couldn't he find any socks in this mess?

It was still four hours before Randy would be by. What was he going to do for four full hours? Was this what retirement did to you? All those years you worked your tail off just waiting for that day when you could take a pension and have all the time in the world to yourself.

No wonder, Jake finally decided, the statistics said that men seldom lived long after retirement.

"I haven't got any fishing equipment here," he told Randy in the driveway. "It's all in storage back in L.A."

"I figured," Randy said grinning, "so I brought two poles."

Oak Creek Canyon—all twenty-odd miles of it—was overflowing with tourists fishing, camping and hiking. It was a nature lover's paradise. But Randy had this special spot; all they had to do was cross the rushing creek one at a time in Randy's waders and they'd find solitude and "the best little trench you ever did see for rainbow trout!"

"You know who first fished these waters? I mean, after the Indians, of course," said Randy as they settled in on the grassy bank.

"No," replied Jake, "but I'll bet you're gonna tell me."

"Says on the tour guides that Sedona was founded in 1902, but long before that the soldiers down in Camp Verde used to come up here to summer camp. You know, the officers, for fishing and hunting."

"A little spa."

"Yeah. We sure didn't have any spas in Nam, did we?"

"Just Saigon."

"Garden spot of Asia."

Time passed quietly. Jake let his body relax as he sat, knees up, fishing pole propped in between, staring silently at the opalescent water.

"Nice spot," mused Randy.

Overhead was a green canopy of juniper and piñon, oak and pine, growing strangely in harmony. Sunlight filtered through, filmy in the late afternoon, dappling man and earth. The mountain smelled of summer, warm and vibrant; occasionally a droplet of creek water, dashed against the rocks, would spray Jake's face.

Now *this*, he had to admit, was more like it.

"Got one!" hollered Randy, coming to his feet as if there was a fire. "Damnation! The son-of-a-gun got away."

"You never could fish," reflected Jake dryly.

"And you never could keep that big mouth shut."

The late afternoon wore on tranquilly. The sun slipped lazily behind the canyon ridge to the west, and a deep green glow settled in the valley.

"I may just stay here." Jake stood and stretched, surveying the two fat rainbows in his creel...and Randy's empty one. "Yep, you never could catch 'em."

"Very funny, Brannigan." Then Randy asked, "How're you killing the time these days?"

"I jog, read. You know."

"Sure. Like you always did." Randy muttered sarcastically. "Truth is, Jake old pal, you never could sit still a minute. Always had to poke your nose in everywhere. And...."

"Always have to be right." They both laughed, having finished Randy's little lecture simultaneously.

"You get bored now with Bobby gone half the day on the swim team?" Randy cast again into the deep blue swirling trench.

"Maybe...some, I suppose."

"A lot, I bet."

"Come on, Randy." Jake eyed him narrowly. "Get to the point."

"I've got a week to fill that undersheriff post."

"Bring a deputy up. You must have some capable hands."

"There is one guy, Kyle, who's dying to get the post."

"So give him the promotion."

"Can't. He's too young, too wet behind the ears."

"So?"

"I want you."

"I'm retired."

"On half pension. And bored out of your mind."

"So what? It's my life." Jake stretched out on the ground, put his hands behind his neck and squinted up into the fading light.

"You're a cop. And a darn good one at that. But then—" Randy glared at his fishing line where it entered the water "—I guess you think you're too good for a town like Sedona. All we get is drunk drivers, an occasional robbery, a hunting accident.... Of course, there is this Twelvetrees case."

"You'll handle it."

"How? I can't close the file on it. Too many unanswered questions."

"In L.A.," said Jake lazily, "we just put those files aside...for years."

"Not in Sedona. Too small a town."

"So solve it, Randy. You're the sheriff and you can't kid a kidder—you're a smart guy."

"Aren't you the least bit curious? I know you too well, Jake."

"So I'm curious. So I'll read about it in the paper when you've got it all solved."

"Hire on with me, Jake. Come on. I'll take care of all the details, get your records from L.A. sent in. Other than the standard physical, you won't have to do a thing."

"No."

"Does that mean yes?"

Jake sat up slowly, raking his big hands through his

thick straight hair. "You know something, Randy?" he blustered. "You really are a pain."

"It's yes, then." Randy slapped Jake so hard on the back it half toppled the big Irishman into the water.

Jake swore loudly. "But I may not stay past summer and I'm not wearing one of your dumb Stetsons!"

ALEX HAD BEEN WEEDING THE FLOWER GARDEN that ran along the front of the white painted porch. Her hair was tied back in a green bandanna and dirt smudged her cheek, the front of her old torn T-shirt and cutoff blue jeans.

She stood, arched her aching back and rubbed her forearm across her damp brow.

"Hot work," said a husky voice.

At first, for an instant, she didn't recognize him. "Jake Brannigan?"

"Yeah." He seemed a little defensive and a little proud, too, like a boy showing off a new football jersey. He wore the sheriff's department uniform: neat Western-cut tan shirt with its three perfect creases in the back, well-pressed, tailored trousers—with brown gun belt, gun and cuffs prominently displayed—tall, polished boots and, to top it all off, a big-brimmed Stetson.

"You've taken the job, then," Alex finally said, a bit uncomfortable, remembering the strange magnetism that had surged between them.

"Randy didn't tell you?"

"I haven't seen him in a while."

"Well, this might just be temporary."

"I see."

"The department's busy. Summer tourist season and all. Just helping out a friend."

"There's the Twelvetrees case...."

"Yeah. Randy's dumped it in my lap."

Alex's face brightened. "But that's great! After all, I mean, you *were* a homicide detective."

"Whoa there, Alex. You realize that there may be nothing more to uncover in this one."

The light left her blue eyes. "I know. But if there's anything, you'll find it."

Jake frowned. "Sure. Well, I gotta get going... work."

"I'll bet you're glad, really," she found herself saying.

Jake turned back to face her again. "Oh yeah, I'm real happy," he growled. She never knew whether or not he was serious.

As she watched him drive off in the sheriff department's white Blazer, she asked herself if he ever, for anyone, let down that prickly guard. And she wondered again what kind of woman would he have been married to.

Just before she was ready to hop in the shower, she remembered thinking that she was going to ask Janet about Jake's wife. But that was silly. And it was none of her business.

"I saw Jake this morning," she told Janet moments later on the phone, "and nobody told me he'd filled that undersheriff post."

"Just happened, Alex. Couple of days ago. Randy's pleased as punch. You can just imagine."

"I'll bet!" How to put it? "Listen, Janet, there's a question that's been rattling around in my mind. ..."

"About Jake?"

"Well, yes...."

"So? Oh come, Alex. I'd ask *you* straight out."

"I know. But swear you won't tell anyone I asked. I wouldn't want Tom to know...."

"Oh dear sweet Tom. Heavens no! He'd be the last person on earth I'd tell."

"No one, now. Swear."

"I swear."

"Tell me about Jake's wife."

There was a long groan on the line. "Darn. Now that's the one thing I don't know much about. Even Randy wouldn't tell me if he knew."

"Really? Why?"

"You know Jake well enough by now to have figured that one out. The man's a closed book. *Really* closed."

"Well, you must know something."

"Oh, I met Linda, all right. Years and years ago on a trip to L.A."

"And?"

"She was cute. Dark and neat and cute. And as cool as they come."

"And?"

"She up and left one day. She packed her bags and split with an insurance agent." Janet thought. "I guess he was a safer bet than Jake. You know a cop in L.A. doesn't keep the most regular hours."

"I guess it must have devastated him."

"Oh, you might say that! He really started to drink then."

"How long ago was that?"

"Six, seven years."

"I see. So he *never* talks about her?"

"Never. And I'll tell you what I think. I think the cute little witch ruined him for anyone else."

Inexplicably Alex's heart sank. "I'm sure you're right about that. He sure keeps his distance."

"Oh," said Janet coyly, "have you tried to get near?"

"No. You know what I mean."

"Sure Alex."

She'd finished her shower and dressed in tan summer slacks and a royal-blue blouse when the phone rang. "It's Randy."

"Oh. . .hi." *Janet didn't. . .?*

"We've got a pretty complete file on Twelvetrees, Alex. I thought you might like to look it over, take a copy up to Bill in Flagstaff."

"Anything new?" she asked hopefully.

" 'Fraid not, Alex."

Disappointment filled her. "All right then, I'll be over. I'm heading up to Flagstaff anyway, so I'll just stop on my way. By the way, Randy, I just saw Jake. You didn't tell me...."

"Well, I figured you'd find out soon enough anyway. He's a good man, Alex."

"I certainly hope so," she said cautiously.

RANDY HANDED HER THE FILE, copies of each enclosed item neatly clipped together. She glanced through the pages. There were photos of the body, all angles, the medical examiner's report, even newspaper clippings from the *Red Rock News*. Then she saw a new item, a deputy's report on his findings after examining a half mile section of riverbank down on Joseph's property. Nothing. Certainly not the rock that had caused Joseph's death. Of course, as Randy pointed out, chances of finding that were as good as finding a needle in a haystack.

"We won't close the file, Alex," he told her quietly. "But I'm afraid there's nothing more we can do right now."

"The county attorney's office won't close it, either. At least," she added, smiling wryly, "I'll do my best with Bill...."

"The rumors still going around?"

"What...?"

"You know, about the Navajo witch?"

"Oh." Alex felt a twinge of uneasiness. "I imagine they'll die down sooner or later. You know, we Indians like to dwell on spiritual matters." She shrugged. "I guess I'll be on my way."

"Oh, and Alex, if anything comes up at all, Jake will be handling it."

"He mentioned it to me."

"Yeah. You know with no local police force in the summer here 'bout all I have time for is administration. I'll tell you," he said, whistling softly, "I'm lucky to have him."

Alex stopped in the doorway, turning to face Randy. "You know, we all expected Kyle to land that job. He has been a deputy for a while."

Randy scratched his head. "Yeah, but he hasn't got the qualifications yet."

"I'll bet he was disappointed."

"Some. But Jake set him straight."

"I'm sure he did."

She ran into Jake in the parking lot of the sheriff's department. He was carrying a pizza box.

It was childish of her, but he had a way of making her feel self-conscious, and she said the first thing that came to her lips. "Busy today?" She realized he must have taken her words as sarcasm because his face hardened.

"Actually," he said flatly, "yes."

"Oh, well then...." She thought, as she made her way toward her car, that this job had certainly put a damper on Jake Brannigan; whereas before he'd been a tough character, now he was just plain nasty.

"Alex."

She spun around, caught guiltily in her musings. "What?" she breathed.

"We're not closing the Twelvetrees file. I hope you understand that."

"It seems to me that's exactly what's happened. Well...I'd better be going."

She wondered later why he'd upset her so—why she'd become unsettled when Randy had said that Jake had set Kyle straight. What, exactly, had he meant? And why did the very sight of him make her nervous? She guessed that in general, she'd been upset about Joseph's case—what there was of it—when she'd run into Jake in the parking lot.

He certainly had been all business. Cold, if she was to put a word to it.

It wasn't until she switched on the car radio, picking up the Flagstaff news station, that she'd heard it: apparently two climbers were caught on a ledge somewhere north of Oak Creek Canyon and had been stuck there since the previous day. The sheriff's department of Sedona, along with local mountain rescue volunteers of Coconino County, were presently exhausting

themselves in an all-out effort to rescue the boys—
four-wheel-drive vehicles, climbing attempts, the department's helicopter. And here she had made a dumb
remark about him having nothing to do! Probably the
pizza had been for the department's rescue team or for
Randy, who would be stuck in the office.

How thoughtless she'd been.

The afternoon sped by. Alex found several new
routine case files on her desk—a burglary, a child-
neglect case, a reckless driver—and mountains of legal
paperwork to be typed. She had no secretary, of
course. Tom telephoned and talked her into dinner
again when she really should have stayed late at the office. Aware of her tendency to push herself too hard,
she often forced herself to put things aside. And her
boss, Bill, didn't help matters any with his snide cracks
about women who worked overtime.

They dined at the Poco Diablo Resort a couple of
miles southwest of Sedona, a lovely serene spot, surrounded by a golf course, tennis courts, swimming
pools, a beautifully appointed terrace overlooking
several ponds, willow trees and all. In the background
were the familiar, jutting red mesas that drew the pho-
tographers.

Alex wore a dress for the occasion and was glad she
had when Tom complimented her on the crimson-and-
white outfit.

"You look beautiful!" Tom had said, standing at
her door, attired handsomely himself in gray slacks, a
lavender polo shirt and summer-weight sports jacket.
He was, Alex realized, an extremely handsome man,
tall and lean—he worked out regularly—with neatly
cut sandy-brown hair that hadn't yet thinned, pleasant
brown eyes, a prominent nose and sensitive mouth.
Any woman would be proud to be seen with Tom.

Alex ate tender Utah lamb. "My red meat for the
week," she told Tom. She even allowed herself des-
sert—a chocolate mousse. After all, she hadn't eaten
much that day....

They talked, over coffee and brandy, on the serene veranda.

"I want to tell you something," Tom said quietly, resting his elbows on the glass table top. "I've never enjoyed a woman's company more than yours."

Alex blushed slightly. "Thank you."

"I'd hope someday that we could make it more permanent."

She sat silently, her heart beating rapidly. Tom had never mentioned a permanent relationship. . . until tonight.

"I'd ask you right now, Alex," he said smiling, reaching across the table to take one of her hands, "but I've still got some things in my life which need attending to."

Her thoughts turned to Mavis and the kids, but she kept silent. And his real-estate business. And his position in the community—school-board member, churchgoer. . . .

"You do a lot," Alex reflected aloud. "Sometimes, Tom, I think you do too much. I have that tendency myself, but I try to be aware of it, and then I don't have a family. You're spreading yourself too thin, Tom. How do you find time for it all?"

"I make the time, Alex. I enjoy it."

But did he really? How good could it all be when he felt it necessary to mention a permanent relationship but had to put it off into the future? And how fair was that to her?

She began to feel slightly tense, and knew that Tom could sense her anxiety.

"Look," he began, "I wish I could ask you. . . to marry me. I honestly do, Alex. But you understand. I just need time. . . ."

"I understand, do I?" She took her hand away carefully.

"Come on, Alex. . . ."

"Have you ever looked at things from my point of view?" She didn't wait for a reply. "Try being in my shoes."

"I have," he said defensively.

"Then you should know that *people* come first. I can't wait forever, Tom. I'm twenty-eight years old."

Tom's hand was rubbing his chin. "When people care, Alex, they should be able to see the other person's side. That's all a part of giving in a relationship."

She wanted to ask Tom what had gone sour in his marriage to Mavis, but she suspected she knew the answer anyway: he'd been too busy starting up his real-estate firm at the time, joining the school board— the same things that were coming between them now.

"Tom," she said quietly, "it's silly to sit here arguing."

"I'm not arguing."

"Well," Alex continued, shifting in her chair, "I am. The point is, when will there ever be time in your life for anything else?"

Her bluntness seemed to stun him momentarily. "I...well, I'll make time, of course. That's a ridiculous question."

"Then you don't think you could stand to eliminate a few things in your life?"

"What? My children, Alex?"

"No. You know I don't mean that."

"Then what do I eliminate? My business? My friends?"

"How about the school board. You spend at least two evenings a week in Flagstaff."

"And let my kids grow up and go to school there? Things need changing in our schools, Alex. I can't stand by...."

"No. I suppose you can't." Her words came out bitterly. She hadn't meant them to. Or, perhaps, she had.

"Can we go?" she asked finally, seeing no way to end the argument. Of course, Tom didn't even think they were arguing....

He asked her to spend the night at his place on the drive back into Sedona.

"I don't think so," she replied, her eyes fastened on the road. "There are some things I need to sort out in my mind."

"Please, Alex." His voice touched her gently in the dimness. "Don't do this. We're good together. You know it. Look, I'll try. I'll really try to pare things down in my life."

She still insisted on his driving her home. And when he pulled into her driveway, she quickly opened her car door and stepped out. But Tom did the same.

"I don't want to part like this tonight," he said, coming around the front of his car. He took hold of her arms, pulling her around to face him. "Alex." His voice caressed her ears. And then his mouth was covering hers and her lips parted, and he was drawing her against him, almost forcefully.

For an instant Alex was caught breathless and excited by him, a man doing exactly what he wanted, with no care whatsoever for proprieties. But as his mouth continued to move over hers, she knew that it was all contrived. He'd probably read the latest how-to-seduce-a-woman book and was implementing chapter four. Her desire fled. She pushed at his chest.

"Don't," she whispered.

"Alex...?"

"I mean it, Tom."

"But I thought...I thought you'd like it. What do I have to do to please you?"

Alex sighed warily. "Just be yourself, Tom. Stop trying so hard to be what you think others want. Please. Just be yourself."

She stood in the drive and watched as he got back into his car and pulled out in reverse, his headlights illuminating her brightly for a moment before he was gone. She turned away and unaccountably her glance was drawn to the garage—to the apartment windows. The lights were on in the living room but the bedrooms were dark. Was Jake reading late? And then she wondered, had he seen them standing in the drive?

A slight mountain breeze caught at her dress and stirred her hair. Somewhere on the dark hills behind, an owl hooted. She was reminded instantly of her grandfather and his stories about the lonely cry of the night owl. She remembered his last words to her, about the fork in the road on which she now stood. Was she coming to a choice in her life, really? It certainly did seem as if everything in her life had changed in the last few weeks, since, well, since Joseph Twelvetrees's death.

She walked toward the porch steps, once again noticing the light spilling from the windows of the apartment over the garage. And coincidentally, wasn't the day they'd found Joseph the same day Jake Brannigan had arrived?

CHAPTER ELEVEN

ALEX TOOK A MOMENT to glance out her kitchen window as she fixed herself a cup of coffee. It was another perfect June morning—clear and blue. Later in the afternoon thunderclouds would pile up on the horizon, threatening and blustering, but the rain would dry up before it ever hit the ground and by evening the sky would be perfectly clear again.

She looked forward to her Sunday ride with Janet despite the many other things on her mind. No dead bodies *this* week, she promised herself with a shudder. They'd go in an entirely different direction this time.

Bobby Brannigan appeared in her line of vision from the kitchen window, hands in pockets, shoulders hunched, walking down the driveway, kicking at pebbles with his scuffed tennis shoes—a forlorn figure, lonely, bored, a kid who didn't belong yet. She felt a surge of pity for him and a little bit of unjustified shame for herself, situated so well here in Sedona. She had friends, a position, security galore.

A sudden impulse shook her; it was put into action before she considered further, a step most unusual for her. It must have been her frustrated mothering instinct, she was to think later.

Opening the back door, she poked her head out, calling after the retreating figure, "Hey, Bobby!"

He turned, his face sullen, his blond hair tousled. "Oh, hi."

"Want to join me for breakfast? I'm making pancakes." She wasn't, but she could remedy that quickly enough.

"Well...." He had obviously been told not to bother the landlady.

"Come on, do me a favor. I hate to make pancakes for one person. It's Sunday morning."

"Gee, dad...." But he was walking toward her already.

"I'd like the company, Bobby."

He sidled into the kitchen, hands still in his pockets.

"Where's your dad?" she asked conversationally as she pulled the box of pancake mix from a cupboard.

"Aw, he's out jogging," the boy said disparagingly.

"Jogging." It was a statement of mild amazement.

"Yeah, he's turned gung ho all of a sudden. Gotta get in shape, he says."

"Because of his new job?" she asked, mixing in egg and milk.

"I dunno. Maybe."

"So, Bobby, I guess you're stuck here now that Jake's the undersheriff." She made her tone light and joking.

"Yeah, I guess."

"So what do you think about it?"

He shrugged. "One place is as good as another when it's not home."

"And L.A. is home?"

"Yeah."

"Maybe someday Sedona could be home. It's a nice place, Bobby. The kids here love it. I went to Flagstaff High School myself, you know."

"Sure, but it's not *my* home."

"I know, it must be real hard to move. What grade are you going into?"

"Ninth."

She poured batter into a hot frying pan, then put butter and syrup and orange juice on the kitchen table. "Sit down. They're almost ready."

The kid looked as if he'd been living on Cheerios and TV dinners. Somehow Jake did not strike her as either a great cook or housekeeper.

"Here's a batch for you," she said, piling several pancakes on his plate. He dug into them ravenously. Poor kid.

"How does your dad feel about his new job? Is he pleased?"

Bobby shrugged, his mouth full. "It's right up his alley. Boy, another cop job. The kids used to really tease me back home because my dad was a cop."

"They were jealous, that's all," said Alex pertly. "You should be proud."

"Aw, he's okay, I guess. He was a good detective," he added grudgingly.

"So I understand. Maybe he'll help me with my new case."

"You mean that... body?"

"Yes, that one."

"Well, if it can be solved, dad'll do it."

He ate for a while in silence. Alex piled more pancakes on his plate. "These are good, Miss Crawford."

"Thanks, Bobby, but it's Alex, remember?"

"Yeah. Say, can we go riding again some time?"

"Sure we can. I'm going this afternoon. Janet and I go every Sunday. Want to come along?"

"I'll ask my dad. Will Cecily be along?" he inquired, eager for once.

Alex laughed. "I don't know. Why don't you call her and ask?"

"Aw, I couldn't do that!" He blushed like a girl.

Alex sat down across from Bobby, leaning her elbows on the table. "Bobby, I hope you don't think I'm prying, but why didn't you stay in L.A. with your mother?"

A cloud settled over Bobby's young features.

"Look, if you don't want to talk about it...."

"I hate my mother." The words were a litany, obviously repeated many times. "She left us. My dad took her to court so he could keep me. But she didn't even care. Then she got married again."

"I'm sorry," said Alex softly.

"Don't be sorry for me! We're both better off without her!"

"Maybe someday, Bobby, you'll understand about your mother. I know she loved you."

"Ha!"

"I understand it's real difficult to be a policeman's wife in a big city like L.A."

"She knew he was a cop when they got married," he remarked sullenly.

"Sure, but that wasn't the same as living with one. Worrying all the time. . . ."

"Nothing ever happened to my dad. He was too tough. All those bad guys and criminals and all were afraid of him. He had a *reputation*."

"You're proud of Jake, aren't you?"

"Yeah, sure. Shouldn't I be?"

"Oh, you should, of course. I'm sure he was very good at his job."

Bobby sopped up the last bit of syrup on his plate. "That was good. Thanks. . . Alex."

"Any time, kiddo."

There was a knock at the back door.

"Come in," called Alex. "It's open."

Jake's head appeared, circled by a twisted bandanna. Sweat darkened his T-shirt. "Sorry to bother you, but I wondered if you'd seen Bob."

"I'm here, dad," called the boy.

"Is he bugging you, Alex?"

"No, really. In fact, I invited him for breakfast."

Jake wore shorts and a T-shirt that clung to his body with dampness; his hair was also slick. There was something terribly primitive about him as he stood on her threshold, breathing a little heavily still. He had strong legs, the heavy thigh muscles of a football player. Alex liked looking at him.

"Well, send him home when he's done. He'll be moving in if you're not careful."

"*Dad.* . . ."

"Jake, he's welcome here. I was going to show him

those books and some artifacts I've found." Why was he always so abrasive?

"Just send him home when he's done, okay?"

She sighed, shrugging at Bobby as if to say "never mind." Maybe Jake resented her feeding Bobby, as if she was insinuating that he couldn't feed his own son. He was a strange, closed man.

"Come on, Bobby, I'll show you the books."

The boy really was interested in Indians. He turned every page reverently, looking at the pictures, studying the old photographs.

"Do they *really* put snakes in their mouths?" he asked once, seeing a photograph of the Hopi snake dance in which the serpents writhed in great clumps on the dancing ground.

"Yes, they do. My grandfather says there's a way of, well, charming the snakes so they won't bite. He used to dance it when he was younger. He was a two-horn priest of the Bear clan."

"Wow. Could I see one of those snake dances?"

"Sure. But not until fall. I'll let you know when it's coming."

"What are the dances for?" he asked.

"To celebrate, usually a seasonal event. Spring, summer, harvest. The Hopis had no sense of time except for the turning of the seasons. They were farmers, and corn was their main crop, so everything revolved around the 'corn mother.'"

"What I can't figure out is why they wanted to live out there." He waved a hand toward the east. "In a desert."

"To the Hopi the desert is a beautiful and plentiful place. They believe they were led there so they would always have faith in their creator who provides the rain they need. It's a kind of life test and their supreme title to the land."

"That's sort of a tough way to live, isn't it?"

"Perhaps. But it gives them peace. They know always how they should think and act. Everything they do is a prayer to the creator. A Hopi lives his religion every day.''

"Is that how *you* live?'' asked Bobby shrewdly.

"No,'' she answered regretfully. "I was raised in the white man's world. Even my mother hasn't followed the Hopi ways.''

"But your grandfather has.''

"Yes. Isn't he wonderful?''

"That's some old man!''

Bobby helped her wash the dishes, something he had obviously not done often, as he was awkward and in the way. Still, Alex thought, it was sweet of him.

They were putting away the last few things when there was a knock on the front door.

"Thanks, Bobby. You've helped a lot. You can quit now,'' she said as she started toward the living room.

It was George Twelvetrees, Joseph's son.

"George, good to see you. Come in,'' said Alex, faintly surprised.

"You're not busy?'' He was a man of medium height with the high cheekbones and black hair of all Navajos. He wore jeans and a plaid shirt, not his usual city clothes.

"No, please, come in. Bobby and I were just finishing the breakfast dishes.'' She indicated Bobby, standing in the kitchen doorway.

"George Twelvetrees, Bobby Brannigan.'' She introduced them. "Bobby is the son of our new undersheriff,'' she explained.

"Ah yes, Randy spoke of him. I stopped by the other day to see if he had come up with anything.''

"Oh, you're the son of that...that man,'' Bobby burst out.

"Yes, unfortunately my father is making more of a stir in death than he ever did in life,'' said George gravely.

"I'm sorry,'' mumbled the boy.

"Yes, well...George, would you like some coffee?'' offered Alex.

"If you don't mind. I stopped by to ask you something."

"Sure, anything. Let me just get the coffee."

Bobby still stood in the same spot, staring openly at George. George nodded, smiling at the boy.

"I guess I gotta go now," said Bobby, but he didn't move.

"Here we are," said Alex, returning. "Now what is it you want to ask?"

"Well, I was back home in Flagstaff—it was Wednesday—when I got an odd phone call. A man named Justin Manor of the Manor Development Corporation wanted to know if I was interested in selling my father's property here. And it was a generous offer, too. Anyway, I'm afraid I was a bit short with the man—told him the will wasn't even probated yet and I'd have to talk to my younger brothers. He didn't seem to mind, just told me to think about it. Then, the next day I got this in the mail." He took a business card out of his pocket, and handed it to Alex. It said "Manor Development Corporation" on it. Underneath was "Justin Manor" and then an address on fashionable Fifth Avenue in Scottsdale.

"I just thought, since you knew my father and you're a lawyer.... Well, we could use the money, but you know that my father would never have sold the land, and he sure wouldn't want us to sell it. I don't trust these speculators a bit, but this one said something that made me consider him more trustworthy than most."

"Oh, what was that?" Absently Alex turned the small white card over in her fingers.

"He said that Tom Farley was his partner in this venture."

"Tom?" Alex's head snapped up.

"I know," said George. "I thought it was strange. I know you and Tom...well...you know each other quite well...."

"George, I know absolutely nothing about this. Tom has never said a word to me."

"I just wondered why they wanted it so badly. The price he mentioned was quite high."

"I can't believe—" She broke off, looking at George intently. "George, if he calls again, play him along, ask some questions, but for goodness' sakes don't sign anything or promise him anything, okay?"

"Sure, Alex."

"I'm going to look into this a little," she said thoughtfully. "I'm glad you stopped by. I'll be in touch."

"Thanks."

George left. Pensively Alex wandered into the kitchen, and noticed Bobby still standing there awkwardly.

"Is he a Hopi, too?" he asked.

"No, George is a full-blooded Navajo. He's a good man."

"Wow, he looked real cool," breathed Bobby. "Well, thanks. I better go on back before dad comes over and drags me out. See you."

"Sure, Bobby, any time."

Alex's mind was whirling with this new knowledge about Tom. Why had he never mentioned this partnership? Usually he told her all about his business dealings, even asked her for legal advice from time to time. She couldn't believe it—Tom and some land-grabbing wheeler-dealer?

Oh, she'd seen plenty in her time. Everyone in Sedona had. Cigar-smoking, perfectly manicured big shots who would rape and destroy the precious land— the dry-country land that was especially fragile—for profit. How on earth could Tom have a partner like that? But maybe she was misjudging this man, this Justin Manor.

There was something that teased the edge of her consciousness, something she needed to remember. She tried to concentrate but it eluded her. It was something about a land speculator. The idea would not surface; she shook her head in annoyance and went outside to do some work in the yard—there was always something to do, and she hated leaving things undone.

When she was pruning the hedge of rose bushes in the backyard, it came to her. Of course. Randy had mentioned that Joseph Twelvetrees had complained about a speculator harassing him. The same one, she wondered. It was logical.

What had she said in Randy's office? "Murdering someone isn't going to get him to sell his land." No, but it might get his heirs to sell, especially sons who did not live in the area. But who could possibly want land enough to murder for it? Wasn't that a little too drastic? Ridiculous, in fact?

And Tom...no, he would never be involved in anything like that. But what if he had no idea...no, that was ridiculous, too.

And yet, she found herself walking inside, picking up the phone and dialing that familiar number. There was a cold lump in her chest, a vague foreboding. Tom wouldn't....

"Hello?" he said.

"Tom." Did she sound a little breathless?

"Hi, hon."

"Do you know Justin Manor?" There, it was out.

He was silent for a heartbeat of time. "Yes, I know him. I'm helping him out on a land acquisition. Alex, what...?"

"Is he legitimate, Tom?"

"Of course. He runs a development corporation in Phoenix."

"How come you never mentioned him to me?"

"Hey," he said, laughing, "what is this, Miss Deputy County Attorney, the third degree?"

"Tom. What exactly are you and this Manor working on?"

"He's planning to build a big resort just south of town. You know, golf course, pool, tennis, condominiums. The works. I've seen the plans. They're really spectacular."

"And where do you come in?"

"Alex, hon, I'm just helping him get the land together. It's my job."

"It's the Twelvetrees land, isn't it?"

Another hesitation. "Well, yes, part of it."

"And the rest?" Oh, wasn't she *hard*?

"It happens to be a piece of property that I own. I bought it years ago for an investment."

"I see," she responded coldly.

"Alex, look, this could mean a lot to me. To us. I've got a lot of financial responsibilities these days. A couple of deals didn't work out so well. I'm stretched pretty thin."

She knew how he hated to admit this to her; it revealed a chink in his perfection.

"Then what's the problem, Tom?"

"Joseph Twelvetrees wouldn't sell. You know those old Indians. . . ."

"Oh, don't I though?" Anger sparked in her voice. "I'm one of those *old Indians*!"

"Alex, you know what I mean."

"Well, he's dead now. What's the hang-up?" Was that her voice—so harsh and brittle?

"Alex." Patient, kind, reasonable Tom. "Look, why are you so upset? This is a perfectly ordinary business deal. I'm a very small part of it."

"Did Justin Manor ever talk to Joseph Twelvetrees?"

"Sure, of course. We both went out to talk to him several times."

"Tom, I've been asked by George Twelvetrees to represent the estate." Not exactly true, but a little white lie was useful right now.

"Oh."

"I'd like to talk to Mr. Manor. Can you arrange it?"

"Good God, Alex, you're really up in arms about this, aren't you? I can't imagine why. Things like this go on every day. It's business."

"Can you arrange the meeting? Otherwise I'll call him myself."

"Okay. All right. He'll be up in Sedona in a few days. I'll arrange lunch or something."

"Fine. I'll see you then."

"Not before? What's the matter with you, hon? You sound like you're angry with me. Was it last night?"

"No, Tom, I'm just a little disappointed in your choice of business partners." And then she hung up.

CHAPTER TWELVE

JAKE HAD SHOWERED and changed by the time Bobby got back from breakfast. He was sitting in the one easy chair, his long legs stretched out before him, reading the *Phoenix Sun*.

"So, you have a good breakfast?" he ventured.

"Yeah. She's got some neat Indian books. Did you know the Hopis have this snake dance...."

"Bob, don't get in the habit of hanging around her house."

"She asked me, dad."

"Sure, *this* time. But don't butt in where you're not wanted. That's a single lady, she's got a boyfriend and her own life. Don't get involved, Bobby."

"Geez, dad, can't I do anything right?" he asked sullenly.

Jake recognized the old resentful tone in his son's voice. He relented, finding the words difficult. "Look, Bobby," he said, letting the paper fall to his lap, "I didn't mean to criticize. It's my own fault, for Pete's sake. I took her up on the dinner offer last week, I guess." He drew a deep breath. "Just don't push it."

"Okay, but I sure don't have much to do around here."

"You will, when school starts." He picked up the paper again, rustled the pages and began to read an article on the trial of a mobster in Phoenix.

"School, oh great!" mumbled Bobby sarcastically, adding, "This neat-looking Indian visited Alex while I was there. A Navajo. He was that dead man's son, Alex told me."

"Hmm," said Jake, deep into the DEA's case against the mobster.

"He was telling her about this man who wants to buy the old man's property. Somebody from Phoenix." Idly Bobby walked to the window, hands in pockets, remarkably like his father.

"That's nice," mumbled Jake, reading.

"Boy, did Alex get upset. I mean, she didn't even know I was there anymore."

"Who?"

"*Alex.* Gee, dad, you aren't listening! And I thought this was your case!"

"Alex what?" Jake looked up finally.

"Alex got real upset when this George Twelvetrees told her about the guy from Phoenix."

Jake was suddenly alert. "George Twelvetrees?"

"The dead man's son. I *told* you."

The paper fell once more. "Tell me again. What about this guy from Phoenix?"

"Some big developer wants to buy the old man's land. Only now he has to ask George because the old man's dead," explained Bobby patiently. "And George wanted to ask Alex's advice because he said he didn't trust speculators—but he thought this one was okay because Alex's boyfriend was in on it."

"Wait a minute. Let me get this straight, Bob. George Twelvetrees had been approached by a speculator from Phoenix who wants to buy his father's land?"

"Yeah, I guess so."

"And Tom Farley is involved?"

"That's what he said."

Jake let out a low whistle, and slowly looked up at Bobby. "You sure you heard this all right?"

Disgust tinged Bobby's answer. "You think I'm dumb or something, dad?"

"No," he replied absently, his mind busy with this new knowledge. He recalled instantly that Randy had mentioned old Joseph Twelvetrees complaining about a speculator bothering him. Was it the same one? Just how badly did this man want the Twelvetrees land? Pretty badly; it wasn't two weeks since the old Indian had died and the man had already contacted his son.

"You remember the speculator's name?" he asked Bobby.

The boy thought. "I don't know. Something fancy. I can't remember."

He'd have to check on that tomorrow at work. He doubted Randy had the name; after all, it had just been mentioned in passing. But he'd bet a bundle that Alex remembered that name. "You said Alex got upset?" he queried casually.

"Yeah, especially when George told her about her boyfriend being in on this thing."

"I just bet," muttered Jake under his breath. He stored it away in his mind: call Alex Monday morning and get the name of that speculator from Phoenix.

After all, it was his case.

As IT TURNED OUT, Jake forgot to call Alex because he got involved in a burglary case on Monday morning. An art gallery had been broken into and robbed of some valuable gold Hopi jewelry. It was a humdrum case, but he had been on it nearly all day, finally tracking down the owner's stepson, who had the stuff in the trunk of his car.

But Alex called him bright and early on Tuesday from home.

"Officer Brannigan?" Her voice was cool and professional.

"Yeah, it's me," he replied, deliberately casual.

"I just wanted to tell you I've got some new information on the Twelvetrees case."

"You mean about the speculator from Phoenix wanting to buy the old man's land?" His voice was deceptively nonchalant. He'd dealt with uptight DA's before.

The quickly indrawn breath came clearly over the phone line. "How did you know that?" She was a little angry, a little confused.

"I have my sources." No sense getting the kid involved.

Her voice was cold now, and tinged with triumph, "Well, then, perhaps you also know that I'm having lunch with him and Tom today?"

"With *whom*?" He sat up straight, losing his carefully blasé tone for a moment.

"With Justin Manor and Tom. Today. Lunch." Her voice was tolerant, the way you'd speak to a child. He felt his temper begin to rise. At the same time he tucked the name away in his brain: Justin Manor.

He took a calming breath. "Look, Alex, I hardly think it's your job to have lunch with this guy."

He heard her light laughter over the phone. "But it *is* my job to do exactly that. I'm gathering evidence on the Twelvetrees case."

"You know anything about this Manor guy?"

"Only that he's approached George Twelvetrees, that he wants to build a resort here and that Tom's involved with him."

"That gives you great confidence in him?" he asked sarcastically.

"I don't think we need to continue this conversation, Officer Brannigan," she stated coolly. "I'll let you know the results of my investigation."

"Hey, you just hold on there, counselor!" Jake began, but before he finished, he realized he was talking into a dead phone. Of all the nerve! The little lady had hung up on him! He was left holding the receiver, listening to a monotonous dial tone, and feeling like a fool.

Of course, he couldn't let it go on that note. He started out of the office, to confront Alex and try to put some sense in her head, but Randy saw him in the corridor and called him into his office.

"Hey, Jake." He had a folder in his hand. "I want you to handle this. Mrs. Sanders at the art gallery wants to drop charges against her stepson. Can you go talk to her? I guess her husband raised a ruckus—it's *his* kid. See what you can do."

"One of those ticklish ones," growled Jake.

"Not exactly homicide," replied Randy, almost apologetically, "but then this isn't L.A., Jake."

"I'll take care of it."

"Okay, just get me the report afterward. I want this documented fully in case the kid pulls anything again. I don't want the county attorney breathing down my neck."

"Sure, Randy."

It took until lunchtime to untangle the messy affair. Jake was unusually patient, trying hard to reconcile all the parties. It wasn't easy. Police work, Jake sometimes thought, was a little like psychiatry.

He was hot and irritable and hungry as he headed home to grab a quick sandwich. He could have eaten downtown, but he was trying to save money and he could check on Bobby at the same time.

As he pulled into the driveway in the big white Blazer that said Coconino County Sheriff's Department on its side, he saw Alex getting into her car.

His first reaction was anger, his second, amazement. She was dressed in a stunning bottle-green dress made of something silky that swirled around her legs and clung to her slim hips. She wore high-heeled sandals and her hair hung down in a shimmering, dark curtain. She looked cool and glamorous and totally self-possessed. Almost a different person. Somehow, that only increased his irritation.

He braked the Blazer harshly, grinding gravel under the tires and sending up puffs of dust. He knew he must have looked like a State Trooper sauntering up to someone stopped for speeding on the interstate—officious, molasses-slow, overly casual. But he was past caring.

She was sitting in her car, the door still open, waiting for him. "Jake," she greeted, nodding impersonally.

"I don't like people hanging up on me." He was aware that his voice was surly.

"And I don't like being treated like an incompetent child. Besides, you have no business interfering with the county attorney's office."

"Okay," he conceded, "but you shouldn't be going off like this half-cocked."

"You wouldn't say that if I were a man," she retorted hotly.

That stopped him for a moment. "Don't be ridiculous. You aren't going to find anything out over lunch."

"I'm going to darn well try." She glared at him angrily. "This is my job, Jake! Don't try to protect me or tell me what to do. I'm not one of your helpless little females. And I'm not your *wife*!"

Her words must have touched a long-suppressed chord in him; he felt outrage flare. Suddenly he was leaning across her, not even aware that his hard-muscled arm brushed her breasts, pulling her car keys from the ignition.

"How dare you!" she cried, getting out of the car and facing him, her chest rising and falling quickly under the green silk. "Give me those keys."

"Not until you listen to me," barked Jake in a low, dangerous voice.

"This isn't L.A.," Alex breathed, her voice quavering with anger. "Don't try those bodyguard tactics with me!"

"You're getting into something over your head. You haven't got any idea. . . ."

"It's none of your business!"

"It's my case."

"It's my case too!"

They faced each other, both furious, neither willing to give way, both consumed with pride and anger and, on Jake's part, worry. The air crackled between them, sparked with taut emotion. Jake's eyes behind his sunglasses were narrowed, his big hands clenched unknowingly into fists at his sides. Alex's eyes shot blue fire, and her stance was as rigidly tense as a cat ready to pounce.

It was Jake who gave in.

He swore under his breath, threw the keys into the

dust at Alex's feet, turned on his heel and stalked to his Blazer.

As he spun the wheels on the gravel and shot backward out of the driveway, he was aware of her still standing there, as if frozen, a graceful figure in a shimmering green dress, staring at her car keys lying in the dust.

He cursed himself up and down in the privacy of the car. He should have known better. That wasn't the way to handle someone like Alex; he was stupid, incompetent, bungling. And Alex Crawford was pigheaded, naive and totally aggravating. It rankled that he'd done something stupid; it rankled even more that she had most definitely won the first round.

And to top it all off, he was still as hungry as the devil!

His police radio crackled to life: "Unit twelve. Respond please."

Jake picked up the small black mouthpiece, depressing the button. "Unit twelve here."

"Officer needs assistance at Oak Valley Bar and Grill on Highway 179, one mile south of town. Code ten-seventy-eight. Repeat, officer needs assistance."

"Roger, dispatch. I'm at Mesquite and Price now. On my way. Unit twelve."

He switched on the siren and flashing lights, and careened around a corner toward the highway. What was going on at the Oak Valley Bar and Grill? And in the middle of the afternoon? Automatically he unsnapped the flap of his holster as he stepped on the gas.

Being so new in Sedona, he wasn't entirely clear where the Oak Valley Bar was—he could only head south on the highway and hope he saw it. He felt the heightened level of awareness, the familiar pulsing of blood in his veins, the adrenaline-charged tingle of nerve and muscle as his body prepared for a crisis. It might not be anything. Then again, it could be his life on the line. You never knew in police work.

There it was! He almost missed the place, then pulled

into the parking lot with screeching tires, slammed on the brakes and leaped out of the car at almost the same moment.

He saw immediately what the problem was: a dozen gaudy Harley-Davidson motorcycles crouched in the parking lot like shiny beetles. Bikers. Mostly they minded their own business, but occasionally they caused problems.

He pushed open the door to the bar, hearing the laughter and rough voices of the bikers. It took a second for his eyes to adjust to the dimness, and hardly more for the bikers to notice him.

"Hey, looky what we got here!" yelled one of them. "Another policy-man!"

Jake saw instantly what had occurred. Kyle Sanchez, the young deputy he'd had words with when he took the job, was in a corner surrounded by laughing, jeering gang members. His hat was off, his hands were handcuffed in front of him with his own cuffs. Kyle looked young and scared; Jake felt a twinge of pity for him, but there wasn't time for that. He took a step into the room, feet apart, knees slightly flexed, hand hovering over his holster. His husky voice boomed out over the noisy room.

"All right, fellas, you've had your fun. Let him go and we'll forget the whole thing!"

One of the bikers, obviously the leader, sidled up to Jake. He was heavy, dressed in black, pimply and vicious looking. "He was buggin' us. Told us to leave. That was not polite at all." His voice was mocking. "So now he can't bother us no more. Why don't you just get on out of here and let us have a good time? We'll turn that there dude loose when we're done."

"You'll turn him loose now and be quick about it," said Jake quietly. His voice was cold and soft and deadly.

"Make me," mocked the gang leader.

The decision was instantaneous: pull a gun and maybe he'd wound one or two, if it came to that, but a man with lead in him could still do damage—and then there were the others. Far better to go for the leader, break his self-assurance.

Jake shot his leg out, hooked the biker's knee and dropped him to the floor. Then he was on him, getting a good right to the unshaven jaw. He heard a howl of shock and anger go up from the room, felt the bones in his hand crack, sensed the blood pounding in his ears.

"Get him!" shouted one of the gang. "No-good fuzz!"

Jake heard the sounds of running feet, curses, a table overturning.

He swung a left to his man's jaw and felt him go limp under him. He stood up, shook his right hand out, and then another one was on him.

It was all instinctive; his reflexes were conditioned from long years of experience, and they still worked, even if his reaction time was a hair slower.

He kneed the first one in the groin, and left him lying moaning on the floor.

Jake hit and kicked, and then it was over. He stood in the middle of the floor, breathing hard like a big fair-haired bear; four men lay around him, two out cold and two groaning in pain. The rest backed away warily, their spirits broken.

Only then did Jake pull his gun from his holster. "All right now, unlock the cuffs, you pansies. On the double!" He held the gun levelly, with two hands, aimed directly at one of the biker's stomachs. "You! Do it now!"

The guy moved quickly, unlocked Kyle's cuffs, and backed off.

Kyle picked up his Stetson, recovered his gun from the bar counter and hurried to Jake's side.

"Thanks," he muttered, holding his own gun on them. "There were too many of them...."

"Never mind, kid, not now," growled Jake, his gun never wavering. "Go call this in. We're going to need a van. Oh, yeah, and an ambulance."

"Holy cow!" A head appeared above the bar. "Is it safe to come out?" The bartender's eyes were bulging, his face pale.

"Sure. It's all over now."

"I called the cops when these here bikers started making trouble, but I ain't never had this happen before!"

"Make a list of the damage, and we'll try to get it out of them," said Jake.

Kyle came rushing back in, breathless, his face slick with sweat. "They're on their way."

"Good. Now let's just take care of these fellas while we wait. Then we can sit down and have a nice tonic and lime."

They ended up shoving all the bikers into the storage room in the back. There were no windows and only one door, which had a stout padlock on it.

Jake had his tonic and lime and fought off the shakes he always got after violent action. It wasn't until the van arrived a few minutes later that his right hand really began to hurt.

"IT'S BROKEN," the doctor stated flatly.

"Damn!" muttered Jake under his breath. Of all the stupid things! Some showing for his first real crisis as undersheriff for Coconino County! They'd be talking behind his back now. He could just hear it: "Big L.A. homicide cop, thinks he's a one-man SWAT team! Broke his hand first time out." Oh, he could hear it now. "Jake Brannigan's losing it. He's old, washed up."

What a lousy day it had been.

"Let me just call my son and then do what you have to do," he growled.

"Hey, dad, I heard it on the radio!" came Bobby's excited voice. "Wow, was it great?"

"Yeah, real great. I broke my hand."

"Wow."

"I'll be a while, Bob. I'm still at the hospital. Can you handle things for a little longer?"

"Sure, dad." He sounded self-important, impressed. "Does it hurt?"

"It hurts like. . . . It hurts a lot, Bob."

"You going to have a cast?"

"I guess so."

"Wow. Take it easy, dad. I'll fix something to eat."

"Thanks, Bob." The kid was really shaping up. Fixing dinner—that was a remarkable offer coming from Bobby. Maybe his son really liked him after all.

"Just let me ask you something real quick. Is Alex's car in the driveway?"

"Just a minute, I'll look." Then, "Nope, no car."

"Thanks, Bob."

"Why'd you want to know?"

"Nothing, just some business."

"Okay, dad."

It was after the doctor had finished putting the cast on his hand that Kyle Sanchez arrived in the emergency room. Jake felt like a fool, his sleeve rolled up, white plaster all over his hand, the ridiculous Stetson on the gurney next to him.

He nodded curtly to Kyle, muttering an unintelligible greeting.

"Is it broken?" Kyle asked.

"Yeah." It was practically a grunt.

Kyle look at him for a time, not saying anything. Then slowly he took off his sunglasses and a big grin split his handsome young face. "I've never seen anything like it," he said, shaking his head in disbelief.

"Like what?"

"Like the way you took those guys out. It was amazing."

Jake looked at Kyle quizzically.

"I really came over here to thank you. You got me out of a bad fix. I was stupid, thought I could handle it . . . ."

"It happens," said Jake curtly.

"I wanted to apologize for some of the things I said—and thought—when Randy gave you the job. I want you to know he was right."

Jake twisted his neck to look up at the young deputy's face. "No problem," was all he came up with.

"I told all the guys in the department what really happened to me and what you did." He shook his head again. "I can't believe it. You against all of those guys."

"It just takes experience," said Jake gruffly, beginning to get embarrassed.

"Will you teach me some of those moves?"

"Heck, kid, any street punk in L.A. knows those tricks. It's not such a big deal."

"The devil it isn't! You're a hero, Jake, a goldarn hero."

"Aw, cut it out."

Kyle tried to drive him home from the hospital, but he refused the deputy's well-meaning offer. He was a little awkward with his hand; it throbbed like crazy, making him grit his teeth whenever he had to turn the wheel with his right hand. What a damned nuisance!

He chuckled to himself at Kyle's reaction—the green kid! A hero—Jake Brannigan a hero! He wondered what Randy would say, but that could wait for tomorrow. He was surprised—no, more relieved than surprised—at being labeled a hero rather than a washed-up bum. Maybe the jogging was helping after all.

What a crazy day it had been.

He was exhausted—still keyed up from the afternoon, but now with a kind of weary restlessness that left him trembling slightly. It was a feeling he recognized from many another aftermath of violence. And the pain of his hand was dragging at him. Oh, he had pills—but he'd only take them in dire necessity. He hated that woozy feeling now.

He still hadn't eaten since breakfast. His stomach grumbled sickeningly, partly from hunger, partly from reaction.

What an ogre of a day.

Bobby had fixed spaghetti—out of a jar—and salad with dressing—out of a jar again. It didn't matter. Jake was so hungry he didn't taste it anyway. And then, when he finished, he felt nauseated again.

"Randy called," Bobby told him.

No answer.

"Your hand hurt?" Bobby asked.

"Some."

"Tell me about it. Were there really thirty guys?"

Jake laughed shortly. "Maybe twelve."

"And was the other deputy really lying on the floor bleeding?"

"No, he was sitting on a bar stool, handcuffed." Jake sighed, too weary suddenly even to take off his uniform.

"How many did you knock out?"

"Two—well, four. They were out of commission anyway."

"Wow."

"Help me get this blasted thing off, Bob, will you?"

"Sure, dad."

Bobby helped unbuckle his holster; Jake couldn't do much with his hand. Maybe he should take a pill after all.

Then it occurred to him; he hadn't even noticed when he drove into the driveway. Heaving himself out of the chair, he moved toward the window.

Still no red Saab.

Where was she?

But he was so tired he didn't even have the energy to worry about Alex. She'd made it quite plain to him that she didn't want protection or advice. So be it.

He must have dozed in the chair. He awoke later with a start. His hand throbbed unmercifully. Outside it was practically dark, and Bobby's door was closed.

He rose stiffly, scrubbing his left hand through his hair. Maybe he'd take one of those pills now so he could at least get some sleep. But he caught himself as he was reaching for the little plastic bottle and instead approached the window.

Her car still wasn't there.

He glanced at his watch: nine o'clock. Was she in some kind of trouble? Was she still with Tom Farley? Maybe she was out with a friend or catching up on work at the office. What business was it of his anyway?

Yet he found himself opening Bobby's door and peering inside. "You asleep?"

"Nah. I'm reading one of Alex's books." He held it up.

"I'm going for a walk, Bobby."

The boy cocked his head to one side. "You okay, dad?"

"Sure. I just want some fresh air."

"Okay."

Jake closed the door quietly behind him, paced across the living room, and thoughtlessly tried to put his hands in his pockets. He winced as his bad hand gave a twinge. Blasted thing.

It was still warm outside; there was no moon to lighten the inky blackness. A soft summer breeze caressed his skin and lifted strands of hair. Jake raised his face into the air, took a deep breath and began to walk down the stairs.

He circled the block, thinking. His head churned with unresolved, conflicting ideas. Reflections lit like a flock of birds, then scattered at the intrusion of another thought, confused and wary: Alex, Bobby, his new job, the Twelvetrees case, Alex, his broken hand, the future. . . .

His feet led him back up his own driveway, but they headed toward the dark porch of the big house, not to the garage. He sat on the top step, his long legs stretched out in front of him, to wait. He could be patient; he'd learned that in many a stakeout.

He never asked himself what he'd do when she finally got home.

CHAPTER THIRTEEN

ALEX HAD BEEN STUNNED WITH RAGE when she'd pulled out of her driveway.

How dared he, she'd kept repeating to herself as she steered the car blindly. Of all the nerve! The scene would flash through her mind again and again: Jake scrutinizing her sharply, her keys in his big hand, his gruff voice lecturing her as if she were completely witless! What in the devil had gotten into him anyway?

She tried to calm herself as she steered through town toward the Canyon View Lodge. It sat virtually on the side of a cliff, five hundred feet above the spot where Oak Creek left Sedona, winding its way south through the spectacular valley. But her thoughts refused to settle, and no matter how hard she tried to summon up that inner core of peace, it eluded her.

"Oh, I'm going to be great at lunch!" she voiced aloud. She could feel her dress against her skin dampening under the arms.

Ahead on the road was a service station. Without even clicking on her turn signal, Alex pulled in, braked the car hard and parked next to the ladies' room. She rested her forehead on the steering wheel, her hands clutching and releasing the wheel spasmodically. How was she going to meet Tom and Justin Manor in this condition?

Finally she stepped out of the car, entered the phone booth and dialed Janet. She had to talk to *someone*.

The phone rang several times before Janet finally answered.

"Oh, am I glad I caught you in," breathed Alex.

"You sound just great! What's the matter?"

"Oh, I don't know. I'm just rattled. I needed to talk to someone." Alex knew that statement sounded terribly strange to Janet, who was always telling her how in control she was.

"Something happen?" Janet's voice brimmed with concern.

"You might say . . . I had a scene with Jake."

"A *scene*?"

"An argument. It was so outrageous, I don't even know how it happened."

"So let's talk it out. Tell me what happened."

Alex could hear Janet rattling pans in the background; she was cleaning up the kitchen. "Look," Alex said, realizing that she had no business taking up Janet's limited time. "You're busy. . . ."

"Come on now, Alex, what're friends for? Besides, my phone cord reaches clear around the house. I spend half my life on the phone and get everything done to boot!"

Alex sighed, embarrassed, and then began to let it out. It did help, just being able to voice her emotions to a friend.

"It doesn't sound terribly professional of Jake," Janet said pensively.

"He was a total jerk."

"And all because you're meeting with Tom and this other man about Joseph's land?"

"Yes."

"Wow. You want to know what I think?"

"I'm not sure . . .".

"I think he was pulling some sort of a protection thing on you."

"That's ridiculous, Janet. Why would he do that?" Then, "No. I'll tell you what I think. He's so chauvinistic he can't even conceive of a woman being capable of doing a little investigation on her own. It never even occurred to him that my job is investigation! That's it. The more I think about it, the surer I am."

"Well," Janet said, "Jake's bad, but not *that* bad. He's had women partners in L.A. Why, Randy even told me that one of his female partners was shot once. Maybe even killed. Yes, that's right," recalled Janet. "Got all sorts of coverage."

"Don't tell me that Jake respects women, Janet. I'm not buying that one!"

"Well, he *doesn't* disrespect them, either," Janet reflected. "I just don't think you two hit it off at all."

"Now there's the understatement of the year!"

"Say," put in Janet, "you really think that Tom and this other realtor put the screws to old Joseph?"

Alex knew that Janet was gloating to hear that Tom might be involved with a shady character. Alex took it carefully. "I never told you that, Janet. All I said was that Tom had been there when this Justin Manor approached Joseph."

"I see. But you aren't having lunch with them to pass the time of day, either."

"And I won't be having lunch at all if I don't get off this phone."

"Who called who?" teased Janet.

Alex was forced to smile. "Thanks. I do feel much better."

"Go have your meeting. And forget about Jake. He's just rude as all get out sometimes, and I'm sure he doesn't even know it. Cops!"

"Yes. . .cops."

The Canyon View Lodge was jammed by the time Alex pulled into the parking lot twenty minutes later. Not only was it unprofessional to be so late, but she had Jake Brannigan to blame for it!

She spotted Tom easily in the lobby: neatly styled sandy-brown hair, white sports shirt under a tan jacket, well-pressed slacks, shoes polished. He looked awfully attractive—a bit edgy, but in his element.

But if Tom looked attractive, he was all but unnoticeable compared to the man standing next to him, leaning casually against a wall, his dark head bent to the conversation.

Was *that* Justin Manor...?

He was tall, six foot anyway, and wore, from what Alex could tell at a distance, only the finest in clothes: a dark-blue cotton polo shirt, slightly wrinkled to perfection, a silk-blend cream-colored sports jacket, linen slacks, Gucci shoes. The gold Rolex around the well-tanned wrist stood out from across the lobby. His face held her frozen for another moment. The eyes were dark blue, like his shirt, the cheekbones high and wide, his nose full and hawklike, with an arrogant curl to his nostrils, his lips thin and unsmiling. Even his casual demeanor lent him an aura of power and knowledge—he was someone not to be taken lightly.

"Alex!" Tom spotted her. "Over here!"

Her feet moved toward them automatically as her gaze met Justin Manor's. She half expected him to study her blatantly with those dark-blue eyes, but he didn't. Still, Alex had the feeling that he was taking in every inch of her—the way her hair swung at her shoulders as she moved, her long limbs, the soft material of her bottle-green dress where it draped over her slim hips.... *Yes*, she thought, *he's looking me over too. He's just not as obvious as most.*

Introductions were made by Tom, who seemed uncharacteristically tense. *He really did need this land deal to go through,* Alex thought. How had Tom gotten himself into financial difficulties? Stretched too thin? And did Justin Manor know that?

They were seated at a well-appointed table by the window, overlooking the panoramic view of the canyon. The hostess knew Justin Manor.

"Nice to have you back again." She smiled at him. "And how is the weather in Phoenix?"

"Hot," he said, returning her smile with his own gleaming white one. Alex noted that the smile never reached his eyes.

"I haven't eaten here in years," Tom was saying.

"You know how it is when you live somewhere. You forget some of the nicer spots."

"Yes," agreed Justin, meeting Alex's gaze.

They ordered—that is, Justin all but ordered for them, having eaten there many times before. Oysters on the half shell, French onion soup, salad *niçoise*.

Impressive, Alex registered.

"Tom tells me," began Justin, "that you and the Twelvetrees family go back a long way."

"Yes," replied Alex, determined not to let her glance waver. "I first met the family when I was attending school in Flagstaff."

"That would be through George."

"That's right."

A good bottle of Chardonnay was brought, the cork was gently removed from the bottle with the subtlest of "pops" and presented to Justin. After tasting the wine, and pronouncing it "excellent," he took the bottle from the steward and poured for them and himself.

"A half a glass will do," said Alex. "I'm working. . . ."

Justin frowned slightly, shrugging broad shoulders. "Of course."

Oysters were not Alex's favorite dish. She did, however, manage to slip one down her throat, sipping on her wine afterward.

"I always have difficulty discussing business with this distracting view," said Justin. "It's one of my favorite spots."

"It is lovely." Alex turned in her seat, glanced at the breathtaking view of the tall red mesa land and wondered if Manor was trying to defuse her distrust. She wasn't that naive, but it was a good try.

Tom was ready for a second glass of wine by the time the soup crocks arrived. "A great year." He smiled, lifting his crystal glass in salute.

Men, Alex decided, did things quite differently than did her sex. Women on a business luncheon would have already been down to the fine print. She wondered if she shouldn't launch in.

Why not? The lunch was great, the company attractive. But it was time. "My client tells me that you've made the family an excellent offer for their father's land."

Justin's blue eyes rose to meet hers. "That's right. More than it's actually worth."

That was direct, thought Alex. "Just a curious question...Justin." She forged ahead. "Why so generous? Why not fair market value?"

"I need the land and I happen to know that the family could use the money, and I don't intend to haggle over prices for months."

Again, very direct, forthright. At least he wasn't treating her like a woman who needed to be coddled. Had she misjudged this man? "And what, if I might ask, if the family doesn't want to sell?"

"Then I'll build elsewhere, Alex." His gaze pinned her with determination. "I may call you Alex?" The question dripped authority.

She smiled inwardly. "Come now, Justin," she said levelly. "All three of us sitting here know that the only other suitable river land for your purposes would situate a golf course too far from town to draw the number of customers I'm certain you'll need."

"Not true." He smiled thinly, and she was struck once again with his aura of power and self-assurance. "As I'm sure you know, Alex," he said quietly, "I'm a very wealthy man. If I were to build my club in a less desirable location, which might draw fewer customers, it would simply benefit me taxwise for a few more years. To me," he stated flatly, "it's six of one, half a dozen of the other. I can use the write-off on my taxes."

It sounded good, coming from him, but she made a mental note to have his tax records subpoenaed by the county attorney.

She turned to Tom. "If Justin builds elsewhere,"

she said smoothly, "then your tract of land remains
idle. Correct?"

Tom shrugged casually. "That's right, although I'm
sure it would only set a sale back a few months, Alex.
I'd live." He drained his second glass of wine and Alex
thought: *No you wouldn't. The loss of the sale would
put you in a real financial bind.*

They sat quietly for a minute, finishing their soup.
Alex barely tasted hers—she was acutely aware of
Justin; the way his eyes would hold hers unabashedly
for a moment, then move away. If this hadn't been a
business luncheon and if he weren't being so direct with
her, Alex would have thought his occasional glances
might have been a sexual invitation. Would he do that
to Tom? Perhaps he didn't know about her link to Tom
at all. But, of course he knew. She suspected he knew a
lot about Tom—and her.

"You visited Joseph Twelvetrees back in late April?"
she suggested.

"Yes. Tom and I drove out there once."

Once, Alex thought, her heart beating just a little
more rapidly. Hadn't Tom indicated that they'd gone
to Joseph's home at least twice? More? And what about
Joseph's complaint to Sheriff Webster: the land speculator from Phoenix who was harassing him. . . .

Push a little harder, she decided, just a little. "If my
client should decide to sell," Alex said calmly, "it will
be because I'm advising him to do so."

Tom's back visibly stiffened but not Justin's—he was
too smooth for that.

"And what are you trying to say, Alex?" he asked.
"That you're interviewing me?"

She smiled sweetly. "Not exactly, Justin. I'm merely
stating a fact. Let me explain."

He nodded, his fine, sensual lips tilted up at one corner.

"You see, the Indians have great concern for land
usage. None of the Twelvetrees family members wants
to see his father's land desecrated by the hands of pro-
gress."

"Of course."

"And they feel that certain stipulations must be agreed upon before a sale." She'd thrown out the bait. Now she'd see just how badly he wanted the land.

"Of course there'd be land-usage stipulations in a contract. I'd expect as much, Alex."

Had he jumped just a touch? Push harder, she thought. "And when would you want to see these usage clauses?"

Justin took a long sip of his wine. "Immediately." Then he said, "The plans for the club house and health facilities are already in blueprint. The layout for the golf course is completed. I'd like to begin construction by late summer."

Alex eyed him coolly. "That soon?"

"It takes years to develop a golf course, Alex. The club house could be erected by next spring—no rush there—but to put together an eighteen-hole championship course is another matter altogether."

She folded her hands together on the linen tablecloth—this must be how the hunter feels before the kill.... "I would suggest, Justin," she said slowly, emphasizing his name, "that to build your country club elsewhere would impose tremendous hardships on you, with respect to both finances and timing."

"Alex!" came Tom's surprised voice.

Her eyes never left Justin's. But his dark head tipped back and he laughed. "Of course it would! But don't forget one thing. Real-estate transactions that go sour are an everyday occurrence in my line. We don't like it, but that's the name of the game, Alex." The laughter was wiped clean from his lips.

Alex sat back. He'd made it sound so easy. She doubted it was.

A strained silence fell between them. Thankfully the salad was served, giving her time to think. It crossed her mind that Justin Manor was a tough customer, smooth as silk, but nevertheless quite steely. Was he serious about real-estate deals falling through everyday? Did his budget allow for it? And if it wasn't quite so simple, then was he capable of resorting to desperate means. . . to murder?

A lump formed in her throat. She put down her salad fork, took a long drink of water and looked at him hard over the rim of her glass. What did a murderer look like?

It was Tom who broke into the prolonged moment. "Why don't we drive over to my office after lunch and I'll show Alex the plans." He seemed to relax a little. "Yes." His eyes met hers. "And you can see for yourself that the layouts are absolutely breathtaking. Every care has been taken to enhance the beauty of the land."

"I'm sure," she replied dryly.

"And you can explain all that to George," he added enthusiastically. "In fact, we'll make copies of the plans and George can send them along to his brothers."

"All right," Alex said, realizing that she wasn't really representing the Twelvetrees at all. Not really. . . . But then she wouldn't miss this chance to take a look at the country club's layout—not for anything in the world. And she couldn't help but wonder how much it had already cost Justin to have architect's renderings drawn up and blueprinted. And how about a complete layout for a golf course? How much had he already spent? Too much to let it all go—to let an old Indian stand in his way? Perhaps, Alex thought uneasily, she was having lunch with a murderer. . . .

She had imagined that the set of blueprints and layouts would be modestly done and would no doubt be quite attractive. But she had hardly expected the glossy portfolio with which Tom and Justin presented her.

As she stood over the real-estate office's planning board, she could not believe the amount of work they had already completed.

"This is hardly just a country club," she remarked aloud.

"It's beautiful, isn't it?" asked Tom, as he pushed

aside one set of plans and unrolled another with plastic overlays indicating future projects planned for the area. There were two swimming pools, multiple tennis courts, a complete health-spa center, gardens, two restaurants on the grounds, condominiums. . . .

"My," she breathed, "and how long would it take to complete such facilities?" It was staggering.

Justin was bent over beside her, his head bowed. He turned toward her. "Six years. Maybe, if we're lucky, five."

"I see." He was so close she could feel his warm breath fanning her bare shoulder. She moved away an inch or two.

"I just hope," said Tom, "that you'll point out to the Twelvetrees the care that's been taken to preserve the beauty of the land."

Alex stood up straight from her position over the planning board. "And how much of this land actually belongs to the Twelvetrees? I mean," she added, "these plans certainly look as if they'll require a lot more than Joseph's twenty acres. . .or your thirty, Tom."

"It's nearly two hundred acres, Alex," put in Justin.

"Who owns the rest?"

Tom looked quickly at Justin, then back to Alex. "Justin does."

She turned toward him. "I didn't realize that."

"Obviously." He smiled, unconcerned. "You see, Alex, I've been acquiring land here under a subsidiary corporation for the last five years." His eyes held her. "But then, that's a matter of public record."

"Yes. It would be." He was big, she was learning, really big. She took a shot. "Yet I can't help but wonder again, Justin, how you could absorb such a loss if the family refuses to sell." She held her breath.

Justin put his hands in his trouser pockets, looking totally at ease. "I told you. I could build elsewhere."

"That's hard to see," she said slowly, without caution. "I mean, what about the land you've already purchased?"

"Spec homes. I'll recoup my losses within a few years."

Alex hadn't thought of that. He made it sound so simple. "Well, then," she said finally, "if you'll give me a copy of these plans, I'll see that George gets them."

"And remember to put in a good word, Alex," said Tom, coming over to her side, and taking one of her hands. "A lot of this, it seems, is in your hands now."

Wasn't it though, she thought. And Tom hadn't even the slightest idea exactly how much!

She withdrew her hand, glanced at her watch and smiled. "I've got to get up to Flagstaff for a while yet today. A hit-and-run case. If you'll give me the copies...?"

Tom nodded. "Of course, just be a minute," and she was left alone with Justin Manor.

"So you're a deputy county attorney?" he said after a few silent moments.

"That's right."

"And you have a law practice on the side?"

"Not really."

"George Twelvetrees isn't your client?" He quirked a dark brow. It seemed that it was his turn now to grill her.

"I have a few select people whom I advise. Friends."

"I see."

The silence stretched out. Alex could hear the copy machine running in the next room and wished that Tom would hurry. Justin Manor, however, seemed totally at ease, leaning back against the planning board, casually studying her.

She shifted from one foot to the other. "Your office is in Phoenix?" she asked finally, not really in the least interested.

"My main offices. I live in Scottsdale, actually, and work out of a branch office there."

YOURS FREE

Two best-selling Superromance novels and a fashion tote to carry them in.

The editors of Harlequin would like to share two of their best-loved books with you, and at the same time, send you a fashion tote bag—FREE!

You'll find plenty of compelling reading in your *free* HARLEQUIN SUPERROMANCES. And you'll find plenty of uses for your *free* Harlequin tote. Take it on shopping sprees or out-of-town trips...to the beach or to the gym...on picnics or overnighters. It's perfect for carrying everything from parcels to your Harlequin novels.

The two Harlequin novels and the fashion tote are yours to keep—**FREE**—just for sending us the postpaid card at right.

More good news! You can also look forward to a long love affair with Harlequin *at a terrific savings.* As a subscriber, you'll receive four newly published HARLEQUIN SUPERROMANCES every month, delivered right to your home up to 4 weeks before they're available in stores. Each novel, over 300 pages of exciting reading, is yours for only $2.50. You save over $1.80 per shipment off the retail price.

Begin your rendezvous with romance right now by accepting our two free novels and tote bag. Rush the attached card to us today!

HSCA

Your rendezvous with romance

Watch as TV talk show Host Russ Marshall betrays author Sara Daniel's trust and love right on television.

Never Strangers by Lynda Ward

Follow through Dr. Robin Mitchell's struggles to convince Dr. Paul Wilcox that marriage is the ultimate expression of love.

Reach the Splendor by Judith Duncan

Free Gifts/Savings Card

Yes, please send me my *free* tote bag and my two *free* HARLEQUIN SUPERROMANCE novels, *Never Strangers* and *Reach the Splendor*. Then send me 4 new HARLEQUIN SUPERROMANCE books every month as soon as they come off the press. I understand I will be billed only $2.50 per book (for a total of $10.00 — a saving of $1.80 off the retail price). There are no shipping, handling or other hidden charges. There is no minimum number of books I must purchase. In fact, I may cancel this arrangement at any time. The tote bag and novels, *Never Strangers* and *Reach the Splendor*, are mine to keep even if I do not buy any additional books.   334 CIS YKEE

Name_____

Address_____Apt. No._____

City_____

Province_____Postal Code_____

Offer limited to one per household and not valid for present subscribers. Prices subject to change.

Mail to:
HARLEQUIN SUPERROMANCE
P.O. Box 2800, 5170 Yonge St.
Postal Station A, Willowdale,
Ontario   M2N 6J3

LIMITED TIME ONLY
Mail today and get a
MYSTERY BONUS
GIFT

Take it, tote it, swing it, sling it —

You'll just love this stylish tote. Perfect for shopping, traveling and your Harlequin novels. Made of durable cotton canvas with two sturdy straps and snap closure. Topstitched. Bottom-gusseted. Natural color attractively highlighted with Harlequin diamonds in lovely shades. A $6.99 value—it's yours *free* along with two *free* HARLEQUIN SUPERROMANCES.

Canada Post
Postes Canada
708

"My parents live in Scottsdale."

"Tom told me."

"Oh."

"Here they are, Alex." Tom came back in, handing her a weighty roll fastened with a rubber band.

"I'll be going, then."

Justin straightened. "I'll see you to your car, Alex." He opened the door for her, half guiding her out to the curb of the downtown Sedona street.

"Alex," he said, his voice low and sincere, "I want you to know something. It might help the family decide."

"Yes?" she answered coolly.

"That time that Tom and I visited Joseph Twelvetrees, he seemed quite amenable to my price. What I'm trying to say is that there seemed to be no problem with him in selling."

"Oh?" She tried to keep her voice calm, in control.

"That's right." He handed Alex into her car. "He even mentioned moving back to the Navajo Reservation to spend his remaining years."

"Is that so?" She wondered if he could detect the skepticism in her voice.

"Yes. He said his boys would just as soon inherit money as land. That they were all settled elsewhere. You might tell them his wishes."

"I might," she managed, thinking of Randy's recollection of the Phoenix land speculator whom Joseph had complained about. There were a lot of things that Mr. Justin Manor did not know. . . a lot. Alex smiled to herself.

She turned on the ignition to her car and looked up into his dark-blue eyes. "Did you know I was half-Indian?" she asked smoothly.

For the first time he seemed shaken. "No," he said, not quite recovered. "Tom never. . ."

"Mentioned it. Then I guess," she said heedlessly, "that it would come as news to you that I understand many things about the Indians...things that are sacred to them."

"Such as?" he inquired very cautiously.

"The land, Mr. Manor. There is nothing more sacred to us than our land." She put the car in gear. "And the last consideration is...money." And she pulled away from the curb.

"IF YOU'RE RIGHT," Bill told her, "and I'm not saying that you are, mind you, Alex, you've put yourself in a compromising position."

Alex shifted in her seat in front of her boss's desk. "Maybe. But isn't my job to ferret out the truth?"

He nodded, his glasses slipping down his nose. "Making cases against suspected criminals is your job, yes, but putting yourself in danger is not part of it."

"How else am I going to get to him? He's real cool, Bill."

"Let the sheriff's department do the legwork. Look up his tax records, see what you can find out about his business dealings in Phoenix, put the screws to him. On paper."

"That won't prove he's a murderer, Bill."

"No. And let's face it, you may never be able to make a case there."

Alex sighed in exasperation. "There's got to be a way."

"I've heard that before."

Alex left his office, the familiar frustration gnawing at her. Bill wouldn't change. What did she have to do to prove herself?

It was too late to contact the Maricopa County Attorney's Office in Phoenix that day, nor could she begin proceedings to have Justin Manor's tax records made available to her office, but Alex did spend an hour typing notes for her file, making sure that she used phrases containing only facts, not impressions, not hearsay.

It was fact that Tom had told her that he and Justin

Manor had visited Joseph more than once...several times, she recalled him saying. It was fact that Manor had lied about that. It was fact, too, that Joseph had complained to Sheriff Webster. And let's face it, she thought, in no way, shape or form would tough old Joseph Twelvetrees have told Manor that he was planning on living out his remaining days on the reservation. One, his land was sacred to him and two, he would never have returned to the reservation. After leaving it decades before, he'd have been totally unwelcome, and he knew it.

Justin Manor had obviously lied to her.

It occurred to Alex as she sat late into the evening at her desk that Bill might have been correct. If Justin had indeed murdered once, he was quite capable of doing it a second time. As she sat there thinking, a chill, a foreboding, crept into her and refused to be reasoned aside.

It was after eight by the time Alex switched off her desk lamp and closed up the file. She sat for a moment in the semidarkness, seeing in her mind a handsome face and two utterly cold, dark-blue eyes resting on her pensively. Quickly she stood, rubbed the chill from her arms with her hands and left the office.

BY NINE the lights of Sedona glowed softly before her as she drove out of the mouth of Oak Creek Canyon and headed home.

She was exhausted, hungry, and needed time to think.

"This has been a day," she whispered to herself as she turned onto her road, almost home, envisioning the soft comforts of her bed.

She swung the car into her drive, turned off the lights, and switched off the ignition. Wearily, she stepped out of her car, walked around the front of it toward the porch and stopped short.

Jake.

He was sitting there, on her porch steps, cloaked in

evening shadows. Her heart quickened at the same moment as she mouthed the words, *Oh, no!*

It all came rushing back in a tide of disturbing memories.

And then he was standing there, watching her intently, his hooded eyes displaying anger even in the growing dark.

"Jake," she began tiredly, her feet moving once again.

"Where have you been?"

His question, the controlled rage in his husky voice, stunned her speechless for an instant. "I...I was at work." But why should she be answering to him? To the big bully who had thrown her car keys in the dust.

"Work?" He moved down the steps toward her. "Work until nine o'clock?"

"Jake..." she breathed, stunned. Had he completely lost his senses?

"Tell me, Alex." He was standing in front of her and somewhere in her mind she imagined that he had gotten even taller somehow. "Where have you been!"

She realized with astonishment that she was—at that moment—frightened. It must have been the aftermath of the day, Justin Manor.... But why did Jake look as if he was ready to strike her?

"Where, Alex?"

"If you must know, I was typing a report on the lunch with Manor," she said defiantly.

"The man could be dangerous."

"Oh come on, Jake. He'd hire thugs to do his dirty work."

"Not necessarily. He's no Mafioso. His type can't trust anyone else."

"You can't possibly know that."

"There's statistics, and you can't take the risk anyway."

She saw it then, half hidden behind his back. The cast. "Jake," she gasped, "you're hurt!"

The hand disappeared farther behind his back.

"Let me see. How...?"

"Never mind," he began roughly.

But at that moment all she could think about was his hand. How had he hurt himself? She reached out, took hold of his arm and forced the hand around to his front. "Is it broken?"

"Forget it."

Alex still held his arm. "How did you do this?" she demanded.

He opened his mouth, presumably to repeat his same warning, but somehow his darkened features changed subtly and anger was replaced....

Unexpectedly, his uninjured arm came around her back and she was pulled against the wall of his chest with such force it nearly knocked her breath away. At almost the same instant his mouth was covering hers, and her neck was forced backward from the violent pressure of his lips.

There was no time for thought or consideration—she would realize later that her knees had buckled and that Jake had been holding her up. All she was aware of, as his lips assaulted hers, was an overpowering surge of warmth deep in her stomach—a surge that swept mind and body along helplessly in its wake. As she stood crushed against him in the darkness, she knew only one thing—she wanted this man more desperately than she had ever wanted anything in her life.

Slowly, slowly, her arms came up to encircle his neck as they stood locked together and then, as her hands reveled in the smoothness of his hair, his lips lessened their pressure moment by moment until they were moving tenderly against hers.

Just as abruptly as he'd swept her against him, he reached up and took her arms away. She was no longer pressed against him but was instead standing alone, her knees ready to give out, her eyes half-closed. He was backing away.

Somehow, somewhere in a shadowy corner of her mind, Alex likened her feelings to being ablaze and then covered with icy-cold water. But the notion had barely formed when she had to strain to hear what he was saying.

"I never meant that to happen," she thought she heard him say, but at that precise moment she was not entirely sure of anything.

And then he was gone, and she was left alone under the growing blanket of stars to wonder if he'd ever been there at all. She reached a hand up to touch her lips long moments later.

Yes. Jake had been there all right.

CHAPTER FOURTEEN

THE PACKET from Deputy County Attorney Alex Crawford arrived at the sheriff's department on Thursday. Jake sat at his desk, staring at it for a moment as a rush of unsettling emotions swept him. He felt as if she was standing there herself, handing him the packet with cool accusation in those startling blue eyes of hers.

He'd been a darn fool to kiss her like that. What had gotten into him?

He turned the packet over with his left hand, swearing under his breath at the awkward cast that was forever getting in his way.

As she'd promised, she'd sent a neatly typed report of Deputy Attorney Alex Crawford's meeting with Tom Farley and Justin Manor at the Canyon View Lodge on Tuesday, June 15. It was totally objective, stating merely that Mr. Manor had a master plan, including blueprints, for a large resort, and that to implement the plan he needed to buy land now in the Twelvetrees estate as well as property owned by Tom Farley to add to a large tract owned by Manor himself. Copies of the blueprints were on file in the county attorney's office in Flagstaff. The office was also in the process of subpoenaing Manor's tax records, articles of incorporation, etc.

But Jake didn't pay much attention to the actual words—not at first. He was still unable to move beyond the images that crowded his mind: Alex in the darkness, yielding, beautiful. The feel of her skin and hair and lips under his, the scent of her, the soft warm movement of her body. Her response—had he dreamed it?—her most remarkable response.

And then he was overwhelmed once more with dread—

ful, paralyzing humiliation. It had washed in waves over him for two days now, two days of agony and indecision: should he call her this very minute and apologize? Should he move, even leave Sedona? Should he ask advice of Janet? But he couldn't do any of those things; his paralysis was all-encompassing and he found himself only able to meet each minute, each hour, each day at a time, plodding doggedly on, trying to regain his equilibrium.

He had been abysmally stupid, his usual brash self mu'tiplied a thousand times. Tough Jake Brannigan—did his reputation include assaulting other men's women? My Lord. And as much as he went over and over the incident in his mind, he could come up with no answer as to why he'd kissed her.

He turned his eyes to the typed report again, trying to make sense of the words. Blueprints, resort, Tom Farley. They danced before his eyes, meaningless. It was then that he noticed the small note clipped to the back of the papers—a pale-blue piece of notepaper with slanted handwriting. "Jake," it read—not "Dear Jake," just "Jake." "Bobby and I have made plans to ride up to the House Made of Dawn this coming Friday after work. If you have any objections, please let me know. Alex."

That was all. Strictly business. Not a word about the incident Tuesday night, not a reproach, just the note—straightforward and terse. It was a relief in a way; at least she would communicate with him, in a manner of speaking. A fresh wave of humiliation washed over him; and he bent his head over the note as if ducking a blow.

"What've you got there?" came Randy's voice.

"Oh nothing much." Jake stuck the note into his shirt pocket. "A report from Alex about her meeting with this speculator from Phoenix. I haven't really had a chance to read it."

"I heard about that. It's a possibility there was some funny business there, but it's awful hard to believe. What do you think?"

Jake pushed his chair back and flexed the fingers of his right hand in the cast. "Oh, I don't know. It's a lead. Alex seems convinced this Manor fellow is worth checking on."

"Think she's doing an all-right job?"

Jake shrugged. "I'll keep on it. But she's pretty sensitive about the department stepping on her toes."

"So I've noticed," said Randy dryly. "That girl can be plenty tough for all her innocent looks."

"Is that so?" replied Jake noncommittally.

When Randy left, Jake turned back to Alex's report and tried to really concentrate. It seemed there was a definite need for the Twelvetrees land. Was it motive enough for murder? It also seemed that Manor was a smooth operator, unflappable and smart. And Farley needed money—she mentioned that in her report, which kind of surprised him. He bet she'd hated to let that little piece of information out! Could Farley be desperate enough to commit murder? He almost had more to lose here than Manor. The man would warrant watching.

And then it occurred to Jake that he was reading about Alex's lover, that she kissed smooth-faced Tom Farley with passion whenever he wanted her to, that Farley had the right to touch her, phone her, be near her whenever the whim struck. Jake felt a swift cold dislike of the man, not that he'd ever taken to him, but now it was more focused.

My Lord, Jake thought, *I'm acting as if I were actually jealous of him!* He shook his head, picked up his Stetson and stalked out of the sheriff's department.

Thursday afternoon was very quiet. Jake wasn't used to lulls like this; the LAPD had always been roiled into a froth over something—internal politicking, political pressure from the mayor, an important case or reams of paperwork to finish by a deadline. He checked the deputies' reports from the day before and drank too much coffee while he read over the night dispatcher's record. He felt his big body fill with restless energy, an impatience to be doing something, an inability to sit still.

His only important case was the Twelvetrees one, and there were no new leads on that. It occurred to Jake that he'd had murder cases like this before often enough—dead ends, no evidence, not a clue—and he had often had his own way of getting a feel for the crime by visiting the victim's home or place of work. It was an odd thing, but even days or weeks later, he could visit the place and feel *something*. It was a kind of sixth sense a good detective had—to feel the vibes of the past, as if the dead person were actually communicating his disquiet to you. He'd never told anyone about this odd talent of his except, of course, his buddies in the department, and then only when he was very, very drunk at McCready's Bar. The *good* detectives had all agreed with him that the talent existed, unspoken, untaught, ridiculous to the layman, but there it was; a detective would never be any good without it, no matter how neat and punctual his paperwork.

Randy was off that afternoon; Jake told Kyle to watch the shop—he could always radio him—jammed his Stetson on his head and left the building once more.

He drove out of town toward the south, enjoying the feeling of being on his own, of following a crazy hunch. He turned down the rutted dirt road toward the river at the crude wooden plank that read Twelvetrees.

This was Joseph Twelvetrees's land. Jake knew it had been gone over with a fine-tooth comb by the deputies before he'd been hired onto the force, but *he* hadn't seen it yet.

There was a stand of tall cottonwood trees by the clear stream, and Joseph's hogan stood on a meadow above the water, its doorway facing the east as all good Navajo hogans did. There was a stack of old firewood, a few shaky outbuildings and a rusted, ancient Ford truck parked nearby.

Jake stopped the Blazer and got out, walking slowly, feeling the air almost as a hunting dog searches for a scent. It was a peaceful place: the river rushed by, the cottonwoods rustled in a faint breeze, insects buzzed and clicked among the brush. Somewhere nearby a magpie gave its harsh call and another answered.

Jake bent, entered the mud-and-brush hogan and waited for his eyes to adjust to the darkness. Everything was still there, just as it had been when Joseph was alive. No Navajo would ever enter the hogan of a dead person; it was left to disintegrate under the summer sun and winter rains.

He got no particular feelings from the hogan—it was a neutral place. Joseph's corpse had had red river clay under its fingernails. The alleged crime had been done by the river then. He tried to picture it in his mind: the old man, silent and unmoving as only an Indian can be, the flashy realtor perhaps showing a thick roll of bills, persuasive, fast-talking. Then... how did it happen? Joseph turning to walk away, his old back as obdurate as a stone wall, infuriating the desperate realtor. A handy rock, a blow, no witnesses within miles. So easy. Then bundling the old man's body into a car—rented, perhaps?—and dumping it where it had been found by Janet and Alex.

It could have been that way.

Jake walked down to the river and felt the red riverbank mud with his fingers. The forensic lab had matched the matter under Joseph's fingernails with this stuff, but then the river flowed miles along red mud banks like this; it could have happened anywhere along it.

As Jake turned from the river, he caught a movement out of the corner of his eye. His body stiffened, his hand automatically hovering over his gun. He heard a rustling in the bush.

"Who's there?" he called to the empty meadow, feeling foolish. Moving toward the sound carefully, he saw nothing but the grass tips moving slightly. An animal? Why didn't it run then?

A brown hide showed through a patch of grass. What...?

"For Pete's sake," he said aloud, "it's a dog."

A sad scrawny mutt of a dog crouched in the grass, its ears flattened in abject fear, its bony ribs showing like flying buttresses. The splotchy brown hide quivered with terror.

"Hey, I bet you were Joseph's dog," Jake said, holding his hand out. "They must've missed you, pal."

The dog crawled a few inches forward on its belly, whimpering once.

"Guess you're hungry and I don't have a thing with me." Jake thought a minute, then went back to Joseph's hogan. There was a stale loaf of bread on a shelf. He carried it back, crumbled it for the poor mutt and watched the dog gobble it up, one eye on Jake every second.

"You've been living on mice and prairie dogs, haven't you, pal?" Jake liked dogs, had always had one as a kid, but Linda refused to have one because they got hairs and muddy footprints all over. Maybe one of Joseph's sons would like the dog; he couldn't just leave it there to starve. "Come on then, let's go. You ever ride in a car?"

He walked away. The dog stayed flattened on the ground, panting with nervousness. Jake sighed, took off his belt and looped it around the dog's neck. "What I have to do in the line of duty," he grumbled to himself, half dragging the terrified mutt to the Blazer.

Not one of the Twelvetrees clan wanted the dog, as it turned out after an hour or so on the phone. He couldn't blame them; dogs were a pain in the neck. He could take it to the pound, but he knew no one would adopt such a sad sack. Jake also knew he was a sucker. What the devil was he going to do with the scrawny thing?

Thursday evening when he got home, he called Bobby out to the car.

"Got a surprise for you, Bob," he said, indicating the back seat.

Bobby opened the back door and turned to Jake. "A dog?"

"We're stuck with him, Bob. He's sort of an orphan. Belonged to Joseph Twelvetrees."

"You mean we can keep him, dad? Wow!"

"I guess so. Nobody else wants him," Jake said with a sigh.

"He belonged to Joseph Twelvetrees? He's an Indian dog?"

"I don't know exactly what *breed* he is, but I guess you could call him an Indian dog."

"Geez, dad! I'm gonna call him Indian. I bet he's smart!"

"He's nearly starved to death. I stopped and gave him part of a sandwich," admitted Jake.

Getting him up the stairs to the apartment wasn't easy. Jake ended up carrying him. Indian ate everything they could scrounge up. Then Jake had to carry him down the stairs while Bobby proudly took the dog for a walk—with Jake's belt, of course.

The poor mutt whimpered until three in the morning, when Bobby finally let him sleep on his bed. Then he seemed happy as a clam.

Bobby had already left for his ride with Alex, taking Indian with him, by the time Jake got home on Friday. There was a note saying he'd be back late. Jake was glad in a way he hadn't had to see Alex again; it would have been very uncomfortable for both of them. He'd only seen her leaving in her car or returning in it for three days now, and she had managed to get in pretty late Wednesday and Thursday evenings.

He fixed himself a hamburger and ate it while reading the paper, cursing his awkward hand all the time. It didn't hurt so much anymore, but it was always in the way. It was a nuisance, a vague embarrassment, even with Randy's talk of putting him up for a commendation.

It felt a little lonely without Bobby. Even if they didn't talk much, it was nice to know he had somebody. He could have gone downtown to the bar where all the deputies hung out, but then he would have had to tell the story of the fight at the Oak Valley Bar again and besides, he didn't drink. Best to stay out of the bars.

He paced restlessly around the small apartment; the four walls seemed particularly confining. He needed to do something, but what? Maybe drive back to the office and do some paperwork? No, they'd wonder why he was putting in the extra time.

It was Friday evening—in the old days he would have gone to a movie with Linda or had some policeman friends over for a barbecue in the backyard of their neat little house. He wondered idly if the renters had gotten the lawnmower fixed yet and what would go wrong next. The air conditioner in the master bedroom was a few years old. . . .

More recently he would have hung out at McCready's Bar on Hollywood Boulevard with the guys, drinking until he could barely navigate his way home. But those days were over, too.

He hadn't bothered taking off his uniform that evening—had merely unbuckled the holster and belt. He would, soon, but he felt too keyed up to do anything quite so ordinary and practical.

Finally he decided to drive downtown and buy himself a magazine—something easy to read like *Field and Stream*—maybe a candy bar. Anything to get away from the stifling apathy of loneliness.

The western sky was a boiling mass of slate-colored clouds above blood-red hills. Funny he hadn't noticed earlier, but the thunderheads had moved in fast. A wind flattened grass in silvery waves, tossed treetops, and swept dust off the road in miniature whirlwinds. He wondered if Alex and Bobby would get caught in the storm. Of course, it could blow over and amount to nothing.

When he came out of the drugstore on Jorden Road, the first giant drops were splattering on the pavement, sending up that dusty oily smell of newly wet asphalt. Jake had to run for the Blazer, keeping his cast protected as it wasn't supposed to get wet. And then the downpour hit in earnest.

The gray curtain closed in all around him as he hurried to roll up the windows; the rain splashed on the windshield, and ran off the hood. Distant jagged lightning lit up the sky, illuminating weird rock formations like flashbulbs; thunder boomed.

A sudden irrational fear took hold of Jake, and he swore under his breath at the thought of Bobby and Alex riding down that rough canyon toward the Websters' ranch. With this kind of storm, no telling what might happen: a horse spooked by lightning and Bobby not such a hot rider, a flash flood down the normally dry wash, a misstep by a nervous horse on slippery wet rocks. And then how many people had been killed when lightning had struck barren rock, spreading and crackling great distances across its surface like living tentacles reaching out for victims? He knew with utter certainty that he couldn't go home and sit in the apartment waiting.

There was no choice, then, but to drive out to Someday Ranch and wait there, or perhaps take a horse up the canyon himself, although with his blasted cast, he wondered just how he'd manage it. The windshield wipers swished rhythmically as he drove out to the Websters'; the rain washed in waves across the road as the big tires of the Blazer sloshed through it. It was getting dark, difficult to see. Jake stepped on the gas, disregarding the conditions. If he was there, he could do something at least!

When he drove into the Websters' driveway he thought the rain was slackening a little. He sprinted across the lawn, got under the porch overhang puffing like a track star and knocked on the door.

"Jake," said Janet in surprise, "come on *in*, for goodness' sakes!"

He slapped the rain off the Stetson's brim and entered the living room. "I just...well, I got a little worried about Bobby," he explained, a touch embarrassed now. No one else seemed in a panic.

"Oh, for goodness' sakes! I should have had Bobby call!" said Janet. "What a dummy I am!"

"You mean...he's here?"

"Sure. Alex saw that it was going to rain, so they started back early."

"Evening, Jake." Randy came into the room. "Quite a night."

Jake managed a shaky smile. "Sure is." Relief thudded in his veins.

"He was worried about Bobby...and Alex," Janet put in as an afterthought.

"Ah." Randy nodded.

"How's your *poor* hand?" gushed Janet. "I heard all about it."

Jake gestured with his cast. "Oh, it's okay. Dumb thing..." he mumbled.

"Well, come on in. Sit down. Bobby's trying to dry his clothes out a little. Randy gave him his bathrobe. It'll just be a few minutes. Want a tonic?"

"Ah, no thanks, Janet." He wanted to ask *where is Alex*—but he didn't dare.

"Oh, come on. Some coffee then?" persisted Janet.

"Okay, sure."

"Cecily asked Bobby to stay the night, Jake, *and* his new dog, too," Janet called from the kitchen. "I'll drive them both up to the swimming meet in Flagstaff tomorrow. That okay with you?"

"Well, I hate to bother you..." began Jake. "He was going to take the bus with the other kids."

"No bother. I'm going up to watch it anyway, and it's so early."

"Well, if it's okay with you."

"Sure."

Jake sat on the plaid couch uneasily. He wanted to see Bobby, say something to his son. He wanted to stay and see Alex, thank her for getting Bob back safely before the storm broke in all its fury. And then again, as much as he wanted to see her in this neutral setting, he wondered for just how long he could keep up the distant facade, pretend that he had never pulled her into his arms. Where was she, anyway?

The back door opened suddenly, a gust of wet cold air accompanying it before it was slammed shut. "Oh boy, is it raining!" laughed a familiar voice. "Look at me, I'm soaked!"

She appeared at the kitchen door, her blue chambray shirt clinging wetly, her jeans darkened with rain. She was bent over, shaking the raindrops off her arms and hands.

"I *told* you to leave the horses," scolded Janet.

Alex straightened, wiped some water off her forehead with her wrist and stopped short with her arm still suspended in the air. Jake could see her whole body grow rigid; he felt guilty. At least he'd been prepared.

"Oh, hello," she finally said. To anyone else the pause would have been unnoticeable.

Jake nodded noncommittally.

"Jake was worried about Bobby," explained Janet.

"Oh," said Alex, retreating back into the kitchen. "Maybe I'll have some of that coffee, too."

He was desperately uncomfortable. Suddenly he felt that he should leave. But that might be awkward too. Randy was asking him about a stolen car they'd found that day, and he tried to answer reasonably.

Eventually Janet came out with the coffee for everyone, and Alex finally sat around the low table with the rest.

"I'm sorry I didn't have Bobby call as soon as we got back," Alex said.

"No, it was my fault," put in Janet.

"No problem," Jake said.

"We got back before the worst of the storm," she went on, meeting his gaze levelly. So it was going to be all polite conversation. He felt a spurt of admiration for her.

"Hi, dad." Bobby came into the room, his clothes finally dry, Indian slinking at his side. "Do you know I'm staying here tonight?"

"Janet told me. You'd better behave yourself, Bob."

"I will. How come you're here?"

"He was worried, young man," said Janet.

"Oh, for Pete's sake, dad." Bobby was mortified.

"It's my fault," began Alex.

"We had a real neat ride, dad," said Bobby scornfully. "Riding in the rain is *cool*."

"Well." Jake stood and picked up his hat. "I think I'll be going now. I just wanted to wish you luck for tomorrow, Bob." He turned to Janet and Randy. "And Cecily too."

"Thanks, dad," he answered casually. "See you tomorrow night."

"Thanks for the coffee, Janet." He nodded to Alex and Randy, and strode to the door.

"Hey, you take care of *that* hand!" Janet called after him, but by then he was out in the rain, leaping over puddles to reach the Blazer, the cool drops hitting him in the face with myriad tiny shocks.

The rain had stopped by the time he pulled into his own driveway and switched the car off. He sat there for a minute in the silent darkness, his hands still on the steering wheel, staring through the refracted halos of raindrops on the windshield. Then his head sank down onto his arm and he remained that way for a moment, feeling entirely drained.

It seemed forever before he had the energy to get out of the car, lock it—left-handed—and climb the stairs to his apartment. It was pitch-black inside; as usual he'd forgotten to leave a light on. He stumbled around, knocking his cast on the table and swearing as the pain shot up his arm.

He finally found the light switch, then looked around at the disorder of the place: dishes in the sink, magazines all over the table, dirty glasses on the windowsill, his unmade bed staring unappetizingly at him from the bedroom. There was a scrap of bright blue tousled among his disordered bedclothes: Alex's scarf. He picked it up, savoring the smoothness of it as if it were her skin—but her skin was warmer, more alive. He'd forgotten to return it to her. Or had he forgotten? Was he keeping it for some incomprehensible reason of which he was totally unaware? He stuck it in his pocket—he'd return it tomorrow. No more games.

He'd have to clean the place up. On Sunday. He and Bobby would do it on Sunday. It'd be neat as a pin, like in the marines. He'd check to see if he could bounce a quarter off the bed covers, teach his son how to make a military bed. Studiously he kept his mind from turning to Alex, to the cool light he'd seen in her eyes that night, to her soft voice explaining.

It must have been a half hour later that Alex's headlights illuminated the driveway. He noticed them because he was standing in the window, idly gazing out over the darkened town.

He didn't move—out of some kind of odd perversity—and watched her dark form enter the back door of the house. The lights switched on; he could make out her shadow in the kitchen, flitting, intangible. Then the light came on upstairs in her bedroom.

What was she doing now? Calling Tom Farley, inviting him over? Undressing, taking a shower, brushing out the gleaming dark mane of hair? He stood there, his mind filled with images, his heart beginning a slow, cadenced beating in his breast, his limbs heavy with a strange restless lethargy.

When he began the short walk to her house, he knew it was not a rational thing he was doing, and yet his feet moved on one ahead of the other and his heart thudded in his ears. He supposed, he told himself, he was going to talk to her—apologize perhaps.

His hand raised the knocker on the door, the white cast gleaming dully in the night. But it dropped, and he opened the door and stepped inside.

He heard light footsteps at the top of the stairs, and felt her presence so poignantly he could barely breathe.

"Hello? Anyone there?" Her voice was low, a little anxious.

"Alex." His voice surprised him with its strength.

"Jake?" The word was an indrawn breath of disbelief. She appeared on the stairs, her wet riding clothes still on, one hand on the top button of her clinging blouse. Her blue eyes were wide with apprehension, her cheeks suddenly pale.

"Don't be afraid," he heard himself say. "I just stopped by...."

Slowly, ever so slowly—it seemed to Jake—in a prolonged movement, she descended the stairs. When she reached the bottom, she gave a little laugh, half turning away. "You startled me."

"You should lock your door."

"So you've told me."

She looked so small, so delicate standing there. Her riding boots were off; she had tiny feet and hands for her height.

"Is anything wrong?" she was asking.

"No." he answered curtly.

"Then...?"

"Nothing." He turned as if to leave, thinking this was crazy. What was he doing there?

"Jake." Her voice, gentle and low, stopped him in his tracks. He turned toward her; she had stepped closer to him, so close he could reach out a hand and touch her smooth golden skin. "Don't go," she whispered softly.

All the air seemed to have gone out of the room. The moment paused indefinitely, unmoving, like a film stopped on a single frame. And then the film moved on—light, color, action returned. Jake felt the breath in his lungs, and the drum of his heart. Alex was in his arms, murmuring something against his chest. He held her tightly as if never to let her go.

Her face turned up to his, glowing, radiant. Her lips touched his, moving and searching for the sweet nectar of his mouth.

Small hands roamed his back, his shoulders, and stroked the hair on the back of his neck. He felt an unfamiliar heat in his limbs, a desperate passion to hold her closer. Her lips caressed his mouth, then moved to touch his neck, his nose and cheeks. He could feel her breath, warm and quick, on his skin.

''Alex,'' he groaned.

She stopped his lips with a finger; her eyes told him to say nothing. Again he sensed the deep passion pent up within her—the same total, uncompromising response she'd given him the other night. It crossed his mind as her lips moved gently over his that Alex did not often let her passion loose. Was it for him, alone? Or was it male ego merely wishing it to be so?

For an endless time they stood locked in embrace, almost desperately searching each other's flesh with impatient hands, as if there were no time but the present moment. Jake had never known such strength of response, either in himself or in another woman. Had they been approaching this moment of uncontrolled desire since she'd opened her door to him that first time?

Their hands never left each other as they mounted the stairs and entered her bedroom. There were no questions asked, no convincing words needed to reassure. Only overpowering desire guided them as Alex helped him first with her clothes and then with his. She stood there before him breathless, her body glowing whitely in the darkness. She was carved with an artful hand, all hollows and curves and shadows, her curtain of dark hair swinging forward as she bent to kiss him when he lay on the bed.

He pulled her down to him, his lips finding hers once more. She murmured something against his mouth; he stroked the lean length of her body and cupped a small firm breast in his hand.

How long had he imagined this scene? How long had his desire for her been suppressed, denied?

She was moaning, her small hands pulling at his shoulders. He felt the desire grow white-hot in him; it had been so long, so long.

There were few preliminaries; both of them seemed to be beyond them, wanting only the ultimate union, heeding only a kind of desperation.

He entered her quickly, her body arching up to meet him. The breath seemed to explode from him as he moved upon her, gently at first, then more quickly and more quickly still as the urgency of his passion drove him on.

She was silk and velvet, warmth and smoothness, moving under him in primeval rhythm.

Time had no meaning. They were locked together in a compelling embrace for a moment, for always. Their movements became more frenzied, wilder. And then he felt the urgency rise within him in an overwhelming tide, and he heard Alex cry out and arch, shuddering, under him. He let himself go, spilling his seed deep within her in agonized glory, bursting with the fullness within him. Finally he collapsed upon her, spent.

He never knew how much time passed after that. He finally became cognizant of where he was when Alex made a tiny movement under him and reality came flooding back.

"Am I smothering you?" he asked, his voice emerging low and concerned.

"A little. You're awfully big, you know." There was laughter and joy in her voice.

He slid off her, kissed her shoulder tenderly and moved upward to her neck, her chin, her eyelids.

He studied her face in the darkness. It was shadowed but he could make out the high cheekbones and straight nose, the dark cloud of hair on the pillow. Her face held a kind of beauty for him that he could not explain to himself. She was mysterious yet familiar, an odd combination of stranger and friend. "Bluebird," he rumbled.

"You remembered," she said, with wonder tinging her voice.

"How could I forget?"

He put his right arm under her shoulders, and drew her toward him, close to his side.

"Does your hand hurt?" she asked.

"No, it's fine." He hated allusions to his hand.

"Were you really worried tonight?" Alex asked then.

"Yeah, I was."

"I don't knew whether to be insulted or flattered," she said, smiling.

"You had my son out there, you know."

"I know. Thank you for worrying." She kissed the cleft of his chin gently.

It took him a moment to get the right phrase out. "I have something that belongs to you."

She gave a low, throaty laugh, snuggling closer.

"No, really."

"What's that?" she murmured.

"Your scarf, your blue scarf." He felt like a fool, keeping her scarf all this time like a lovesick cavalier.

"My scarf?"

"It was tied to the road sign that day."

"Oh!" She smiled against his chest. "*That* one. I'd forgotten all about it."

"I untied it from the sign. Then I guess I just forgot to give it back. It's in my pocket."

"Oh?" She raised herself up and leaned over him, studying his face with an impish smile on her lips. "Is that why you came over here tonight? To return my scarf?"

"No," he grunted.

"Somehow I thought not," she said with a grin, sliding back down into his embrace.

They lay together like that for a long time; her breast rose and fell rhythmically, her breath whispered against his chest. It felt good, lying there so close to her; he hadn't realized how much he'd missed the feel of a beloved woman next to him.

Then a cool tremor seemed to chill his body. "Alex?"

"What, Officer Brannigan?" she teased.

"What about Farley?" There, it was out.

She was silent for a heartbeat of time. "That's not your problem, Jake."

Silence.

She raised herself on one elbow. "It has nothing to do with us. Please, Jake."

He released a breath he'd been holding. No need to act like a jealous idiot. He knew the unique experience they'd just shared; no one could take that away from him.

"Okay, forget I said anything."

But an infinitesimal rift had come between them, spoiling the perfection.

"Jake, please," she begged.

In answer he leaned over to kiss her and felt her immediate response. She was so smooth, so supple, so utterly open to sensation. She touched him everywhere with quicksilver fingers, arousing him instantly once again. He crushed her to him, pressing her slim body to his chest, but she had a kind of whipcord strength that resisted his unknowing power. Their lips ground together, their tongues entwined, her fingernails dug into his broad back in ecstasy.

And they came together again with fire, with whimpers of passion, with sweat-slick bodies and panting breath, unable to stop the tide of fate that washed them along in its urgent undertow.

CHAPTER FIFTEEN

THE ROOM WAS SWATHED in purple light and silence. It was *qoyangnuptu*—the first face of dawn. Alex stirred gently, enough so that she could see his face and the quiet, peaceful rise and fall of his smooth chest. The length and power of his body held her spellbound as dawn's premier glow slowly gave way to the yellow phase, in which man's breath could be seen.

She could just make out the details of his shadowed features; the slight, sad furrow to his brow even as he slept, the strong, straight nose, the pronounced cleft in the square jaw. A fine-looking man, virile, strong, a man who moved with the confidence and instinctive ease of the mountain lion. Her ancestors, she thought, would have found this "white eyes" a powerful adversary.

He had changed somehow, since she'd first seen him that morning on her doorstep. He walked taller now, seemed less bowed under a burden of disillusionment. He'd lost that city pallor and developed tanned crinkle lines around his eyes from the Arizona sun. He was like a man coming out of a prison or a hospital, regaining health and vitality. He was leaner and fitter looking. Sedona was good for him. She wondered what his life had been like before: his job, the people he'd had to deal with, his ex-wife, Bobby's problems.... She found she was one of those women who was jealous and possessive about a man's past, about the life he'd had before her. Suddenly she wanted to ask him a thousand questions and knew she couldn't ask even one of them. But there would be time for that later.

Her fingers reached across the pillows, touching the

fair mustache so delicately that he never stirred. He could still use a haircut, she mused, smiling to herself, and the mustache needed to be trimmed. A shave, too, but then he'd do that when he rose.

Finally Jake moved, cleared his throat a little and threw his well-muscled arm across the flat plane of her stomach. Alex could feel her breasts rising and falling a little more rapidly at the contact. She snuggled closer.

Then she was kissing him, her slim fingers tracing the strong rugged lines of his face as the room became bathed in a soft red glow, *tálawva*—the swiftly passing time of day when man stands naked and revealed in the fullness of creation.

"Tálawva," Alex breathed against his lips, and Jake pulled her to him forcefully. "Good morning, Jake," she whispered in contentment.

He groaned something, his husky tone a warm and welcome sound to her. How could she once have found this man harsh and distant? He was a bear, a big growling animal that was all soft inside. She twisted her fingers in his straight hair, kissing him thoroughly as she rose above his torso slightly, until only their lips met and her breasts teased the smooth muscled wall of his chest.

Words of endearment formed in her mind as his lips moved down the silky column of her neck; aloud she voiced them in Hopi, then in words that he would understand. With no heed to his damaged hand, and with the ease that comes only with great strength, he lifted her from above him and placed her carefully on her back.

"Your hand?" Alex breathed against his whiskered chin.

"It's fine." But she suspected that it must still throb and ache.

With his uninjured, rough-skinned hand, Jake slowly explored her smooth flesh, the contrast of rough against silk making the breath catch in her throat. She moaned softly, impatiently, as he stroked the curves of her belly, her hips, and the long leanness of her thigh.

In awe, she watched the muscles moving fluidly beneath his flesh, the powerful cords flexing on his neck, his wide shoulder blades and down the length of his strong back. She closed her eyes and ran her hands across those muscles, committing them to memory.

Time and space ceased to exist, and only an eternity remained to explore each other. Alex knew somehow that her whole life had been slowly moving toward this singular moment. Had she finally chosen that path of which her grandfather had spoken?

Yes, she thought, *yes!* This is what the wise old man had seen—he'd known all along. She couldn't believe she'd fought so hard against her destiny.

It was finally Alex who took the initiative and brought herself on top of him, arching the small of her back to receive him—a primitive gift from the gods. Her breathing quickened in cadence with their rocking movements and she felt him filling her, then parting, then filling her again—as if her body were at one with the earth, and life-giving water moved against it, abated, then lapped at her shore once more. She thirsted desperately, needing the inevitable flood to come and wash her away with its powerful tide.

And the tide rose and she felt herself giving in, no longer craving but instead letting it wash over her, carrying her along as if she were a mere pebble in its wake. Softly, with calm acceptance, she allowed herself to be swept over the crest and washed under, moving along with the flow. Jake, too, rode that tide and was carried away, sated, to peaceful shores.

They lay together, entwined as one being, in that refuge that was caressed by the white light of early day. Neither spoke. Words seemed without meaning; only the soft rise and fall of their chests mattered, the peaceful aftermath of love.

Eventually Jake broke the enchanted spell, throwing his long legs over the side of the bed, and running those big hands through his rumpled hair. "It's almost six-thirty," he said.

"I know." Alex sighed, propping herself up on an elbow, watching him with loving fascination glowing from her sapphire-blue eyes.

Jake turned to look at her for a moment and Alex wondered what thoughts ran through his mind. Were they the same as hers? *I love you,* she wanted to say, but held back, sensing that the moment was no longer quite right. She'd tell him later. They'd have all the time in the world.

"Mind if I shower?" asked Jake, picking up his uniform shirt.

Alex nodded, and lay back in bed again, content. "The towels are in the vanity drawer. And don't get your cast wet." She smiled warmly at him.

"I won't." He paused in the bathroom door. "Alex..." he began, but then seemed reluctant to continue.

She listened to the running water knowing that she, too, must rise, but she far preferred to lie there, content, envisioning the water streaming down the well-toned muscles of his back and strong, lightly furred thighs. It saddened her a little, knowing that he was washing away her scent. But there would be other times, many, many times....

She heard him turn off the water, and draw the shower curtain aside. She nearly dozed off. But then he was standing there in the bedroom fully dressed, his hair dark from dampness, needing to be combed better.

Alex smiled, stretching. "It seems so natural being together like this, doesn't it?" she half-whispered, reluctant still to move.

But Jake did not return her smile. "Alex...I...."

His tone, and an unaccountable stiffness in his carriage, gave her cause to awaken fully. Slowly she sat up, inadvertently pulling the sheet up over her nakedness.

"Look," he began again, walking toward the window. "What happened here...between us...."

"Go on," Alex breathed, sudden foreboding clutching at her belly. "What is it, Jake?"

"Look, I don't say things so well but...."

"Try, Jake." The moment stretched like spun glass between them. "Tell me what's...wrong."

"It isn't going to work."

Tears, hot and burning, pressed against her eyelids suddenly. "What are you saying?"

"I'm no good for you." Turning his back to her, he half leaned against the window frame.

"You're what I want, Jake. You *are* good for me. I know it." But she knew by the set of his shoulders and the stiff manner in which he folded his arms that he hadn't heard her. He was not listening. "Jake," she said, "please. Don't do this."

"I'm all used up, Alex. I can't try again. I'm sorry."

"Your marriage...?"

"Yes," he interrupted gruffly.

"But I would never walk out on you," she said fervently, from the bottom of her heart. "Please... trust me."

"I can't. I'm sorry." He turned toward her, cradling his broken hand with the other. "I'm sorry if I hurt you."

"Hurt me...." Her voice rose. "I'd say you're hurting us both, Jake. You can't do this. I won't let you. I...I know you care." But she couldn't meet his penetrating green gaze. "Please. Let's try?" How could she make him understand?

"No. I'm not going through that hell again. And I care enough for you not to put you through it, either."

The tears finally spilled onto her cheeks. She was losing him. With angry fingers she rubbed the tears away. "Then what happened here, between us...was just physical. You felt nothing more?"

"Yes. No, Alex. You know what I mean."

"No, I don't! I don't work like that, Jake! I can't just shut it all off like a water faucet!"

"Alex..." He took a hesitant step toward her bed.

"I won't let you do this, Jake Brannigan. I won't let some woman who wrecked your life years ago ruin our chances."

"You don't know what you're saying. I told you," he said, raking a hand through his hair, "it's no good. That's it, Alex. I'm not getting involved."

"Jake...." She was begging, she knew, but it didn't matter. "Please...."

He looked as if some tormented invisible hand had carved his features. And his voice, when he spoke, was deadly, horribly earnest. "Don't try to change me, Alex. You'll end up hurting worse than you can imagine. What happened last night was my fault. Let's face it." He smiled, pathetically. "I flat out wanted you. Any man would."

Something snapped in her and the pain turned to rage, instant and terrible. "Get out," she whispered fiercely. "Get out of here and out of my life! Now, Jake Brannigan! Just go!" Blue flames sparked in her eyes.

"I'm sorry," he said finally, his throat closing over the words. "I've hurt you...."

"You bet you have! Now, get out and leave me alone!" She turned away from him. "You're a coward, Jake, a used-up old coward."

She could feel his eyes on her, sad, disillusioned. "Maybe I am."

Then she heard her bedroom door click open and close gently. In her hurt and anger she believed that she hated him, but in her heart she knew that hate was just the other side of the coin from love, one as consuming, as intense as the other.

His footsteps seemed to echo, crashing in her mind, as he walked down the steps slowly, opened the front door and closed it. And then she heard him crossing her porch, the old boards creaking.

Jake! her heart cried. *Oh Jake...!*

There was another sound then. A car turning into her drive, she registered somewhere in her mind. But who...?

Moments later she heard voices, male voices, below her window in her drive. Lethargically she rose out of bed and pulled her long blue robe off the chair, putting her arms into it as she went to the window.

Her heart squeezed. Tom. Dear Lord, it was Tom! And he was standing there, in front of his station wagon, saying something to Jake.

She clutched her robe to her breast as Tom's gaze rose from Jake's face to her window. She wanted to run, to slam her window and crawl into a hole and die, but she was held rooted to the spot by Tom's accusing glare.

His eyes finally dropped to Jake's face, and she could hear him say something, then swear coarsely.

"That's none of your business," she heard Jake reply in the gruff voice. Then Jake turned, as if dismissing Tom.

It all happened quickly, but to Alex, who was still held immobile, each ensuing motion of the two men seemed isolated in time—like a movie frame frozen before her horrified stare.

Tom grabbed Jake's arm, his injured one, and Jake turned slowly back to face him, a thunderous, deadly look seizing his features.

"You don't want to do this, Farley," she heard Jake say.

Then Tom swore again, calling Jake names that burned in Alex's mind. Jake was looking at his arm where Tom's hand still held it.

Jake finally snatched his arm away, turning once again to walk up the drive. That was when Tom shoved him, hard, from behind.

"No!" The word tore itself from Alex's lungs. "Stop it, Tom!" She ran down the stairs, reaching the back door just in time to see Jake stumble, then quickly catch himself, spinning around to face his attacker.

"If that's what you want," she heard Jake say. Then his left fist shot upward—lightning quick—and he caught Tom squarely on the jaw. Even as Tom was falling, hitting the dusty drive, Alex was aware of her own cry escaping her lips.

Tom sat on the ground for what seemed an eternity to Alex, holding his jaw, red stains showing finally on his fingers. Jake was still standing there, hovering over him, evidently waiting to see if Tom was going to get up.

"Stay down," she heard Jake's deep voice say. But Tom didn't. He couldn't, Alex realized, not Tom Farley; if anyone was watching it wouldn't *look* right! How dare the two of them do this! As Tom began to get up, his glance caught Alex's for an instant, and she felt suddenly as if she could punch Tom herself. How dare he! She became aware, too, of several windows going up in the neighborhood, of two children stopped on their bikes in front of her drive. She heard herself crying to Jake not to hit him again, but the words failed her in a surge of rage and mortification.

Both men stood there, half crouched, ready to do battle.

She had to stop them somehow.... "Please, Tom! Jake!" she managed to cry. "For heaven's sake, stop this!" But both men ignored her and Tom went for Jake again. Jake ducked Tom's flying fist, spun around and tripped Tom as he was lunging for Jake a second time. Tom was sprawled in the dirt once more.

This time, he stayed down. All the while Alex was crying, pleading for them to stop.

She stood there, half out of the door, praying that Jake would just leave, that Tom wouldn't try to get up, that the whole horrid scene had never taken place.

I could kill them both with my bare hands, she thought.

Finally, mercifully, Jake turned around and stalked up the drive, but not before his green eyes had looked up for a fleeting moment, catching her horrified stare.

After it was over, she turned, gulping in air, sagging against the doorframe. A minute later she forced her feet to move, trying not to think about Tom, about the neighbors, about Jake....

She walked back into the kitchen, feeling shaky all over, unable to sort out the thoughts crowding her mind. Anger tinged sorely with humiliation still coursed through her as she heard the door open behind her, knowing instinctively that Tom would be there.

He stepped angrily into the house past her, his shirt dirt stained and missing a button. Blood welled from the cut on his already swollen jaw.

Alex took a deep breath. "I'll get some ice," she said, unwilling to meet his accusing eyes.

Tom followed her silently to the kitchen table, where Alex wrapped ice into a clean towel and handed it to him.

Not another word was spoken.

It was finally Tom, as he sat down at the table, who broke the strained silence. "How could you have done that?" he asked, wincing as he pressed the cool towel to his jaw.

"Me?" Alex accused. "When you stand out in my driveway and start a fight? And you're asking me how I could do that?"

"Forget the fight." His eyes shifted away.

"Oh, I'll forget it all right, Tom Farley, but will the neighbors?"

"I don't care about them!" he declared, and Alex was taken aback: Tom not care about what people thought—that would be the day. "I just want to know what *he* was doing here, at this hour? As if I don't already know."

Alex leaned against the counter, folded her arms stiffly and fought the surge of renewed anger. "My life is my own, Tom."

"What about me? Didn't it even once occur to you that you were making me look like an idiot? And I don't just mean the fight, Alex."

"It's my life, Tom," she repeated.

"You did it because I can't marry you right now."

Alex couldn't help but laugh, a cold, hard sound, alien even to her own ears. "You really believe that? You think I'd stay with another man just to prove something to you?"

He looked at her bitterly. "Yes."

"I'm glad you think so highly of me."

"Why else would you have done it?"

He was so blind, she thought. Hadn't Tom realized that their relationship had been going stale? "I did it, Tom, because I care about that man." Did she, though? Alex was forced to wonder. After what Jake had done to her that morning, how *could* she care about him?

"So that's it?" Tom was saying. "You've switched loyalties?"

"I'm my own person. I'll do as I like." What was the point in trying to explain?

Tom lifted his gaze to meet hers. "Alex," he began, "you probably can't see it yet, but you're making a mistake. He's not for you. Why . . . Brannigan is nothing but a thug dressed up in a uniform."

"That's enough. You don't have the least idea what you're talking about."

"Don't I!"

"No."

"Look, I need to think about all this. I need some time. And I'm not saying that I don't forgive you."

Alex smiled grimly. "I don't want your forgiveness, Tom." He just would never understand. Not Tom. Everything had to be by the book.

Alex has made a grave error, but in time I'll forgive her.

"Tom," she said slowly, "it's over. It was over a long time ago. I don't need or want your forgiveness because what I did with Jake is something that I wanted to do. I'm not ashamed and you can just keep your forgiveness to yourself."

He simply sat there, staring at her, his mouth open. "I never thought you were this hard," he finally whispered.

"I'm not hard, Tom. I'm only being entirely honest with you."

"Call it what you like."

"I am. Would you rather I stood here and lied to you?"

"No." Then he paused, weighing the situation. "Do you . . . love him?"

Alex thought. How could she honestly answer that when Jake had taken the beauty they'd shared and thrown it in her face? She looked at Tom for a few long moments; she wanted to give him a truthful answer but could she? She didn't know herself.

"Do you?"

"I don't know," she said carefully.

"Did you ever love me?"

"In a way, Tom, I did. How can I know? We never talked about it, did we?"

He shook his head. "No."

"Then that's it, isn't it?"

"I guess," he replied slowly, "that it's over." Then he looked up at her. "I hope you won't hold any of this against Justin Manor, I mean, I hope your feelings toward me won't go against our land deal."

As Alex returned his gaze, she asked herself how she could ever have trusted him, given herself to him when he needed to ask her something like that! Was that why he'd come? Just how desperate was he?

"You'll give those plans to George Twelvetrees, won't you, Alex?"

"Yes," she breathed. "And my feelings for you or for Jake or for Justin Manor have nothing whatsoever to do with George Twelvetrees."

"I'm glad." He tried to smile. "I didn't really think that you'd let this whole mess stand in the way. I mean, you're a real professional, Alex."

She sighed. "I'm sorry you felt it necessary to

ask. In fact, Tom, it leaves a bitter taste in my
mouth."

"Alex, I . . . ."

"Don't." She straightened abruptly and strode out
of the room.

IT WASN'T OFTEN THAT ALEX INDULGED in self-pity. It
simply wasn't her nature. But that morning she wal-
lowed in it. She cried, she cursed Jake and Tom and
men in general, nearly swearing off them all until it
struck her that that was precisely what Jake had
done—sworn off women.

Still it hurt. Terribly. And it seemed that nothing she
did would soothe her frayed nerves or suppress the
pain he'd caused her. It was so stupid of her not to
have seen it coming—Janet told her as much, she'd
seen all the little signs herself in Jake—the cynicism,
the disillusionment, the way he'd been closed to her
when they'd first met. Yet still she'd befriended Bobby, made herself more attractive to Jake. It galled her
to think of the day she'd put on makeup, the day of
Janet's party. And it had all been for Jake Brannigan!
Cop. Bully.

It must have been afternoon when Alex was weeding
the small flower bed in front of her house that she
heard Jake's car pull into the drive. Her back stiffened, and she refused to turn around in spite of the
stern talk she'd given herself that morning. She knew,
of course, that because of the proximity of their living
quarters, she'd run into him—often. And she'd told
herself that she would behave maturely. She might
never come to terms with the way he'd treated her, and
his reasons certainly seemed those of a coward, but she
had finally decided that he'd been honest with her. For
that she couldn't fault him.

Now, Alex told herself, all she had to do was learn
not to react to her own deep feelings when he was near.

"Hey, Alex!" she heard, refusing to turn around.
She just couldn't. Not yet. "Alex!"

It was Bobby, she realized, her heart sinking. Yet she knew she mustn't let him see her anguish. Bobby was her friend. She turned a little from her bent position, forcing a smile. "Hi, Bobby," she called, and saw that Jake was nowhere around. He'd gone to the apartment, then. Good, she thought.

"How's Indian?" she asked, seeing the skinny dog at Bobby's side. He seemed glued there permanently.

"He's fine. Do you think he looks any fatter today?" asked Bobby.

"Well, not yet. Give him a few days." Bobby had told her all about Jake finding Indian. There *was* a soft spot in Jake's heart then, but perhaps it was only for dogs, not for people.

"How was swimming?" she asked, fighting the tension within her.

Bobby sauntered over. "Diving. I suppose it was all right."

"You think you'll make the team?"

"Yeah. Why shouldn't I?"

"You don't sound terribly excited." She went back to pulling the weeds.

"Yeah, well, dad's got me on a bummer."

"Oh?" Alex couldn't stop the question from pouring out. "What do you suppose is the matter with him?" Of course, she told herself, Bobby wouldn't know, but a secret little part of herself wanted Bobby to say that his heart was broken.

"Don't know what's got him so mad. Wasn't me, though. Maybe it's his hand."

"Well," said Alex, "don't worry, it will pass. Things do, you know." But even after Bobby had left, Alex couldn't keep from wondering just how long her own anger and pain would prevail.

She finished her work, walked to the back of the house where she hung her tools and glanced up toward the apartment windows, cursing Jake Brannigan under her breath.

CHAPTER SIXTEEN

JAKE HAD PICKED UP his telephone in the sheriff's department countless times to call Alex, but each time he'd replaced the receiver without dialing.

What was he supposed to say to her? *I love you, marry me, live with me?* He knew he couldn't say the words or live through that torment another time.

Alex had hit the nail on the head: he was a coward. But it was a good thing for her sake that he already knew the score. It would save her a lot of pain in the long run and that was worth her hatred. At least, he told himself often enough, it sounded right. How noble of him, he thought once, realizing that he had a hundred cop-outs for the way he'd treated her—one not any better than the others.

And so he did nothing—but burn inside. He'd remind himself that desire was a candle, tall and firm and pure at first, but in time it ended up in a misshapen flickering blob, used and misused until it was finally discarded.

By Saturday afternoon he was ready for the department's dispatcher to call him with a mass murder—anything to take his mind off the mess he'd made of his own life—not to mention Alex's.

He found himself in Randy's office by three. "Got a minute, Randy?"

Randy looked up from a stack of police reports. "Sure. Sit down."

"I've been thinking."

"That's good."

"How would the department feel if I drove on down to Phoenix and did some checking on Alex's friend, Justin Manor?"

"It's out of my jurisdiction, Jake." Randy shrugged. "Sorry."

"Okay, then. I need two days off this week. Personal."

Randy looked up again, his eyes narrowing. "Look, Jake...."

"Just give me two days, my own time."

Randy studied him slowly for a moment. "I'm not bailing you out, Jake."

"I won't need bailing out."

"Sure."

Jake walked to the door but turned on his heel abruptly. "Oh, and Randy?"

"What now?"

"Can Janet watch Bobby? And that blasted dog of his?"

Randy mock frowned. "Sure. She won't mind. Anything else I can do for you, good buddy?"

"No. That's about it."

It was an easy two-and-a-half-hour drive Sunday afternoon down through the high desert country into the tremendous valley that housed Phoenix, Tempe, Scottsdale, and Sun City. An easy drive—but as the altitude dropped and the shimmering valley floor seemed to rise up to meet him, the temperature rocketed. One hundred and two degrees. And that wasn't even *hot* for Phoenix in June—just seasonal.

Jake thought he was going to die in the old Pontiac. And to make matters worse, it was unlikely that he'd find any admissible evidence on the Twelvetrees case. If this Justin Manor were involved in the old man's death, then most likely the speculator had covered his tracks only too well. His kind always did. Still, Jake did have an idea or two. Call it that old sixth sense! He knew where to look.

Rooms in Phoenix were a dime a dozen in the summer. Only a nut would vacation there or visit in that heat, and the lodge owners knew it. He took a room in Mesa, another one of the small towns of the greater Phoenix area, centrally located between Phoenix and

Scottsdale. Immediately after checking in, he threw on his swimming trunks and cooled off in the palm-shaded pool, noticing that even the colorfully planted grounds around the motel were parched in the summer sun. Then he changed into clean clothes—a white shirt and khaki pants—and sat on the side of the bed to make a few calls. The main thing he needed to know was how Justin Manor operated. To find that out was simple—go to one of his country-club resorts, hang out, ask a few questions. Simple. Basic police work.

He found out quite easily from the switchboard at Manor Development Corporation that Mr. Justin Manor was owner and developer of three golf-and-country-club resort complexes in the greater valley area. Jake decided to visit the closest one, on the eastern edge of plush Scottsdale, Manor Resort Estates. Pools, condos, an eighteen-hole golf course, tennis courts. Very chic, very expensive.

At eight, he drove out Scottsdale Drive and located the lush estates easily. Now all he had to do was find someone talkative—a bartender, an old-timer, someone who knew the ropes.

The main bar that adjoined the club dining room was a model example of Southwestern Indian art and clean Spanish-style architecture: tiled floor, tiled archways, white stucco walls, soft lighting on the Western and Indian artifacts. There was even a genuine Remington spotlighted behind the bar. In spite of himself, Jake was impressed.

"Hi." Jake nodded at the bartender as he took a cushy seat at the immaculate blue-tiled bar. "Tonic and lime, please." He smiled, glancing around in feigned interest. "Nice place."

"Yeah," said the white-haired, tan-faced man. Jake suspected that the bartender had had his fill of tourists for the season. Maybe this wasn't going to be so easy after all.

The simplest approach, Jake decided, would be to put himself on the man's level. "Yeah," began Jake, the only customer there. "I tend bar myself at a resort, but this place is plush all right."

"Oh yeah?" The white-haired man moved the ubiquitous bar rag up and down the counter's surface. "Where's that?"

Jake smoothly proceeded to tell the man the biggest pack of lies the poor fellow had ever heard. Still, the guy bought every one of them. Finally, after about half an hour, when the pianist in the far corner began a second set of Manilow songs, Jake casually brought the conversation around to exactly where he needed it. "How's a guy like this Manor fellow acquire so much land? Man, I can't even imagine the kind of bucks it must take."

"Big bucks'll buy you anything," replied the bartender.

"Yeah," said Jake, shaking his head, "but what if, say, you wanted a piece of land—you know, for the eighteenth green or something—and you couldn't get the owners to sell? What would you do, move the whole resort over?" And Jake laughed.

"Naw. People always sell for the right price."

"No way."

"Sure they do, buddy. And if they don't then you just make 'em a deal they can't refuse."

"Godfather style?" Again, Jake shook his leonine head. "That went out in the sixties, man."

"Think so?" The knowledgeable bartender smirked. "Then you're pretty naive, buddy."

Jake put on his shocked, innocent mask. "Come on. You don't mean to say this fellow, Manor, would threaten someone if they refused to sell a stinking little piece of land. No way."

The bartender leaned over the counter conspiratorially. "Yeah, well, how do you think Mr. Manor got where he is? By being a nice guy? And I'll tell you something else, folks used to try to take him to court for harassment when he first came to the area...I was here, buddy...."

"And?"

"And each and every one of them changed their minds before the court dates."

"You mean... they sold out to him?"

"You see the eighteenth green out there, don't you?" The bartender nodded toward the huge picture window.

Minutes later, Jake was gone.

HARASSMENT. Jake looked through the files of the Maricopa County library's newspaper section on Monday morning and found exactly what he wanted. It had taken four hours.

Actually the bartender had exaggerated some— Manor had only been sued twice in the past ten years. Still, both cases had been suddenly dropped before the set court day, and apparently the owners of the land had agreed to sell. The prices were not mentioned but Jake imagined that the frightened landowners would have taken a pittance.

Jake looked up from the microfilm scanner, grim lines etched in his face. And to think, Alex had lunched with the guy....

Cortez and Robinson. Those were the two families involved in the dropped lawsuits. Jake couldn't find the right Robinson listed anywhere in the phone book, but Miguel Cortez had a number and street address somewhere in Phoenix.

Jake left the cool confines of the library and crossed the blistering hot parking lot to his car. His shirt was drenched through by the time he'd found the street on his city road map. After he'd actually driven to the address on McDowell Road, not only was his shirt soaked but the back of the driver's seat was as well. "Great climate," he swore under his breath.

Maria Cortez was a pretty little plump Mexican woman of about thirty-five. Her husband, she told Jake at the door, was not home but she expected him any minute. Jake doubted that, but admired the woman for using her head and telling him the lie. In this day and age, women couldn't be too cautious.

"You want my husband for a plumbing job?" she questioned, still peeking out around the door.

"Not exactly." Then Jake decided to level with her—not all the way, of course, but enough to gain a measure of her trust.

He pulled out his ID card and Coconino County badge and told her he was investigating a fraud charge on Justin Manor, fearing that if he mentioned a murder investigation, she'd panic.

But even the name Justin Manor was enough to make her close the door in Jake's face.

It didn't matter, however, because Maria's fear told Jake all he needed to know. He turned to leave, realizing that he was half dying of thirst, when he saw a truck pull into their narrow drive. *Cortez Plumbing* was stenciled on the passenger door. So her husband really was coming home.

Jake identified himself to Miguel Cortez in the same manner as he had done with the man's wife. And all the while he could see Miguel's eyes darting to a window in the front of the house and back to Jake.

Nervous couple, Jake thought, feeling sorry for them both, and at the same time deciding that Justin Manor really ought to pay.

"If Manor threatened you in any way, shape or form," Jake said carefully, "just let me know. That's all I'm asking. No one needs to ever find out I was here. Okay?"

"If I tell you," the short dark man said, "then you leave?"

"That's right. I'll drive out of here, and you'll never hear another word about this."

"You˜know," the man said cautiously, "I would kick you off my property if I did not hate that gringo so much."

"I understand."

"Where were you guys when Manor threatened my

wife over the phone and had the bank call in my loan?"
Miguel Cortez spat on the driveway. "You come
around here a year later and ask me questions? What
you gonna do, put him in jail?"

"Look, I'm sorry, Mr. Cortez. This is a new case for
me. I'm with the sheriff up in Sedona. We're trying to
pin something on Manor. You've answered my question, I guess." The poor guy—the cops couldn't protect
everyone, everywhere. There were always the helpless
innocent ones who suffered. He felt sorry for Miguel
Cortez, but he'd needed verification. He turned to
leave, then heard Cortez call after him in a frightened,
angry voice, "And don't think I'll go to court and
testify, either!"

Jake turned back, to reply gravely, "That won't be
necessary, Mr. Cortez."

"Good." The man subsided, his voice calmer. He
opened his hands in a very Latin gesture. "I am not a
coward, Mr. Brannigan. But I have Maria and my three
children."

Jake smiled sympathetically. "I know." Then he
said, "And thanks. Watch the news, Mr. Cortez. I
think our friend is ready to take a fall."

"I'll light a candle, Mr. Brannigan. *Vaya con Dios.*"

IT WAS EIGHTY-EIGHT DEGREES in Sedona when Jake
pulled into the Someday Ranch drive late on Monday
afternoon.

Paradise, Jake thought. Compared to Phoenix, a
mere two hours or so away, this was heaven.

Bobby was watching TV with Cecily, eating popcorn,
draining a Coke. Indian lay by his side like a moth-eaten
brown rug, panting. "Hi, dad."

"Hi, Bob. You behave yourself?"

"Sure." Then he went back to the TV and Cecily.
Jake suspected that for the first time in his kid's life, TV
came second.

"How was the trip?" Randy asked, coming in the
front door from work.

"Told me what I needed to know."

"Such as?" Randy walked him out onto the patio for privacy.

"Such as the fact that if Justin Manor wants something, he'll go to any lengths to get it."

"Like murder."

"Maybe."

"Any hard evidence?"

Jake frowned. "Not yet. But I don't like Alex mixed up in this. She's got the guy believing that the Twelvetrees land deal is in her hands. Stupid little...."

Randy shook his head. "It's her job, Jake."

"To put her neck on the line?"

"If that's what it takes. She's dedicated."

"Yeah."

"And how else is anyone going to force his hand, Jake? You tell me that."

Jake said nothing.

Bobby was quiet on the short drive to Sedona, absently stroking the dog's ears.

"Cat got your tongue?" asked Jake.

"Nope. Just thinking."

"About?"

"Life in general, dad. Gee, can't a guy think without getting in trouble...?"

"You're not in trouble, kid, but if you keep it up..." he growled.

"Okay, okay. Cecily...well...she wants to...you know...go together."

Jake smiled but quickly wiped it away. "So? How do *you* feel?"

"Geez," whistled Bobby. "I feel like a trapped man!"

"Tell me about it," said Jake under his breath. "So tell her no."

Silence. Then, "I don't want her to hate my guts."

"So take her out. You know, a movie, a baseball game...."

"I know, dad!" he interrupted disgustedly. "I'll just have to think this out."

"You do that, kid."

"Dad?" said Bobby before they pulled into their drive. "I know you're tired and all, but how about a decent meal? I mean, Mrs. Webster spoiled me. Three squares a day."

Jake shrugged. "I'm not much at the grocery store, am I?"

"Or in the kitchen," added Bobby without thinking.

Jake shot him a hard glance, but relented. "Okay. Dinner for two, out though. We'll go to a restaurant."

"All right!"

"You can even pick your poison."

"Now you're talkin', dad."

A night out with Bobby, a relaxing night, might do them both good, Jake thought. If anything could.

"Just one thing," said Bobby as he stepped out of the car, pulling the mutt out after him. "I don't want you giving me advice about this Cecily thing. I can work it out myself."

"That's fine," said Jake pensively. "I'm no one to take advice from anyway."

CHAPTER SEVENTEEN

ON ALEX'S SUNDAY-AFTERNOON RIDE with Janet she heard that Jake was taking a couple of days off. Janet mentioned casually in passing that Bobby Brannigan was staying with the Websters while his father was gone somewhere.

Alex's first reaction was vast relief that she would be spared seeing him; her second was that she'd miss dreadfully the sight of his big form coming and going from the garage apartment.

She'd been on the verge of confiding in Janet all afternoon, but she couldn't bring herself to do it. What she felt was still too raw and painful to discuss with anyone, too ambiguous in her own mind and heart even to put into words. Tom had asked her if she loved Jake. She had answered, honestly, that she didn't know. The emotional turmoil she was going through, however, told her that whatever it was she felt for Jake Brannigan, it was very strong. She was coming to the realization that you could be *in love* with someone who did not respond in kind—but you could only *love* someone who loved you in return. It was a subtle distinction, but a valid one. She knew she'd get over Jake Brannigan eventually, but with him gone, even for a short time, it would be easier.

At least now she had a goal, an emotion to recapture in a future relationship, sensations to look forward to. That, she told herself, was good.

What wasn't so good was the anguish she felt, the questions that plucked at her mind incessantly, the loss of self-respect and the constant wondering and worrying about where he was, what he was doing, what he was thinking and how he felt.

"What's with you today?" asked Janet as soon as they headed away from the barn.

"Nothing. What do you mean?"

"You look tired. Feeling all right?" Janet's round face radiated genuine concern; she couldn't fake anything.

"A little tired maybe. I've been working hard on the Twelvetrees case."

"On the *weekend*?"

"Sure. I've been taking notes and things." A pure, outright lie.

The horses ambled lazily across a wide field cut by a dry wash. Belle seemed to feel her rider's lack of enthusiasm and had to be prodded to keep up with Poncho.

"So how's Tom?" The inevitable Sunday question—Alex had been awaiting it with foreboding ever since she'd mounted up.

"Tom and I are, well, not seeing each other anymore, I guess you'd say." No sense beating around the bush.

"Good," said Janet firmly.

Alex looked at her friend closely. Did Janet know anything? "Just *good*?" she said. "Nothing else?"

"No," replied Janet airily, kicking Poncho into a trot. "Nothing else."

Alex had to kick Belle twice to catch up. "No advice for the lovelorn?" She tried to speak lightly.

Janet turned to her, saying matter-of-factly, "You aren't lovelorn. You *never* loved Tom Farley in the first place."

Alex was silent a moment, mentally going over her relationship with Tom. "You know, I think you're right, Jan."

Thankfully, Janet let it drop; Alex had the feeling her friend wanted to ask a lot of questions but was shrewd enough to bide her time.

Alex couldn't resist asking about Jake, though, trying desperately to keep her voice casual. It was like a scab, not yet healed over, that she was picking at, unable to stop. "So how's Jake doing as undersheriff? Is Randy pleased?"

"Well, you heard about the thing at the Oak Creek Bar."

"Yes."

"Jake's quite a guy when he's pushed, I guess. Randy's going to put him up for a commendation."

"That's nice." Pause. "Then I guess he's staying in Sedona."

Janet shrugged. "Who knows? Jake could take it in his mind to leave, I guess. Of course, there's Bobby. He's doing well on the diving team and all. I know Jake's happy about that." Janet turned in her saddle, speaking earnestly. "That kid needs a mother very badly. It's a shame."

"Yes, it is." Alex felt herself flush, ridiculously. She prayed that her hat hid it, that Janet didn't suspect.

ON MONDAY MORNING she began researching Justin Manor in earnest. Copies of his tax records and data on real-estate holdings, corporate relationships and his holding companies, arrived at the Flagstaff office. She had to slug through the piles of information.

She found out a few interesting facts: the Manor Development Corporation had paid no income taxes whatsoever for three years, claiming depreciation and business losses; real-estate taxes—very large sums— were in arrears on two properties that were close to being foreclosed upon; he owed vast sums of money on several properties on which he had already built hotels or resorts.

Then there was the complex structure of his company. He was the head of the Manor Development Corporation; however, he was also in a separate partnership with a Los Angeles contractor named Lou Travilli, who together with Manor, owned four hotels. There were also ties with a Mexican pharmaceutical company and an ex-wife, Lois Manor, who had something to do with a holding company.

It was all very complicated. But one thing was clear from his IRS returns; Justin Manor was in very deep, stretched to the breaking point. Very soon one of his creditors would demand payment and his whole empire would come crashing down around his ears. Of course, it was possible he could pull it off—perhaps with a very successful resort in Sedona. But Mr. Manor must have been a little nervous at this point. And frustrated—one piece of Indian property holding up the whole deal.

Alex pushed her glasses up to massage her eyelids, then leaned back and tapped a pencil against her teeth.

She pulled out her address book and dialed a number from it, was switched from secretary to secretary and finally got the person to whom she wanted to speak.

"Maricopa County Attorney. Dick Moore here." He was the attorney, Alex knew, for the greater Phoenix area.

"Hello. This is Alex Crawford, deputy county attorney in Flagstaff. I'd like some information on the Manor Development Corporation or on Justin Manor, president of that corporation. I'm working on a case here."

"Well, Miss—or is it Mrs. Crawford?—let me take down the information, and I'll get back to you as soon as I can."

His voice was just a little condescending, a bit oily. It was a common reaction, she'd found, among members of her profession when dealing with a female. Play the little girl along and see what cute things she'd come up with. She gritted her teeth and refused to let it get to her as she explained precisely what she wanted.

"Thank you so much, Mr. Moore. I'll be awaiting your call, then."

The return message from one of his deputies came late that afternoon, just as she was about to leave.

Mr. Manor owned extensive property in Scottsdale and Phoenix—but she already knew that. He was president of Manor Development Corporation and in partnership with Louis G. Travilli, etc., etc. Impatiently Alex, tapping her foot, listened to the voice on the phone. She knew all that and more.

Then her foot stopped tapping and she sat up straighter in her chair, scribbling notes: Manor Development had been the defendant in two lawsuits, it seemed. The Maricopa County Attorney's Office had begun to make cases against Justin Manor on behalf of two complainants on charges of fraud and harassment. This had gone on over a period of ten years, ever since Manor had moved into Scottsdale. Strangely enough—and even the deputy on the phone sounded puzzled—the cases had been dropped by the complainants before they had come to trial.

"Very interesting," murmured Alex, half to herself. "And you will send me photostats of the clerk's records?"

"Yes, Miss Crawford, Mr. Moore has arranged all that."

"Thank you so much." Thoughtfully Alex hung up, staring unfocused across her office. My, wouldn't she just like to get in touch with one of those complainants! And she would, as soon as she got the list from Phoenix. What exactly had caused them to drop the charges against Manor—coercion, threats, physical violence? This case was definitely getting interesting.

She should let Jake know about this new development, she realized, but he was gone for a few days and she'd rather have concrete information to report to him. It was going to be difficult if they had to work closely together on this case, but she couldn't give it up now. It was too important—and she had a gut feeling that she was on to something.

Before she left Flagstaff that afternoon, she drove over to George Twelvetrees's house, hoping to catch him home. His wife, Madge, heavily pregnant with their second child, let her in.

"It's nice to see you, Alex," she said, smiling.

"Is George home, Madge? I've got some business with him."

"He's out back mowing the lawn. Let me get him."

"Oh, don't bother. Just show me where he is and I'll find him."

She nodded. "Just make sure he finishes mowing when you're done."

"I will, I promise." Alex remembered her mother saying something similar about her father—scolding and loving at the same time. She had a moment of fresh pain that she could not know that feeling, at least not soon.

George turned the power mower off when Alex waved to him.

"Hi, George."

"What brings you by?" he asked. "Not that you're not welcome."

"I wondered if you'd heard from Justin Manor again."

They moved to a flagstone patio and sat down on lawn chairs. George took off his baseball cap and wiped his forehead. "He called once. I said I was going to speak to my brothers. He was pleasant enough."

"I've found out a few unsavory facts about the man." She told him about Manor's financial problems and about the lawsuits.

George whistled, then leaned toward her. "Alex, do you really think he wants that land enough to...well, to...."

"I don't know anything yet, George. We can't jump to conclusions. It looks like Manor and Tom Farley both need that land very badly. That's all I can say now."

"You realize where this is all heading?" George pinned her with his dark eyes.

She found it hard to meet them. "Yes."

"Okay, not another word. I'll leave it to you." He paused. "Do you think this Manor would...do anything, you know, to convince me?"

"Not yet. Just, for goodness' sakes, don't let him think you know anything."

"He's dangerous then."

"I didn't say that."

"Look, Madge is alone here with Tommy all day, and she's just about to have a baby, and...."

"George, please don't be overly alarmed. I'm working on it. So is the sheriff's department."

He leaned back, smiling crookedly. "They didn't help my father, Alex. And all that witch talk—well, what do *you* think?"

"I don't have an opinion yet. Unfortunately, I have to stick to facts."

"What about the claw marks? Did Justin Manor do *that*? Or was it a witch?"

"We don't know yet, George, but we'll find out, I promise you."

"I have to trust you, Alex. Be careful."

"I will. Let me know when Madge has the baby, please. Oh, and she says to finish mowing the lawn."

George laughed. "She would!"

As Alex drove down Oak Creek Canyon, her mind only half on the drive, she tried to sort out her thoughts. She was getting closer to a solid motive, she was sure. But then her brain would rebelliously refuse to concentrate, and she would see Madge Twelvetrees—happy, ready to give birth, with a husband who loved her and a small child who needed her. Would she rather be like Madge? Would she, *could* she, give up her career, her hard work to be a mother and wife? Would that be enough for her? But was her job enough for her? Could she ever have both?

She shook her head, curling a lip in disgust with herself. It was academic; no one wanted her to be a mother or wife. Wasn't that the first step?

And then another idea gripped her. George Twelve-trees had a very valid fear of Justin Manor. And if George was worried, shouldn't she be more concerned? After all, she had literally told both Justin Manor and Tom that a sale was pending on her decision. Was that above and beyond the call of duty? No, she decided; it wasn't. Joseph had been her friend. She wasn't about to let Justin Manor intimidate her! She'd get to the bottom of this case, no matter what!

THE PHONE WAS RINGING when Alex walked into her house. She grabbed it, sure the person on the other end would have hung up already.

"Hello?"

"At last!" cried Janet. "You are *definitely* working late these days."

"Hi, Jan. What's up?" She sank down into an armchair, threw her purse onto the couch and kicked off her shoes.

"I just called to invite you out to La Pinata for dinner. We're all going. Come on and join us."

"Oh, I don't know, Jan. I'm beat."

"So much the better. You won't have to cook."

Alex thought for a moment. Maybe company would do her some good, keep her from sitting home alone, brooding, watching for a light that would not go on in the apartment behind her house. "Okay, sounds great. What time?"

"We're leaving in half an hour. See you there at seven-thirty."

"Great, see you."

The Websters were already sitting at a big round table in the homey Mexican restaurant when Alex walked in, dressed casually in summer tan slacks with a lavender blouse double-belted around her waist. Her hair swung loosely at her shoulders. Randy waved to her across the crowded room and she smiled, making her way past the filled tables to where they sat.

"Hi, Alex," said Janet. "Look who we found here."

Alex hadn't noticed in the busy, noisy restaurant—there were two other figures at the table with the Websters. Her heart contracted, and her throat seemed to close with an audible click.

"Hello, Alex," Jake said in that deep, husky voice that she knew could turn soft and intimate during lovemaking.

"Hi, Alex," Bobby said with a grin.

"Hello," she managed, knowing her smile was lopsided and her face frozen. "I. . .I thought you were out of town for a couple of days."

Jake stood to pull a chair out for her, his face grave and still, his green eyes hooded, the way they'd been when she'd first met him. "Just got back."

"Oh."

"Isn't it funny?" piped up young Brian. "They were gonna eat at the same place we were, so we can all eat together!"

"How nice," murmured Alex as she slipped into the chair. It was next to Jake but she had no choice about that. She was aware that Janet was studying her intently, as if wondering if something might be wrong.

Bobby and Cecily had their heads together, Randy and Jake were discussing something about cars, and Brian was reading the menu to everyone in a clear, loud soprano. Only Janet and Alex were rather quiet for a time.

"A pitcher of margaritas," Randy said to the waitress, "and bean dip."

"Tonic and lime for me, please," put in Jake.

How could he just sit there, so unconcerned, so cool? Alex wanted to jump up, to scream, to hit him, to put her face in her hands and cry. She was terribly aware of his big body next to her: the large, capable hands that could be so very gentle, the too-long fair hair, the breadth of back and chest, the length of corded muscles in his legs. She knew his body so well now; it had been almost a part of her. And yet she could only sit there, smiling politely, as tense as a cornered doe.

They ordered. Alex hadn't looked at the menu; she asked for the same thing Janet had ordered. It didn't matter. She stared at her nails, pushed her black bangs back nervously, and rubbed at the crust of salt on the rim of the glass of the tart margarita, that fine concoction of lime juice and tequila, triple sec and crushed ice. Janet shot her a questioning look; she smiled back blandly in answer.

"You get anything more on the Twelvetrees case?" Randy asked her eventually.

"Yes, as a matter of fact I did. I'll send you a report in a couple of days," she replied, failing to understand the significant glance shared by Randy and Jake.

"Good. Good," said Randy.

"I went to see George today. George Twelvetrees. That's why I got home so late." She was talking merely to prove that her mouth could still move, that her tongue could still form words, her brain make sense.

"No shoptalk," remarked Janet. "Randy...."

"Okay, okay." He laughed.

Maybe the second margarita did it, Alex would think later. Whatever caused it, the evening took a turn for the better after the food came. She decided it was ridiculous to act like a scared little mouse just because Jake Brannigan was there; she would *not* mope and fade into the woodwork. She had just as much right as anyone at that table to enjoy herself— maybe more.

"Hey, Alex," Bobby was saying to her, "next time we go up to the House Made of Dawn, can Cecily come?"

"Of course, but she's been there a dozen times."

"I'd love to." Cecily grinned shyly.

Alex recalled the last time she and Jan and Cecily had been up there. Cecily had been bored with the "old place." She smiled inwardly. Watch out, Bobby!

"Did you know," Bobby was explaining to Cecily, "that a Hopi boy has to make a journey alone on foot to the Grand Canyon and back to prove he's a man?"

"Most cultures have a manhood ceremony of some sort, Bobby," said Alex.

"But this is really neat. And the Taos Indians believe there is a giant who walks on their mountain, but nobody can see him, and every boy has to go to the mountain alone and look for the giant's footprint. And then he can call himself a man. Isn't that cool?"

"It sure is," agreed Randy.

"Are you going to look for the giant's footprint, Bobby?" asked Cecily, her tawny eyes big and round.

"You bet I am. And maybe I'll find it, too. I'm just about the right age, aren't I, Alex?"

"I suppose so...."

Then the men and the two boys got to seeing how much hot sauce they could put on a forkful of their enchiladas and tacos. Janet made mock-disgusted noises; she'd seen the act before. Cecily urged Bobby on until his eyes were red and his nose raw. Randy laughed, drinking glass after glass of cold water. Jake, who'd broken out in a sweat, ordered three more tonics before he was through and Brian nearly cried.

Alex ate little; usually she loved the food at La Pinata, but she knew she was only putting up a good front by laughing with the rest at the men's antics. How nice it would be to have a ready-made family like this and good friends like the Websters, she dared to think.

"I ate too much," groaned Janet, "as usual!"

The plates were cleared away. The last remnants of the dinner remained on the table—mute reminders. The bill sat facedown on a small tray in the center of the round table.

Alex began digging in her purse for some cash; it was an unspoken rule that she went Dutch treat with the Websters. Randy didn't make *that* much money. But a big hand covered hers.

"I'll get it," Jake growled.

"I couldn't possibly..." she began, wishing he'd take his hand away. Her skin crawled under his touch.

"I insist." He reached over and took the check. "My treat everybody. I owe you."

"Jake," Alex said quietly, intensely, "please don't make a scene. You don't owe me a thing. I'll pay my own way."

He turned his full gaze on her and she could see, for the first time, an ice-cold spark of anger in his eyes. She drew back as if struck, and fell silent, appreciating suddenly just why Jake was so good at his job. She'd pay him back later; a scene right now would do her in.

Randy was protesting uselessly. Jake insisted coldly, adamantly, unmovably. Finally Randy gave in, throwing his hands up in despair. "So go on and do it, pal," he said, laughing. "I'll get you another time."

"Sure, no problem."

"Thanks, Jake," put in Janet.

Alex had to say something polite too, but the words stuck in her throat. She swallowed, managed to mumble, "thank you," and felt Jake's cold gaze brush her for a moment.

The Websters disappeared, waving, into their station wagon. Jake and Bobby walked toward the old Pontiac. Alex waited for a few minutes, not wanting to arrive home the same time as the Brannigans in case she might have to say something to Jake; even a goodnight would be too much at this point.

She finally pulled into her driveway, berating herself for acting like a lovesick adolescent. My Lord, she was avoiding her own house, for goodness' sakes! Angrily, she got out of her car, grabbed her purse and turned toward her porch.

"Alex." The voice was low, barely above a whisper; it stopped her in her tracks, melting the anger like wax under a flame.

He waited there in the shadows of the porch, just as on that other night that had started it all. She wanted to turn and run, flee from him and her own feelings.

He stepped out of the shadows. "Sorry if I startled you," he said carefully.

She was utterly silent, waiting. What on earth did he want with her now? Hadn't he had everything he desired already?

His eyes were hollow in the darkness, his mouth a dark slash; a faint light burnished the line of his flat cheek. "Look," he said, "I just wanted to say that I didn't know you were going to be there tonight. By the time I found out it was too late."

Was it an apology? "I'm sure you were just as uncomfortable as I was," Alex said coolly, pleased that her voice was strong and under control.

"It won't happen again."

"Good." She began to brush past him, fumbling for her keys in her purse.

"I'm sorry." His voice rumbled in his chest, familiar, painful.

"Oh, don't worry," she said airily, "I'm sure we can manage to act like civilized people. Don't you agree?"

"Yeah."

She was at the door now, acutely aware of his tall form behind her. "Good night, Jake," she said firmly, stepping inside and closing the door carefully behind her.

By ten o'clock she was propped up in bed reading a magazine, holding herself together tightly. She tried not to glance toward her bedroom window, through which she could see the glow from the apartment. But it was there, a beacon, reminding her of him with every breath and every heartbeat.

She jumped when the phone rang, knowing instantly that it was Jake, so strong were her thoughts in that direction. As her hand automatically reached out for the receiver, she told herself over and over that it wasn't Jake, it couldn't be him....

It was Tom.

"Alex, hon." It was as if nothing final had happened between them. "I've been trying to get you all evening."

"I was out."

"Oh." She could imagine him licking his lips nervously. "Well, I just wanted to see how you were. It's been a few days...."

"I'm fine, Tom," she said wearily. What did he want?

"Good." He cleared his throat. "Alex, have you, ah, made any decision on the Twelvetrees land?"

"Oh, for goodness' sakes, Tom, did you have to call me up at ten o'clock at night to ask me that? I'm tired. I've had a rough day."

"I'm sorry, hon, I just wondered. Justin has been phoning me ever since last week."

"Tell him to back off, Tom. I need more time. Tell him...." She paused, thinking a moment. "Tell him that I'm checking up on his corporation to see if he's bona fide."

"Well, of course he is, Alex."

"Just tell him that, Tom." That should force his hand. "Good night, Tom."

"Good night, Alex, hon."

She hung up, tossed the magazine to the foot of the bed and let a sudden, unaccountable rush of tears flow hotly down her cheeks.

CHAPTER EIGHTEEN

ON THURSDAY MORNING the flowers arrived—twenty-four of the most beautiful white, long-stemmed roses Alex had ever seen. Strangely, significantly, one blood-red, closed bud rested in the center of the fragrant mass.

Who on earth . . . ?

She put on her glasses, picked up the small white envelope enclosed in the box and opened it, pulling out the card. It read simply, "Hope your mother is feeling well."

Mother, she thought. But her mother's heart condition was well under control. She stood in her living room for several long bewildering moments.

Suddenly a terrible hand of dread clutched her. "Oh my Lord, no!" she breathed, racing to the telephone.

Her hands were fumbling so badly she had to redial twice, but finally she heard the familiar ring on the other end of the line.

It rang and rang. Each time Alex's heart jumped in her breast. Answer, please, just answer it, she cried silently.

"Hello?" At last!

"Dad?" whispered Alex.

"That you, Alex?"

"Yes . . . I . . . Is mother there?"

"Of course, dear. Are you all right?"

"Is she well, dad?"

"She's fine, honey. Now what's this all about?"

Alex let relief flood her. "It's a long story, dad. I don't know quite where to begin."

"It's your dime, dear. If you want to just tell me from the beginning?"

Her father was an ex-county judge from Coconino; he'd heard all sorts of stories from all sorts of people through the years and Alex knew one thing—she'd better tell it to him straight and stick to the facts. She began with Joseph's death—the fact of which he was already aware—and the claw marks indicating Indian vengeance. She went on to Tom's involvement and received a flat "I see" from the hard old judge. And then she told him about Justin Manor's involvement, his tax records and the lawsuits brought against him in the past.

"You could have saved yourself some time, Alex," he said sternly, "and asked me about Justin Manor in the first place, instead of going to the Maricopa County Attorney's Office. Everyone in Scottsdale who reads the papers knows about Manor."

"He's awfully shady, dad."

"That's putting it mildly." Then he said, "So why this concern about your mother? Let's hear all of this, Alex."

Now came the rough part. "I told our Mr. Manor that the Twelvetrees land acquisition depended on my decision after I'd done some research."

"You didn't!"

Alex swallowed hard. "I did. It *is* my job, dad. Remember, I represent the people. George asked me for advice."

"Good Lord, Alex," he grumbled. "So you've had a threat . . . ?"

"A note in a box of flowers, just now."

"About your mother's health?"

"Yes." She felt like weeping, like tearing her hair out—like killing Justin Manor on the spot!

"Dear Lord . . . ."

After much debating and some family arguing, they decided that the best step was to take Alex's mother, Sarah, up to the Hopi Reservation to visit for a few days.

"She's been promising to visit her father anyway,"

stated Judge Crawford. "But I'll tell you, Alex, I don't like running from this one bit."

"It's for mother's sake, dad. And we'd better not tell her, either."

"All right, but you know that Hopi brain of hers. She'll know something's wrong, and she'll worry herself sick about you."

"I know," Alex said with a sigh. "But you'll handle it."

"You be very careful. This sort of terrorism is not easy to deal with nor can you prove a thing at this stage of the game. Luckily, however," he added, "the police already are only too aware of Justin Manor's methods. They just can't seem to nail him on anything. You know how witnesses are when they get threatened."

"Yes. But I'm one who doesn't scare so easily. I'm just sorry you and mother got involved."

"So am I."

"I'll be coming down to Scottsdale, dad, just as soon as I notify the office here and get Bill's okay."

"You're coming to Scottsdale? What on earth for?" he blustered.

"To trace where the flowers originated. It was FTD. Now's the time to push our Mr. Manor."

"You can call from Sedona."

"No. I'll get better results in person. I'll be careful. And besides, when the time comes, the police will back me up."

"Don't you go near Manor, Alex, and I mean that. Get what you can and back off. Let the police take it from there. It's their territory."

"I will. I *do* know my duty."

There was a moment's pause on the line. "Alex," her father said slowly, "you wouldn't be trying to put a feather in your cap?"

"What do you mean?" The shrewd old fox, she thought.

"You know exactly what I mean. The police in

Sedona could check those flowers out just as easily as you can.''

They could, Alex knew, but that meant calling Jake. And deep in her heart she wanted to break this case wide open herself, prove something to Bill, to them all. And, too, the division of detective work between the agents of law enforcement and the county attorneys was often a little nebulous—thus the frequent conflicts between the two offices.

"This is my duty,'' she stated finally. "They've had their shot, dad. They haven't come up with anything.''

"And I wanted a son.''

Alex could almost see her father's smile. "Listen,'' she said, thinking quickly, "leave the key to the house under the mat, and I promise I'll let you know exactly what's going on. I'll call John Longstretch in New Oraibi—he'll give you a message. I'm betting Justin Manor will panic, especially when I let him know through Tom that the sale is off.''

"Don't be a guinea pig, Alex. Promise you'll get police protection for yourself if and when the time arrives.''

Alex agreed completely and listened to a curt lecture from her father on how not to give in to terrorism and still protect herself and then, of course, on precisely where her jurisdiction ended and that of the police department began. When she finally hung up, she felt renewed, almost exhilarated—gone was the fear and dread that the note in the flowers had initiated.

She thought about her father's parting words: "Our system of justice works. It's simply a matter of following a careful procedure and not deviating an inch.'' He was right, of course. And immediately she made a mental list: call Tom—let him know the land sale was off, then talk to Bill about going to Phoenix immediately; *that* might be a problem. Bill was always opposed to anything she wanted to do. Maybe she'd just avoid the argument altogether and tell him she had to see her parents. And then she remembered, her excitement mounting, that she should check with the local florist shop and get the originating address of the FTD order. She could make her calls, pack her bag and be ready to leave in an hour, maybe less, if Bill didn't give her a particularly hard time.

It was all so simple. ABC. And Justin Manor, when he found out from Tom that there would not be a land sale, would be forced to make a move. Oh, he might not run right out and come for her, but she was banking on him eventually having to deal with her. She'd have to let the police in on the whole thing soon.

She glanced at the box of lovely flowers half wrapped in green paper still sitting on the couch, and the thorny red single rose lying in their midst. How very clever of Mr. Manor, she thought, an inadvertent chill seizing her—the pure white body, the blood-red hole in it....

Tom was shocked when Alex called him at his office. "You...you don't know what you're doing!" he shouted over the phone, losing control completely. Alex wondered just how long it would take him to dial Justin Manor's number in Scottsdale. Then she told him about the flowers and the note, and he totally fell apart, accusing her of being crazy.

"Justin would never do such a thing! You've lost your mind, Alex!"

"What about Joseph's death," she tossed in.

"An accident! Alex, please...!"

"If you'd use your head, Tom," she said calmly, "you'd realize that Joseph's death was a little too convenient."

"I...Alex, I'm telling you, you've got Justin all wrong."

"I don't think so. I'm just disappointed that you're so blinded by money that you're willing to be a part of his organization." It was futile, Alex realized, to try to convince Tom—he'd just have to learn the hard way. A part of Alex still cared for him—they had been close friends, lovers—but each day that passed since the parting left Alex wondering more and more what she could ever have seen in him.

Finally she hung up, drained of all emotion for Tom save pity. She could picture him dialing Justin Manor at that very moment; the mental image left her with ambiguous feelings.

Bill, of course, was skeptical. "Don't go near Manor. Do your little research and get your little tush back up here. We don't need any trouble with that man. We'll get him legally, Alex."

She hated the way Bill talked to her, the distrust he had for her judgment and abilities. Her own father trusted her more in this situation.

"I'll do my best," she told him tightly, and then gave him her parents' number and address and hung up.

The easiest task she'd had that morning was telephoning the Sedona florist to get the address of the Scottsdale flower shop where the roses originated. She had decided a personal visit was definitely in order. What if the person who had purchased the expensive roses was untraceable? Had paid in cash. . .? Had Manor himself ordered them or sent some flunky?

Well, Alex told herself as she stuffed a few clothes in an overnight bag, she wouldn't think about that now; she'd face each problem as it arose. Possible danger to herself. . .? She'd be careful, just as she'd promised Bill and her father; she'd visit the florist and that was all. The rest she'd leave to the proper authorities.

She had a good head on her shoulders; she knew what she was doing. Exactly.

The flower shop was located near downtown Scottsdale, on Indian School Road. Alex parked in the small shopping center lot, barely feeling the intense heat rising from the pavement as she stepped out of her air-conditioned car—all she could think of at that moment was the success of her mission. How sweet the word sounded to her. *Success. To be able to pin Joseph Twelvetrees's death on Justin Manor. . . .* The idea she might be in a dangerous position, and reminders that her own personal affairs were in shambles were suppressed as she swung open the door to the shop and stepped into the fragrant coolness.

"May I help you?" asked a very attractive middle-aged woman.

Alex stepped up to the counter. "My name is Alexandra Crawford," she began, "and this morning I received twenty-four white roses and one red one delivered by my local florist in Sedona." Alex smiled. "I was told that the order originated in your shop." Alex produced the embossed envelope from the Sedona florist.

"Yes." The lady returned Alex's smile. "I recall the order. It was a little unusual," she reflected, "what with a single red rose."

Alex tried to keep excitement from creeping into her voice. "Can you tell me, please, who purchased the flowers?"

"Now let's see...." The woman tapped her polished nails on the countertop. "It may have been cash." Then she pulled a manila file folder from beneath the counter and began to flip through purchase orders. Finally she lifted one of the orders out of the pile. "Yes. It was cash...but I'm sorry, there was no name."

"No name on it?" breathed Alex, her heart sinking.

"Well, it's not necessary on a cash purchase." The woman shrugged. Then suddenly her face brightened. "But I do remember the woman had been...."

"The woman?"

"Yes, she was driving a large car...a station wagon, I recall, because she left the keys on the countertop and had to come back in."

Alex thought quickly. "Do you remember anything else about her? I mean, would you recognize her?"

"Well...I do remember the lettering on the side of her car. It said, Manor Development, something like that."

Alex's pulse rate soared. "Manor," she whispered.

"Yes. I'm sure now. Why, come to think of it, everyone around here has heard of Mr. Manor."

"I'll bet they have."

"Was there a problem with the flowers? I mean...."

"Oh no, no," Alex hastened to explain. "They were absolutely lovely." And by the time Alex had pushed open the shop door and was met by the blast of one-hundred-five-degree weather, the poor saleslady was thoroughly perplexed.

A powerful urge swept Alex as she got back into her car and switched on the air conditioner. She wanted to confront Manor immediately, but she remembered her promise to Bill and her father. And really, what would that produce? He'd simply talk his way out of the whole thing.

No, she decided, she'd wait him out—let him stew over Tom's call about the Twelvetrees land. Let him sit and mull over his options for a time.

It was nearly three when Alex pulled into her parents' shrub-lined driveway in Scottsdale.

Instantly anger tinged with worry crept into her bones.

Their Buick was still in the garage!

She hurried out of her car, half-stumbled over the cat lying in the shade of the walk and pressed the door-bell.

Why hadn't they left? He'd promised....

"Alex!" said her dark-haired mother, smiling. "We were hoping you'd get here before we left." Sarah Crawford stepped aside to let her red-faced daughter in.

Immediately Alex caught her father's eye. "I thought you were going to get an early start," said Alex, trying to control the tremor in her voice.

"Well," said her father significantly, "your mother saw no reason to rush off."

It was difficult to hide her impatience, but to let it

out would tell her sensitive mother that something was indeed very wrong.

"I don't know why your father is insisting that we leave for New Oraibi today," Sarah was saying. "He usually hates the trip." Turning to her white-haired husband, she continued, "And here I could spend the rest of the day with Alexandra."

"We're leaving, Sarah," he said in his stern voice, "as soon as you get those bags packed. I told you, I have to be back by Tuesday."

Sarah shrugged delicately boned shoulders, her dark, Hopi eyes smiling at her daughter. "See what I have to put up with? But we'll leave New Oraibi early and stop at the Sedona house on Monday night, dear. Then we'll visit all evening. Perhaps we can all have dinner. You invite Tom."

Alex would have told her about Tom—but why launch into that? She'd tell her mother Monday night, when there was time. When, she hoped, this whole sordid mess would be over.

Sarah left them in the living room and went to finish packing, calling over her shoulder, "Now there's lots of food in the refrigerator and the pool was cleaned last week, and oh, there's a huge sale going on at Goldwater's Department Store."

Alex sighed, smiling, as she kicked off her sandals. "Mother is something, isn't she?" she remarked to her father.

"The best."

They sat out back by the pool, in the shade of her father's prize palm. It was always a lovely spot; a flagstone patio, potted cactus plants, juniper, three tall royal palm trees for shade.

"Are you going to tell her, dad?" asked Alex, pushing her dark bangs aside.

"She knows something's up. You know her, however. She's been taking all day to pack just waiting for you to get here."

"To see if I'm in one piece?"

"I suppose."

Alex told him about her visit to the floral shop in Scottsdale, about the woman who had purchased the roses driving a Manor Development vehicle.

"A note like the one he sent," said her father, "proves nothing."

"I suppose."

"It would never stand up in court."

"I know that, dad."

"So I take it you called Tom."

"Yes. I told him the land deal is off."

"And he'll call Justin Manor?"

Alex frowned. "Yes, Tom will call him because it still hasn't hit him that Manor is no good. Tom can be so incredibly blind."

"I told you that a year ago."

She tried to keep her hackles from rising. Parents!

"Then won't Manor be pushed into a corner? I mean, Alex, there's no telling what he'll do next."

"I can guess at that, though. He'll have to do some hard thinking. Let's assume that he was the one who killed Joseph. Then he'll have to decide if it's worth going to those lengths again."

Judge Crawford frowned deeply. "And he'll target you."

"Maybe. But remember, he doesn't know where I am. And when I get back to Sedona, the chances are that he'll keep threatening me. Remember, he did visit Joseph several times before he acted."

"I hope you're right."

"I'm sure I am. And if he does try to threaten me, I'll get it on tape, and I'll have him on harassment."

"Should be able to make that stick," he reflected.

"Oh yes, it'll stick, all right."

They both knew, of course, that Manor might resort to a more violent means, as he had done with poor old Joseph Twelvetrees. But Alex was prepared to let the sheriff's department in on the whole thing as soon as she got back to Sedona. Why take unnecessary chances? Would Jake feel it his duty to watch her twenty-four hours a day? Wasn't that how it was all done? Cops and robbers.

She told herself that she'd face that possibility when it arose. And, too, she could always ask Jake to put someone else on as watchdog. It didn't *have* to be him.

"All ready," called Sarah from the patio door.

Alex walked them out, promising to feed the cat, lock the doors and pour out the unused milk from the fridge. It all seemed so trivial in the face of her real concerns, but she smiled and nodded nonetheless.

"You call us," said her father. And they were gone, safely away, just in case.

She did lock the front door carefully behind her, thought about driving back to Sedona instead of spending the night, but decided she was too tired. It had been a long, nerve-racking day. The longest of her life.

Around six she took a swim in the buff, then lazed on a lounge in the warm evening sun. It felt good, an incredible indulgence in the face of so much tension. And she managed to drift, her thoughts coming to peaceful rest as she envisioned the House Made of Dawn. Her house. The sun would be setting soon there, casting giant red shadows on the crumbled home of the Ancient Ones. Somewhere a hawk would rise on an ascending shaft of air in the valley below. Later an owl would cry into the setting sun, the moon would rise softly in the eastern sky and the night creatures would begin their prowl, at one with the cyclic changes of the Earth.

Alex awakened at seven, walked into the house clad only in her towel, went to the guest room and lay down on the spread. It was a full twelve hours before she again opened her eyes.

At NINE on Friday morning Alex telephoned Bill in Flagstaff.

"Where are you?"

"At my parents' house, in Scottsdale."

"Everything all right?"

"Perfectly fine. And I managed to find out that Manor did have those flowers sent."

"Good...although the note hardly proves harassment. So you're on your way back to Sedona?"

"Soon." Alex smiled to herself. "Actually, later this afternoon. I thought I might do some shopping."

"Shopping!"

Alex laughed, her blue eyes sparkling. "Why not? Let Manor stew for a while before he can reach me."

"You know," said Bill, "you're getting a bit cocky. Watch it."

"I will," said Alex dryly.

She hung up and dressed in a tan linen skirt and shell-pink silk blouse, taking more care than usual with her appearance—a touch of deep-blue eye shadow, a little mascara, a dab of lipstick.

After all, she was going shopping! She was as carefree that morning as a bird. As Chosóvi. Yes—she was a bird.

The surge of power that kept coursing through her that afternoon did not escape Alex. She walked in the open all over the Old Town of Scottsdale, through the famous galleries and chic jewelry shops, the trading posts that sold every imaginable trinket for the tourists, the numerous restaurants and expensive gift shops. And all the while she felt like a daredevil. Justin Manor's office was a mere three blocks away, on Scottsdale's plush Fifth Avenue.

Strangely, her feet carried her in that direction. Certainly she had no intention of actually entering his office, but the temptation of just strolling by was too great to resist. She could envision him, sitting at an expensive desk, his handsome features contorted in rage as he dialed and redialed her home telephone.

If he only knew!

The actual experience of walking past his building left her jittery and as high as a kite. She stood at the corner of his block taking in deep breaths, pleased as punch with herself, the blazing hot Arizona sun turning her eyes to a deep sapphire blue. She felt triumphant, self-confident—yes, cocky.

Finally she left Fifth Avenue, strolled to the hot-pink-fronted ice-cream shop on Scottsdale Drive and entered its deliciously cool atmosphere.

"Can I help you?" asked the pretty little waitress in her cute pink uniform.

"Yes," said Alex, "I'll have a hot-fudge sundae." But she caught the girl. "Oh, miss? Would you make that a double scoop? I suddenly feel like indulging myself." And Alex smiled brightly.

CHAPTER NINETEEN

"Wow, IT'S GOING TO BE HOT OUT today," said Bobby, opening the screen door to the apartment and letting Indian in ahead of him.

"Don't slam the door," grumbled Jake automatically, a split second before the door slammed.

"Sorry, dad."

"Where have you been?" Jake sat on a kitchen chair in his running shorts. He had Friday off and had taken a leisurely jog. It was actually beginning to feel good now, even with the cast in the way.

"Oh, over at Alex's. I taped a TV show I wanted to watch."

"I told you not to bother her." Jake's voice turned rough.

"She isn't home, dad. She must have gone somewhere. Her car was gone all night. And she said I could use her VCR any time, remember?"

Now that he thought about it, Jake realized her car hadn't been there since yesterday morning. Tom Farley? He replied with a little more irritation in his voice than he'd meant to. "I don't like it, Bob. Your traipsing around in her house when she's gone. Don't do it again."

"Geez, dad." Bobby sat down at the table, picking at a crust of toast on a plate. "There was this big box of flowers in her house. She must have some rich boyfriend."

"Flowers?"

"One of those big long cardboard boxes like in the movies all filled with white roses. Real strange too. There was one red rose in the middle of all the white ones. But she didn't put them in water. They were all wilted. I wondered if I should put them in a vase or something. What d'you think, dad?''

"For Pete's sake, Bob, don't touch anything in her house! Were you snooping?'' Jake turned angry green eyes on his son.

"No, dad. They were just lying right out there on the couch. Honest.''

Jake used his left hand to untie the bandanna knotted around his head, and wiped at the drops of sweat on his temples. "Did you notice who they were from?'' He hated to ask, but the words left his lips before he could prevent them.

"There was this funny note with them.'' Bobby looked down at his hands, abashed. "I couldn't help reading it. It was just lying there, dad.''

"Yeah, so what did it say?''

"It said, 'Hope your mother is feeling well.' ''

"That's all? No name or anything?''

"Nope, just that. Is that why Alex went away? Is her mother sick or something?''

"I don't know, Bob.'' Jake stared into space, wondering. He'd been sure the flowers were from Farley, but wouldn't he have signed the note? And why hadn't Alex put them in water? Roses were expensive.

"Bobby.'' Jake paused, wording his request carefully. "Look, I know I said you weren't to go into her house when she was away, but I'd like to see those flowers. Can you let me in?''

"Sure, dad, I trust you. But why do you want to see them?''

"Call it a hunch, Bob. It may just turn out to be important.''

They walked the short distance to the big house. Bobby found the back-door key over the door ledge— Jake could have found it himself—and they went inside, Indian slinking along with them, a panting brown shadow at Bobby's knee.

It was more of a shock than Jake had realized. Her

scent pervaded the house, faint and tantalizing. There was a coffee cup and a plate in the sink. A chair was pushed back from the kitchen table. Had she left in a hurry then? He recalled with utter clarity that she had stood right there by the sink; he had stood over there. They had kissed once, passionately, at the foot of the stairs. But those thoughts were futile.

"Here they are, dad," Bobby was calling from the living room.

He walked into the other room and looked down at the florist's box of roses lying open on the couch. At least two dozen pure white roses, wilted now, and one crimson bud in the center of them—like a drop of blood.

He picked up the plain white note—the envelope was gone—and read it: "Hope your mother is feeling well." That was all.

He knew instantly who the flowers were from, recognized the unspoken threat of the note and felt a stab of fear for Alex.

He swore under his breath, guessing instinctively that Alex would have left for Scottsdale like a shot after receiving the flowers—either to check on her mother or to do something insane like confront Justin Manor.

"What's the matter?" asked Bobby.

"Bob, I'm going to have to go on back to Scottsdale. Today. Think you can stay with the Websters?"

"I guess so. At this rate I haven't got much choice. I'm gonna have to go steady with Cecily."

"Hey, Bob, don't mention the flowers to anyone, okay?"

"Okay. I won't. Does this have anything to do with your case?"

"It might. Just keep it quiet. I have to trust you, Bob."

"Don't worry, dad." There was real pride in his voice, a mature ring to it.

Jake got on the phone to Randy at the office, explaining the situation. "Can I take the Blazer? I'll die in that old Pontiac. No air conditioning."

"If it's in the line of work, pal."

"It is."

"Okay."

"And tell Janet to expect Bobby and that blasted mutt tonight. I'll be back tomorrow. And, good buddy, thank her for me."

"Sure, sure. Be careful. If I have to get you out of a mess, it's your head. *Or* if the county attorney's office gets on me about harassment of one of their deputies...."

"Don't worry. I'll walk on eggs."

"Yeah, that I can just see!"

"Tomorrow, Randy."

The drive down the plummeting superhighway to the desert floor was pleasant in the air-conditioned Blazer. But Jake was worried and didn't really enjoy the trip. He'd called the county attorney's office in Flagstaff and checked out where Alex had gone so he didn't end up on a wild-goose chase. She'd left word she was staying at her parents' house in Scottsdale—he had the address.

What would she do first? Where would she go? Would she confront Manor right away? The man was dangerous. And he had threatened Alex, indirectly, through her parents. If Jake was any judge of character, Alex wouldn't take it lying down. Not her. She'd fly into a temper. He could see her as she'd been that previous Saturday morning: two spots of red on her cheeks, her eyes shooting sapphire sparks, her small hands clenched into fists.

And she was good at her job—she'd flushed Manor all right. It's just that she couldn't possibly know what kind of a monster she was dealing with. That man would kill for his own gain without compunction—he wouldn't even hire someone else to do his dirty work. No. Justin Manor would leave no loose ends at all. One old man dead meant less than nothing to Manor.

If Alex stood in his way, he'd destroy her just as easily—and with just as little evidence implicating him.

He found himself stepping on the accelerator a little too heavily. Randy would definitely not like his under-sheriff to get a ticket for speeding. A cynical grin caught at Jake's lip. But he could probably get it fixed. Official business, of course.

Scottsdale crouched, desiccated and gleaming, under the blasting desert sun. The heat was an entity unto itself; it felt solid as a wall to Jake as he opened the car door. It made everything seem a little unreal, removed from him.

He looked up at the building that housed the Manor Development Corporation on Scottsdale's posh Fifth Avenue. It was a two-story white stucco building, very solid and prosperous looking. The deep-set windows were of tinted glass and a small, unostentatious brass plaque advised one of the offices inside.

Jake took a deep breath, feeling the searing air bite into his lungs, and pushed open the door.

Coolness drenched him like a thrown bucket of water. A pretty young receptionist sat at a polished oak desk.

"May I help you, sir?"

"I'd like to speak to Justin Manor."

"What is your name, please? Do you have an appointment?" her voice was singsongy.

"The name's Brannigan. I don't have an appointment, but I think he'll see me. It's official business." He flipped open his wallet, showing his Coconino County Sheriff's ID.

"Let me check and see if Mr. Manor is in today." She could have been a robot, a smooth-skinned, externally feminine humanoid of some sort. She pressed a button on a state-of-the-art communications console and spoke into the speaker.

"Mr. Manor will see you now, sir. Right this way." She led him to a tiled alcove where an elevator waited. An *elevator*, in a two-story building. She pressed "two" for him and held the doors apart as he stepped in.

Justin Manor's office was Southwestern chic to the extreme. Indian rugs, sand paintings and photographs of desert scenery filled the walls. The decor was quasi-Mexican: stucco and dark beams and deep-set windows and tiles. One side wall boasted a huge painted mural of a golf course, a complex of club buildings, pools and tennis courts in an elegantly landscaped setting. One of Manor's resorts, no doubt. On another wall were extensive oak bookshelves containing a large number of leather-bound tomes and a few Indian artifacts, including a kachina doll. Everything was expensive and in perfect taste; it was just all a little new, a little too well put together for Jake's taste.

Under a priceless Navajo rug that hung on the opposite wall stood the man himself, tall and straight and dressed in pleated white pants, tennis shoes and a polo golf shirt in the palest of pinks.

He advanced, his hand held out, a wide welcoming smile on his exquisitely tanned face. "Mr. Brannigan." His clasp was as perfect as his smile—not too weak, not too strong, confident, masculine, reassuring. Jake was impressed despite himself.

"And to what do I owe this visit?" he asked in a resonant voice, indicating the chair opposite his polished teak desk. He seated himself, steepling his fingers, and leaning forward with keen anticipation.

Jake folded his tall frame into the chair. "I'm undersheriff up in Sedona. I'd like some information if you don't mind." He tried to keep his tone even; the man wouldn't need much of an opening to turn it to his advantage.

"Certainly. Is that," he questioned, gesturing delicately to Jake's cast, "due to your profession or merely to a sport?"

"A little of both, you might say," replied Jake without a moment's hesitation.

"Ah."

"The information, Mr. Manor?"

"Shoot." He was steady, open.

"Have you seen Miss Alexandra Crawford recently?"

Manor looked surprised. "Not since, let's see, last Tuesday in Sedona."

"Not yesterday or this morning?"

"Certainly not."

"Did you send the lady some flowers yesterday? Some white roses?"

"Mr. Brannigan, are you here to investigate something besides the lady's admirers?" His voice was sure, full of laughter.

Jake persisted, his tone never changing, his expression as still and closed as a winter pond. "Did you?"

"I believe I had my secretary send some flowers. I'm engaged in a business deal with Miss Crawford."

"Does that include sending expensive flowers and threatening messages, Mr. Manor?"

"I beg your pardon. I did not threaten the lady. I would never do a thing like that."

"Then what concern of yours is her mother's health?"

Justin Manor rose from his chair, came around to the front of his desk and leaned back on it, his legs out in front of him, his tanned arms folded across his chest. "I happen to know the lady's mother has a heart problem and has had for years. Would it not behoove me to inquire politely after her health?" He leaned forward a little. "Mr. Brannigan, let me explain to you how I work. I prefer to get my customers and potential business associates on my side. I flatter them, send them gifts. It's a small price to pay for good relations and cooperation."

"And you send roses to your male business associates as well?"

"Certainly not." Justin smiled. "I send them bottles of Courvoisier and golf clubs."

"Also with unsigned cards?"

Manor looked puzzled. "Wasn't the card signed?"

Jake let the question pass. Manor was slick. His little stunt with the unsigned note wasn't meant to hide the fact that he'd sent the flowers; it was intended to intimidate and to threaten.

"Well, Mr. Manor," began Jake, rising from his chair, "I just want you to know one thing. We don't want you or your resort in Sedona. Miss Crawford will not accept your offer on behalf of the Twelvetrees, nor will anyone else. Your kind is not wanted in our town. Keep out of Sedona and keep away from Alex Crawford." His voice had not risen an iota. He made his statements calmly, coldly, totally without inflection.

Manor smiled thinly. "I hear you, Mr. Brannigan, but I do not concur. I will have that land, and Sedona will have a resort. There really isn't much more to say, is there?"

Swiftly Jake reached out his good left hand, grabbed the front of Manor's pale-pink shirt and had him leaning backward across his desk in an eyeblink of time. It was done so quickly, so cleanly, that Manor never had a chance to retaliate—he was occupied with supporting his and Jake's weight on his own arms so that his back wasn't broken over the sharp edge of the desk.

Jake put his face close to Manor's, smelling the expensive after-shave. "You stink like a woman, Manor," he growled roughly. "Stay out of my town and don't lay a finger on any of the Crawfords, or I'll see you in hell." He shook him, as a dog shakes a rat and felt the pale-pink fabric under his fingers tear. "If you ever set foot in Sedona again, you may only end up in jail and you'd be real lucky at that." He dropped Manor onto his desk, sending papers flying to the floor.

"You'll be sorry you ever laid a hand on me, you fool," ground out Manor hoarsely as he heaved himself up. He was pale, and his whole body shook. "Don't stand in my way, Brannigan."

But Jake merely turned on his heel and strode to the doorway. He opened it, paused on the threshold and half turned. "We'll get you for Joseph Twelvetrees, you know. Eventually," he said matter of factly.

"Get out!" rasped Manor.

Jake closed the door gently behind him and took the elevator down, passed the plastic receptionist with a smile and a nod and left the Manor Development Corporation offices.

The heat smote him a soft blow. He walked to his car, got in and started it, and pulled out into the tourist-clogged traffic. He knew from previous experience that he'd have to stop soon because the shaking would set in, and it would take a while for him to calm down.

He pulled into the parking lot of a bar: The Cowboy Saloon—another adobe-and-tile creation. His hands shook; tremors traveled up his arms to his shoulders. He sat there for a second or two, taking deep breaths. Then slowly he walked into the darkened haven.

The bar was gleaming wood, the bartender carefully impartial, the customers few at that hour.

"What'll it be?"

Jake hesitated a split second. My God, wouldn't a beer and a whiskey taste good! "Tonic and lime," he said gruffly.

He sipped slowly, carefully. It calmed him just to sit in the cool dimness, to hear the quiet conversation of the two men down the bar. Bars were universal; he could have been in McCready's back in L.A. an hour before the day shift was out. He ordered another, beyond temptation for the moment. Gradually the spasms relaxed and tired emptiness replaced the high-tension adrenaline rush.

Jake tried to review the facts. He believed Manor's statement that he hadn't seen Alex. Somehow, you got the feel for truth after twenty years of pursuing it. That was good. If he got hold of her this evening, he could convince her to go back to Sedona, not to confront Manor. The man was dangerous, no doubt about it. A real shark.

Unfortunately Alex might let their abortive personal relationship prevent her from seeing the logic of the situation. She had set herself up as the rabbit, and the dogs would be after her. Now it was time to let the professional law-enforcement people take over. Her job was purely investigative, and she'd done it. Exit county attorney, stage right.

He considered going to the Scottsdale police, but he had no proof whatsoever—not yet—and he'd appear foolish. He'd done that once or twice as a rookie: rushed in with no hard evidence when he knew the person was guilty. It was a humbling experience.

He tried to divorce his feeling for Alex from his knowledge of how best to handle the situation. It was difficult. He wanted her out of there, away from the line of fire. The image of Joseph Twelvetrees's dead body pervaded his mind. They could find Alex like that—somewhere, all alone, caught by that slimy creature.

Jake looked around the dim quiet bar for the public telephone and reached into his pocket for the number of Alex's parents.

He'd better be pretty convincing—this would be harder than getting through to Justin Manor. Of that he had no doubt.

CHAPTER TWENTY

ALEX WAS STILL GLOWING when she let herself into her parents' house late in the afternoon. But she was hot and dusty and her feet hurt. She'd reconsidered driving home that night. After all, it was the weekend. Her time was her own. A dip in the pool would feel fantastic. Then a light dinner, and maybe she'd even go out to a movie. Up in Sedona they got movies a few months late, and even then there were relatively few compared to a big city. Yes, maybe a movie. . . .

When the phone rang she wasn't at all surprised. It would be one of her parents' friends with a last-minute invitation for a Friday-evening cocktail party or perhaps a golf game for her father for the weekend. She'd have to let their friends know they'd gone for a long weekend to, say, Lake Havasu City.

"Hello?"

"Alex." Just her name, nothing else—in that deep gravelly voice she knew so well.

"What do you want? How did you know. . . ?" But of course, her office had told him. "What is it?"

"I'm in Scottsdale, Alex."

"You're what? How dare you follow me? What do you think. . . ."

"If you'll just keep quiet for a minute, I'll tell you." There was no hint of emotion in his voice. It was the voice of the perfect interrogator or cross-examiner, totally under control.

"Go on." She tried to keep the anger from her voice, replacing it with coldness.

"I found out about the flowers and the message. I've seen Manor."

"I don't believe this!" Alex stood and paced the length of the phone cord, unable to put her thoughts in logical order. Anger overrode reason. "First you spy on me and go into my house. Then you follow me. How dare you!"

"Bobby saw the flowers, Alex. And your office told me where you were. All nice and aboveboard."

"Oh, Mr. Big City Detective again! Terrific! And just what did you get out of Manor, may I ask?"

"A little satisfaction. Now, listen to me, please, Alex. I'm about two miles away from you. I'm driving over right now to get you, and you're not leaving my sight until you drive back to Sedona." His voice was masculine, the epitome of reason. It irritated her beyond belief.

"I will not! *You* will not! Leave me alone. I'm doing my job and I'm getting somewhere! It's none of your business!" She felt helpless tears of rage fill her eyes.

"I've made it my business. And I have a few things to tell you about this Manor. You have no idea who you're playing with."

"He doesn't know I'm here, Jake," she tried to explain patiently, but her voice quavered with anger.

"He will soon enough."

"How? Don't be ridiculous!"

"Believe me, Justin Manor can find out anything he wants. He can call your office just as easily as I did. Don't be a fool, Alex." She could tell, even in her fury, that he was trying very hard to remain reasonable. And she hated to admit it, but his last shot hit the bull's-eye.

"Oh, *darn* you, Jake Brannigan! Why can't you leave me alone!" It was a childish wail, and she knew it but it didn't matter.

"Because you're in danger, Alex. Believe me."

"I find it exceedingly difficult to trust you about anything." She succeeded in keeping her voice under control this time.

There was a moment's pause. "I understand, but trust me on this...please."

She knew it was hard for him to beg her; she heard the grating tone in his voice and was glad for any discomfort she might cause him. She sighed, massaging her forehead with her fingers. "Did you really go to see Manor? You've blown the thing wide open then. You should have waited."

"I saw him but, believe me, you'd already blown the case wide open. You set yourself up. That was unwise, Alex."

"I did it on purpose, you fool! How else do you think we'd ever get him?" She took a deep breath. "Oh, never mind! I don't have to explain myself to *you*."

"We're supposed to be working on the same case. What do you care which one of us gets him? You're not trained to be a target, Alex. I am. It's very simple. Now, will you wait there while I drive over?"

"No! Don't you dare!"

"You're not safe." He was still trying to be patient, but it was a strain. "Look, forget about. . .us. Manor wouldn't think twice about removing you if you got in his way."

"He wouldn't dare touch me."

"It's my job to protect you."

"Protect me!" She laughed. "All you've ever done for me, Jake, is hurt me." Her voice failed, breaking at the end. She hated herself for being so weak.

"Alex—" His voice stopped short. "I'm coming over. Lock your doors and windows."

"Oh, for heaven's sake, don't be so melodramatic!"

"I'm not. I mean it. See you in about fifteen minutes, Alex." Then the phone went dead in her ear.

She stalked around the cool, quiet house, alternating between rage and frustration. Her immediate thought had been to leave—just leave—and let Mr. Jake Brannigan find the house empty. But she couldn't stand the idea of running away from him. Run away? Alex Crawford had never run from anything in her life! She absolutely couldn't do it.

She'd face Jake, face him down, enjoy his defeat, grind her metaphoric heel in his face. He had no right!

Angrily she strode into the bathroom, splashed cold water on her face and pulled her hair back into a barrette. *This* time she wouldn't put on a smidgen of makeup. He wasn't worth it. Her skirt was wrinkled from the long hot day. Did she have time to change? What for? To impress Jake Brannigan? She gave a bitter little laugh into the empty air, then merely smoothed her skirt down over her hips with her hands and tucked her blouse in more neatly.

She sat stiffly on the white sectional sofa in the silent living room, starting at the sound of every car that went by, waiting for him.

She heard his car pull into the drive, heard the door open and close, heard his footsteps approach the front door. She held herself still, refusing to budge. The door chimes went through their tune once, then twice. Halfway through the third time she stood, took a deep breath and went to open the door.

He was just as big as ever, just as broad—maybe a little slimmer in the waist, a touch leaner in the jaw line than when she'd first seen him. His blond hair was shorter now, his mustache trimmed more neatly. He looked a little tired; but his face had no expression on it whatsoever: neither anger nor welcome nor worry.

He stepped inside without a word, taking in the foyer and living room at a glance. Alex knew he'd remember every detail.

"Your folks?" he asked.

"They're up on the reservation with my grandfather."

"Did they know about the note?"

"My father did."

"Had they been contacted by Manor?"

"No."

They stood on the pale-green carpet, both of them stiff with each other, like two strange dogs circling, their hackles raised.

"You're coming with me. You can't stay here to-night."

"I will *not!* Who do you think you are?" She backed off a step, feeling heat flush her neck.

Jake scrubbed his left hand through his hair; a frown shadowed his face, then passed. "Okay, I'm sorry. *Please*, for your own safety, come with me."

"No." She turned her back on him deliberately and began to walk to the sofa.

He was after her in a split second, his hand grabbing her arm at the elbow. "Alex, listen to me, for God's sakes! This is no game."

She turned as cold and hard as ice. "Get your hand off me. Don't ever touch me again."

He pulled his hand back as if burned. "Sorry," he mumbled. He walked over to a white damask armchair and flung himself down in it. "Alex, I'm tired. I've had a long day. I can't afford to let you stay here alone. If you won't come with me, I'll just stay here."

She felt a traitorous stirring of pity for him, but banished the weakness furiously. "This is not my house, Jake. You can't stay here."

"I'm sure your father wouldn't mind your having police protection, Alex," he said wearily. "I'll take my chances on that."

She was silent. Jake had her there. She only knew she couldn't bear him to stay with her. What could she do? She couldn't exactly remove him physically.

"All right," she relented sullenly. "But I was going to go out to eat."

"Fine. Wherever you want."

"Alfredo's." It popped into her mind without thought. What did it matter anyway? At least it was a way to get him out of her parents' house.

He followed Alex to the restaurant in the Blazer; she insisted on driving, refusing to go in his car. He gave in, apparently not feeling it was worth the argument. She experienced a slight spurt of satisfaction at getting her own way in this small matter, then just as quickly felt childish and ridiculous.

The restaurant had a fountain in the courtyard, but one ate in the upstairs dining room, on the roof actually, that was open to the evening sky. In each corner of the area stood an Aladdin's lamp with a flame that leaped gracefully into the air.

Alex and Jake were quite early and the place was only half-filled. It didn't seem to matter what one wore; the restaurant wasn't formal at all. There were people at the bar in tennis clothes and shorts, so Alex didn't mind her wrinkled skirt and blouse. Jake didn't seem to care where he was anyway; he was obviously only along to placate her.

She ordered a white wine. Jake had the inevitable tonic and lime.

"Can we talk now?" he finally asked.

"Go right ahead," she replied scornfully. "Let's hear your words of wisdom."

He leaned forward, keeping his deep voice low. "I want you safely back in Sedona under Randy's protection."

"You want? What about what I want?"

"Alex." He started to say something, then shook his head. "Look at it this way. It's time for you to bow out. You've done a great job, but now I take over. I may even have to call in the Scottsdale police. This is not a job for a deputy county attorney. Even your boss would agree with me there."

He was so sincere, so logical she almost believed him. "I just want to know why you took it upon yourself to follow me, to spy on me."

His hooded green eyes held her gaze. "I knew about the flowers and the note, and it's my case. I had to follow up. No matter who it had been, Alex."

No matter who it had been. The words made her heart falter a little in spite of herself.

She narrowed her eyes and shot a barb at him. "Not if it had been a man!"

"Yes," he corrected wearily, "even if it had been a man."

She didn't believe him, but let it drop. "What did you ask Manor?"

"I asked him if he'd sent the flowers," said Jake off-handedly. "And if he'd seen you today or yesterday."

Alex couldn't believe her ears. "You asked him if he sent the flowers?"

"Yeah. His secretary did it, he told me. And the note about your mother was merely *courtesy* on his part."

Alex was about to say something outrageous when the waitress arrived and she had to study the menu quickly, choose something, anything. "Steak au poivre," she said, her eyes touching upon the first thing on the list.

She heard Jake order something—she couldn't remember what—because his words kept echoing in her mind. He'd asked Manor outright about the flowers! She'd assumed he'd deny it! And here she'd been trudging around in the heat to locate the florist—to prove Manor had sent them. And she'd gotten her proof, but now it was ashes in her mouth. All she'd had to do was ask Manor. She felt like an utter fool, a dunce.

"Alex?" Jake looked puzzled, a little worried. "You okay?"

She must have been silent for too long. She took a long sip of her wine and set her glass on the table. "I found the florist who sold those flowers," she said in a small voice. "The lady remembered his car."

Jake looked at her closely. "You did this today?"

"Yesterday."

"That was good work."

"It was pretty easy, actually." Her blue eyes met his squarely. "But it seems all I had to do was ask."

"It's corroborative evidence. That's fine." Was there a trace of condescension in his voice? "He even knew about your mother's heart condition, Alex. I take it she has one?"

"Yes." A whisper. "Not too serious though."

"You see what I mean? He can find out anything he wants. He's like a spider with his legs on strands that tell him everything he wants to know." Jake leaned across the table, touching her hand gently with his fingers. His cast lay between them like a white flag of truce. "I want to help you, Alex. Can you believe that?"

She averted her face. "I guess so. It just seems so unfair. I've been sweating over this for weeks now and you blithely go in and *ask* him. I suppose," she said scornfully, "that he confessed to Joseph Twelvetrees's murder too."

"No." Jake leaned back. "He didn't do that."

"What else did you get out of him?"

"Well, not much as a matter of fact. He said something that got me a bit angry, and I'm afraid I got a little rough with Mr. Manor."

"You did?" Alex's eyes were wide. "Did you hurt him?"

"Only his pride." Jake's lip twitched a little under his mustache. "I think he got the idea though."

"You didn't get hurt, did you? Your hand?" Her eyes fell to his cast.

"Would it matter to you if I had?" His hooded green eyes searched hers, but his voice was steady and low.

"Well, I don't like anyone to get hurt. Don't be silly, Jake."

"Not even Manor?" Was he teasing?

"I would like him to be tried and convicted in a fair court of law."

Jake gave a short laugh. "There's a lawyer for you." He leaned forward, resting muscular forearms on the table. "Let me ask you this. What if, because of some technicality or lack of evidence, he went free after being brought to trial? What then?"

"I'd have to go with our system, Jake."

"What if he called you every night and threatened you and your family, seeing as you'd been the star witness for the prosecution? For years. What then, Alex?"

"I would hope I'd make a better case against him than that," she said through stiff lips.

"Ah," he said disgustedly, "guys like Manor should be shot on sight."

"But Jake," she replied softly, "I don't notice you out there shooting. Why not, if you really believe that?"

"I was tempted today, let me tell you. Only shooting's too good for him."

"I'll tell you what *I* think. I think your bark is a good deal louder than your bite."

"Maybe," he growled, subsiding.

Alex finished her glass of wine, staring out, over the city built around an ancient desert oasis, at the lengthening shadows of early evening. Soon there would be a glorious sunset on the western horizon, the kind of spectacularly brilliant sunset that occurs only in the desert. It was something about the dry desert air, she'd once heard. She wished she could enjoy it.

"Can I have another glass of wine?" she asked.

"Sure. This meal is on the Coconino County Sheriff's Department anyway."

"Is it?"

"Yeah. That way we won't have to argue about who pays."

She almost smiled. But this time she wouldn't say a word.

Her glass of wine arrived, then their meals. She really hadn't wanted steak—she rarely ate meat anyway. But suddenly she was starving, even after her double ice-cream sundae.

Jake had ordered some kind of fish, but he left half of his potato and didn't touch the crusty French bread. Alex was almost embarrassed at the way she cleaned her plate.

Dusk settled over the desert floor, resting on the shoulders of the dust-dry hills surrounding them. In the west, futile thunderheads amassed, reflecting the pinks and purples and crimsons wildly.

"It's beautiful," breathed Alex, feeling drowsy, full, and relaxed from the wine.

"In L.A. you never could see the sunset. There were buildings in the way, or smog."

"Do you miss it?"

"What—L.A.?" He looked surprised. "I miss a few good buddies. My partner for the last five years. The city—no."

"Will you stay in Sedona?" she asked idly.

"I don't know. It depends."

"On what?"

"A lot of things."

He wouldn't be pushed, she realized.

"Alex, will you get a room in my motel tonight? I mean," he added quickly, "for your protection. I'd feel a lot better if you were in the same motel. That house has a hundred ways in."

"Oh Lord, you're going to start that again." She almost wanted to laugh; he was being so absurdly serious.

Jake had an odd expression on his face, half-solemn, half-embarrassed. "I'd like to know you're safe. I've been. . . well, pretty worried about you."

"Jake, I wish you wouldn't."

"Blast it all, Alex, I can't help it. I care about you."

The words stunned her. A warm feeling surged in her breast, flooding her cheeks with pink. "Jake?"

"This is hard for me, Alex. I have to protect you—it's my job. But there's more. I need to know you're all right." He turned his face away suddenly, a muscle ticking in his jaw. "Just give in this once, Alex. It won't kill you."

She was silent, searching his face. "Jake, what you're saying is. . . ." She hesitated, then felt the need for final, irrevocable truth. "You're not telling me the truth and you're not even admitting it to yourself, Jake. If I go to your motel with you, I'm giving up. . . everything that is me. I'm afraid of what will happen. And it will, Jake. You know it as well as I do. I've been putting you away from me and now you come bursting back into my life. You can't play with me like that.''

"I'm not playing with you, Alex." There was real pain in his eyes now; his voice was low and full of emotion. "What do you think I am?"

"I don't know. A man who's been through a lot, a man who's afraid to take another chance."

"Come with me, Alex. Now. Forget all the rest." It was a groan, a kind of plea for help. He reached out his hand and touched her fingers again. Her skin burned from his nearness.

"I can't," she whispered, but her voice sounded weak and ineffectual even to her own ears.

He stood, threw some bills on the table and took her arm under the elbow firmly, pulling her out of her chair. They stood toe to toe, gazes locked in anguish.

He broke the impasse finally. "Please, Alex, I need you."

She felt suddenly lost in a whirlwind of conflicting emotions. He needed her! The words were from his heart. It was no longer a simple matter of her dignity and self-respect; both seemed somehow trite in the face of Jake's spoken need.

Alex met his gaze in the growing darkness. "It cost you a lot to say that, didn't it?"

His lips barely moved. "Yes."

He had, that hot summer's night, reached her own heart, melting it until it was all soft and warm and utterly his. Later, later she might regret her decision—but now, Jake's need overwhelmed all else. There were many things in life one regretted, but without those dim, undefined impulses, would it be worth it after all?

Moments later they walked down the stairs to the entrance close together, as if afraid to be parted from each other.

"My car," Jake said. "Leave yours here."

"That'll confuse old Justin if he's watching!" She laughed suddenly, but she wouldn't have been parted from Jake even for the short drive to his motel.

Alex gave in totally to her instincts. She couldn't keep her hands off him as he drove. She had to feel his warm skin under his shirt, his mouth, the tickling mustache, his muscular thighs. He turned his head to kiss her, but it was almost impossible to watch the road at the same time. They laughed together like children at the awkwardness of it. She leaned her head against his chest, put her arms around him, kissed the smooth skin and the blond hairs on his chest where she'd unbuttoned his shirt.

It was all pure sensation: his breath on her hair, the car swerving around corners, the feel of his thigh muscle tensing as he braked, the feel of his skin under her lips—utterly familiar, utterly self-indulgent.

He unlocked the door to his room. Alex had no idea where it was or its name or anything else—it was merely a place they could be alone, to fulfill themselves. She was breathless, buoyed high with excitement; no man in her life had ever made her feel this way.

Nothing mattered; neither cared about anything outside of the four walls of the motel room. He undressed her carefully, kissing her neck, her breasts, her stomach. She moaned in desire, wanting to make love right now, yet wanting to hold off until neither of them could stand to wait any longer.

There were few words between them. It was all inarticulate sounds, the rustle of fabric sliding on skin, quick breathing, hands caressing a shoulder, an arm, a waist, a leg.

She pulled off his clothes, kissed his chest and strong neck, breathed in the scent of him. They joined powerfully, like a storm that finally breaks after threatening for hours. At first, they moved together slowly, reveling in the feel of each other's flesh, in the sensation of being fulfilled. They were opposites drawn together, creating a whole.

Then little darts of pleasure began to stab in Alex's belly, arrows of pleasure-pain that shot outward stronger and stronger until her body shook with them, controlled by a power entirely outside of herself.

Jake rose and fell with her, his big body totally in unison with hers. He gave her his entire self, driving her onward to a height of response. She knew the wonder of what he was doing to her, with her, but she could only thank him with small cries and touches and the quivering intensity of her response.

It shook her again and again, until she was drained and exhausted, gasping for breath.

"Oh," she sighed, finally back to herself.

Jake merely kissed her earlobe in answer, rolled over on one elbow and drew his fingers across her stomach.

"You're wonderful." Her voice was a fragile wisp of sound.

"So are you." He leaned over, kissed her lightly on the lips, and stroked her black bangs back from her face.

Alex was afraid to say another word, afraid to shatter the delicate mood that lay between them. They fell asleep like that, their arms around each other, their breaths mingling.

When Alex awoke it was pitch-dark in the room, and she had no idea where she was for a moment. Then she felt Jake's heavy leg over hers and remembered it all. She lay there in the dark room, knowing she loved him, knowing, too, that he must love her. His body could not lie to her, nor his whispered words, his caresses, his care for her pleasure. She envisioned a future for them— idyllic, satisfying. They could have children together; it would be good for Bobby. They'd enlarge her house. Everything would be wonderful. Janet would be thrilled... her mind flew on the wings of happiness, like her namesake, Chosóvi. Did all women dream like this when they'd just been with a man they loved, she wondered.

"Jake?" She shook him gently, desperately waiting to share her love with him.

"Umm." He rolled over toward her, sleepily flinging his arm over her. His cast thumped against her hip bone.

"Ouch!"

He was wide awake then. "Alex, I'm sorry. I forgot..."

She laughed ruefully. "That's okay. I'll live."

"The darned thing is a nuisance. I'll be glad to get it off," he growled.

"Ah, that's more like the old Jake I know." She paused deliberately, then finished her sentence, "and love."

She felt him stiffen inadvertently and pull away from her, not bodily, but mentally.

"Does it frighten you to speak of love?" she asked, determined to have it out with him.

"Yes," he said flatly.

"Because you were hurt?"

Jake sat up in bed and swept his hand back through his blond hair. "Look, Alex, I find it really hard to talk about. Can we drop it?"

"No. If you can't even talk about the pain of your divorce, how will you ever move on to loving someone else?"

"I have no intention of ever loving anyone else."

"Thank you so much, Jake. I guess you've answered any question I might have."

"I'm sorry," he mumbled, "that's me."

"Well, it doesn't have to be!" Alex snapped on the bedside light, slid out of bed and gathered her scattered clothes. She felt sick—wounded in a vital spot, but she held herself proudly as she began dressing.

Jake looked at his watch. "It's after midnight, Alex. What do you think you're doing?"

"I'm leaving."

"You can't. It's not safe."

She turned on him then, her blouse half-buttoned, her hair tangled. "Don't tell me what I can do, Jake. And don't try that protective bunk on me either, you coward. I'm not buying it."

"Alex...."

He got up, and she turned away from the sight of his

naked body. Grabbing her purse, she rushed to the door. "Don't try to stop me, Jake," she said fiercely. She opened the door and walked out into the black velvet night.

CHAPTER TWENTY-ONE

"A COWARD," Jake groaned to himself.

So what was he supposed to do? Forget about the past, pretend that Linda hadn't torn his guts out? How could he ever forget those terrible days of pain and loneliness? How could he chance living it all over again, and with Alex?

Simple. He couldn't.

He looked at his watch face in the darkness. One in the morning. How many times had he looked at a watch in the small hours of the morning and felt the same hideous futility? Thousands of times, a never-ending river of nights, all slowly moving, all painfully lonely. And Alex could be there, beside him, stretched out in naked wonder, slumbering quietly, her small firm breasts rising and falling gently, beautifully, her raven-black hair spread out on the white pillow, her dark eyelashes lying on her cheeks like delicate, miniature fans.

So beautiful, so giving, so alive....

"And she could be mine," Jake whispered harshly, smashing his good fist into the wall beside the bed. *She could be mine.* He'd practically forced her to leave—no woman of her spirit and pride could possibly have stayed after he'd so blatantly rejected her. Now she was out there in the dark, hot night, alone and helpless. He'd have to go after her in a minute, as soon as he got himself under control.

He dressed and took a walk in the still-warm hours of very early morning. With his useful hand jammed into his pocket he strode the empty streets of Scottsdale cursing himself, cursing Alex for what she had come to mean to him, cursing the world in general for its cruel,

brutal realities, promising himself he'd go after her—
soon.

The liquor store just seemed to materialize in front of
him. Like a scene from "Twilight Zone." Jake's body
broke out in a sick sweat. His hair became plastered
wetly to his head, his shirt glued to his back. The door
swung open and he heard a voice in his head say:
"Come on in, Jake. There's sweet oblivion waiting. I'll
solve all your problems, and it won't have to hurt anymore." He pulled a wrinkled handkerchief out of his
pocket, mopped the sweat off his face and neck and
fought the voice for long agonizing minutes. He shook
his leonine head, clearing it, and walked on. But the liquor store eventually shimmered, dreamlike, in front of
him again and he could see that bottle of Irish behind
the wavering glass like a beacon in the ugly black night.
And then he saw Alex's youthful face—and his own
seamed one suddenly superimposed itself over hers and
he knew then, with terrible insight, that he was all done
in. Jake Brannigan was a washed up old hulk, and it was
pointless to keep fighting the truth.

He bought the Irish whiskey from the blank-faced
storekeeper, tossing his ten onto the counter and picked
up the brown paper-wrapped bottle reverently, as if it
were a long-lost buddy.

And then he walked out into the dry hot blackness,
leaned against the wall of the store and felt a strange,
burning sensation behind his ears. He swallowed hard
several times, then walked on quickly, unthinking, his
feet carrying him back to his motel room.

It sat there next to the gray-faced TV and dominated
the deathly silent room. He picked up a glass he'd used
earlier for a Coke, walked into the bathroom to rinse it,
caught sight of himself in the unforgiving mirror and
quickly turned away, swearing under his breath.

When he strode back into the bedroom there *it* sat,
all-powerful, his friend, the only pal on earth who understood him really, his crutch, his lifeblood—sweet,
welcome forgetfulness.

He touched it. His fingers were oily, sweat slicked against the smooth cool glass. Quickly he retracted his hand.

Jake turned his back abruptly on the friend sitting there and walked to the chair next to the door. He tried to keep his eyes off his waiting buddy, who seemed to be calling his name in a part of his mind that Jake had forgotten existed.

It's just a bottle, he told himself, *a bottle of amber, fragrant poison.* But his friend spoke back harshly. "I'm your friend," it repeated over and over. "I got you through a lot of bad times. Don't reject me."

Jake swore out loud, viciously, ran a shaking hand through his sweat-dampened hair, swore again, and promised himself he'd go after Alex in a minute.

Then he paced the room feeling as if the friend had eyes, which followed him, as if the old friend knew, could read his mind. With each pacing step the room seemed to grow smaller and the friend's size and stature proportionately larger.

It was three in the morning when Jake unscrewed the cap from the bottle and five minutes past three when he stood in the shower and let the cold fingers of water wash the sick sweat from his flesh. At three-thirty he stepped out and wrapped a white towel around his naked, wet torso. When he reentered the bedroom the beacon on the counter next to the TV seemed somehow smaller but the ordeal was not yet over.

He fought the urge with all his renewed strength but that good buddy of his was powerful and, like a magnet, it seemed to sap the strength from Jake all over again.

At five he took another shower, thinking to himself, *Just one. I can have just one and then I'll drive over to Alex's and face her.*

At five-thirty he walked into the bedroom, picked up the bottle, threw the cap on the soft carpeting and put the friend to his lips. He took a deep swill, his head tossed back, the long muscles in his strong neck working hard as he gulped down the burning amber liquid, praying all the while for mindless oblivion.

JAKE AWOKE with a convulsive start, sitting straight up in bed, his naked body half in and half out of the sheets.

And he remembered the feel of the blazing liquid going down his throat, the race into the bathroom and his head hanging over the toilet until his stomach was spasmed from retching.

He guessed that afterward he'd collapsed, exhausted, on the bed. He really couldn't remember.

He looked at his watch. Seven thirty-five. He went to the counter, picked up the bottle and walked into the bathroom. He stood there for a moment before tilting the bottle and watching the golden liquid swirl into the bowl, spinning as it disappeared down the drain.

And then he went back into the bedroom, picked up the telephone and dialed nine for an outside line.

"Hello?" came her familiar voice. It was slightly constrained. He realized he'd been holding his breath in case she didn't answer the phone, in case Manor had been waiting there for her in the dark the night before. And it would have been his fault if anything had happened to her—all his fault.

"It's Jake." He heard his own rough voice. "We've gotta talk." She hung up.

He sat there like a complete, naked idiot, the receiver dangling in his hand. He got up, dressed and then redialed. The phone rang for five minutes before she picked it up.

"Don't hang up." He tried to keep his voice even, controlled; still, this was Alex, innocent, brave Alex on the other end of the line. Lord, how she must hate him! "Look," he said, "I'm coming over."

"Over my dead body."

"I mean it, Alex. We'll leave your car and take mine back up to Sedona. It's not safe for you here anymore."

"No," she answered adamantly.

"Look, we can . . . talk, on the way, if you like."

"Oh, I see," came her strained voice, "and I suppose you've changed your mind...you didn't mean the things you said last night."

"Alex, I . . ."

"Don't you dare say another word to me!"

"Alex, please. . . ."

"Please nothing! You don't have any idea how much you...you've tormented me, Jake Brannigan." But there was no anger in her voice, only pain.

He squeezed his hand in the cast until he could feel nothing else but a hard, throbbing ache. "We need to get you away from Scottsdale, Alex. Use your head. You can't stay there in that house...alone."

"I'll leave." He heard her breathe. "I'll go soon."

"Now. I'm coming over, and you better either be gone or I'm dragging you out of there and I mean that, Alex. I don't care what it takes."

He heard her little laugh. "Oh, you mean that you'd hurt me, Jake? I don't think I'd even feel physical pain anymore."

"Alex. . . ." But she'd already hung up.

It was over a half hour before he'd checked out of his motel and driven to her parents' address. When he pulled into their drive, he was relieved to see Alex's car gone. Of course, that didn't mean that she hadn't parked it down the road to trick Manor and was now sitting in the house, brooding, gloating, whatever it was a woman did when she was feeling as rotten as he was.

He walked to the front door, pressed the bell and got no answer. Then he tried the door. Locked. He was ready to turn and go when he thought, Where do children learn to hide keys under doormats? From their parents, of course.

He lifted up the corner of the grassy doormat and spotted the house key. "Some people never learn," he grumbled under his breath.

He entered the house, feeling slightly guilty at the thought of Alex's absent parents, but alert for signs of a struggle, or of Alex herself. All he encountered was the big orange cat that nearly tripped him as he walked down the hallway. It startled him and his hand went automatically to his nonexistent holster. Then he laughed embarrassedly into the empty air.

The expensively decorated house was empty, as far as he could tell. He checked out back, saw the elegant oval-shaped pool and wondered if Alex swam there often. For long moments he stood staring at the turquoise-blue water, fantasizing. He imagined Alex breaking through the glassy surface, her dark head shining in the desert sun, her delicate tanned shoulders sparkling as if diamond covered, her small but firm breasts teasing his eyes beneath the rippling water, the long smooth limbs, the womanly dark triangle. . . .

His face contorted in a grim self-loathing frown as Jake walked back into the cool house and checked around once more.

If he'd really believed that she hadn't left for Sedona, he'd have checked more thoroughly, seen her suitcase sitting, closed, on a rack beside the guest-room bed. As it was, Jake's mind was filled with the image of Alex in the swimming pool, and his eyes swept right over the small blue suitcase lying there in the open for any fool to see.

But then, things might never have happened as they did.

THE DRIVE BACK to Sedona seemed too easy, but he was speeding, his thoughts pinned on Alex, wondering why in the devil at his rate of speed he hadn't caught up to her. Perhaps she had stopped for lunch somewhere in the cooler, twisting hills above the scorching Phoenix valley. Or maybe he had passed her when she'd stopped for gas. Could be a lot of reasons. Maybe she hadn't left the valley at all. But Jake put that unsettling thought from him quickly.

Alex was a smart woman. She wouldn't have stayed around Scottsdale alone like that, not after their conversation the previous night.

The previous night—Alex furious, Alex soft and warm and giving. Her mouth opening to cry out her passion in the throes of love....

Jake nearly passed the entrance to Someday Ranch, so desperate was he to pull into her driveway in Sedona and see her car there. No matter what had happened between them, her safety came first and foremost. If anything happened to her....

Bobby had already left the ranch to go on his solo overnight accompanied, of course, by Indian, when Jake arrived.

"I'm worried about him," Cecily said at the door. "I mean, Mr. Brannigan, he's awfully new to camping and stuff like that."

But Jake was not too concerned. "He's a pretty tough kid, Cecily. If he survived on the streets of L.A., I suspect this will be a breeze." The kid had come a long ways in a short time.

"Let him grow up," said Randy, coming to the door. "You know, kids have got to have some freedom, some leeway to make mistakes, to learn. Hey, come on in."

Jake grimaced. "You sound as if I've got him tied to the old apron strings."

Randy laughed. "Not hardly, Jake, not you!"

"Say, can I use your phone?"

"Sure. There's an extension in the den."

Jake dialed Alex's number, twice, but both times he received no answer, only the empty, monotonous ring.

Randy was standing in the doorway, his arms folded across his barrel chest. "You calling Alex?"

"Yeah. But she's not back yet." He hung up the phone, his shoulders sagging. "Blast it all."

"I take it she left before you."

"Yeah. Or at least," reflected Jake gravely, "it looked like it. Her car was gone, I checked her parents' house...."

"She'll be along, Jake. Alex is a pretty sensible woman."

Jake thought, *Maybe so, but she's really upset now and who's to blame for that. . . ?*

"You want a beer?" asked Randy. "Oops, I forgot. How about a tonic?"

The men walked out to the patio behind the house and sat on the comfortable wooden lawn furniture. "Janet's at the grocery store," Randy began. "So now's a good time for you to fill me in on the trip to Phoenix." He looked at Jake hard. "You know, you look like you got run over by a truck down there. Problems?"

Jake sat back in his chair, groaning. "That's putting it mildly."

"With Justin Manor. . . or Alex?"

"Both," he admitted grudgingly.

"So?"

"I saw Manor, all right, at his office."

"How'd it go?" Randy took a long drink of his beer and settled back, closing his eyes against the bright afternoon sun.

"It went all right, I guess. At least," reflected Jake, "I think he got my message. . . ."

"You rough him up?"

Jake fell silent for a moment. "Some. Not bad enough."

"And?" Randy suppressed a smile.

"And I told him to stay away from Sedona and Alex. I guess I told him that eventually we'd nail him on the Twelvetrees murder."

"Think we will? I don't know, Jake. It's a tough one. He'll have to slip up somewhere 'cause we've got nothing hard to go in with for an indictment."

"Slip up?" Jake laughed cruelly. "That's a joke! We've got Alex out there—God knows where. Sitting like a duck on a pond!"

"You really think Manor's gonna go for her?"

"He hasn't got a choice, Randy. He's gone too far now, and he'll lose everything if she stands in his way." Jake's hooded eyes beneath the sunglasses stared out across the desert vista. "Yeah, I'm sure he'll make a move. And soon. Call it an old cop's sixth sense."

"Alex better get herself back here," said Randy in a deadly serious voice. "And when she does, we'll put someone on her twenty-four hours a day."

"Yeah. If and *when* she gets back." Then Jake unfolded himself from the chair. "Mind if I try calling her place again?"

"Go ahead." Randy's eyes followed Jake's form carefully as he entered the back door.

Jake dialed again. Twice. Still no answer. He began to worry, more, he realized, than was actually necessary at this point. For all he really knew, Alex might have stopped on her way out of Scottsdale to go shopping for something. It was a Saturday. Women always shopped on Saturdays, didn't they? And when they were upset, they bought a hat. Or was it shoes?

"She home yet?" asked Randy when Jake returned.

"No."

"Look, if you don't mind my saying so, pal, you seem a little rattled."

Jake looked at his friend quietly for a minute. "I am worried. We all should be."

Randy shifted his large frame in his seat, and appeared to be thinking. "You think you're a little more worried about Alex than you would be over some Joe Blow out there?"

"What's it matter?" retorted Jake gruffly.

"Thought we were friends here, Jake." Randy fixed him with his gaze.

"What're you driving at?"

"You. . . and Alex."

Jake's first reaction was one of anger. He'd always been really private and he didn't like anyone, even his best friend, prying into his business.

Randy sensed his mood. "I just thought you might want to talk. You look pretty low right now, partner. I'm only offering. . . ."

Jake backed down, just a notch. "There's nothing to say. I'm pretty low. That's all."

"And how does Alex feel about all this?"

"All what?" he shot back irritably.

"Come on, Jake. You and Alex both looked like you might break if someone touched you at dinner the other night in that Mexican joint."

Jake shook his head. "That obvious?"

"Yeah. It's all Janet's been talking about since." Randy groaned, rolling his eyes.

"Well," said Jake, "you saw it all then. I guess I made another mess out of things."

"Your fault, huh?"

"Sure. Isn't it always?"

"You mean Linda?"

"That's exactly what I mean, pal. I'm not good for anyone anymore. Guess it's a fact of life."

"You know, you amaze me, Jake. You have one bad experience with a woman—and a pretty hard woman at that, if I might say so—and you're ready to lock yourself up and throw away the key. It's pretty sad, if you want my opinion there, buddy."

"I don't want your opinion."

"Well, you got it anyway." They both sat silently glaring at each other for a long tense moment.

It was finally Randy who eased off. "Guess I shot off my big mouth again. Sorry, Jake."

"No problem."

"No. I mean it. It's none of my business what you do with your life or Alex's or anybody's."

"That's right."

"So all I guess I'm trying to say is that I wish you wouldn't be so hard on yourself."

Jake shrugged. "I guess it's the way I am. If I could change," he growled pensively, "I would."

Randy looked at him for an uncomfortable moment. "You could at least try."

THE TWO MEN AND CECILY helped Janet in with the groceries—a week's worth for the family.

"How can four people eat all this?" mumbled Jake, lugging in a huge sack of dog food over his shoulder.

"Easy," declared Janet. "And I'll run out of milk by Tuesday." Oddly, the family setting, hauling in the groceries, Randy's complaints about the cost, made Jake feel curiously envious.

"Stay for dinner?" called Janet from the kitchen.

Jake shook his head. "I don't think so, Janet, but thanks anyway."

"I can't afford to feed him," put in Randy, shaking his head at the eight sacks of groceries.

"Well," replied Janet, joining them on the front porch, "Bobby should be back tomorrow morning. I'll get him to call as soon as he gets in."

"Good," said Jake. "The more I think on it, the more I'm sure he'll do fine."

"Oh, Mr. Brannigan," piped up Cecily, "I still think I should have gone with him, but Bobby wouldn't let me. . . and neither would mom."

The three adults watched her go, shaking their heads.

Jake drove the department's Blazer back to the sheriff's parking lot and started up the old Pontiac. His mind was now consumed with one single thought: would he find Alex's car in her driveway?

He drove the short distance across town doing at least ten miles per hour over the speed limit, swearing under his breath at the slow-poke tourist traffic jamming the main road. A woman driver yelled at him once to slow down. Jake never heard her.

And then he was on Alex's road, and he could see the top of the house over the trees and the entrance to the drive.

He pulled in.

Her car was not there.

But then, he hadn't really believed for one moment that it would be.

About seven that evening, when she still hadn't arrived back, he let himself into her house with the hidden key. It had been a long afternoon. He'd read a little, dialed her parents' number in Scottsdale a dozen times, worried about Bobby's safety on his overnight camping trip and stood staring out his window into the driveway for longer than he cared to think about.

And so he'd walked down the outside steps of the garage and crossed the lawn to her kitchen door and stood there.

The house seemed dismally empty. It was as if she'd been gone forever. Even her scent had faded in the soft red glow of evening.

He strode into the living room, glanced around, walked to the front window and looked out into the drive. Finally he stood next to the couch, staring down at the dead roses.

Idly he picked one up. The blood-red one. His unfocused eyes stared off into the middle distance, and he thought about Randy's words—that he *could* change. He thought about the bleak future and he tried, he tried as hard as he could, to envision Alex in that dreary scenario but somehow he could still only see desolation.

He dropped the rose, missing the box and scattering faded petals on the couch and floor, turned, and walked slowly out of the silent house.

CHAPTER TWENTY-TWO

THE ONLY REMNANT of reason that had remained to Alex that morning told her to leave as quickly as possible. Under no circumstances was she about to sit in that house and wait for Jake. She couldn't. Wildly, she had looked around at the plush pastel interior. She had fifteen or twenty minutes, she figured, no more, and she'd have to be gone.

She dashed into the bedroom, grabbed a navy-blue skirt from her small suitcase, a blue-and-white polka-dotted blouse and some high-heeled sandals. She was about to run a comb through her hair when the phone rang.

"Blast it!" she swore. Was it him again? Probably not. It could be her father, worried about her. She grabbed the receiver on the second ring.

It was George Twelvetrees from Flagstaff.

"Alex, I'm sorry to bother you, but something's come up. I've been trying to track you down since yesterday."

"What is it, George?" She hoped she didn't sound impatient, but her eyes wouldn't budge from the hand of her watch moving inexorably toward the time Jake would drive into the driveway.

"I got your number from your office. I hope that's okay. Yesterday my wife got a huge box of flowers. White roses with one red one. Must have cost a fortune. But there was this note. Very odd. It wasn't signed and said 'Hope your newborn child will be healthy.' That's all. Alex, I have a bad feeling about those flowers."

"George, I got the same flowers. It was Manor."

"I knew it!" George sounded alarmed. "Alex, I've got to protect my family. Maybe we should. . . ."

"George, listen. We've scared Manor. That's exactly what I wanted. Don't worry. He's in Scottsdale right now. I'll take care of it. Just don't give in. Don't do anything!"

"Alex. . . ."

"Please, George, trust me."

"You sure? If anything happens. . . . I'll tell you, it really upset Madge. That's all she needs now."

"I know. I know. We'll have him soon though. Look, I'll go see him today. I'll tell him you're thinking of selling but that I want to look into it further. Then he'll leave you alone."

"Alex, you sure that's a good idea? I mean, when I think of my poor old father. . . ."

"Don't worry, I'll take care of it." Hurry, George, be convinced, please.

"Okay, I guess you know what you're doing."

"See you, George. I'll call on Monday. I promise."

In a panic, she grabbed her purse and sunglasses and raced out of the house, checking only to see that the door was locked. For a second she was afraid her car wouldn't start, but it did. She backed out of the driveway too fast, spun the steering wheel and raced away down the street in the quiet early morning. She could have sworn, as she careened around the corner of the block, that she saw the white Blazer in her rearview mirror. But she couldn't be sure of that.

She turned onto Scottsdale Drive, got lost in the traffic and drew her first breath in what seemed like ages. She was safe. Jake could never find her now.

She pulled into the lot of a Village Inn, carefully parking her car in the back of the building, just in case *he* drove by, and went inside.

She sat at the counter and ordered coffee and an English muffin. She felt safe there—one insignificant person in a crowd. Idly she flipped through a newspaper left on the counter by a previous customer.

She read the headlines, "Gulf War Intensifies." "Temperature to hit 109, possibility of rain showers by midweek." She saw the words but didn't really grasp the meaning. It was something to do.

She had another cup of coffee and began to think about George's phone call. Manor must be getting really desperate—or was it Tom? No, Tom would never do anything like that; he would worry about what people would think. Besides, Manor had admitted to Jake that he'd sent her the flowers.

A slow anger began to burn in her breast. How dare Manor send a note like that to Madge Twelvetrees? It was brutal, sadistic. The man was a monster, just as Jake had said. She could not really fathom such a person; Justin Manor held no reality for her except as a criminal to bring to justice, an abstract idea.

She'd told George she would see Manor today. Now, anger burned so brightly within her that she couldn't possibly leave Scottsdale without seeing him. It was Saturday. Would he be home? His office would be closed but he might be there—he might be anywhere. Yet Jake had seen him yesterday....

It was still early but she didn't care. She went to the public phone by the rest-room door, found the Scottsdale phone book and searched under *M*. Yes, there was Justin Manor, Lois Manor, Manor Development and another number for Manor Resort Estates. She'd try them all if she had to even this early on Saturday morning.

She tried his home number first. It rang five times, and then a recording came on in Manor's resonant, cultured voice, which was carefully devoid of any regional accent. "I'm not at home at the moment, but if you'll leave a message at the tone, I'll get back to you. Darcy, I'll meet you at the club at five for tennis."

She decided not to leave a message, since she could always do it later if necessary. Then she pulled a scrap of paper from her purse and scrabbled for a pen. She wrote, "Darcy 5:00 P.M., the club." What club? She could try calling some tennis clubs in the area if she hadn't found him by five. At least he was in town. That helped.

It turned out to be absurdly easy. She dialed his office, and he answered immediately.

"This is Alex Crawford. I'm in Scottsdale. Could I see you today?"

Manor gave a rich throaty chuckle. "So soon, Alex? I am so glad you've decided to see reason."

She'd let him think that was it, that he'd scared her, or that George had insisted. "I'm sorry I have to disturb you on Saturday, but I'm going back to Sedona later today."

"Quite all right. I work seven days a week. My job never ends, Alex."

"When?"

"About one o'clock. Ring the bell by the front door—it's locked."

"All right. See you at one."

"I'm looking forward to it. Goodbye."

She looked at her watch; she had nearly four hours to waste. She was afraid to go back to her parents' in case Jake was waiting for her, she'd shopped yesterday and the county attorney's office in Phoenix was closed.

She ended up going to the zoo in Phoenix, walking along the hard-baked, dusty paths between the rolling hills of the zoo terrain. She loved the animals and the small children's reactions to them, but mostly she sat on a bench in the shade, nibbled on her popcorn and thought of what she was going to say to Justin Manor.

At one o'clock sharp she was ringing Manor's bell, keyed up from the long wait. Manor came down to the lobby to let her in. He wore pale-beige slacks and a white crushed-cotton camp shirt with lots of pockets and buttons and epaulets. A stunning man, a beautifully turned out, classy figure of a man: tanned, virile, well-muscled, tall.

"Nice to see you again, Alex." He took her hand, held it for a moment but did not shake it as he would have a man's. His grasp was reassuring and warm. "So glad you could make it." As if he'd invited her to a party.

He led her to an elevator, and it made her a touch uncomfortable to be closed in with him in the confined area. How silly of her.

She sat on a sofa in a corner of his office; he sat across the round smoked-glass table from her.

"Now, what can I do for you?" She noticed that the smooth, vaguely sexual overtones she'd felt so strongly in Sedona were still there, but subdued, as if Manor had other, more important fish to fry. Or, perhaps, since Jake, she was immune to his silky charms.

She smiled sweetly and gave her prepared statement. "My office in Flagstaff has asked me to look further into this land deal involving Manor Development. Coconino County is very careful who they award development permits to. You understand, I'm sure. So they know that I am here today." Her eyes met his coolly and locked with his blue gaze. Oh, he knew, all right, exactly what she meant: *touch me and you'll never get away with it.*

"Of course," he soothed.

"In spite of my client's willingness, I have advised him to refuse the sale because of lack of information."

"I can give you any information you need right now."

"Wonderful. My office would like to know, for instance, what provisions you've made for housing over two hundred employees. And there is a concern that your pro shop is in a flash-flood area."

"I'll have those points looked into first thing Monday morning. Anything else?" He smiled pleasantly.

"Perhaps you can tell me, Justin, exactly why George and I received flowers and insinuating notes."

"Insinuating? My dear Miss Crawford, nothing could be further from the truth. I was merely sending my fondest wishes to both of you. Your mother is, I take it, quite well?"

"Quite." Then she continued. "I want you to be

aware that the decision not to sell is my decision entirely and that I take full responsibility for it."

"I only hope I can still change your mind then." He was unruffled, cool.

"I doubt it."

He shrugged. "Excuse me, would you like something to drink? A beer or a mixed drink? Fresh-squeezed orange juice, perhaps? I'm going to have some myself."

"Why, yes, orange juice please." Oh, she'd play his little game all right....

He went to an alcove and opened a small refrigerator. She had time to notice the wall mural, a priceless kachina doll, a very good Navajo rug and a full bookshelf. Casually, she stood and moved around the room, as if appreciative. The books caught her eye: *The Fourth World of the Hopi*, *The Navajo*, *Indian Legends of the Four Corners Area*. And several mysteries by the famed Navajo writer, Tony Hillerman. There were some anthropological studies that Alex's mother had, as well.

Then Manor was coming back with a tall glass of juice and a white smile, as if they were the best of friends.

"I was admiring your kachina," she said quickly. "It's Mausau, isn't it?"

"Yes, the bloody-faced guardian of this lovely fourth world. I found that one at Hotevilla."

"A nice piece," Alex murmured, taking the glass from his hand.

"I keep it to remind me how fleeting our world really is. Soon, you know, the fourth world will be destroyed by war and the fifth world will be created."

"Yes, so my grandfather tells me."

They were playing a game, a very clever, ultra-civilized game: If I make a statement that has a double meaning I get a point, but if you, in turn, make a triple-faceted statement, you score higher. Meanings behind meanings, words twisted, shaded, tortured into unfamiliar forms. Oh, she could play his game.

She sipped at her juice. "You seem to be an expert on Southwestern Indians, Justin."

"Only in a very modest way," he smiled.

"We're working on a difficult case up in Sedona. There has been a man killed, seemingly by a Navajo witch. I wonder if you could cast some light on why someone would try to make it look as if a witch had done it. And how he made the claw marks." She stared at him fiercely, thrilled by her own temerity, her heart beating madly.

Manor laughed. "I have a very superficial knowledge of Indian lore, Alex. It's more along the lines of how to recognize a good rug, an old carving, something like that. I'm afraid witches are quite out of my realm. I'm surprised you can take that stuff seriously."

"The Indians believe it."

"But you don't?" he asked.

"No." She declared flatly.

"Well, I'm truly sorry, but I can't help you. If you want advice on whether or not to buy a rug, I'd be glad to oblige."

"I think I'd better be going now," Alex said. "I'm to meet a friend for lunch at three."

"A little late for lunch, isn't it?"

"Not at all. I sleep late."

"No more questions? I'll let you out then."

The elevator again—she wondered whether he noticed that she stood as far from him as possible. The empty, echoing lobby.

"Goodbye, Alex. I do hope you change your mind about the land sale."

"It's unlikely. I think it would set a dangerous precedent."

"Not at all." He smiled. "But you're entitled to your opinion, naturally."

She stepped out onto the hot pavement, heard the

heavy oak door click shut behind her and walked brisk-
ly away into the sun-baked streets of Scottsdale.

BY TEN O'CLOCK Saturday evening Jake was looking out
of his apartment window every five minutes. He didn't
mean to, but his eyes strayed rebelliously toward her
driveway as if on a timing clock.

Jake paced the small apartment, thinking. Her
parents. Where had she said her parents were? The
reservation, with Fred Kwáhu. How in the devil did you
get in touch with someone at the Hopi village of New
Oraibi? Fred certainly had no phone. But there had to
be a way—for emergencies.

He dialed the sheriff's department switchboard. The
girls on night duty there knew everything—or could
darn well find out.

"Coconino County Sheriff," a voice answered.
Somehow not being totally alone gave Jake a ridiculous
boost.

"Hi, Annie, it's Jake. Having a quiet night?"

"Oh, just the usual—a car accident on seventeen and
a couple of drunks at Tico's." He could hear her snapping her gum over the line.

"Anyone hurt in the accident?" he asked casually.
He had visions of Alex run off the road, smashed,
bleeding. . . .

"An old couple, out of state. The guy fell asleep, I
guess. The ambulance just picked them up."

Jake felt relief wash over him. "Say, Annie, how do
you go about getting hold of someone at New Oraibi?"

"You got a girlfriend there?" Annie asked teasingly.

"Sure, sure. And she likes to be called at midnight."

"What's up, Jake?"

"Nothing much. Just checking on something."

"Let me see. New Oraibi. Yeah, there's a guy there
that has a phone. His name's John Longstretch. But he
sure isn't going to appreciate a call at this time of
night." She snapped her gum extra loudly as if to punc-
tuate her sentence.

"You got that number, Annie?" You had to handle the night girls carefully—they had a certain way of being cranky if you didn't. It must have been the hours they worked.

"Lemme see." He heard the rustle of pages. "Sure, here it is. 575-4200. John Longstretch. And, Jake...."

"Yeah?"

"You better tell me what this is all about tomorrow. I hate mysteries."

"I'll tell you, I promise. Thanks, Annie, I owe you."

The fact that it was almost midnight didn't even faze Jake by then. He dialed the number and heard the distant ring—over and over. Maybe John Longstretch wasn't home. Maybe....

"Hello?" A groggy voice answered. "What in heck do you want?"

"John Longstretch?"

"Sure is. Now what's going on here?"

"This is Undersheriff Jake Brannigan from Sedona. I'd like you to do me a favor."

"What time is it? Do you *know* what time it is?"

"Yes, Mr. Longstretch, but this is important. I need to get in touch with Judge Crawford."

"He ain't gonna like this. You sure it can't wait?"

"I'm sure, Mr. Longstretch. It's official business."

"I'll have to go get him at Fred's. It'll be a spell."

"No problem. I'll just hang on here."

It must have been nearly twenty minutes that Jake waited, his heart thudding, his mouth dry, his fingers drumming on the tabletop. It felt like an eternity. He wondered whether this was all a waste of time, a fool's errand. He wondered if Judge Crawford knew anything at all about his daughter's whereabouts. He wondered if the judge would be so irritated he'd hang up on him or so worried he'd have a stroke.

"Hello?" The judge's sleepy voice, tinged with alarm, came on the line.

"Undersheriff Jake Brannigan here, Judge Crawford. Sorry to disturb you so late...."

"It's Alexandra, isn't it?"

Sharp man. "Well, I'm just attempting to locate her, judge. Can you help me at all? For instance, has she contacted you today?"

"She's not back in Sedona yet." It was a statement.

"No sir."

"She left a message with John Longstretch this afternoon. Just a second." Jake could hear him talk to John in low tones. "About six or seven o'clock. She told him that she was going to think things out before she went back to Sedona and that we weren't to worry."

Jake's heart lurched in hope. "Do you know where she went?"

"Hold on." The judge spoke with John again. "She called it one of those Indian names. John says it means the House Made of Dawn."

"Ah." Jake drew in a deep breath. Of course. "Thank you very much, judge."

"Is she in any danger?"

"I'm sure she's not, sir. I just wanted to check."

"Are you going to try to find her—now?"

"Yes, sir."

There was a long, pulsing silence on the line. "You call me when you find her, young man. No matter when it is."

"I'll do that, sir. Thank you very much."

When Jake hung up, his palms were damp. It could be nothing. She'd gone up to her favorite place to heal herself, to find peace. He understood that perfectly. It was just that she was totally unprotected, totally alone up there.

And then it struck him like a hammer blow: Bobby was up there too! Bobby had hiked up there Saturday afternoon to spend the night alone. It was his Indian rite of manhood.

Bobby—his son—up there in the dark lonely canyon. Maybe he was camped somewhere else and in the dark no one would see him. Maybe.... And then again, there might be someone else up there, the night walker, the wolf who killed, the witch who destroyed for no reason at all. But Jake knew the reason, and he had to find both Bobby and Alex before that other person—or thing—did.

It was twelve thirty-five. No time to waste. Maybe too late already. No! His mind recoiled in horror. He couldn't lose everything he loved like that. No!

His brain worked furiously, efficiently. He was dialing the number before his thought was finished. "Annie, it's Jake again. Is Kyle on tonight? Good. Put him on, will you? Thanks, Annie."

"Kyle Sanchez."

"Kyle. It's Jake. Look, can you do me a favor?" He explained precisely what he wanted: was there an outlet onto the highway for the dirt road that went up the canyon behind Someday Ranch to the old cliff dwelling? There was. Could a car drive it? Part way, depending on the spring runoff. Would Kyle drive up there, follow the road as far as he could and report back by radio if there were any cars up there? Particularly a late-model red Saab.

"This serious?" asked Kyle.

"Could be. Then again, it could be nothing. I'll be down at the department. Call in as soon as you can. And Kyle, step on it."

"Roger."

Jake hung up and rubbed his left hand over his face. He was tired and keyed up, on the edge of panic. He took a couple of deep breaths to fight it down. He retrieved his gun and holster automatically from the bedroom, slammed out of the apartment and drove down to the sheriff's department.

It would be at least forty-five minutes, maybe more before Kyle called in. And then, it could be nothing. Maybe there was no car there at all, maybe only Alex's. Then what?

He waited, pacing the floor of the sheriff's department, drinking innumerable cups of coffee until his nerves jittered and his heart jumped at every ring of the switchboard phone, every scratch of the dispatcher's radio.

"Take it easy," said Ken Ryan, the other night-duty officer. "It can't be *that* bad."

Jake didn't answer as he finished another cup of coffee.

"Hey, if it's that bad, maybe you should call Randy."

"Not yet," rasped Jake. "I'll know the time."

There was another scratch on the dispatch radio. "Unit ten here."

It was Kyle! Jake rushed to Annie's desk and hung over her shoulder while she answered. "Go ahead unit ten."

"I am approximately five miles east of Highway 179 south of Bell Rock. There is a red '82 Saab, Arizona license plate number Harry, Able, Mary 692 parked here. There is also a metallic-blue Lincoln Continental, Arizona plate number John, David, Mary, Zero, Zero, Zero. Both are empty and locked. Over."

Jake grabbed the mike from Annie's hand. "Kyle! Anything else at all? Signs of a struggle? Footprints?"

"Too dark to see. Just two locked cars, both with cold engines. That what you wanted, Jake?"

"Yeah, that's it. Thanks. Stay where you are. I'm sending reinforcements. Hang in there, Kyle. This may be a long night. Over."

"Okay, boss, but send up some coffee and doughnuts at least. Over and out."

Okay. Now he knew the worst. There was no need to check the owner of that blue Continental. Any idiot could figure that one out: Justin D. Manor would drive a Continental—it fit him—JDM-000. He needed to get to the cliff dwelling fast. It was one-twenty. Alex had parked there hours ago most likely. How long? She had called John Long tretch at six or seven. A long time. Not too long, he prayed.

Sunrise was at around four-thirty or five in the morning—three hours—too long to wait. What could get him there sooner? What could navigate a dark, treacherous canyon?

It came to him suddenly and then there was no hesitation. He dialed Randy's number and waited impatiently through one ring, two rings, three rings. . . . "Come on, Randy," he muttered into the receiver.

"Webster here." He sounded alert, fresh. Maybe he was just used to calls like this.

"It's Jake. Listen, I need a helicopter right away."

"Jake, you crazy?"

"Deadly serious, old buddy. I need a pilot—a good one—and a helicopter with searchlights."

"What's up?"

"Alex Crawford has gone up to her cliff dwelling, and Manor's after her. It's too long to explain, but it's going down, Randy. Bobby's up there too."

Randy gave a low whistle. "Okay. The nearest helicopter is up in Flagstaff. It'll take time. . . ."

"We don't have time, pal."

"I'll do the best I can. They've got to round up the pilot, probably fuel up, check her out, fly down here. There'll be some hot tempers over this. It better pan out."

"Trust me, Randy."

"Yeah, yeah. I'll call Flagstaff, then I'll be down."

"Sure thing."

Jake had Annie ring up some of the deputies. He wanted two Blazers to meet Kyle and drive up to the head of the canyon. They were four-wheel-drive vehicles with winches and high clearance, so he figured they'd be able to negotiate it. Just in case. No one was going to get out of that canyon without their knowing it.

Randy called back. "It'll take time. The helicopter's missing on a cylinder. There are plugs there, but they haven't tuned it yet."

"Damn!"

"They said an hour or so."

Jake ground his teeth in frustration. Maybe the

Blazers would get there first and be able to do something. And then, maybe it would be too late—but he wouldn't even consider that.

"Hurry," he ground out between clenched teeth. "Hurry up."

He wondered what was going on up there in the dark canyon, in the House Made of Dawn. He prayed, foolishly, futilely, that Alex's ancestors would protect her, that Bobby wasn't involved at all.

And he wondered just how he would live if the only two people he loved in this world were harmed.

CHAPTER TWENTY-THREE

BY THE TIME Alex had spotted the interstate sign for Bumble Bee, halfway home, she knew she had to stop. She hadn't slept a wink the night before once she'd left Jake, and she was really afraid she'd fall asleep at the wheel. She finally spotted a rest area ahead with some shade trees—it was the hottest part of the late afternoon—and had pulled off the road.

She had actually slept.

It couldn't have been more than an hour, but it helped. She glanced at her watch: six o'clock in the evening. A faintly cooler breeze ruffled her hair through the open window of the car. She felt so stiff and hot and sticky that her physical discomfort almost overshadowed her mental turmoil.

She went to the rest area's ladies' room, splashed cold water on her face and combed her hair, redoing the rubber band that held it back. Since she couldn't meet her own eyes in the water-spotted mirror, she got only an impression of paleness and eyes shadowed by dark smudges. She looked like a hag; she felt like a hag.

Jake was waiting for her back home in Sedona, she knew, probably furious she hadn't shown up yet. If he was worried—and she gave him credit for worrying; after all, it was his job—*if* he was worried she didn't care. Let him stew. She'd confronted Manor herself and she was still alive and kicking.

She realized slowly, as she drove up north on the twisting mountain highway, that she could not go home, right next door to Jake. She needed some time to set her mind straight, to search once more for an inner core of peace that was growing further away every day.

She thought instantly of the reservation and her grandfather, but her parents were there and they'd ask too many questions. She needed time—and peace.

It came to her: the House Made of Dawn. She could drive in as far as the car would go, then walk. She knew where the dirt road up the canyon started at the highway; she wouldn't even have to bother the Websters. She didn't want to see them—or anybody.

She could sleep a little there, perhaps, see the sun rise and the golden rays touch the crumbled chambers, think, make some decisions. She needed a link to the past to regain her balance, a steadying touchstone to get her through this time. She had to decide what to do about Justin Manor, but amazingly, even overshadowing that, she needed time to recover the courage necessary to face Jake Brannigan again.

She stopped for gas once, got a soda pop but turned away from the snacks with nausea. She thought better on an empty stomach anyway.

She remembered that she had promised to call her father before she left. It had slipped her mind. She phoned John Longstretch from the gas station and asked him to give her father a message: she was going to the House Made of Dawn to sort things out. She was fine, perfectly safe and would be home in the morning. It was easier to give the message and hang up than to talk to her father.

She almost missed the unmarked turnoff just north of Someday Ranch. It was only a pair of tracks, really, across the dry red earth, but she saw it in time and pulled off the highway. Dust rose in a red plume behind her car as she drove slowly up the winding dirt track. She tried to avoid the rocks—all she needed now was a flat tire! It was a tedious, difficult drive, and more than once she wished she was on horseback.

Dusk fell and she switched her headlights on, driving even more cautiously. Eventually she came to a washed-out gully across the road that she didn't dare navigate in her car. She got out, stretched, and watched a lopsided moon rise in the east, nearly full. Digging in her small suitcase, she located a pair of slacks, her tennis shoes and a sweater. It would be cool later; already the air had lost its fierce daytime heat. She wished she had a flashlight in her car, but there was nothing nearly so practical—only some books of matches, an old comb and a road map. As she was locking her car, she thought she heard the distant sound of a car engine below her somewhere—probably a four-wheel-drive vehicle on one of the dead-end spurs leading back to the highway.

Shafts of moonlight brightened the canyon floor as she began to walk. She was surprised at how light it really was. Had her ancestors hunted under a summer moon such as this? Or held their spring festival, Soyal, to celebrate the renewal of life, and danced long into the warm night? She had no fear of the dark; the clicks and rustling, the swish of wind in a tree, the trickle of water nearby were welcome sounds to her ears. It was as if centuries had slid off her shoulders and she could feel the quiet thaw out her tension. Yes, this was a good idea. But she would not think yet about anything. She would simply let her body take her where it would, sensing the night noises, the caress of a breeze on her warm cheek, the scent of piñon and sage and dust.

An owl hooted from somewhere. Alex smiled in the darkness; it was night and an owl was a good omen. Her feet found the path easily, instinctively avoiding rocks and branches and cracks in the dry earth.

Once she stopped short and listened—an animal moved in the brush behind her, a coyote perhaps, or a wildcat. It would not bother her, she knew. Man walked alone on the red earth, threatened only by the bear and the wolf, but most often by another human being.

It took an hour and a half or so, Alex guessed, to reach the bottom of the cliff. She could not see the House Made of Dawn but she felt its presence keenly. Just above her were the familiar, comforting broken walls, tumbled roof pales, walls, stairs, rooms. She could sit there waiting, thinking, watching the sun rise across the canyon until its long fingers reached above the canyon rim to gild the ancient pueblo with glory. By then she would have straightened her problems out, made her life orderly again, as it had been before Joseph Twelvetrees and Jake Brannigan. She could do it.

She climbed carefully up the steep path, endlessly glad that she'd be descending it in daylight. Going down would be much harder in the dark. The moon cast geometric shadows on the chambers of the cliff dwelling, pale silver and steel gray and black angles—squares and rectangles and arrow-straight horizontal and perpendicular lines. Only the gap left by a fallen rock occasionally marred the purity of its ancient form.

Alex sighed, sat down on a wall and felt the silence and tranquillity of the place fill her. She could not fathom why the Navajo were afraid of the Anasazi cliff dwellings. There was no fearful magic there, no witches, no frightening presence of any sort. She felt only harmony and peace.

Her watch, she thought, said eleven o'clock, but it was hard to read by moonlight. It didn't matter....

She felt tired, physically tired, and curled up in the still-warm floor of a chamber to sleep for a time.

It was the chill that woke her, but she rubbed her arms and felt refreshed, renewed. It was as if she'd come to some decisions in her sleep. Her mind worked efficiently all of a sudden, as clear as the night air around her. Things began falling in place. Justin Manor could be indicted on several counts of harassment—she'd find the people who had dropped cases against him, dig up the facts, convince them to testify. She'd somehow prove he was in Sedona on the day Joseph was killed. She'd press his creditors to call in his loans if she had to, let his business partners and clients know how shaky his empire was. She'd attack from all fronts—legally. It might take a couple of years, but she'd get him on one charge or another. Maybe even a grand jury would be convened to look into Manor Development Corporation from top to bottom.

Then there was Jake. She realized, very simply, that she didn't have to do anything about Jake at all. It was his decision. She'd let him know how she felt, and now it was entirely up to him. He could come to her, he could pack and leave, he could try to ignore what had gone on between them. Jake Brannigan had to do battle with his own demons and vanquish them or go under in defeat. It was all up to him.

As Alex sat on the low wall looking out over the canyon, her knees hugged to her chest; it occurred to her that there was a tenuous paling of the eastern sky. It was a mere impression, no more. Then it became more definite—a glow, a vast source of energy just below the horizon. The sun creator of the Hopis. It was *qoyangnuptu*, the first phase of dawn.

How many of the ancient ones, the one- and two-horn priests, the kachina spirits, the troubled clan leaders had sat there in centuries long past awaiting the dawn and the answers to their questions?

Then she heard, breaking the pristine silence, the faint but distinct noise of a stone dislodged. Was it a small animal, an owl? Her senses sharpened, and she strained to hear a repetition of the noise. For the first time a touch of anxiety pricked her.

There! Another faint scuffle, a stone scratching across another? Alex's heart squeezed. A great pale-golden fan spread across the eastern sky above the ancient mesas now, and she could see trees and rocks outlined, the rim of the opposite canyon wall silhouetted against the sky. *Sikangnuqa*, the yellow light that reveals man's breath.

Her own breath came fast; she sat paralyzed, listening, listening. Another scuffle, without doubt a footstep, scratching on the stones of the rough, climbing path up the steep cliffside.

All the chilling tales came back to her in a rush—the tales of her childhood at her grandfather's knee—of demons and demigods and snakes that spoke and birds that had extraordinary powers, of sorcerers and spirits.

The claw marks in Joseph's throat, unreasonable, inexplicable, the talk of the witch. The witch that was a wolf or a man, an evil being that needed no reason to kill. Was it the witch after her?

Another pebble scrabbled across the ground, closer now. She couldn't scream, couldn't move. The sky lightened imperceptibly, throwing elongated shadows across the canyon, jagged lines and stripes of light and darkness. She strained desperately to see down the path, but it was still bathed in shadow. Her heart pounded drumbeats in her ears: the witch, the witch, the witch. . . .

The disturbance moved even nearer and a shadowy figure materialized out of the canyon, looming huge over her, indistinct and terrifying. Her muscles finally reacted and she sprang up, whirled, and tried to run, but a hand of iron was on her, spinning her back around. In the eerie half-light of the reddening sunrise she finally saw his face, a desperate face, monstrous in the quickening light, so horribly familiar.

She tried to break away from his grip; she heard a scream coming from her own throat. He said nothing but held her arm, pulling her closer and closer. Then she knew with horrifying clarity what he was going to do. He was going to push her off the cliff to her death and they'd find her with her throat savaged by wolf's claws.

"No!" she screamed, hitting at him with her free hand, kicking, struggling.

But his grip only tightened; he was so very strong, as strong as a witch, a wolf man. She screamed again, heaving herself away from him, but tripped, fell heavily on the hard ground and dragged him down with her.

"There's no one to hear you," she heard him say, and she knew it was true. No one. She was filled with a momentary sharp-edged regret, but there was no time.

He was pulling her along the ground, dragging her to the low wall that rimmed the edge of the great drop to the canyon floor. She grabbed onto anything she could, a rock, a crumbling doorframe, a corner of the build-

ing, but her fingernails broke and the ancient adobe
crumbled. He dragged her slowly, inch by inch, inexorably to the edge, to her death.

She dug her heels in, twisted and pulled, but his grip
never slackened. He only slapped her hard with his free
hand so that her head snapped around and her ears
rang. Her breath came in short, tearing gasps, and her
heart felt ready to burst.

Somewhere in a far recess of her mind she thought
she heard a scraping behind them on the path, but that
couldn't be. She twisted desperately, forgetting the
faint noise in her terror. But there it was again, and a
voice. Wasn't that shrill youthful voice—a familiar
voice somehow—yelling something?

Bobby Brannigan!

Her mind could not work quickly enough to account
for his presence; there was only time to register overwhelming amazement. The man had succeeded in dragging her to the parapet. Nothing lay before her but dark
emptiness.

"Bobby!" she screamed, gasping, "help me! Bobby!"

There was a scuffle and a shorter figure was flailing at
her attacker, trying to drag him away from her. There
was also the sound of a dog growling viciously and a
small brown shadow darting in to snap at his pant leg.

But the man gave a short harsh laugh and held Bobby
off effortlessly with one arm, kicking the dog.

"Alex!" yelled Bobby. "Leave her alone! Alex!"

He had her on her feet now, pulling her upright, forcing her over the edge. She kicked, punched and twisted,
terrified of the drop that was so close she could feel the
cold dark void reaching up for her.

Alex would never remember precisely when she first
heard the distinctive chopping sound made by the helicopter's blades as they beat at the air. But it seemed suddenly that the whole world was filled with the whump,
whump, whump of the hovering copter, the wild
whirlwinds of dust kicked up by the blades, the shud-

dering noise of the motor bearing down upon them, the blinding cone of light.

In the suffocating whirls of dust she could just barely see someone leaning out of the helicopter's door with a bullhorn, shouting something. But she couldn't hear above the roar, and the rushing backwash blew her hair into her eyes, blinding her again.

Her enemy looked up too, jerking her arm to pull her closer to the edge. His grip slipped infinitesimally as Bobby's dog attacked once more. Then suddenly Alex reared back, pulling away from him with all her strength, and she felt his hands slip a little more. Bobby was there, a rock in his hands, battering at the man's head while the dog snapped at his ankles.

Alex was shocked at the ferocity of her own attack. Blinded by dust and glaring light, deafened by noise, she struck at him frantically again and again. The man stumbled, and she shoved at him furiously, nearly losing her own footing at the crumbling edge of the cliff. Bobby hit at him again with his rock, then threw it in desperation, striking him on the cheek. The dog darted in to attack once more.

Then the man seemed to arch backward, as if reaching for the rapidly rising sun creator. The dirt at the cliff edge crumbled, and he was tumbling over. Even above the terrible sound of the helicopter, they heard a frightful scream tear itself from his throat, as his body plummeted down, down.

And then there was absolute stillness.

CHAPTER TWENTY-FOUR

THE SILENCE WAS EAR SHATTERING.

There was no helicopter, no blinding light or pounding rotors, there was no more sound from the darkly shadowed void below. There was only the frantic thudding of her heart and dawn's quickening light.

It was a long time before Alex became aware of the hard red earth beneath her hands, of the strangely peaceful chirping of a bird somewhere, of the reassuring dust-dry smell of the crumbled ruins.

And Bobby.

She turned her head slowly to see him crouched near her side, one arm around his dog, and she could discern his deathly white face and a purple bruise darkening already on his jaw.

"Bobby," she breathed, moving toward him. "Oh, Bobby!" The whisper became a sob, breaking the ghostly silence. She sobbed out his name again and again and held him to her. "Bobby...Bobby...."

The red light in the east intensified unheeded as the woman and boy clung to each other, desperately seeking comfort in the aftermath of the horror.

Long minutes later, the questions finally poured from Bobby's throat. "That man was trying to kill you! Why was he trying to kill you? Oh...Alex!"

But she couldn't talk, she couldn't explain. Not yet. Her own mind was still consumed with unanswered questions. Hadn't there been a helicopter there? Had she dreamed the whole nightmarish scene?

"The helicopter," Alex breathed. "Bobby, wasn't there a helicopter?"

"It flew down into the canyon," the boy said, gulping. "Why was he trying to kill you?"

Slowly they stood together, but Alex found herself sagging against a crumbled wall, staring mutely at her scratched and bleeding hands and then out across the brightening canyon. Quietly she tried to explain to Bobby the situation, but reasonable words kept failing her, only to be replaced by more sobs.

"It's all right," Bobby soothed once, holding her to him. "I wonder where the helicopter went?"

She shook her head. "I don't know." She could still feel Manor's hands on her, dragging her relentlessly. She shuddered with horror and couldn't stop trembling.

"It's dad, I'll bet," said Bobby.

"He couldn't know," Alex whispered.

"Sure, he knows everything. Everything important that is."

And as they talked, the full red dawn—*tálawva*—broke over the canyon as if to witness the violence that had been done to its House Made of Dawn. It touched Alex with silent warmth and light.

And then Indian barked at the big pale owl riding an ascending current of air from the canyon floor—an owl, hunting too late for its nocturnal habits, an odd, other-worldly creature in the bright light of the new day. It was the soul of someone, a lost soul, searching forever for rest and peace, Alex knew. She felt goose bumps rise on her arms even as the sun warmed her.

As the owl finally disappeared from sight Alex became aware of noises below them on the path leading to the House Made of Dawn. Indian barked once more.

"What's that?" said Alex, alerted.

"The men from the helicopter," Bobby guessed aloud as Alex hugged him closer to her. "Dad, I'll bet."

Alex saw him finally. Leading a handful of police officers, threading his way quickly through the ancient ruins toward them. He looked so strong to her in the awakening light, so capable and familiar and rugged—even his ravaged features gave her a kind of security.

Tears filled her eyes.

"Jake," she whispered, "Jake...."

JANET, OF COURSE, HAD TO HEAR it all. "And to *think*," she gushed from her seat on the family patio, "if Bobby hadn't been there...*and* his dog!"

Jake shook his blond head. "That's the last time he's going camping alone. Manhood rite! It's lucky both he and Alex weren't harmed." He looked sternly toward Randy, who nodded in agreement.

"And that man—" Janet grimaced "—what's his name?"

"Justin Manor." Alex's blue eyes caught Jake's for a prolonged moment.

"Yes, Justin Manor," Janet went on. "Can you *imagine* how desperate he must have been to think he could get away with such a thing?"

"He darn near did," mused Randy. "If it hadn't been for Jake and Bobby and Joseph Twelvetrees's crazy mutt." He laughed ruefully, taking a sip of his early-afternoon beer. "And to think I just about told Jake where to get off when he woke me up this morning and asked for a helicopter."

Jake frowned. "Well, except for Manor's trial, it's over now."

"Amen to that," breathed Alex.

Randy shook his head. "And what really slays me is that Manor lived through that fall!"

"Yes," breathed Alex.

"Were you relieved when they found him on that ledge?" Janet asked Alex.

"More than you can know."

"He should have bought the whole farm," complained Jake under his breath.

Alex's eyes snapped up to his. "No," she said firmly. "It's better this way. Let the courts handle him when he's healed."

"Lawyers," grumbled Jake.

"You know it's better. No one deserves to die like that, Jake."

"Well, what do you think he was trying to do to you?" put in Randy.

The two women exchanged glances before declaring simultaneously, "Cops!" Yet Alex understood—in a way, Manor did deserve to die for the dreadful, inhuman things he'd done. But the system works, she reminded herself, and a jury of his peers would decide his fate. In a way, she pitied him: a man blinded by worldly wealth and power when wealth was all around them, every day, in each golden blade of grass. . . .

It was just about then that Bobby, with Indian and Cecily on his heels, bounded out of the kitchen door. "Wait till you see this, dad! This will seal Alex's case in court!" cried Bobby.

Behind them was Kyle, and in his hand was a large clear plastic bag. As he approached the four adults, Alex's heart squeezed with unaccountable apprehension.

"Jake," she whispered.

"I'll have a look." Jake shot her a reassuring glance as he rose from his seat. Then, along with Randy he approached Kyle. "Interesting," was all he said as the men looked at the ominous contents of the plastic bag.

"What is it?" Janet came to her feet. "Is it some sort of evidence?"

But even before the men announced what Kyle had found on the canyon floor, hundreds of feet below Manor, Alex knew exactly what was in that bag. "It's the wolf claws," she whispered. Alex, too, rose from her chair but instead of heading toward the excited throng she walked pensively in the direction of the Websters' corral. She could hear their voices still as she leaned her elbows against the rail and tried to will the tenseness from her weary muscles.

An image flew through her consciousness then, the owl rising in the morning light. She'd thought it was Justin Manor's soul, but now she sensed—in that repressed, uncivilized corner of her mind—that it was instead dear old Joseph's soul that had finally taken wings from its earthly bondage and sought that mystic somewhere of which only the Indian knew.

"Have you had a chance to talk to your father yet?" Jake was standing next to her, his green eyes fixed on her profile.

"I called as soon as I got here. They'll be here later this afternoon."

"Kyle never should have brought those claws here."

"It's all right." Alex forced a wan smile. "They *are* evidence."

"Manor'll be nailed for sure."

For a time they stood together, elbows on the corral's rail, silently looking out over the expanse of desert beyond. The sun was intense now, at its summer zenith, brutalizing the land, sapping its moisture, causing small, scurrying animals to take shelter beneath the scant shrubs and rocks. Beyond the valley floor sat the giant mesas, striated and shimmering red in the day's heat, forming an illusive horizon against the brilliantly azure sky.

"You know, Jake," said Alex finally, "It's always the land, isn't it? I mean, men will do anything to possess it."

"Some will."

"Even my ancestors," she went on pensively. "The way they revered and cherished it was a kind of possession."

"Yes, in a way. . . ." Jake turned toward Alex then, quietly studying her. "Alex," he said finally, his deep voice more ragged than usual, "I'd. . . I want to talk to you."

She turned her blue eyes toward his face.

"Look," he began, "I. . . I'm not much with words. . . but this morning, well, I . . . ." The words failed him.

Alex smiled sympathetically. "I know. . ."

"No you don't!" he said harshly. "I'm a blind stupid idiot! I felt as if my whole life was flashing past my eyes when I saw you and Bobby struggling with that. . . ." And he used a terrible word then.

"Jake," admonished Alex.

"Sorry. But I don't know what else to call him."

"Go on," she urged softly.

"I don't know." He raked a hand through his straight blond hair. "I guess what I'm trying to say. . . ." She could see him swallow hard, the muscle ticking in his strong jaw. "I . . . I'd like to make it up to you."

"What, Jake?" Her heart was beating a little too strongly.

"You know."

"I don't know. Tell me."

"I've been a fool. You know, Alex, like you said, a coward."

"And . . . ?"

He looked at her with a dangerous light in his eyes. "You aren't going to make this easy, are you?"

"No." Even then her heart was singing. Say it, her eyes begged, say it Jake.

"Damn it all, I love you, Alex!"

She thought wildly, insanely, that his harshly spoken statement was the most beautiful thing she'd ever heard. Sudden tears sprang to her eyes. She took his reluctant hand in hers, and smiled to herself when his uneasy gaze remained fixed out across the desert expanse.

"And I love you, Jake Brannigan," she whispered ardently.

"Well," he said finally, uncomfortably, "guess we ought to talk about this."

Alex laughed, a light, sunny impulse. "I don't want to talk, you big dumb Irish cop."

"Neither do I," he growled, and she was swept into those arms and crushed against his chest as her heart blazed, at one with the primeval glory of the sun.

ABOUT THE AUTHOR

Molly Swanton and Carla Peltonen, friends and partners from Aspen, Colorado, write contemporary and historical romances under the pseudonym Lynn Erickson. *The Faces of Dawn*, their second Superromance, entailed extensive research into the history and customs of the Indians of the American Southwest. Their latest effort demonstrates once more that blending intrigue and romance is definitely their forte!

Books by Lynn Erickson

HARLEQUIN SUPERROMANCE

These books may be available at your local bookseller.

Don't miss any of our special offers. Write to us at the following address for information on our newest releases.

Harlequin Reader Service
P.O. Box 52040, Phoenix, AZ 85072-2040
Canadian address: P.O. Box 2800, Postal Station A,
5170 Yonge St., Willowdale, Ont. M2N 6J3

Enter a uniquely exciting new world with

Harlequin American Romance ™

Harlequin American Romances are the first romances to explore today's love relationships. These compelling novels reach into the hearts and minds of women across America... probing the most intimate moments of romance, love and desire.

You'll follow romantic heroines and irresistible men as they boldly face confusing choices. Career first, love later? Love without marriage? Long-distance relationships? All the experiences that make love real are captured in the tender, loving pages of **Harlequin American Romances.**

What makes American women so different when it comes to love? Find out with **Harlequin American Romance!**

Send for your introductory FREE book now!

Get this book FREE!

Mail to:

Harlequin Reader Service

In the U.S.	In Canada
2504 West Southern Ave.	P.O. Box 2800, Postal Station A
Tempe, AZ 85282	5170 Yonge St., Willowdale, Ont. M2N 5T5

YES! I want to be one of the first to discover **Harlequin American Romance.** Send me FREE and without obligation *Twice in a Lifetime.* If you do not hear from me after I have examined my FREE book, please send me the 4 new **Harlequin American Romances** each month as soon as they come off the presses. I understand that I will be billed only $2.25 for each book (total $9.00). There are no shipping or handling charges. There is no minimum number of books that I have to purchase. In fact, I may cancel this arrangement at any time. *Twice in a Lifetime* is mine to keep as a FREE gift, even if I do not buy any additional books.

Name   (please print)

Address   Apt. no.

City   State/Prov.   Zip/Postal Code

Signature (If under 18, parent or guardian must sign.)

154-BPA-NAZJ

AMR-SUB-2

Readers rave about
Harlequin American Romance!

"...the best series of modern romances
I have read...great, exciting, stupendous,
wonderful."
—*S.E.*, *Coweta, Oklahoma*

"...they are absolutely fantastic...going to be
a smash hit and hard to keep on the
bookshelves."
—*P.D., Easton, Pennsylvania*

"The American line is great. I've enjoyed
every one I've read so far."
—*W.M.K., Lansing, Illinois*

"...the best stories I have read in a long
time."
—*R.H., Northport, New York*

Names available on request.